TUTU

TUTUOBA

SALEM'S BLACK SHANGO SLAVE QUEEN

PRINCE JUSTICE

Cover Photo: Nerissa Irving
Photographer: A.J Alexander

Books also written by Prince Justice;
THE BLACKWORLD: EVOLUTION TO REVOLUTION
(2006)—Non-fiction
MOTHER OF ALL EVILS (2007)—Novel

TUTUOBA:
SALEM'S BLACK SHANGO SLAVE QUEEN

First Edition
TUTUOBA: SALEM'S BLACK SHANGO SLAVE QUEEN
An AU Media Book published by arrangement with Booksurge LLC
AU Media, 12 Durninghall Business Center, Earlham Grove, London U.K. E7 9AB

Visit www.booksurge.com to order additional copies.

TUTUOBA

Dedicated to my Mother, Esther Olufunke Faloye, my aunts, sisters and sistas...and to all those strong women keeping it going on...

I

JUNE 29, 2010: ATLANTIC OCEAN

She pulled off the headphones and irritably shoved them with the channel guide into the pocket behind the front seat. In an effort to sleep or relax for the umpteenth time, Tutu stretched her long legs and sank further into her seat. She was somewhat tense and despite wide variety of offerings, she could not find anything on the channels to suit her taste or at least soothe her nerves.

Jazz would have been ideal, she thought, having used it to relax since her boyfriend introduced it to her in college. Only God knows who puts things together on airlines, from the music to the food! Tutu sighed. It was becoming apparent sleep was not going to come easily, as she kept reopening her eyes and fidgeting.

To add to her irritation, every time she opened her eyes, they met with those of a middle-aged Indian man. The man sitting two seats away was staring at her whenever she looked up. She caught him a couple of times ogling her cleavage. Nasty old man! She thought and threw him a dirty look as she pulled a blanket over her well-endowed chest, although she knew that wouldn't necessarily stop the staring.

Tutu Barbara Oba was accustomed to advances from the opposite sex, being an attractive woman with a smooth, golden well-sculptured oval face. A face accentuated by her long locks and clear intelligent eyes. Standing at five feet ten inches, Tutu had a sexy figure that boasted ample breasts, an equally ample, but taut rear with a small waist. These and other qualities triggered off desire in men and jealousy from some women.

Sometimes, she enjoyed the attention and even flirted, but at present she was in no mood. He had tried to strike up a conversation with her, but she curtly put an end to it. Moreover, sitting between them was a middle-aged woman whom she suspected was his wife, since he didn't make advances until she was miles away in dreamland.

How I wish I could join her, she mused, but it was not going to happen easily after all the months of anticipation, fear and drama. She had come a long way and all types of surprises and disappointments had beset her journey. As Tutu fidgeted in her seat, her mind wandered from the beginning of her decision to leave to the concoction of a scheme to pacify her obstinate father.

And mother! She sighed as she thought of the struggle with her mother. Who would have thought mother would come to be the greatest stumbling block? Tutu sat up in her seat, her face a mixture of anxiety, fear and confusion as she let down her locks and did a few neck and shoulder exercises to ease the tension. How could she expect to relax when all she had been hearing for the last few weeks were warnings of danger and evil?

"We shall see wickedness!" Or was it evil the psychic had foretold? She had heard and said the word over a million times, but had never stopped to think of the meaning phonetically in her language and was sure that none of her friends at home or elsewhere, would have ever thought of it. As a matter of fact, only a minute percentage of the speakers of Africa's largest indigenous language, Yoruba, had heard such interpretation of America from the late enigmatic singer and political activist, Fela Kuti. America pronounced slowly in Yoruba as in "A Ma Ri Ka" means we would see wickedness or evil.

She was aware through her education that the Yorubas and Ibos suffered the most from the American slave trade, but that is history, she argued! In the second millennium with thousands, if not millions, of her contemporaries emigrating to the Western world and seemingly making headway for themselves, she didn't want to entertain historical perspectives which had no direct relevance to her present day needs and objectives.

Unfortunately, her mother kept haranguing her over some unexplained danger the psychic claimed to have forecast. How this danger or evil was to manifest itself was never explained, yet she was expected to shelve all her plans. Of course, she remained adamant, which led to a serious rift between them. Now, she wished she could have parted in a more amicable way with her mother, her close confidant.

Now, she was feeling lonely and scared! Mother was never really headstrong unless she was absolutely sure of her point. And that was the scary part, she thought, now that she had her own way. Being a very determined young lady, she knew she had a habit of digging in her heels, once she made up her mind. Tutu was her Zodiac sign, Capricorn—The Goat. It was only after successfully barging her way through opposition that she sometimes had second thoughts, like she was now having.

She asked for a soda from a passing flight attendant, who promptly obliged her and gave her some peanuts to go along with the drink. As she brought the drink to her mouth, she noticed her hands shaking.

"Oh, My God!" she whispered under her breath, "I am all nerves. Why is this happening? Why am I all tense?" she worried and having every reason to.

After all, this was not the first time she was traveling abroad or in a plane. She had been all over Europe, even if she had never been to the United States of America. Nor did she really believe the historical hogwash her mum, and to a lesser extent the old psychic, tried giving to her.

Hmm, America! Amarika! She smiled. Or did she believe? She wondered. No, of course she didn't, she was too modern to believe, but she still felt uneasy. As her mind continued to wander, she gradually felt more relaxed, and was on the brink of dozing off, when she was disturbed.

JUNE 29, 2010 NEW YORK, NY
There were about 100 or so guests in the large hall that glittered with glass chandeliers and diamond necklaces worn by the well-heeled partygoers. All the guests were formally dressed

in black dinner jackets and designer gowns typical of a gathering of the movers and shakers of society. In the background was a glimpse of the New York skyline, which could be seen through the glass walls and open balconies, although nobody was taking particular notice of the scenic view.

Apart from the busy waiters moving around to cater to the needs of the super-rich guests, everyone was grouped in twos and threes discussing politics and high finance. The guests ranged from bank chairmen and presidents to the mayor, governor and many senators.

Everyone appeared to be in good spirits, at least as much as their status would allow them to show in public. This was one of the first parties to break the monotony of what had turned out to be a very bitter winter and wet spring, even by New York standards. But where better to break the ice than at the party of the chairman of the largest bank in New York, America, if not in the world?

George Forrest, scion of the distinguished family that owned Empire Bank, called and organized the cocktail party, which was a shortlist of the crème de la crème of old money. Heirs and contemporaries of family businesses, financial and political dynasties could be seen talking and mingling everywhere as he walked around weaving in and out of conversations.

George Forrest, looking well sun tanned at the beginning of summer, could very well pass for someone in his early forties, although he was soon to celebrate his sixty-fourth birthday.

"Look who we have here! My dear Senator Hankel," he said ebulliently, as he shook the hands of the tall, silver-haired senator from Kentucky. He kissed the hands of the senator's young, beautiful wife, before turning back to give him a cursory glance. "You're looking far better than the television has been making you look recently. You are…"

"Thank you!" the senator answered effusively, adjusting his tie as if he was standing in front of a mirror. "You aren't looking bad yourself for a 30-year-old," he said, pausing for the light laughter to subside. "I asked about you and was told you were on vacation in Bali. I can see it has done you quite some good and..."

"Yeah, I guess one needs to step back from everything once in a while and take a good rest. I'll see you before you leave, but if I don't, I'll be sending down our contributions through the normal channels. Keep up the good work! In the meantime, enjoy yourselves. Excuse me!"

He had barely finished his sentence, when he sighted someone nearby, whom he greeted with equal warmth. To an observer, he was just being a perfect host, making small talk to keep the party moving, but this was only a half-truth. There was something going on under the surface.

Just down the line, he placed his hand gently on the shoulder of a slightly shorter, thickset man that sported a black suit with a dotted blue bow tie.

"Make your way to the room with blue ribbons on the door. The meeting starts soon!" The younger man nodded and discontinued his conversation with the politician he was talking to.

In a smaller Scandinavian-style room, which had a different view of the New York skyline through its glass windows and walls, there were plush chairs and sofas around a long cream marble coffee table. Seated in some of the chairs were men of varying ages, ranging from late thirties to late sixties, although they all emanated wealth and power. A few were standing along the wall sipping their cocktails, either looking out into the night or lost in thought.

The door jerked open and a portly man in his late forties with a jacket, slightly tight in the midsection, entered. With a fat Cuban cigar burning between his fat lips, he smiled, as he looked around taking in the familiar faces sitting around the table. "Who called this meeting?" he bellowed. "And what for? I have a busy itinerary..." He was interrupted by George Forrest's voice, coming from behind.

"The drinks are not going anywhere, Jack!" Forrest said boisterously, attracting everyone's attention. "I called the meeting," he admitted and made his way to a vacant seat. After gaining everyone's full attention, he continued.

"A serious matter has been brought to my attention, which I believe is of paramount importance to everyone and our continued existence. It is so..."

"Another tax increase?" someone queried cynically.

George Forrest smirked, "No! Worse!" He sighed pensively. Pausing, he contemplated how best to present his information.

"I was told by my wife, Mrs. Quincy and your wife," he said, pointing vaguely to one of the elderly men seated across from him, "that there is a force heading towards this coast, whose main objective is to put everything we've worked and stand for in great jeopardy!" There were sharp intakes of breath across the room.

"Has the force been identified, so it can be isolated and negated?" asked the cigar-smoking, large-bellied Jack Michaels arrogantly. Chairman of a heavy manufacturing multinational firm, Jack was legendary for his ruthlessness in both business and personal dealings, but sometimes overplayed the role, while trying to live up to expectations.

"No! It's not that easy, but the women are working on it, at this present moment," Forrest answered gloomily, rubbing his hands together nervously as Jack slightly startled backward, but said nothing.

"Sorry, I don't understand," the youngest member of the clique confessed. He was in his late thirties and had just taken the reins of his family's business empire, due to his father's death in a plane crash a few years ago. "You said there is a force heading towards us that is supposed to threaten our well-being, and its counteraction is being placed with our womenfolk?" he asked, gesturing with his fingers to stress his confusion.

"May I ask what kind of force is this that warrants the bravery and ruthlessness of our women?" he asked with loads of sarcasm as a small wry smile twisted the corners of his mouth.

"They are the best to handle it," Forrest insisted testily, not amused by the snide comment. He leaned forward to place his cup on the table before continuing.

"There have been fears of a return of this force for some time. It has been known to come every 160 years, bringing along with it great disruption whenever it appears. Apparently, it is due once again and we seem to have been hoping against all odds that we won't experience it again. Last week, we received confirmation that it was surely heading towards our shores."

"And what is this force, or whatever, supposed to do?" asked a bespectacled man in his fifties, wearing a black pinstriped suit.

"Well, we don't know for sure, otherwise our job would be much easier. Going by precedents, I guess it could be quite ominous. For the older ones among us, I guess your parents would have told you a bit about our history, which is not common knowledge. The first experience is what is known in the history books as the Salem witch trials in Massachusetts."

"Sir, I think we all know that the Salem witch trials were a travesty of justice and there were no witches. Moreover, I don't think anyone in this day and age believes in that medieval rubbish," the youngest man said derisively.

Anthony Pierce, a lawyer, who fancied himself as being worldly and intelligent, could not believe his ears.

"My young man, as much as you might disbelieve it, there is more to life than meets the eye. If you disregard all that you can't see, it will be to your detriment," a slightly irritated Forrest reproached him. "It is unfortunate that your father, Eric, could not teach you all he would have wished to before he moved on."

He recomposed himself and continued, "Contrary to present-day beliefs, a whole lot happened in Salem, Massachusetts that was never publicly admitted. The real Salem witch was never identified and terminated but believe me, there was definitely a force at work. There was a whole lot to do with the supernatural and what is never told in that story was how it changed the course and destiny of this nation and the western world as a whole. Thanks to their determination and versatility, our forbearers, were able to turn an ugly situation around, otherwise we would never have dreamed of the prosperity we are now accustomed to," Forrest slowly elucidated.

"One of its effects was a shift of finance and business from Massachusetts to the New York Islands in order to distance themselves, if only psychologically, from the myriad problems of the mainland, especially slavery and religious fervor. The example of Britain's progress, due to its separation from mainland Europe and its religious and political problems, informed the decision and many others afterwards all the way to Hong Kong."

The man in the pinstriped suit rose and walked to the windows as he asked tentatively, "So how do we identify this threat? Do we know where it is going to strike?"

"Unfortunately, we don't! Which is why I called the meeting. At this moment, the women are working hard in the other room to identify and counteract this force. At the same time, we have to make contingency plans and be very, very alert," he sternly warned them.

The second youngest of the group, a man in his early forties who normally wouldn't have been invited to the meeting and had kept quiet all along, cleared his throat and spoke in a deep voice. "Being in charge of the security arrangements, I can reassure you that all our systems are in tip top condition and can confidently say we are up to any problem!"

"That's nice to hear, but I would rather not be too confident! This is not like anything, we have encountered in recent memory," Forrest warned.

"I am sorry, but I don't see how any person or force, could upset what we have in place. We are not a small outfit that some witch or whatever can derail. No matter how strong!" the young heir, Anthony Pierce contended. He explained himself further, when he saw the derisory looks around him. "For example, in a worst case scenario, even if this force were to kill the business leaders, we have reached a state in our development where there will always be continuity and it will be a futile exercise and sheer waste of lives for the force to take on such a doomed venture."

"You can never fully rationalize the supernatural! Don't you know how many people were killed or destroyed in Salem and elsewhere?" one of the elderly men questioned him tetchily. He was annoyed by what he saw as the younger men's impertinence, but they took no note of his irritation. After all, everyone was invited in their own capacity as the leaders and protectors of their families and their interests.

"But why does this force choose us and where does it actually come from?" Anthony asked, still baffled by what he was hearing.

"Her background is shrouded in mystery due to the officials who did not want the whole truth out, because of their fear that it might incite the slave populations at the time. Contrary to official reports and historical records that she was an Indian slave from Barbados in the Caribbean Islands, what my grandmother told me was that she was from the heart of Africa, from the Yoruba.

"At the time, Africans made up ninety-nine percent of slaves in the West Indies, where her master was supposed to have brought her from. Although she was supposed to be a bit lighter in complexion than the average African, she was definitely a dreadlocked Yoruba woman," he explained carefully.

"And who are these Yoruba? Or what is it?" asked Mr. Andrews, the man with the blue bow tie.

Forrest smirked as he took pride in enlightening people. "Presently, it is the largest indigenous African group and language...."

"I thought Swahili or Hausa were..." Anthony interrupted.

"No!" Forrest shook his head forcefully and sighed deeply, before continuing pedantically. "Although Swahili and Hausa languages are spoken more widely, they are basically Arabic inspired trade languages, African languages mixed with the languages of their conquerors, the Arabs. They are not original African ethnic groups, but peoples living in the grassland fringes of the African forest. The languages are to Arabic like what the various types of English spoken by Africans in the Americas is to Queen's English."

"Like Ebonics!" Anthony quipped.

"Yeah! Anyway, before the advent of Europeans, the Yorubas used to be the major peoples, gold traders and rulers of the forest area of Africa. There are also claims that they were the Pharaohs of Ancient Egypt..."

"Rubbish!" Jack Michaels interrupted. "How can you believe that?"

Forrest shrugged. "Well, they argue that most Egyptian Pharaohs, especially Osiris was called an 'Auni' in the 'Book of the Dead', which is what the Yoruba's have always called their foremost king and spiritual leader in Ife. Coptic traditions also mention a god-king Shango from Ife and Egypt means sheep in both Greek and Yoruba, which is what the Nile area has been known to supply them from antiquity till today!" Forrest told them and raised his hand to stop being interrupted.

"Anyway, whatever they might have been in Ancient Egypt, their forest homeland was to later experience the worst of European slavery. They possibly would have been annihilated, if not for the intervention of this force, which struck an insidious and fatal blow at the heart of slavery," Forest said sternly, but despite raising his hand and voice forcefully, the security chief interrupted Forest's concentration as he waved a cigar around gesturing for a light.

After pausing for him to light his cigar, Forrest continued, "At the time, millions had been shipped to the sugar plantations of the Atlantic coast of Brazil, which spread to the Caribbean islands as the pace of development increased. This was followed by the south of present day USA, where slaves were used for cotton, tobacco and rice. The next and last in line to be brought under cultivation was the Northeast coast, the land between Washington DC and Boston."

"This is getting interesting," the young lawyer interrupted him jokingly as he moved his chair closer.

Using the opportunity to take a sip, Forrest continued, "Cultivation would have resulted in the people being completely decimated, considering the numbers that would have been required. Bear in mind that would have meant every piece of land on the eastern shores of the Atlantic being cultivated by slave labor. It was for this reason that the force allegedly from Mother Nature was dispatched," George Forrest explained to the younger men.

"So what happened? You mentioned she struck a blow at the heart of the slavery system. How?" The security chief, Bill Jones, inquired with keen interest.

"Well, it is not fully proven, but it is believed she struck various blows and planted seeds that had far reaching effects. At her first place of call, which was in Jamaica, Britain's largest sugar producer, she was alleged to have sowed the seeds of rebellion. This was the Maroon rebellion, which would eventually force Britain out of the sugar market, due to its disruptive impact and the resultant high cost of maintaining law and order."

"Britain, as a result of this, became abolitionist and pressured all other countries into abandoning slavery. This was due to Britain's comparative disadvantage with the losing of its sugar producer, which at one time earned it more income than all the other colonial income combined." He paused again to take another sip from his glass.

Clearing his throat, he continued, "Here in America, she ensured the Northeast coast would remain the barren coast to prevent it from going along the slavery route, which all other lands on the Atlantic coast had followed. It was this Northeast area that championed and fought the slavery cause against the south, Massachusetts being in the forefront to discard the system shortly after her presence. Actually the judge, Samuel Sewall, who sat at her trial, shortly afterwards became one of the first white abolitionists."

"Wonderful! So why was this never known to the public and what happened or who were those hanged in Salem?" Bill Jones asked incredulously.

George Forrest smiled. "Today, it's called damage control or limitation!" He paused, as he seemed to be enjoying their looks of incredulity. "We couldn't come out and say that a slave girl had given us a bloody nose. It would have caused mayhem and dissent among the huge and growing black population."

"I understand all that, but what I don't understand is, why

now? There is no more slavery anymore! What's the bloody problem?" Jack Michaels asked irritably.

"It's true there is no more slavery, but the people will tell you they are under adjusted slavery. They argue that after slavery came colonization, after which came the International Monetary Fund's Structural Adjustment Program, the S.A.P., introduced in the 1980s throughout the black world. The program backed by us resulted in the killing of their economies, abject poverty and mass migration here and in Europe. They call the SAP the slavery-adjusted people and many are bitter about it. Moreover, they accuse the West of imposing leaders on them that sell out their interests. So this might be the bone of contention, but we are neither sure nor willing to find out!"

In another room on the same floor, which appeared to be a boardroom, twelve women sat around a long polished table, lit with candles. Just as their husbands quietly excluded themselves from the partying, so had the ladies unobtrusively excused themselves to the room for their meeting.

The ladies were in their late forties to early sixties, with Mrs. Forrest, who was seated at the head of the table, appearing to be the oldest. Mrs. Forrest was the daughter of an old distinguished Bostonian family, who married into another old money family of New York. Formerly of the Lawrence family that made its fortunes from the cotton mills of New England, before diversifying into arms, she had brought her family fortunes together with those of the Forrests, being the sole heiress of her family.

All the other women were also of the same breed that had also married into respectable families. The combined valued of their jewelry alone could offset the national debts of many third world nations. Although the flashy jewelry and smiles they had worn moments before at the party were now replaced with serious, worried looks. There was a heavy and tense atmosphere in the room.

They had now congregated in the room for 45 minutes discussing their plans for the evening. A few were first timers and very apprehensive about the planned proceedings with fear written boldly across their faces. Even those who weren't novices, but had heard stories of what had once transpired in similar circumstances, were scared.

"We need absolute concentration and I must warn you, this might be the toughest thing we have ever endeavored to do." Mrs. Forrest paused to look around the table to see, if she had everybody's concentration. "If you all understand and are ready, I guess we should get on with it and confront this threat to our families. Let's all link our energies." She stretched out her hands, linking them with those seated next to her and they formed a complete circle for what was to be a séance.

Mrs. Forrest started some incantations in a low voice, which gradually increased in intensity and decibels. "I call to you of the great beyond..." As she spoke, a mild spring wind from the Atlantic Ocean gently blew in, causing the candles on the center of the table to flicker.

At last, Tutu made her first successful attempt to sleep, but was disturbed once again, this time by early morning sunrays that were reflected into her eyes by some movement on the wings of the airplane. She thought she saw some metallic movements on the wing, but couldn't be concerned as she stretched to pull down the visor in frustration. Still half asleep, she heard a rumble to which she paid no attention, but before she returned her hand to her lap commotion ensued.

Suddenly, the plane took a near 90-degree dive, prompting panicked cries. Her carry-on luggage slid from under her chair and hit her calf, with a sharp protrusion stabbing into her calf at the same time as a bag from nowhere hit her on the head. Almost immediately, the plane evened out for a second or two, before making a steep climb, also of nearly ninety degrees.

There were screams all round the plane as people not in their seats flew across aisles. The seat belt signs started flashing, but many people weren't even in their seats and tried grabbing onto anything, including a few oxygen masks that were released from the overhead cabin.

Once again, the plane took a steep dive, making trays, bags and a few toddlers fly forward. One lucky toddler landed right on Tutu's lap, smiling. He thought it was a game. The Asian woman sitting beside her woke up in shock and was speaking Punjabi or some other Asian language, while Tutu could not even utter a word in any language, as bile rose in her throat.

She heard the pilot announce, "Everyone please remain in your seats! We are experiencing extreme turbulence due to pockets of varying air pressure..."

"For real? That's news!" someone shouted sarcastically from somewhere behind her, but could hardly finish his statement before another dip. More oxygen masks dropped from the overhead cabins. Screams for help and prayers rent the plane, while many people just squeezed their eyes shut waiting to die.

Tutu was quiet. An observer might have thought from her blank expression, she had dropped into a state of shock. In fact, she had slipped into a trance, or more accurately, was experiencing a sense of déjà vu, but somehow it was no longer an airplane, but a ship!

On the ship, there was also pandemonium, with screaming people all around her being thrown or running towards her. Tutu was wearing traditional African wear, with a blue top and a matching wrapper around her waist. There was a raging storm, actually a ferocious hurricane, but the strange thing was she remained unaffected and calm, apart from her locks blowing wildly.

Afterwards, she appeared to be alone on the deck, everyone else having escaped to the lower decks or washed overboard. Strangely, instead of escaping from the ferocious wind, she was moving towards it, towards the hull. She moved effortlessly as if she was in a trance with her lips moving slowly and her hands outstretched.

Tutu startled awake from her reverie and found she was in her airplane seat and rubbed the side of her head, which was slightly sore. She was mystified that amid all that was happening at present, she was having daydreams, which she could not in the least begin to explain. Yet they seemed so real. Once more, she rubbed the side of her head and noticed there was a little blood. Apparently, a flying piece of luggage had hit her in the temple, knocking her out of the reverie.

The airplane was still making wild dives and climbs and in despair, she held firmly on to the toddler, still on her lap. Her seat belt was nearly torn loose from her seat. "Oh! God!" she cried as her mind raced through her life. She now thought of her mum and remembered the scary words of the old psychic, whom she had viewed as a "player hater," a "trouble making old hag" and every other hateful thing.

In the midst of the commotion, with people and objects flying around, she tried to recollect everything that the psychic had said. This was not an easy task, since she had never really taken note of the psychic's words. She had viewed everything suspiciously and saw it merely as an exercise to upset her carefully laid plans!

Some people talk of life-threatening experiences and how one's entire life flashes across one's mind vividly at the point of death; this was one such instance. As scenes of her meeting with the psychic flashed, she recalled asking whether or not she would die, but couldn't remember whether the psychic gave an affirmative answer.

Psychics! She hated their dishonest tactics. They always gave vague messages and riddles. At the same time, she had claimed to see a lot of benefits, she had also said she saw a lot of death and danger. However, the psychic had advised her to go on with her plans and gave her two rings, which were supposed to protect her.

Initially, she had no intention of bringing along the rings, being skeptical, if not disbelieving, of the whole premonition. It was her mother, at the last minute of her departure who had begged her to abide with the psychic's advice. Coming from her mother, who had become a nervous wreck, trying everything she could to halt the journey, Tutu just couldn't refuse her last request. Even then, due to her stubborn streak, she didn't follow the exact order. She wore the rings on fingers of different hands, rather than on the same finger as advised.

The plane took its longest dive, which caused louder screams. Tutu clasped her fingers in despair, rubbing them together in prayerful submission. Suddenly, she stopped and drifted away into what seemed to be another trance. Her face became blank, her sharp intelligent eyes appearing miles away, but her lips slowly started to murmur. In a whisper, she started what could be called an incantation.

"The hands of evil shall not bind me, as no hand can bind the wind nor dam the rain. The rain, the wind and thunder go hand in hand helping one another! Help me the gods of nature. Help me, Shango, god of thunder!"

There was a monstrous clap of deafening thunder followed by an immediate calm. The loud clap was taken by most in the plane as a crash. Many fainted, while others with their eyes open thought they were dead, especially with the eerie silence that followed. The clap jolted Tutu out of her trance-like state and she momentarily looked around, not knowing where she was or what had happened.

Suddenly there was a loud clap of thunder followed by the sound of shattering glass. Momentarily, there was silence due to shock, before screams and panic rented the air. Anthony Pierce was the first to reach the door and run into the ballroom, closely followed by George Forrest and others. The guests were milling around a door from which screams were coming. George Forrest hastily made his way through the shocked guests, some of whom were calling for help using their cellphones.

On entering the room, he was met by the ghastly sight of bleeding women with cuts and various wounds. A few were lying unconscious on the floor and everything was torn apart by what appeared to be a massive explosion. The long mahogany table was shattered beyond recognition and a few fires were starting to spread.

"Call 911. Get the fire department and the paramedics!" Anthony Pierce shouted as he pushed people back to create a

path for those bringing out the injured. "Everyone move back!
Move toward the exit. There has been an explosion and a fire!"
The word explosion caused further panic as people stepped
over each other in order to escape from what might have
been a terrorist bomb. This caused problems for the arriving
emergency staff.

Eventually, the emergency team made their way to the
women, whom they placed on stretchers. George Forrest stood
by his wife as she was carried onto a stretcher, frail and bleeding
from a number of wounds. Lying on the stretcher, she stretched
her hand to her husband, who took it and gently squeezed it to
let her know he was by her side. She pulled him towards her as
she tried to speak.

"She is here, I saw her face!" she said feebly." I think she
is going to Boston, get on the phone." She paused to cough
and continued, "Find out all flights that are coming in from
Lagos, Nigeria. It is...." She collapsed before she could finish
her statement.

2

The pilot soon re-established contact with the air traffic controllers, who thought the flight had been lost forever. At the control tower, they were baffled by his report of extreme weather since the seven other planes in the area reported calm conditions. The pilot declined an offer of an emergency landing facility since he had regained control of the plane and thankfully the injuries were not too bad. There were four people unconscious and many others had sustained minor cuts and bruises. Most importantly, the plane was still intact and the pilot believed it to be capable of a safe landing.

In the cabin, people settled in their seats as the flight attendants went around administering first aid and trying to make the passengers comfortable. Tutu politely declined offers of treatment or refreshments as she thought of her experience. She was confused and frightened and couldn't explain her reverie of a ship in troubled waters, which seemed quite surreal.

Due to her recent experience, she started viewing life from a very different perspective. Life had been good to her and like most people she had gone through it without really questioning its essence. So far, so good, she had no reason to question it up until now, being the first child of her upper middle-class family. She had grown up as a slightly over-pampered daddy's girl and did not lack any love from her mother.

Her father, Mr. Oba, a successful lawyer trained in London, was well to do by any standard and was one of the few who could still maintain his affluent standard of living. This was despite the widespread poverty and falling living standards across Africa, induced by the forcibly imposed Structural Adjustment

Program of the International Monetary Fund (IMF) and Western-world banks.

The economic program, which included massive currency devaluation among other things, resulted in a substantial cut in the real incomes of over sixty Black nations in Africa and the Caribbean Islands. Luckily for Jaiye Oba, also an economics graduate of the London School of Economics, he had investments and legal retainers in Europe that were unaffected by the fatal economic policies at home.

It was this income that enabled him to provide Tutu and his family with the little necessary luxuries, like her designer clothes and Toyota at college. The unspoken, but painful reality was that, although they were enjoying a reasonable standard of living at present, the future was very bleak for Tutu and her generation. The family was eating into its wealth to keep up appearances.

Ever since the over 5,000% devaluation, its resultant and corresponding inflation, Tutu and her generation realized that the only way to earn a decent living comparable to that of their parents and what they were used to was by emigrating to the western world. Tutu had to 'follow the money' or otherwise she would be lucky to command a $5,000 per year salary, despite her degrees in law and economics.

Tutu had always possessed ambitions to be successful like her father and believed she wouldn't go wrong if she followed his career route. This was not difficult being an intellectually endowed child. She thanked God for her family that was able to send her to the best of schools. By age 10, she could fluently speak three European and two African languages.

Although she had made up her mind on her career choice, for as long as she could remember, this caused disagreements within the family. Her mother, who had been consulting the psychic since Tutu's birth, wanted her to study medicine because the psychic said she would bring great benefits to people and saw death around her.

This was the first drawn out battle between mother and daughter. "Lawyers do nothing good for people." "Lawyers are liars." "That is not a good profession for a lady." These were but a few of her mother's arguments, which did nothing but harden her resolve.

As far as she was concerned it was profitable and provided them with a model home. Home being the eight-bedroom mansion with a swimming pool and lawn tennis court in Victoria Island, Lagos, situated just 300 yards from the Atlantic Ocean. Contrary to outsiders' expectations, the affluent surroundings did not make her complacent, if anything, it drove her ambitions further.

In reality, it is nearly impossible not to be firmly rooted in one's goals in a city like Lagos, where ancient and downtrodden houses and areas existed side by side with multi-million dollar Beverly Hills-style homes and developments. This juxtaposition served as a constant reminder that if she didn't make a success of herself, she could end up on the other side of the fence.

Like most of her colleagues, she had always wanted to prove herself and succeed in Nigeria. Despite her generation's fascination with the United States she, like many others, had only wished to visit to enjoy the hip-hop culture that she had grown up with. Now, it was not cultural awareness, but economic reality that was leading to the emigration of millions of her peers.

A few were reportedly doing well, since the majority was well educated, making the African ethnic group the most educated immigrant group in the U.S (forty-five percent graduates) and U.K. Although, most of them were shut out of the system, having to turn to menial jobs, taxi driving and ultimately crime, which was the basis of her parents' initial fear and grounds of disagreement.

Her father flatly rejected the idea, "There is absolutely no way I am going to spend all that time and money to give you a good education and have you working in McDonald's," he paused as he chewed on some food. "Or even worse, doing credit card fraud, drugs or prostitution, hell no!" Her father said and stormed out of the house, too upset to finish his dinner.

This incident occurred during the last Easter break, when

a discussion grew into a dispute over her plans after graduation. The debate culminated in her telling him, "I am checking out!" meaning she was leaving for the western world.

"There are over a hundred million people that need your services here!" said her father, shaking his head disdainfully, "All your generation thinks about is money, money, and money! It is heart-rending, the brain drain this nation is enduring. Such a waste!"

Tutu resented the scathing criticisms she was constantly subjected to over her generation's culture. Her father criticized everything from the lyrics of the rap music she played, the clothing she wore and even the language she used. She often argued with her father. Defying her Yoruba upbringing, which placed great reverence on complete subservience to elders, she debated him as if he were a courtroom foe, her peer and not the father she'd always been taught to revere.

"This is no time to be idealistic, Daddy! This is about reality and how to achieve a successful existence," Tutu replied defiantly. She paused, and it would probably have been advisable to stop there.

Instead, she continued, "I don't see you being idealistic by giving up your foreign income to the good and benefit of the poor!" This made him implode and leave the dinner table and house for the country club, where he vented his anger and frustration on the snooker balls.

After his exit and their supper, her mother called her to the living room, before she could escape to her room and music, "Tutu, come around. We need to talk," she said gently, being a quiet and easy-going person by nature.

"Yes, mother!" she answered defensively as she stood at the doorway, "Mum, I know what you have to say, but I am sorry. There is nothing you can say to change my mind," she said with her hands on her hips.

Tinu smiled faintly at her obstinate child as she readjusted her head-tie diligently. Although mother and daughter looked very much alike, the difference being in the older woman having aged graciously and with no locks, the similarities were merely superficial, with Tutu taking after her father's volatile temperament. Tinu Oba, a successful accountant was quite diplomatic and tactful. Despite the fact that she was much less emotionally volatile, she always ended getting things her way.

Wearing a shiny, gray gown with black embroidery, a matching head-tie and colorful African beads as jewelry, Tinu remained smiling as she patted the empty seat by her side. She gestured to her daughter to sit down beside her, which Tutu refused as if it were a trap.

Tutu knew of her mother's gentle persuasive powers and was unwilling to have her change her mind. Her best line of defense against such powers was in not listening or she knew her wall of resistance would collapse.

"No, Mum! Thanks I prefer standing," she said, also refusing to lock eyes with her mother and looked toward the ceiling instead.

"Are you quarrelling with me? You are shunning me, baby?" Tinu feigned surprise and hurt. "Come on!" she urged softly, breaking through the resistance as Tutu grudgingly sat at the edge of the seat next to her.

"Listen! I always tell you that a woman should be diplomatic and not militant. The cool collected persuasive feminine charms always win against militant and forceful men. We women are still in control, but you can't let them know."

Placing a hand on Tutu's shoulders to placate her, she said, "Tutu means cool. Why can't you answer to your name, instead of being Shango's fiery dreadlock?"

The tenderness of her mother's approach made Tutu lose her resolve and she burst into gentle sobs.

"But mother, you heard what he said. Everyone is gone. I want to leave. There is nothing left for me here. I am..." Tutu lamented.

Tinu wiped the tears off her weeping daughter's face with her sleeve. "Yes, I know your worries, and God knows I have been expecting this argument to come up for some time. I have been dreading the clash of my two hotheads." She paused to sip her drink and raised her hand to stop Tutu from interrupting while she drank.

"I see both points of view clearly. You know your father and I studied abroad and know how difficult it is to break into the system there, especially as a black person. Moreover, since you did not study there, it would take double the effort to break..."

"I do have friends who are doing quite well over there!" Tutu countered.

"Yeah, but not a good percentage and you can't gamble your life on poor odds. I do have a better idea, of which I know your father wouldn't disapprove, since all he wants is your success."

Tutu sat upright and attentive, "What is it?" she asked eagerly and Tinu knowing she had her daughters full attention decided to milk it, while it lasted. Slowly, she took another sip from her lemonade.

When she finished she cleared her throat, "The best and only amicable way is to apply for a postgraduate course, LL.M or whatever. Your chances of getting your footing on the corporate ladder will increase, when you have proven your abilities in their academic world. Such a plan would appeal to your father."

Tutu nodded in agreement as she thought of the brilliance of the plan. "I will try, but I gathered that it is not that easy to gain admission into good schools over there. I will surely try!" she promised and hugged her mum in appreciation, already thinking of how to tackle the hurdle.

"God will help you!" Tinu said, as Tutu was about to leave. "One more thing, baby. I am a bit concerned about your love life. Ever since that boy, Emeka, left for the U.S, you haven't dated anyone. I hope you are not waiting for him. You see all the beautiful girls on the black American shows, I wouldn't trust any man among them," Tinu said lightly, although she was a bit worried about the prospect of her daughter's heart being broken.

Tutu smiled. She had been expecting her mum to ask about this for some time. "Don't worry! I am not waiting for anyone. In fact, we broke up before he left."

A lie! She had expected him to keep in touch after entering

the States on a visiting visa, but he disappeared off her radar, despite all his promises. "I have just been very busy," Tutu compounded the lie.

"You can't be too busy to take care of your heart. Find time to socialize!" her mum advised, as Tutu set out to seek admission into a U.S law graduate school.

"We should be landing at Logan International airport, Boston in approximately ten minutes. It's 12.40pm local time and 75 degrees Fahrenheit with dry, clear skies. Please, if you need any assistance, do not hesitate to inform a flight attendant..." The pilot's announcement disrupted her thoughts about her mother and all she had left behind.

Following the announcement, Tutu jumped into action like her fellow passengers. Gathering her carry-on luggage, she once again felt anxiety building up. *God, this is it! This is the beginning of my new life* she thought excitedly and was somewhat apprehensive, this being the first time she was venturing beyond her family's sphere of influence and control.

The plane landed smoothly without any further incidence to the relief of all on board, and the passengers filed out past the flight attendants at the exit. Tutu nodded amiably to them on her way out, although she believed she was being given a suspicious look by some of the attendants, something she initially noticed during the flight. She had heard stories that some attendants report suspicious travelers to the authorities, especially on Nigerian flights.

It was believed that drug smugglers, especially those who had swallowed their contraband to avoid detection, refrained from eating or drinking, in order not to disturb the swallowed packages. She couldn't really be bothered with what anyone thought, but she found it rather annoying to be regarded as a drug smuggler.

Moreover, she knew she was bound to arouse suspicion with her expensive jewelry and designer clothing. She was sporting a blue, straight fitting Armani exchange jeans, which showed all her curves and a loose FUBU blouse, which showed a bit of cleavage. This was against her mother's advice that, "Whenever you are traveling, you dress formally because you never know, whom you might meet and give a wrong first impression."

Tutu would not bulge on the matter. "I am not dressing in some sissy good girl fashion. It's a long flight, and I want to feel at ease," she snapped, weary of what she saw as her mother's constant faultfinding.

"You never listen! I don't know what's easy about those tight jeans and that blouse," her mother complained loudly. This was something out of her character, but understandably so, being worried over Tutu's insistence to travel.

Mr. Oba, sensing a chilly and edgy situation, "Ladies, ladies, let's move on, please!"

That was at Muritala Muhammed Lagos Airport. Now, moving slowly along the immigration line in Boston's Logan Airport, Tutu was conscious of herself and vulnerability.

"Next! Next!" She heard distantly until someone nudged her from behind and she realized that it was her turn at the immigration desk. Disoriented, she fumbled with her luggage, attracting stares from some officials and travelers standing around.

The waiting immigration official looked at her disdainfully as she rushed awkwardly to the booth. "Passport, please," he demanded in an officious monotone and stretched out his hand to collect the documents, she placed on the booth. Tutu stared at the man, who was examining her documents with a hint of cynicism and thought he looked familiar.

"What's the purpose of your visit? Holiday?" The officer had red robust cheeks that showed signs that he was a heavy drinker. In his late thirties, Martin O'Brien, as his nametag read, had put on more than his own fair share of weight. Bald-headed with wire-rimmed glasses that sat daintily on an extra large nose, O'Brien had an aura of a cynicism.

An Irish Bostonian whose family had settled in Massachusetts right after the pilgrims, he didn't like the influx of recent immigrants, especially the dodgy ones. High on his list were Nigerians and Jamaicans. This one had a Nigerian passport and Jamaican hair, he thought amusedly.

There had been a memo circulated to watch out for Nigerian travelers and over the time, he had stopped many from entering. His motto was "when in doubt, exclude." Having absolute power at the point of entry meant no recourse to justice and a wasted airfare.

"Here on holiday?" he repeated impertinently.

"No! To stay...em...eh, to study" she stuttered, not knowing how to explain to him, since his facial expression showed he obviously didn't want to listen. Before she could finish, he stood up. "Please follow me," he ordered and made his way to an unmarked door.

Inside the room was a pretty blonde lady of medium height and features, who seemed to be the complete opposite of Mr. O'Brien in temperament. Dressed in a green uniform that did justice to her figure, she looked at Tutu as she came in and gave her a pitiful smile, which Tutu acknowledged with a slight nod.

"Another one!" Martin O'Brien whispered in her ear, before sitting at a nearby table. Gesturing to Tutu to take the chair across him, "So Madam, tell us your story. Where did you get the documents from?" he asked derisively.

Leaning forward in her chair as if she couldn't hear him properly. "Story?" Tutu repeated loudly, shocked by the allegations, "Get documents from?" still lost for words, before finally regaining her composure. "Of course, where everyone gets them from," she answered, looking very cross as she rallied from the shock.

O'Brien was enjoying himself and continued as if everything was normal, "Where would that be...Oluwole? Where please? We don't have all day as you can see, we are quite busy!" he said sternly. "I will appreciate it if you can answer questions quickly."

Tutu took a deep breath before answering, remembering her mother's advice about being cool, and then with all the charm she could muster. "I got my passport and visa through all the right channels. I am no criminal. I am a student lawyer and have been offered admission into graduate school." Finishing her statement, she stared at him and it was obvious to her, he was neither listening nor interested.

"Yeah, right!" he murmured without looking up. "You didn't fill in, where you will be staying," he looked up querulously from the green landing card she had filled.

"I don't know the specific address. All the arrangements were made by the professor, and I guess I will be staying with him initially."

"Whoa! You'll be sleeping with the professor from the word, go! Girl, that's what I call a good student," he said sarcastically and laughed.

That was enough to tip Tutu over the edge and she had a good mind to punch him in the face. "You know, you are just a nasty, good-for-nothing fat bastard, and I demand to see your supervisor!"

"Sorry, no can do! I am the alpha and omega of who you are going to see in America. Just hold on, let me process your papers and we will set you on your way." He rose and collected the papers together: "One way to Lagos!" He said and chuckled before leaving. Tutu remained silent and stared blankly as she experienced a brief flashback

This time, she and some people were walking down the gangplank of an old ship and as they approached the end, there was a man who looked very much like Martin O'Brien, who was barking out orders. When she got to him, he stopped and examined her lustfully, running his fat fingers over her. "Hmm, I think I will keep this one for myself," he said, as he continued to fondle her disrespectfully.

Flustered, Tutu spat in his face, "Bastard!" she said vehemently.

Angry, he raised his hand to strike her, but someone shouted from somewhere behind her, "O'Brien, keep the bloody line moving before I keep your job for myself."

Tutu broke out of the brief flashback, as the blond immigration officer returning to the room, slammed the door behind her. Tutu couldn't help, but wonder what the flashback meant. This was getting rather scary and baffling, she thought. Shortly afterwards, the woman finished with the Indian traveler and Tutu overheard her say, "I am sorry for the delay. Here you go. I wish you a pleasant stay in the United States of America" as she led the man out.

Lucky man, she thought dejectedly, wishing she could be in his shoes. The thought of being deported back to Lagos after all that had happened was disheartening, but from all indications from Mr. O'Brien, that was what was going to happen. Oh God, she cried as she crossed her fingers at the back of her head in despair, trying to figure out where she went wrong and whether she could salvage the situation. Why had the guy turned against me? Maybe I should have followed mother's dressing advice, she kept wondering. After all, it was her advice that had got me past father's initial objections.

Following her mother's advice to apply for a place in a postgraduate school, she had set about it as soon as she returned to campus after the Easter break. Being her final semester at the University of Ife, she could hardly wait to graduate, since all the euphoria she'd experienced when starting at the beautiful university campus had long dissipated.

The university was located on the fringes of the historical town, Ile-Ife. Ile-Ife meaning the "land of love" is according to Yoruba mythology, the Garden of Eden and spiritual home of Africa's largest indigenous peoples. Fresh students at the university were flooded with euphoric experiences, starting from the greeting at the end of the Ife-Ibadan expressway, which read, "Welcome to Ile-Ife, the cradle of humanity", to the various new architectural designs alongside ancient artifacts as well as its natural scenic beauty surrounded by seven hills.

Normally, the sweet experiences continued until the rigorous academic drilling the university had a reputation for bogged them down. As the university center came into view as

Tutu returned from her Easter break, her heartbeat seemed to falter as she thought of the mammoth task ahead of her. She headed to her room, where she dropped off her things and immediately made for the library at the university center.

She knew for her to get an admission into an Ivy League university, she needed an average of B-pluses in her forthcoming exams. This was no easy mission in the university in which, because of its closed utopian society, the professors appeared to turn into sadistic, megalomaniac slave-masters.

Some of the professors often told their students, "A is for God, B plus is for me, B is for geniuses, the rest of you could fight for the other grades."

On reaching the library that evening, she made a list of the American Ivy League colleges and sent out letters requesting for application forms or outright admission. Then she settled down to the most rigorous campaign of her life, seldom having time to go home or partake in the rich social life of the campus.

After her final exams, she returned to Lagos about two hundred kilometers southwest, where she anxiously waited for the results. Tutu was overjoyed, when the results arrived and she made a first class with an A average. God is definitely on my side, she thought, when on the same day, letters arrived requesting her to send her results for various postgraduate programs.

She started law school for her Nigerian Bar exams after she sent off her results. The law school being based in Victoria Island enabled her to attend from home, although she was hardly at home, due to the demanding nature of the program.

Actually, it was not only the rigorous program that kept her from home, since she could easily cope with anything after being through the University of Ife. Her absence from home was mainly because the family atmosphere had turned rancorous during the summer, while she waited for her exam results.

Her father was caught having an extra marital affair from which he had fathered a child. This led Tutu to bury herself deeper into her books in an effort to bury her hurt feelings. Thankfully, law school went very fast and before she knew it, the one-year program drew to an end.

Shortly before Tutu's bar exams, on the 16th of May, two incidents occurred that changed the monotony.

Tinu had a recurring nightmare in which she and Tutu appeared to be in the nearby prestigious, Eko Hotel, normally filled with foreigners, mostly Caucasians, sunbathing and conducting business deals.

In the dream, they were discussing business with some white Americans, when suddenly some of them as well as those sunbathing attacked Tutu and tried to drown her. Tinu tried fighting them off her daughter, but to no avail, although as she was about to give up, it seemed help came from an unidentified source.

Frustratingly, she never saw the conclusion, despite having the dream thrice overnight, each time waking up in cold sweat. Troubled by the nightmare, which she could not interpret, but believing it to be portent, she set out to the one person she had come to trust.

Twenty-five years ago, when Tinu was still single, a woman approached her on the streets, informing her that she was carrying a powerful miracle girl, who had a mission to take on very powerful people and bring lots of changes to the world. She will be a *'Dada'* the psychic told her—the Yoruba name given to people born with natural hair locks and believed to be spiritually powerful.

Tinu, who didn't know she was three weeks pregnant, discounted her as a fraud trying to hoodwink her. She had rudely dismissed her to be surprised a few weeks later, when she realized she was pregnant.

Tinu did not see the woman again until a day after Tutu's birth, by which time she was greatly troubled by the veracity of the forecast. Not only was the baby a girl, but she also possessed the hair locks the psychic had forecast and her birth was as difficult as foretold.

On her reappearance, the psychic, called Iyaagba, meaning top or senior lady, informed her that the baby was a reincarnation that came every seven generations to help the poor and oppressed. The last messenger was not born in Africa, but in America and her kind had actually not been seen in the land for fourteen generations. She was to be named Tutu Barbara, Iyaagba told a perplexed Tinu.

She informed Tinu that when the time came, her baby would be called upon to take on the battle for justice. She was not certain when exactly this was to occur, but she guessed it was likely to be very early in her life. As Tutu grew up, Tinu consulted with her from time to time whenever she was troubled and was usually placated.

Therefore, she set off early the next morning without an appointment, which was not often required in Africa, due to the predominantly open extended family culture. Nevertheless, it seemed the psychic was forewarned. Tinu met her sitting outdoors on her balcony with an extra seat and two bottles of coke, one unopened.

"I have been expecting you!" she called out jovially to Tinu as she arrived and they exchanged greetings. "How's my Dada?"

As Tinu sat down and was about to talk, the psychic interrupted her. "Open your drink and relax. You don't have to say it; I can see it on your face. You have been having dreams? I have also had similar dreams," she said solemnly. "Dada's time has finally arrived!"

"What time has finally arrived, Iyaagba?" Tinu asked agitatedly, "I thought all that had been done with," she cried in agony, remembering the predictions at Tutu's birth.

"No, it hasn't! I thought it would have occurred a bit earlier like in her first coming, but apparently it didn't."

"Oh! My God! Please what can you do to prevent it? I can't allow anything to happen to her. She is my only child and life," Tinu begged, falling to her knees in desperation, while the older woman looked and shook her head in dismay.

"There is nothing we can do to change destiny, especially this one. All we can do is to help her prepare. Anything else would be a futile exercise," she said with all the sincerity she could summon. She tried to placate Tinu by using her hand to gently soothe the back of her neck as she wept on her lap, where she had placed her head as she knelt beside her.

"No, I can't allow this. She is only an innocent little girl. She can't be expected to take on the world's problems and its wicked, powerful forces. Why must it be..," Tinu implored tearfully.

"Come on! Get hold of yourself. You knew this would happen," the psychic snapped a bit too sharply. "And what do you mean, "She is young"? The gods have chosen her and if the gods are backing her, no one can stand against her. Haven't you heard of David and Goliath? Please stop this negative rubbish!" the psychic said peevishly and stood up to go indoors, leaving behind the emotive mother.

Tinu got hold of her emotions and found her way out of the building to return home, where her worst fears were to be confirmed.

On her arrival home, Tinu was greeted with loud rap music. The servants told her Tutu was in a celebratory mood, which she found rather strange since she knew it was neither her birthday nor were there any exam results to be celebrated at this time of the year. Curious to find out the cause of the celebration, she headed towards Tutu's room.

On entering Tutu's room, before she could ask, Tutu ran up to her and hugged her. "Mum, thanks for the advice, it's happened! I've got an admission to Franklin Pierce College," she shouted joyfully as she waved a letter in her mother's face.

The letter had arrived from the New Hampshire College, offering her a place in its postgraduate program specializing in intellectual property law. This was a great coup for Tutu, as Pierce was one of the foremost colleges in intellectual property and copyright law. Tutu was ecstatic and expected her mother to be joyful, but instead she looked faint and depressed as she sat down.

"What's wrong, mum?" Tutu asked with some concern in her voice over her mother's strange reaction.

"Nothing! Let's hope your father agrees," Tinu answered weakly, deciding not to voice her fears, especially in light of Tutu's high spirits, knowing fully well she would react adversely.

She thought of how she will explain her sudden change of mind after leading her on over the past year, although she had thought the danger was long past. She decided her husband would have to disappoint Tutu.

Unfortunately for Tinu, her husband was unhelpful. He did not want to be at loggerheads with Tutu, who had distanced herself from him ever since the breaking of the scandal. He was even overjoyed, when the next morning a letter offering a full scholarship arrived, thus exempting him from the high cost of tuition.

In addition, another letter of admission arrived from Harvard Law School, although without a scholarship. Tinu realized she was left with no choice, but to voice her objections, which, as expected, were not taken kindly by Tutu. Tutu, in turn, played on the rift between her parents and once again switched loyalties by returning to her former daddy's girl relationship. Much to Tinu's chagrin, she was placed on the outside, while preparations were being made for Tutu's departure. Therefore, she thought the only way she could stop it was by frightening Tutu with the facts.

She decided to take Tutu to the psychic for her to hear from the horse's mouth what lay in store for her on her journey. Getting Tutu to follow her was no minor feat.

"What's the point? She's probably going to say something stupid to scare you into giving her money like they all do," was Tutu's reply, having never met the psychic. In the end, she agreed to go to satisfy her mother.

On their arrival at the psychic's house, they were seated in a modestly furnished medium-sized living room, while they waited for the psychic. There were two old, brown leather loveseats, a sofa and an armchair arranged around a heavily scratched coffee table in the center.

In one corner of the room stood a mahogany cabinet with a 24-inch brown paneled television that looked well over twenty years old. On the long television cabinet and on the wall behind it were a few family and personal pictures, mostly in black and white prints that appeared to have been taken several decades ago.

While waiting for the medium, the teenage girl that ushered them in and informed them that the psychic was busy, served them drinks and tried to make them comfortable. There was a stony silence between mother and daughter, before they were ushered into an inner room decorated this time in the traditional African way, with beautiful multi-colored mats to sit on and stylish calabashes on the wall. Around where she was sitting there were various statues, which appeared to be more religious in nature than for decorative purposes.

"Good afternoon, my dear, I guess you are preparing for your journey," the psychic smiled and greeted Tutu warmly from where she sat near the ancient carvings.

"Iyaagba, that is why I brought her to see you! You know I am against the trip, following your revelations and I will be grateful, if you can tell her yourself!" Tinu said before Tutu had a chance to reply.

The psychic smiled smugly, "True, there are dangers, but isn't life a dangerous journey in itself for everyone. No one knows what life has in store for us. I believe she will do fine," the old woman said philosophically to Tinu's consternation.

"Please Iyaagba, what dangers are these that mummy keeps talking about?" Tutu asked despite her skepticism. Her curiosity was piqued by the woman's philosophical statement that didn't support her mother's stance.

"Well, you can't blame your mother for being worried. It is hard for a mother to let go. As for your question, I can't specifically say the dangers, but I know that you have been chosen to carry out some tasks in which you will face some very powerful people. It will be hard, but you'll not be alone and in the end, hopefully you'll prevail."

Tinu shook her head in disagreement. "You know that before good prevails, lots of the good or innocent die, or are sacrificed. Why should the sacrifice be from me and my only...?" she asked in frustration.

The psychic sighed irritably, "Listen, I told you about this, years ago," she snapped at Tinu with a cold stare. "She's got some work to continue and you should be there to make her strong, not to mess things up."

"What work are you talking about that I am to continue and where?" Tutu asked, being confused by the discussion between the older women.

"You will be shown everything in time, the future, present and past. One thing I know regarding your past and probably future is that you have to absolutely refrain from alcohol. That was the cause of your, and many other people's, downfall the last time! Alcohol was used to weaken our defenses and even the strongest ones will easily fall, once alcohol lets down their guard. Those who choose you will show you where you are coming from and going."

"I know where I am coming from and going to," Tutu answered saucily as she was beginning to get irritated by the drama. Her attitude surprised the older women, while it prompted a smile from the psychic, tears slowly rolled down her mother's cheeks.

"That's the attitude, my child! *Dada o dada to o*" the psychic retorted with a hint of sarcasm. Meaning, *'the dreadlock person is not as good as you'* since *Da* meant good in Yoruba, *'Da Da'* very good and *Dada* a person with dreadlocks.

"Dada!" the psychic slapped her forehead faintly as she remembered something. "Lest I forget, I've got something for your protection until you are strong enough to stand for yourself. It will give you the necessary links you might need."

She reached for something under the statues and brought out two brass rings, which she set before her. Tutu did not venture to collect them, but her mother did.

"Wear them both on one finger at all times and never ever remove them, whatever you do!" Iyaagba sternly warned her. They departed soon afterwards.

On the way home in the car, Tinu broke down and made a heart-rending plea to Tutu to cancel her travel plans, but Tutu ignored her. Once again, she tried to involve her husband, but he did not want to cross his daughter on what he believed to be mere superstition and disguised sentimentality.

Frustrated, she broke down emotionally and turned antagonistic to both daughter and husband, rarely coming out of her room. Eventually, she realized she couldn't change fate a few days prior to Tutu's departure and decided to spend the last few moments in harmony with her daughter, helping with her shopping.

On the eve of Tutu's departure, after her send off party, Tinu went into Tutu's room and had a heart to heart talk with her. Before leaving, she handed over the rings saying, "Since you are bent on going, please follow the psychic's advice and always wear these rings. Please do that for me and yourself!"

They hugged and Tinu went back to her room, where she lay awake through the night, crying as she thought of the dangers Tutu would face.

3

That was last night Tutu thought, while waiting in the room for O'Brien, pending her imminent deportation. Despite her hard work and plans, she would be forced to return home. With her hands clasped behind her head in despair and the rings glittering as they touched, she did not know when she fell into a trance and her lips slowly moved in a whisper.

In the next room, O'Brien settled down to fill in her exclusion papers, a task he enjoyed immensely, but before proceeding, he decided to make a cup of coffee at the other end of the office. This was the back office for the immigration officials and was not open to the public. It was an open plan office with three rows of desks strewn with papers, files, a few personal photographs and each was equipped with a computer, although most of their owners were not at their seats.

Whistling blissfully in the practically empty office, he rinsed his cup, taking no notice of a hand-written "out of order" note stuck to the coffee maker, he plugged it to boil some water. Nor did he notice the frayed cord's slightly exposed wires when he plugged it into the wall outlet with his damp hands.

O'Brien never knew what happened as he received the shock of his life. The voltage passed through him and flung him across the room. He cleared the first two desks, but coming down, he hit his head on the sharp edge of the third. O'Brien landed on the back of his neck with a sharp thud, followed by a computer which fell on him, although he never felt it because he had already passed out.

A lady across the room, who had kept her head down all the while, busy completing her paperwork was the one startled into raising the alarm. He was rushed to Boston General Hospital.

Tutu was brought out of the trance by the commotion that ensued due to the accident next door, but she had no idea of what was happening. She had to wait for another 45minutes before the lady she had seen earlier walked into the room.

"Oh! You are still here," the blond lady, Maria Straw, said in surprise, when she saw her.

Tutu shrugged in resignation, "I am waiting for the man that was attending to me."

"Uh, let me find your papers. Mr. O'Brien is ill disposed and won't be able to take care of your case anymore. Let me see, uh," Ms. Straw scratched her scalp absent-mindedly as she left the room to check for her passport.

She returned shortly afterwards with Tutu's papers, "Do you know what was...." She paused as she read through the letter of admission.

"You are here for an LL.M program. That's nice! My brother and my boyfriend are studying for the same degree. It's nice seeing a woman doing the same," she commented as she read through the documents.

Having perused the papers, she looked up with a baffled expression on her face. "I wonder why Martin was holding you up. It all seems fine to me. Excuse me for a minute," she rose and left the room with the papers and returned two minutes later.

Handing over the papers with a smile. "I am sorry for keeping you waiting. Welcome to the United States," she shook Tutu's hand and led her out of the room. Tutu was at a loss for words and just beamed in appreciation.

When Tutu reached the baggage reclaim area, all of her fellow passengers were gone and her suitcase was the only piece of luggage on the conveyor belt. She quickly shifted the heavy

Louis Vuitton suitcase onto a cart and made her way through customs.

By the time Tutu came out into the arrival hall, Professor Parris was already tired of waiting and holding up a placard with her name on it, at the exit. He never met students at the airport nor even did half of what he had done towards helping her secure admission. It was as if an invisible hand was compelling him to take an extra step every time, despite his reluctance.

He had just returned into the hall after a quick smoke and didn't have the placard up, but amazingly recognized her as she walked out, despite never having set eyes on her before. It had something to do with the peculiar and somewhat familiar way she walked, the way her knees knocked, that made him look at her face. Their eyes met and locked, both of them puzzled by the de ja vu. The professor broke the awkward silence.

"Hi, I guess you must be Tutu," he said nearly sure of the answer as he offered her a hand, which she shook with a shy smile.

"And you must be Professor Parris, who I must thank very much for everything," she said warmly, despite her confusion.

She could have sworn she knew him from somewhere, but couldn't place the face. "Why does everyone look familiar around here," she thought as she subconsciously rubbed her forehead, which was throbbing slightly due to the pressure from her experiences over the last couple of hours. Tutu was too exhausted to brood over anything. She was grateful that she had overcome her flight and immigration ordeals and there was someone, who appeared to be nice and willing to help.

The professor helped her with the luggage cart and led her toward the parking lot. As they got out into the open, there was a loud thunderclap, and it began to drizzle. He made small talk about the weather in Boston, which had experienced heavy snow during the winter and continuous rain in spring.

"How was your journey?" He opened the door to his Toyota Camry and loaded the luggage into the car.

"Please don't remind me," She said in anguish. "It was hell.

At one point, I thought I was going to be refused entry, which was why I came out late."

Turning into the slow moving traffic of interstate 93 South that led into downtown Boston, Professor Parris said, "I bet you must be very hungry, unless there has been a drastic change in airline food menu and quantity."

Tutu nodded her reply in silence, and he asked what she would like to eat.

She shrugged indifferently, being too physically and emotionally drained to feel hunger or think and if she tried, she felt she might just collapse from exhaustion and fear. The recent events had made her realize how vulnerable she was in her new country of residence. Fortunately, her host didn't mind and, feeling rather awkward, he tried to ease the tension by being talkative.

"I don't think it's fair to start you on junk food, you are going to have more than enough of that between lectures and lunch breaks. I know an excellent Chinese restaurant near South Street downtown and if I am right the Chinese are complete in their world food domination. They are everywhere in the world," he said, obviously trying to make her relax with his light banter. He could feel her tension and sensed there was something bothering her.

"That's quite true. They are even in remote towns across Nigeria," she answered loosening up a little bit. "I do love Chinese food."

"Chinese food it shall be," the Professor said. The law professor, Samuel Parris was a divorced 49 year-old Bostonian who, despite his slightly graying black hair, still possessed an impressive, athletic physique standing at six feet one inches. He had a boyish charm with his clean-shaven strong square chin and soft hazel eyes.

Samuel Parris had married his college sweetheart in his late twenties, but after a few years and two kids, he and his wife, Helen had agreed to an amiable divorce. They separated due to growing apart, a direct result of their different career pressures. Due to his easy-going nature, the wife took everything and moved to California with the kids, whom he rarely saw. His son and daughter were now both in college.

Although Samuel Parris was regarded handsome and desired by many a woman, he had not dated anyone in a long while. After the divorce, he had dated various women, some from his college, but soon began to totally immerse himself in his work, leaving little or no time for emotional relationships.

His main social interaction was with his family, who he had moved back to join in Salem after his divorce. With the kids living 3,000 kilometers away and the house sold, he resigned his lecturing post at New York University and came back to his native Massachusetts, where his family had a long history dating nearly as far back as the pilgrims.

Originally from England, his forebears had settled in Salem, before moving a bit to the south of Boston and then back to the northern limits of Boston and to Salem. The Parrises had a long tradition of being clergymen and women until the late 19th century, when many of them went into the law profession.

In his generation, they produced four lawyers, two of them, his brothers currently living in Dallas and Seattle. The fourth one, his aunt's son worked in New York, while the professor stayed with his aunt in Salem. At present, there were about ten other Parrises in and around Salem.

The Parrises were all gifted orators and raconteurs, who enjoyed performing for an audience. The professor often joked that maybe his children would be the first Parrises to make it to the big screen with their move to California.

He had a three-bedroom house off Main Street in Concord, New Hampshire, which was a few minutes away from Franklin Pierce College, where he lectured. While he spent most of the week in Concord, he stayed with his aunt and family in Salem during weekends or whenever he was less busy.

Turning off route 93 at the South Street exit, they drove around for nearly twenty minutes, before finding a suitable parking space. After settling down in the restaurant and having run out of small talk, he suddenly turned officious.

"So, tell me your plans!" he asked, looking straight into her eyes, like a stereotypical professor, a sudden transformation that unsettled Tutu and made her hide eyes behind her locks.

Lost for words, she held back for a second or two, "Uh, I want to take a postgraduate course and see if I can find myself a good job, probably through the college," she quavered, sounding neither convincing nor confident.

Samuel Parris with a slight wry smile on his face decided to drill her, at least, if she was not going to respond to small talk, maybe a bit of questioning would loosen her up, he thought.

"So let's put it this way, if I or someone else could offer you a job right now, will you cancel your plans for the postgraduate course?" he baited her.

Tutu thought for a while before answering, because she did not want to give the wrong impression and luckily, the serving waiter gave her some leeway.

"It depends on a number of things. I won't mind studying intellectual property or corporate law, but it's often said that education is a means to an end, and I will really love to work in the law field." Pausing to see his reaction, she shifted uneasily, not knowing whether she was giving the wrong impression.

Nevertheless, she continued, "To tell you the honest truth, I applied for an LL.M in order to leave home and the poor economic situation. I am eager to apply my knowledge and skills in the real world after studying all my life and earning two degrees."

She was still unsure of how she had fared when she finished due to his blank expression. Instinctively, she had followed her mother's advice: "When in doubt, tell the truth; there is nothing like sincerity". She could even hear Tinu's words ringing in her head. She didn't want him to feel she was shifty person and a waste of his effort though.

Following a short thoughtful silence, "I see where you are coming from, although I won't be offering you any job, at the moment," he said with a small mischievous chuckle over having sufficiently rattled her.

"Did you apply to any other programs?" Prof. Parris asked, dropping the drilling game, which pricked his conscience, knowing she was feeling vulnerable. "Just a matter of interest," he quickly added.

"Yes, I applied and was admitted to Harvard," she replied with a tinge of pride.

"So why did you choose Franklin Pierce over Harvard? Most people will do the opposite."

"First and foremost, the scholarship I was awarded there and secondly, which is more consolatory, I was told Franklin Pierce has the best intellectual property program. All I need is a program that will give me a sound footing in the legal or corporate world," she answered, sounding more relaxed and confident.

"Well, the scholarship is for any reputable postgraduate law degree and was not offered or attached to any particular school," he explained to an attentive Tutu. "Secondly, as you know Harvard has a world class graduate program, which although it might not specialize in intellectual property, could open more doors in the corporate world," he paused for a sip of his wine, "I will advise you to keep your options open, because..."

"Open? How long do I have?" she asked surprised.

"Not very long, I am afraid, but I mean till you look around Boston and Concord. I have been offered a two-year visiting professorship in Harvard, which I intend to accept. While I am in Boston, you can stay in my house in Concord as long as you keep it clean. Otherwise, if you choose Harvard, you are welcome in the Parris' family home in Salem on the northern outskirts of Boston, until you find a nearer residence in Boston, Cambridge or Brookline." With that, they ate in silence.

After lunch, they went to Salem where they were to spend the night, before going up north to Concord, New Hampshire. He told her he had a meeting in Boston the next morning, otherwise they would have gone straight to Concord.

Professor Parris drove to the family home, a big gray building, which had recently been refurbished and renovated. Actually, the structure had experienced too many renovations, additions, and even one major reconstruction after a fire nearly razed it to the ground.

The result was an architectural eyesore that had no shape and various floor levels. Although, classified as a three-story house, which it was in some parts, there were only one or two floors in some other parts of the building. Tutu had a strong eerie feeling of deja vu as she saw the area and the house.

"This whole area seems familiar. Was it in a movie or documentary?" she asked as they unloaded her luggage.

"Salem is notorious for a witch hunt in the seventeenth century, so you might have seen it on television or at the movies. One of my ancestors was in the middle of it all and so was this house," Samuel Parris answered as he opened the door, while Tutu kept looking around.

As they set the luggage down at the bottom of the stairs in the corridor leading to the living room, Tutu sighted an ancient flowery candelabrum. Suddenly, she let out a painful shriek and clutched around her collarbone, falling to her knees in obvious pain. Alarmed, Samuel ran over to her side, asking what was wrong.

"I felt a sharp stabbing pain in my neck" she said, wiping the cold sweat that had accumulated on her forehead, while she steadied herself and regained her composure. "I am okay! It was just a passing pain. Maybe I pulled a muscle carrying my suitcase," she said as he escorted her into the living room, where he introduced her to his aunt.

His aunt, his dead father's sister was about 80years old and frail. Auntie Theresa had taken care of the professor and his brothers since they lost their parents in their teens. Tutu greeted the old woman, who answered her with a slight wave as she watched television.

Parris suggested Tutu take a nap and offered to take her out to Boston later in the evening to see Boston's nightlife. Retiring to the guestroom on the second floor, Tutu tried to have a brief nap, but could hardly sleep because she kept having nightmares.

The injured women from the Empire Bank building were taken to New York University Hospital, where some were placed in the intensive care unit. Mrs. Forrest was revived when she reached the hospital and was classified in a critical but stable condition. She was not allowed to see her worried family members, not even her husband, who had followed the ambulance. He was kept waiting outside until her wounds were treated and the physician gave permission.

He left after two hours of waiting, while he continued making inquiries and giving orders on his mobile phone, with regards to his wife's last request. He found out there were three flights coming from Nigeria landing in Boston, New York and Washington D.C. Although, those arriving in Boston and to a lesser extent D.C, looked more likely to be carrying the girl, due to their time of arrival.

Forrest didn't return to the hospital until late in the afternoon after being told that his wife was ready to receive visitors. In the waiting room, he met the young Anthony Pierce, who was just about to leave, but changed his mind and decided to go in with George Forrest to see his wife. Pierce was eager to hear the details of the macabre incident, which he knew would most likely be discussed around Mrs. Forrest's sickbed.

In a semi-private room, they found Mrs. Forrest covered in bandages and attached to an IV. She looked like a pale and frail memory of the vibrant woman, glittering with diamonds and laughter a few hours earlier. Her voice was very weak, but she made a strong effort to speak when she saw her husband choke up on tears upon seeing his partner of nearly 40 years.

"I am okay and will be out of here soon. Don't bother yourself, George," she said, trying to sound brave for her husband's sake. It had always been like that between them, she being the stronger one. "Did you find out anything?"

George Forrest managed to get hold of his emotions and spoke, "There are three flights coming from Lagos, but only two are likely since the third just landed a few hours ago. I gave orders to exclude all first time female visitors, and I am expecting some feedback anytime from now."

As if on cue, his mobile phone rang to the consternation of a nurse, whom he ignored as she complained about the use of mobile phones on hospital grounds.

After a brief chat, he hung up and walked back from the window to her bedside. "Ten women were excluded in Dulles airport and a couple in Boston, but our man in Boston suffered a serious electrical accident and was taken to hospital. Let's hope, she was one of those barred and not..."

"Oh No!" Mrs. Forrest cried in anguish, attracting a passing nurse and others to her side, but she waved them away. "She is here, she is in Boston! She killed that man. She will not let anyone stand in her way," she shook her head despondently, while her visitors stood in silence, not knowing what to say.

Anthony Pierce broke the silence, "But how can you be so sure, Aunt? Massachusetts is no longer the economic center, thanks to her." He asked, not out of his normal inquisitiveness or argumentativeness, but out of his concern for her health. She was looking worse by the second since hearing the news.

"I am sure. She might be trying to start where she stopped. I thought over it and realized I shouldn't have sent weaker spiritual beings after her. One of her powers is through electrical currents, either through thunder or electricity, and that poor man was electrocuted."

Anthony couldn't resist going further, "Correct me, if I am wrong, because I have being reading up on the Salem Witch Trials and her victims, if we could call them that according to Mr. Forrests version. They were mostly killed by hanging, weren't they? Or is..."

"One of the African gods she worships is Shango, the god of justice and thunder who died by hanging according to Yoruba mythology. The Salem girls affected by sorcery complained of convulsions, which are electrical impulses to the brain. There were many other unpublicized occurrences. Thunder and lighting, you know, are electrical in nature," she explained to Anthony.

"Thunder is a strange thing to worship," he wondered aloud in fascination.

"You must have heard of Santeria in the Bronx, the way of the saints, a mixture of Christian saints and African gods. It's the fastest growing religion here in New York and Miami and has vast followers in Brazil, Cuba, and other South American and Caribbean Islands. They have seven main gods, Yemanja, the sea goddess, Ogun, god of iron and industry, the most popular one Shango, known as Saint Barbara, the thunder god...uh. I can't remember the rest," he tried to recollect, but shook his head and threw his hands up in defeat.

"I only know Osanyin, the healing god called St Joseph and Orunmila, the supreme god called St Francis", Mrs. Forrest contributed.

"Anyway, they are mainly naturalists. If you ever visit southern Nigeria or other rainforests, you will not find it strange they worship thunder. The medieval people took to worshipping the most volatile and recurrent element in their environment. They do not have hurricanes, snowstorms or any other disturbing weather element, apart from thunder and God knows you ain't seen or heard anything till you experience it," Forrest told Anthony, pedantically.

He explained further that all Africans being naturalist worshipped prevalent environmental factors. Further north from the Yorubas, especially Ancient Egypt, which was dry and with no thunderstorms, they worshipped the Sun god, Amon, who baked the earth into desert.

"Amon is also a Yoruba deity. Coptic traditions talked of Shango, god of thunder, the King of Kush. Kush is from Kuoso, meaning 'didn't hang!' Forrest said. "According to some historians, it was from the Sun and other naturalist's gods and beliefs that Judaism, Christianity and Islam took their roots. Christians say Kushites were children of Ham, while some Muslims say the Yorubas were Nimrod, Ham's son, the great hunter!"

"It appears there was a whole lot unpublicized, which I need to know since she has now returned and we may need to go after her," Anthony commented, trying to provoke further discussion.

"Yes, that's true and I'll tell you all I know, but it is not a good idea to go after her. That was the mistake many people made back then, that cost them their lives. Although I guess I must do something," she said as she tried sitting up in the bed, "This is what happened...."

At about seven o'clock, Tutu rose from her troubled sleep and began making preparations for their planned outing. After bathing and dressing, they departed for downtown Boston, first stopping at the Boston Harbor, which was packed with revelers enjoying the warm summer evening. Later, they walked over to nearby downtown Boston, where they ate supper, before leaving for a nightclub.

Samuel suggested going to Officers, an Essex nightclub on the northern outskirts of Boston. He told her he had not been to any nightclub or party in over a year, which was evident in his ebullience, when they arrived at the club.

Officers' nightclub was a medium sized, racially mixed hip-hop club with lots of middle class young people enjoying themselves, although the middle-aged professor mixed easily.

Initially, Tutu held back and remained tense, but she soon relaxed, mixing and enjoying herself, managing to put all her earlier worries and troubles behind her. Soon she felt she was back in Lagos, with the familiar music and merriment, which before her academic life got hectic two years ago, she enjoyed every weekend.

"Have a drink, Tutu," Professor Parris offered as she returned from the dance floor. He was pouring from his second Moet champagne bottle and was getting a bit loud and unsteady, obviously enjoying himself to the hilt.

"No, thanks, I don't drink alcohol," she answered shyly as she dropped into the seat next to him, exhausted. She realized how much she had missed partying, she had once been a party animal, but the University of Ife had gradually turned her into a bookworm. Now everything seemed, so distant and at last, she was in America. She was pleased to be with African Americans, who appeared to be more affluent and educated than she had expected from the stereotypical image she had received.

"Nonsense, champagne isn't drinking alcohol, it's uh..." he said loudly, pausing to search for the right word, "Celebration! Come on, don't be a spoil sport."

For a reason, he couldn't explain, he found himself more and more endeared to her since her arrival, despite his initial resentment of going too far for an unknown stranger in Africa, but on seeing her, he felt like he was reuniting with a long lost friend.

"No, I am really not supposed to..." she stopped mid sentence and reconsidered the offer, especially as he feigned hurt feelings. She did not want to do anything to displease her host, landlord and probably lecturer. In fact, she felt he was more than a host and was growing fonder of him by the minute. Like him, she was beginning to feel like an old friend, "Okay, I guess one drink won't kill me," she laughed coyly and accepted a glass from his extended hand.

"That's the spirit!" Samuel enthused, obviously pleased she was relaxing and joining the flow of things. He ordered some chicken wings to snack upon and they had a few dances together, after which he insisted on refilling her glass twice.

To her dismay, as she was really enjoying herself and getting slightly tipsy, she was told the club was about to close. She was told, according to Massachusetts State law, all clubs must close by two a.m.

They left the club at about 1.45 am. Still in high spirits, she talked about back home and her nightclubbing days. She told him that in Lagos, clubs stayed open till six in the morning and the night would probably just be starting. It showed desperation if you left home for a party before midnight, she explained as they chatted on the way back home from an enjoyable evening, despite its brevity.

When they reached home and both staggered through the front door, Prof. Parris said goodnight and retired to his room. With Tutu's head pounding and her speech slurred, she managed out of sheer determination to get to her room on the second floor.

She fell onto the bed and passed out as soon as she stepped into the room, but after about forty-five minutes, she got up to change into her nightgown. Getting her gown out of her suitcase was no easy task, but she finally managed to extract it. Stripping naked before putting on the gown, she moved like she was on automatic pilot and because of that, she did everything she used to do at home in Lagos. She removed her bangles, chains, earrings and her rings, including the ones given to her by the psychic, before lying in her bed.

She had dozed off for a while, when she startled awake, believing she heard someone call her name. She could hear voices in the corridor, she thought, when she once again heard someone call her name in a familiar voice, which she couldn't exactly identify. It seemed the person was calling outside her door and after the third time, she decided to check. When she opened the door, she saw nobody, but as she was about to close it, the voice once again called her. This time it came from the staircase.

Hesitantly, she walked toward the staircase, but saw nobody and decided to peep through the railings to see whether there was anyone in the living room downstairs. In order to get a proper view, she had to go down a few steps. On her second step, she sensed some movement behind her, but before she could identify what it was, she was roughly pushed. She flew down the stairs screaming, which stopped as she hit the ground falling on the candelabra, which pierced her neck around the collarbone.

Before she collapsed as her vision blurred, she saw two old ladies. One of them, Mrs. Forrest, was obviously very happy, while the other shook her head sadly.

"You were warned about alcohol, this is not what we expected of you. You should know better that...," she said.

"Who are you? Where am I? Warned off what? Who am I?" she asked weakly as her vision continued to swim.

"Listen! I will tell you everything!" the disappointed lady

said and offered her a hand, but by that time Tutu's eyes had closed as she heard rushed footsteps faraway. Tutu rose to her feet with the help of the woman and looked on, standing next to the old woman, as Parris frantically shook her lifeless body.

"This is how it all began in your previous life...."

4

JANUARY 1670: WEST AFRICA

It appeared that the heavens were exploding as thunderclap after thunderclap rent the gloomy sky, with each one trying to outdo the previous one. A couple of fires were started as thunderbolts struck everywhere and everything in the rainforest that had just experienced a long dry season.

To an outsider, it would appear Armageddon had finally arrived, but most of the locals continued their business unperturbed, with the exception of a few people with guilty consciences fearing that Shango, the god of justice and thunder, was out to strike them down for their crimes. The thunderstorm was heavier than the normal rainforest storm expected at the beginning of the raining season, and most people's unruffled countenances could probably be linked to a local saying, "The falling heavens will not be fall on only one person's head".

As the heavens raged, there was a young woman going through a greater disturbance, wishing the heavens could actually come falling and end it all for her in the front room of a newly built hut. She was going through labor pains that went on for hours, despite all traditional means employed to induce birth all day. Even those scurrying around to help her took no particular notice of the raging heavens with pain and turmoil being so close and personal.

Lying on a colorful mat in the middle of a large room with red mud bricks decorated with calabashes and statues, her friends and family stood around praying something could be done to deliver immediately. Close to midnight after eighteen hours of trying everything, the midwife of twenty years threw up her hands in exasperation.

"I do not know what is going on, but I have never come across such a difficult birth," she admitted to those around her as she stood over the agonized mother-to-be. "I think we'd better call the Chief Priest before it is too late," she suggested, acknowledging her first defeat in two decades. A teenager was immediately sent to get the town's chief priest.

Not too long afterwards, the chief priest arrived with his oracle, "It is only you that can get me out of my house at this time of the day and in such conditions," he said grumpily as he sat down to set his oracle. The slightly bent man with plaited hair was believed to be the most supernaturally powerful priest in the land and specialized in the Shango sect, although he also used Ifa like most Yoruba religious practitioners. The Yoruba believe in the Ifa Oracle that is used to consult the gods. The Ifa Oracle is consulted using cowries or stones, which are interpreted by the priest.

In Yoruba religion, there is the supreme god, Olodumare at the center of their beliefs and there were many other lesser gods, who are like saints who intercede on their behalf to Olodumare. Each of the lesser gods has its own domain or area of specialty, like Shango, god of thunder and justice, or Ogun, god of iron and war.

Shaking sixteen cowries in his palms as he chanted, he threw them onto his board and tried to interpret their dispersal like the astrologers read the dispersal of stars.

"Hmm, no!" he said ominously. He picked up the cowries and shook them in his palms once again like dice and threw them out. Looking at their positions as they came to rest, he had a wry expression on his face as he squeezed his eyebrows together pensively.

"No wonder the heavens have been raging all day," he observed aloud to himself, shaking his head in dismay. Looking up from the oracle, he pointed to the laboring mother as he spoke to her family gravely. "That is one hell of a woman, one who could struggle with the heavens and still remain standing."

"What does that mean?" asked her husband impatiently, presently not in the mood for the long theatrics and proverbs of the Ifa practitioners.

"Hold on, boy!" the old man snapped, throwing him a scornful look. "I am bringing out a bird from my pocket, and you are asking whether it is black or red. Be patient and let me bring it out alive before you start inquiring about its color!"

"Sorry, sir!" the embarrassed older members of the family chorused, apologizing on behalf of their impetuous son, who kept quiet with a cynical expression on his face.

"As I was saying before I was interrupted, the woman is struggling with the gods over their beloved one. The baby in her womb is the favorite child of Shango, and he is definitely not happy giving up his daughter to this wicked world. That is why he has been spitting fire all day," he told his amazed audience.

"So what can be done? Please help us appeal to him," begged the mother-in-law. "We will make any sacrifice or whatever is required."

The Chief Priest consulted his oracle once again, while everyone watched in silent anxiety. "Oh! Oh! This is different from anything I have ever done. He does not want any sacrifice," he told them, pointing at the oracle as if they could see for themselves. Everyone drew in sharp breaths in trepidation as they heard the prognosis and looked at him expectantly for a solution. "He wants me to lead her to an intersection, where three roads meet. His daughter...a Dada has I can see...will only come out, where three worlds meet under the watchful eyes of Shango," he told them. Seeing a flash of contemplation on their faces, he continued, "Otherwise, she and the baby would be meeting the gods at home. She will die trying. I don't care if you open her up."

"But, Sir how can she walk in this rain and..." her husband pointed out, but was interrupted and cautioned by some elders, who tugged on his Dashiki.

The priest hastily gathered his things and got up. "I don't have time for haggling. I have just married this young woman that is using up all my energies. I have to catch some sleep. When you are ready, you know where to find me," he said haughtily as he made his way out.

Some members of the family blocked his way pleadingly and pulled him back, "We are sorry, Baba. You know these young generations are stupid. Please forgive him. We shall prepare her immediately and lead her along with you."

The Chief Priest shook his head defiantly. "That you will not be doing. It is only her and I going," he objected sternly. The family looked at each other quizzically and made a quick decision, as the midwife that they all relied on nodded in agreement. They helped the agonized woman onto her feet and gave her a long scarf to cover her head. Her family could only watch apprehensively as she followed the Chief Priest into the thunderous night.

Leading her slowly to the prescribed junction where paths from two kingdoms and the ocean met, the heavens continued to rage as they proceeded. Eventually, they reached the junction in the middle of the forest, and he told the expectant woman to kneel down. Reciting incantations as he shook various charms at the skies, the ferocity of the thunderclaps increased several times over.

"You gods can not refuse this young woman, who has promised to take utmost care of whatever you give her. One whose scalp shall never know a blade. If she lets anything happen to what you give, you can take her life in anger. Please give her a chance. Shango, I know you are the stubborn one, but please!"

At that point, several thunderbolts flew from the skies and struck inches away from the laboring mother, forming a circle of fire around her. Whether it was the striking thunderbolts that terrified her or the labor pains, she let out a long deafening scream. The shrill ended as the raging heavens calmed and the only sound was that of a crying, newly born Dada baby.

In the early hours of January 7, 1670, Tutuoba's parents received her into the world like most newlyweds with joy, pride and hope, despite her troubled delivery. Both parents were scions of distinguished local families with huge parcels of land and property.

They lived on the outskirts of a town of nearly twenty thousand people called Ijebu-Ode. Situated on the fringes of two empires, Ijebu-Ode was around 25 miles north of the West African coast of the Atlantic Ocean, on the south fringe of the Oyo Empire and to the extreme west of the Benin Edo Empire.

Tutuoba's father, Akin, was given a large tract of land on which he built a house, and he farmed on the rest. This was quite different from most people in Yorubaland, who cultivated a large commercial farm on the outskirts of their town, with a smaller mainly provisions farm in their backyards, thus enabling them to enjoy their cherished urban life. Due to this, Akin's family initially viewed him as a recluse, but they soon realized it was mainly due to his wife's profession.

It was in this house, he was to comply with the dictates of tradition, which was an elaborate naming ceremony for his firstborn. In Yorubaland, a child has to be named on the seventh day by the elders of its immediate community.

On the seventh day of Tutuoba's life, elders from both parents' families and friends started arriving as soon as the day broke. Wura's mother was the only absentee, having mysteriously disappeared when Wura was young, suspected to have been kidnapped by slave raiders. Everyone else congregated in the large living room, while last minute arrangements were being finalized.

Food was being prepared in the open courtyard at the back, although not to be served till after the ceremony. It was believed that wishes, prayers, curses or other spoken words were more effective early in the morning, before anything was eaten. Therefore, since a naming ceremony was to give and bless the new baby with goodwill and wishes, it was held first thing in the morning, before breakfast.

With everything in place, the ceremony commenced with the mother and her baby seated in the middle of the room behind an array of various foodstuffs, each having its significance. Her

father-in-law started the ceremony with blessings, each blessing
tied to a particular item, which he took from a bowl, tasted and
gave the baby to taste. He took honey, which being sweet was
to give the baby, sweet experiences throughout her life, salt was
to bring sharpness and give a tasteful life. After passing through
all the items, he named the baby and threw money into a bowl
of water.

The maternal grandfather and parents did likewise, after
which other elders, according to their importance, threw money
in the bowl of water and announced their choice of names. They
used cowry shells for money since gold was too easily available,
and they slowly accumulated in the bowl as everyone took
their turn. The names, potent with meaning, were decided by
examining family history, present circumstances and future
wishes.

As people dropped their names, they stopped to
congratulate the baby and her mother, and gradually the noise
level increased as people discussed and food was served to those
who had completed their duty.

As the line drew to an end, it came to the turn of a scruffy
middle-aged woman, who was about third to the last. Raising a
high-pitched voice above the din, she said, "This is an exceptional
Dada child, who has come to wreck havoc upon us. She wants
to take us on, the keepers of the underworld and I wish her no
blessings, for the soil of the underworld shall burn her feet and
the sun shall burn her scalp." She cursed the baby as she wagged
a finger at the mother and child.

Everyone was shocked and silent, except for a man, who
tugged on her sleeve, "No, I shall not remain silent, but rebuke
the one that wishes to wage war on the womb. She that wishes
to rule the underworld shall be nothing more than a slave!" she
proclaimed ominously and hurriedly left, before anyone could
regain their composure and harass her. On her way out, people
heard her hiss and shout, "Amon! Amon! Taboo!"

For nearly a full minute, everyone remained silent, while
the mother sobbed quietly.

"That is a lie!" the man, who was next in line, Wura's distant relative, said defiantly, breaking the silence. "I, Adegbite, the chief priest of Egbado, name this beautiful girl, Tutuoba. For the world shall be a cool and calm spot for her, it shall be like the shade of an Iroko tree and she shall live like a queen," he enthused in an effort to countermand the old witch's curse, although he had initially planned to name her after her mother, Wura. Everyone heartily said Ase (amen) to his prayers, in an effort to save the day. Tutu meaning calm or cool was to negate the curse of a troubled existence, while Oba meant king or leader to counter the slavery curse, although people mostly used the shortened form, Tutu to address her.

Afterwards, people asked about the identity of the woman, but no one seemed to know, where she came from or who invited her. The only person that knew who she was and what she was referring to, by claiming that the child was to wage war on her womb, couldn't say anything.

Food and entertainment were served, but the mood had been spoiled and the guests quickly ate up and left. Wura tried playing the host, but couldn't wait for the crowd to disperse. She had things to do in light of the disruptive occurrence. As soon as the guests dwindled to close family members, she took the baby indoors to lay her down.

Looking at her baby, Tutuoba, who was sleeping peacefully and oblivious to the trouble caused by the strange woman, Wura fondly rubbed her cheeks and quietly said, "Don't worry, nothing will happen to you. I shall protect you with everything I have." *First of all, let me go and deal with that mad dog*, she thought and kissed Tutu on her forehead. The baby smiled from her sleep as if she heard everything, although Wura believed she was passing wind. She got up and left.

Her destination was the town center, the residence of the Iyalode, the head of the women. Every town in Yorubaland had an Iyalode, whose main function was the organization and welfare of women, especially the market women. This Iyalode in particular, among other things headed the women's secret cult of which Wura was a junior member.

Wura was an herbalist, who although mostly practiced

from home, often went to the huge king's market. She joined the cult to help her supernaturally, whenever her curative medicine failed. Already, there were rumors of Wura's supernatural powers, but there was never any evidence to support the claim. The rumors had increased with her increasingly successful practice, but they were not new to her since it wasn't unusual to suspect women with light skin of supernatural tendencies. It was Wura's light complexion and fine features that earned her the name, Wura, meaning gold.

The light complexion turned red with rage as she headed to the Iyalode. The more she thought of the incident as she proceeded in the hot sun, the more she boiled with rage. How dare her, she fumed, at least she should have been consulted in private, instead of the public embarrassment and shock. Such utterances were known to destroy a child's future and that of its family's. The father's family could send the mother and child away in an effort to ward off evil and bad luck. The community could even stone them to death on mere accusation of witchcraft.

This could prompt an investigation into her herbal and curative practices, bringing about unwarranted scrutiny, false accusations and malicious attacks, she thought. This was undeserved, she believed, since she was no evil witch.

The Iyalode, a much older woman, whom everyone treated with reverence, was sitting in her courtyard, when Wura arrived. Dressed in a colorful, thick-threaded woven, ceremonial attire called Aso Oke and covered in decorative beads, she invited Wura to sit down beside her. Wura ignored the gesture and blurted out her story, standing. The Iyalode listened attentively to Wura's complaints as she slowly fanned herself and, when Wura finished, took her time before answering contemplatively.

"I have heard all that you have to say and would be lying, if I say I haven't heard the other side. Actually, this was why I stayed away," she held up a hand to stop Wura from interrupting as she chewed a kola nut.

"It's our Osanyin priestess, Omodele, who saw the vision, and you can't blame people if they are jittery about such things.

You heard of the incident shortly before you were born, when four women were accused of witchcraft and stoned to death. If your Dada child is truly going to cause us trouble, we are going to have defend ourselves, before it's too late."

"I respect your wisdom, Iyalode, but we are no evil witches and, in addition, how can my own child destroy me? No matter how wild a dog is, it doesn't bite its owner. Therefore I believe, one should examine the messenger closely, since the message doesn't make sense," Wura said. She had cooled down enough to sit next to the Iyalode as a messenger interrupted their conversation. He prostrated in reverence to the Iyalode and delivered a message from the King, thanking her for some gifts he recently received from her. The young messenger ran off immediately after he fulfilled his errand.

Once he left, Wura continued in a lower tone. "If you remember, it was only a couple of months ago that we were contemplating expelling Omodele for abusing her powers and rumors were rife that she had turned evil. You cannot pass a sentence on my baby on the utterances of a mad dog," she protested mildly, hoping to win over the town's most influential woman.

"But this was supported by Adunni, who also claimed to have had similar revelations," the Iyalode countered her argument irritably, not enjoying the position in which she was being placed. If she did nothing and the child came to disrupt and destroy them, she as the leader would be held responsible and accused of laxity. On the other hand, she didn't feel comfortable cursing an innocent baby, which was the reason she stayed away from the ceremony.

Wura sighed exhaustedly. "You know those two are of a kind and would always support each other," she pled with the chief, but realized that her mind was made up.

"All I know is that they said the child is a witch hunter and that the witches she hunts are not evil ones, but those that work for the benefit of their communities, which is what we are. If that is the case, she has to be stopped, before it is too late!" the Iyalode insisted.

Frustrated, Wura sprang to her feet. "If anybody or anything harms my baby, there will be war that no one has ever experienced before!" she said threateningly as she wagged her finger.

"No one talked of harming anyone, but she will have to leave our midst when she grows up enough to cause any havoc."

"How? What do you mean leave? Where is she to go? This is her home and land," Wura angrily stamped her feet as she removed her head tie and wrapped it around her waist in a confrontational posture.

"Don't worry, that could be arranged," the Iyalode said smugly as she bit on her kola, unruffled by the raging mother's histrionics.

"I mean it, if anything happens to her, there will...." She shouted angrily as she furiously wagged her finger, before the Iyalode, jumped to her feet and confronted her.

"Who the hell do you think you are? Coming into my yard, shouting and threatening me. Answer me! Who do you think you are talking to? Is it I or your mama?" The Iyalode moved closer to her till their noses were barely an inch apart and stared defiantly into Wura's eyes.

"Don't you dare come here with that attitude or I will have your head taken off for the birds to snack upon. I am trying to look out for what is in the best interest of everyone and you come in here threatening me. How dare you!" she hissed and walked indoors. "When you finish, take your two left legs and find your way out."

Wura, out of respect and confusion, was speechless as she left.

Wura went home more frustrated, angry and fearful for her baby's welfare than she had been when she left home. When she got home, she went straight to her room, where she'd left Tutuoba. Looking on the mat and around the nearby pile of clothes, she couldn't find her.

Due to her already troubled mind, she went berserk, shouting and screaming obscenities as she threw herself on the ground, alarming everyone around, including some guests, who were still partying.

"They have taken her! They have taken my life," she cried disconsolately.

Among those who ran to her aid was her sister-in-law, who had Tutuoba in her arms. When Wura saw Tutuoba, she was embarrassed and quietly took her from her sister-in-law. The family members, who witnessed or had heard of the earlier incident, understood her fears and looked at her pitifully.

This was the beginning of an overprotective relationship between mother and child, which bordered on paranoia. Wura hardly let Tutuoba out of her sight, making her sleep on the same bed to the displeasure of her husband and constantly waking up in the middle of the night to check on her.

Tutuoba grew up to be a loving and loveable precocious child, always willing to learn or help. She always watched her mother with keen interest as Wura went about making herbs and concoctions, being a well respected, albeit unusual herbalist/doctor, since it was more of a male profession. She was her mother's carbon copy and her immediate family always joked that the resemblance was due to the fact that she was always under her mother's wings.

This arrangement is believed to have prompted her father earlier than expected into marrying another wife, who also lived in the same compound. Over the years, the compound was increased to include other quarters, all surrounded by one fence. In addition to a new wife, some of his brothers moved in, in order to be able to fully cultivate the vast land bequeathed to him by the family.

Tutuoba was twelve in the dry season of 1682, when a tall, charming missionary by the name of Reverend Samuel Parris came into the town to seek converts. The clergyman, in his thirties, had just converted from being a merchant before coming to Africa from Jamaica. His change of heart didn't be extend to his looks, as Parris' tall, strong build and piercing eyes still made him look more like a sailor than a priest.

Reverend Parris moved to Ijebu-Ode from nearby Ketu, where he had escaped being lynched. This was a problem he had experienced once before and was very bitter about. His bitterness was not directed towards the people, who he found to be very hospitable and open, but was directed at his fellow Europeans in his former trade.

Whenever he reached a new African town more often than not, he was accepted into their midst without any qualms. Then he gradually would build his congregation. His plan was always the same—teach the children and teenagers English Language and convert them, for they are the future leaders who would direct their people into the Christian fold. Unfortunately, whenever he was getting comfortable and hopeful, slave raiders disrupted the peace of the town and his plans.

Usually, these towns would not have had any contact with Europeans, and when these raids happened, fingers were always pointed at him. It was hard to convince the people that he knew nothing of the raiders. A scapegoat was always needed and, as the only Caucasian, he was the best candidate.

On moving to Ijebu-Ode, he organized the children and taught them under a big Iroko tree, not too far from Wura's house. His favorite pupil was Tutu, a lanky girl with an engaging and endearing personality who was always eager to learn and soaked up everything he taught like a dry sponge. She had a talent for languages and picked up English rather fast, since it fascinated her.

Her intricately weaved dreadlocked long hair that was alternately wrapped in cloth, or adorned with colorful beads often fascinated Parris. It was obvious to him that Tutu was a special child doted upon by her mother.

This was a problem. Her mother was not at ease leaving her for long periods of time. Initially, she would not have it and Tutu had to sneak out to listen to him, which many a time earned her a cuff on the ear or even the occasional flogging, when her mother was in a bad mood. Fortunately, the floggings subsided after some time, although not completely. That is, until a major incident occurred that moved the reverend and her mother closer.

In July 1683, at the peak of the raining season, which also is that of the mosquito-breeding season, Reverend Parris caught the illness that gave the West African coast its notoriety as the white man's grave—malaria. Samuel Parris had been feeling weak and nauseous for a couple of days, when he collapsed under the tree where he was teaching Tutu and her peers. While other kids ran away laughing, Tutu ran to fetch her mother, who came to his aid at once. With the help of her brothers-in-law, they carried him to Wura's quarters.

When he was revived, he was told that he had malaria, which he had heard was a fatal disease. Many Europeans at the time believed that it was contracted from the drinking water and, although the locals did not narrow it down to the mosquito, they had their own cure. The average European shied away from this remedy due to its horrible taste and their lack of faith in the people's ability to cure a sickness that was as common as the flu.

When Samuel Parris was given the bitter concoction made from various herbs, he rejected it. Initially, Wura let him have his way. She couldn't be bothered over a grown man who, due to his stubbornness and pride, refused to be treated. When she realized he was getting worse, which was greatly depressing her daughter, she decided to take matters into her own hands.

Samuel was not the only one she had seen refuse the treatment. Many younger Africans often behaved likewise and she decided to treat him like one of them.

To do this, she needed Tutu to communicate with him, since Wura couldn't speak English. Normally, he spoke to her in his watery Yoruba or through her daughter. Wura instructed her daughter to tell him she was giving him an ultimatum: drink the concoction she placed by his bedside or face the indignity that was heading his way.

After the ultimatum expired, she entered the room with two heavyset women with massive bottoms and grabbed hold of him. One sat on his legs and the other on his torso, effectively pinning him down, while Wura held his head and forced his mouth open. After pouring a sufficient amount of the bitter concoction into his mouth, while laughing at his weak protests, none of which they understood, they left him to sleep for several hours. They returned to repeat the same process.

By the end of the following day, there was significant improvement in his health. The fever had subsided and he could muster enough strength to talk in Yoruba, which he did as soon as they returned to give him another dose.

"Please don't sit on me, you will break my bones the way you are going," he begged and turned to Tutu in English, "Tell them, I will drink anything they want, but please don't sit on me."

The women laughed heartily when Tutu interpreted his plea and told him to go ahead, which he quickly did. By the end of the week, he was back on his feet as strong as ever and forever grateful to Wura for saving his life. This would not be the last time.

The Reverend Parris and Wura became friends and she was more relaxed over leaving Tutu in his care. He returned to teaching under the tree and increasingly enjoyed his stay, especially with the help of mother and daughter. This blissful existence continued for the next few years until one day when things suddenly changed for the worse.

Slave raiders came up what they and many others called the Slave Coast via one of its numerous rivers and wreaked havoc on the peaceful town.

One evening in September 1686, as kids played outside the palace, one of the king's children and some other kids were kidnapped by the raiders. This brought about great indignation throughout the town. Unfortunately, it was directed towards Parris, the only white man in town. Especially, when some people said they saw some white men giving orders to some notorious coastal peoples around the river. The king ordered the people to bring the heads of all Europeans in sight, a command which they, especially the aggrieved parents, sought to carry out.

Fortunately for Parris, Wura was in the palace on unrelated

business, when she heard of the order. Believing in his innocence, she ran to where he was teaching Tutu and told him to follow her. Due to the language barrier that required Tutu to interpret, he barely escaped with her, but not before they were sighted by an approaching mob, which gave chase. They ran into Wura's quarters, but the mob surrounded the compound demanding the head of the child murderer.

Luckily, Tutu's father, Akin, arrived in time to pacify the mob that was becoming extremely agitated and threatening to burn down the compound, if the white man was not produced. In an effort to placate them, he asked whom they had seen with the white man, but fortunately they didn't know.

In the meantime, Wura hid Parris under a heap of clothes in her room. When she realized that the mob could not be pacified and might be brought in to search, she decided she had to get Parris out, unseen. It was impossible to disguise him due to his color, so she had to find another way. She racked her brain for a solution, but none was forthcoming. Eventually, it was Tutu who came up with a solution.

Tutu suggested hiding him in the large laundry basket, which they had to squeeze him into. Then Wura called upon another woman, who with Tutu helped her load the basket onto her head and she made out she was going to the stream, to do some laundry. With Reverend Parris in the basket, which daintily sat on her head, she passed through the mob and headed to the stream. Shortly afterwards, Tutu's father bowed to pressure to have his compound searched, which was done thoroughly, but to no avail.

With Tutu in tow as usual, they reached the stream, where the Reverend was set down. He was very grateful to mother and daughter and he made a hasty departure, before someone from the town saw him and raised an alarm. Tutu was tearful and he was heartbroken to once again leave those he had learned to love.

Tutu and Wura watched him make his way upstream, before making their way back home. They were to face the wrath of

Tutu's father, Akin, who had learned from someone at home that they were part of the conspiracy to hide the white man.

Tutu was morose for days over the loss of her friend, the only one who had successfully taken her away from under her mother's wings in her sixteen years of living. She once again returned to her mother's vigilant watch, since the only reason her mother had even relaxed her restriction was that he was European and definitely had no ties with the members of her cult, who had threatened her daughter.

Tutu never forgot about her friend, the Reverend Parris, but gradually returned to her normal self as she grew into a tall, beautiful young woman.

5

Although Tutu's town was to enjoy some tranquility for a while after the September 1686 incident, occurrences that resulted in the departure of the Reverend Samuel Parris were on the increase in the numerous surrounding towns and villages as time went on.

What had started as an amicable business and cultural relationship, with the arrival of the Portuguese in 1448 and their warm acceptance by the people and the King of Benin Empire, was to deteriorate into chaos over the next few centuries. The Benin Empire was one of the three most prosperous and heavily populated forest kingdoms, the others being the Oyo and Kongo Empires. Benin's walls were several times longer than the Great China Walls.

Following their arrival in Benin City in the mid 1400's, which culminated in mutually profitable trade, the discovery of America changed the economic situation for both sides. Sugar, derived from the tropical plant sugarcane discovered in Africa, was first cultivated by the Southern Europeans with the use of slave labor on the tiny islands off the coast of North and West Africa. Eastern Europeans, mainly Slavs were initially used as slaves, before the gradual introduction of African prisoners of war.

These islands were not enough to satisfy the skyrocketing demand and as fate would have it, a much larger land for sugar cultivation was found by accident in the Americas in 1497. The same winds that had brought the marauding Arabs from the north to West Africa blew Columbus ships from West Africa to America. The tropical eastern coast of South America, being climatically similar to the West Coast of Africa, was ideal for sugar cultivation.

The catch was that the vast lands needed slave labor, which due to various problems with the indigenous Indians, was sought in West Africa. Initially this was supplied with the prisoners of war, but as more American land was put under cultivation, the numbers supplied were insufficient and African leaders weren't overly interested in fighting for more captives. The high demand for slaves soon brought about a conflict of interest between the Europeans traders and the African leaders.

The authentic African leaders realized that the slave trade would deplete their kingdom of able-bodied labor required to promote and protect the economic and social interests of their empire. Moreover, all other aspects of trade were on a downward trend; therefore, after protracted disagreements, the Europeans were banned from the Benin Empire in 1515. This resulted in chaos as the European traders refused to accept no for an answer.

Guerrilla warfare and terrorist tactics were waged on African towns and villages for slaves, as Europeans armed criminals living on the coastal fringes of the empires. Some led forays into the interior for slaves, while others living within the empires usurped the power structure with the help of arms, took over and gave their European sponsors a free hand. Although the armed sellouts were less than one percent of the population, their gun power was overwhelming and decisive—with over 400,000 guns provided by Europeans every year.

By the end of the first hundred years of transatlantic slavery, which had produced relatively low numbers of slaves, mainly to Brazil, there was to be a marked increase in the demand and capture of slaves as other Europeans, mainly the British, French and Dutch, joined the trade.

With the Dutch invasion and capture of the Northeast coast of Brazil in 1624 from the Portuguese, the sugar plantations spread to the Caribbean Islands of Hispaniola (Haiti and Dominican Republic), Barbados, Jamaica and Cuba by 1650, requiring more slave labor.

In addition, the British, French and other northern Europeans also took over the North American continent for cultivation. The British declared a colony in 1609 in North America, the present day United States, and although, it was only the Deep South around Louisiana that was conducive to sugar cultivation, with time other African crops were discovered and introduced. Tobacco and cotton were grown from the mid-Atlantic coast to the southernmost areas through plantation agriculture, which also relied on slave labor from the West Coast of Africa.

In West Africa, during the first century of transatlantic slavery, the outlying savannahs overran by Arabic Muslims initially supplied the largest percentage of slaves, mainly non-Muslim original Africans, through Senegambia. However, the area soon became deserted as their inhabitants fled into the forests, therefore turning the slavery focus on the forest heartland empires of Benin and Oyo. The Muslim 'Whitemen of the desert' were to constantly attack Oyo Empire protruding into the savannah, while the Christian Europeans were to arm Yorubas coastal cousins on its western boundaries protruding into the Dahomey savannah. Also, a civil war was eventually caused in Benin that was to be won by a proslavery kingship candidate.

The increase in demand for slaves brought about by the emerging powers of Northwest Europe, also led to the challenge and demise of the Portuguese monopoly of all European trade on the West African coast. Although, unlike other areas in Africa and America, the vast population, resources and social organization of the Benin and Oyo Empires prevented any further European state monopolies and the area became free for all by the 1680's.

This was the situation that prompted the increased occurrences around Tutu, Ijebu being on the fringes of both empires and not too far from the Slave Coast.

Anthony Smith was among those involved in the free for all trade, especially after the demise of state monopolies. This was the British merchant's tenth trip to the Slave Coast. It was a very lucrative trade for him, and he had been able to acquire his own ship and go into partnerships with plantation owners in the West Indies. He built mansions in London, Jamaica and the outskirts of Boston, despite the fact that he was broke and gaunt, when he came on someone else's ship on his first trip in 1677.

In 1687 at the age of thirty-four, the tall, portly, red-haired Englander with a pronounced Teutonic nose, was already considering retiring from the route which, although lucrative, was fraught with dangers, especially health risks from malaria. Over a quarter of the crew dies whenever they stay on the continent for long periods of time, usually three weeks or more. Most people attributed the fever to the drinking water, but despite precautions in drinking water, he still suffered losses, which he was beginning to associate with the insects. Although, which of the numerous biting insects, he did not know.

Due to this, he decided he would be spending the minimum time possible on land, especially in the interior. He intended to head back to the coast once he finished conducting his business. If possible, he would not even sleep on the land. This was possible now that he enjoyed a higher level of prosperity and could delegate duties to his subordinates and the African coastal criminals that did most of the work.

This was with the exception of the return journey and stop at Elmina for the gold trade, which due to the low weight in relation to its value could not be trusted to anyone. Such blind faith could result in being robbed blind and could return him to penury.

It now seemed like ancient history to him when he was living in poverty, and had started with two guns and a lot of courage, seeking passage to the Guinea coast with three other friends. Two of the friends were now dead and buried in Africa, while the last had retired and gone into business in Liverpool.

They had sailed up one of the numerous rivers that flowed through Yorubaland into the Atlantic Ocean and berthed on the outskirts of a town. The area known as the Egbado corridor, lying between the two major rivers that flowed through Yorubaland, held one of the heaviest population densities in the world.

The town, like most towns in the world, had a concentric layout, with the market, the business and administrative (palace) centers located in the middle. In the middle of the night, they selected a detached settlement in its suburbs, which they stealthily surrounded to carry out their business.

Their business being the capture of Africans by surrounding a settlement and setting fire to the thatched roofs of houses on the outer circle. This naturally causes panic to the sleeping residents, who run helter-skelter into traps and the waiting hands of the slave raiders.

Smaller settlements, many of which act as satellites to bigger towns, were often favored, due to the number of raiders that were needed to effectively surround them. With people surrounded by fire, there is utmost panic and mayhem, further exacerbated by firing gunshots into the air, causing people to trip over themselves in an effort to escape, while falling into traps.

Women, children and the weak were the ones most vulnerable to capture and a raid like this could net anything from 10 to 100 people, depending on the number of participants in the raiding party. With guns to protect themselves from regrouped search parties, the raiders swiftly left the area by marching their captives to their waiting boat.

On his first trip, Anthony Smith got 60 captives, although 52 were successfully loaded onto the ship. Normally, about twenty percent escape or are shot at close range to instill fear and order among them or at a rate of one a day until they boarded the ship and left shore.

Anthony Smith and the rest of the team set sail for nearby Elmina coast, The Gold Coast, where they exchanged their cargo with some Portuguese middlemen for gold. The new African landlords of the gold mines didn't have the labor to run it and resorted to buying the former landlords as slaves to work in the shafts.

Anthony Smith and friends got a good deal for their slaves

after which they set sail for Liverpool, where they sold their gold. With his proceeds from the sale of gold, he was able to pay his debts, make a down payment for his own ship and attract enough investment to help him further his business objectives. In a short while, he was ready to return, employing enough able men to help sail and raid as well as buy enough ammunition.

On his second trip, he carried out seven raids capturing one hundred and sixty, but effectively shipping one hundred and forty-two of which he only sold twenty-nine in El Mina, due to the poor exchange rate for gold. Prices of slaves greatly fluctuated depending on the occurrence of war, which for a long time served as a source of slaves. Although even in the best of times, slaves attracted relatively lower prices when sold on the African continent. Therefore, Anthony Smith sailed to the Americas, where top money was being paid for his cargo.

On his way to North America, he stopped in Jamaica, where he sold seventy for money and sugar and then onto Annapolis. Slaves sold for one ton of sugar or seventeen pounds in the Americas compared to three pounds in Africa. In Annapolis, he sold the remaining forty-three for money and bought tobacco.

On his return to England, he made a fortune and being an astute businessman, he repaid his debtors, invested in a small arsenal of arms and loads of tea. With the tea, he first set sail for Boston, where he sold it for the exorbitant price that was being offered. From the proceeds of the sale, he bought land and set the building of a mansion in progress, before departing for West Africa via Jamaica, where he loaded rum.

By his fifth trip, Anthony, now married, had already acquired immense wealth and he set out to do what the major companies were doing. This was to be his longest trip and his mission was to get African help in his slave raids and like the big companies, the plan was to secure and arm one of the numerous fishing villages or a band of social misfits.

After a few weeks of sailing around the extensive waterways of the West African coast, he found a fishing village that hadn't yet been taken over by other slave traders. The fishing villages, most of which are built in swamps at the mouths of rivers flowing from the hinterland, are elevated above water by stilts. The people survived by selling their catch for food and other necessities in the hinterland, but were usually separated from the mainland civilization of which they were often resentful and jealous.

The fishing villages were very vulnerable, being easily subjected through the stopping of their means of livelihood and communication by the destruction of their boats. Knowing this, Anthony Smith riddled their boats with bullets and with the introduction of alcohol, their morality and resistance was gradually weakened, while the 'stubborn troublemakers' were summarily terminated.

With the termination of their economic mainstay, many of the fishermen resorted to raiding towns in the interior for food and kidnapping slaves for sale for guns and rum. Finding themselves in a vicious circle of the slave trade, with guns and alcohol, most became violent maniacs and dipsomaniacs.

Anthony Smith soon became rich beyond his wildest dreams as a coal miner's son and hoped to retire either to the tea trade between England and New England, the sugar business of the West Indies or the Asian spice trade. He was hoping this would be one of his last trips to the Slave Coast, not only because of the malaria fever, but things were getting tougher for the sole proprietor, who in order to make maximum profit had to do much more. He had lost quite a number of men on his various trips and his fishing village was fast dwindling.

Starting with fifty men in 1684, they were now only fifteen, some were killed during raids, while others escaped to live on the mainland, in search of a more fulfilling existence. He did not wish to spend another long period on the continent trying to secure another fishing village since his previous endeavor had cost him the most number of men through malaria, up to date. Therefore he had to escort his raiding party, which included a number of his crew due to the paucity of African raiders.

Having to move inland, he was apprehensive of the increased danger he faced, in addition to threat of the fever. Many families and villages were beginning to arm themselves with modern weapons, in response to the onslaught that came as a result of the free-for-all trade. The increased availability of arms had already cost him the lives of some fishermen raiders.

It's funny how things change, he thought as he made his way through the forest, the villages attacking historically unfriendly villages for slaves, which they exchanged for arms to protect their families. Who said they were dumb savages? Given the right circumstances, even animals would do whatever is necessary to survive, he thought with a smirk on his face, which quickly turned into a frown as he swatted an insect on the back of his neck.

Maybe I should start selling arms, he wondered aloud as he called for a rest after two hours of walking through the forest. Slumping under a tree, exhausted by the humid hot weather, he swatted another insect on his arm.

"Bloody suckers," he swore aloud as he killed yet another insect. This is my last trip, he decided as he took a swig from his bottle of rum. Its bad enough fearing the fever, now I have to be scared of looking down the barrel of a rifle held by a Negro, from its wrong end.

Going on to 18, Tutu was blossoming into a tall beautiful young lady, still accentuated by her long stylistic dreadlocked hair, but striking a more gentle and graceful posture. Her elaborate Dada hairstyles also accentuated her long neck, which sometimes appeared to be an uneasy link between two heavy parts, especially when her hair is styled upwards. Tutu, like her mother, was endowed with large breasts and upper body as well as a fairly big rear. Like her mother, she also had two knuckle-kneed long legs.

With the religious use of the traditional "black soap", the African chewing stick and oils from the north, Tutu's smooth chocolate skin and engaging smile were beginning to cause a few flutters in the hearts of many young men in the area. Her family was beginning to receive queries from interested families, and was thinking of arranging a marriage probably to one of the sons of a local well-to-do family.

Her mother was still overprotective of her and she never lacked anything, although she was beginning to show her resentfulness over her restricted movement. She was usually prevented from going to play and wash in the nearby river with her age mates. Unfortunately, she remained her mother's only child having lost two children during pregnancy, although she had seven siblings by her stepmother.

Tutu not only resented her mother's stifling love due to its restrictions, but also because to the resultant derisive gossips. She heard of the incidence at her naming ceremony and there was a cruel rumor that attributed her lack of immediate siblings to her. Some said her mother was the first witch, according to the predictions, that Tutu had attacked and waged war on her womb.

Surprisingly, despite these cruel rumors, Tutu's attitude to strangers and friends was warm and open, being a good-natured person that enjoyed the company of others. The highlight of her day was usually the song singing and storytelling under the moonlight just before bedtime, from which she derived an immense sense of belonging.

As time heals wounds, both physically and socially, Wura healed the rift between her and the market women, especially those of her secret cult. She rejoined their ranks a few years ago due to persuasion and promises that they would no longer pose any threat. Although she refused to let down her guard, she decided to leave the past alone.

On meeting days, which were usually held at night, she always made arrangements for Tutu to sleep in one of her paternal uncles' quarters. Because she could not tell anyone her secret, she feigned illness as an excuse to have Tutu sleep in other quarters within the large compound. Fortunately for her, the covens were irregular and far apart, occurring once every month or two.

Before leaving, Wura always insisted on practically tucking Tutu into bed at her uncle's to put her mind at rest while she is away. Then she would return to her quarters, pretending to have retired for the day, while waiting for everyone to do likewise before leaving.

Tutu disliked being made to sleep in her uncle's rooms that were more crowded and less comfortable than her mother's quarters. As fate would have it, she recently stumbled across her mother's scheme, when one night she mistakenly returned to her own mat half-asleep after going for a pee outside.

Curious, she decided to find out what was going on, and the last two times she discovered her mum was nowhere to be found, but never brought it up with her or anyone else. The next time it occurred, she decided she would return to her mat after what seemed to be an hour or more, when she knew he mother would have left.

That was tonight and she crept back to their area without alerting anyone.

Anthony Smith stifled a yawn after waking up from a quick nap designed to recharge his energy. "It's getting rather late and we better start moving, before it's dawn," he said aloud to no one in particular, but for the benefit of the whole party.

The faster we get out of this Godforsaken place the better, before the bloody fever catches on, he thought, I don't want a plot on the White man's grave. He was hoping that he would be able to leave for shore tonight, having been reassured by his scouts that there was ample prey to be captured with minimal danger.

Struggling to his feet and brushing the dust off himself with his hand, Smith checked his weapons and signaled his readiness. Some members of the team quickly rose to their feet and woke up the others still asleep. Stretching and yawning, they made preparations to move on to their raiding sites.

Setting out, they decided to work their way westward, before heading south toward their ship. The raids were expected to take nine hours. They had traveled quite inland to ensure they could get as many people as possible in a short period by attacking sites that had not been frequented by other slave raiders, at least not recently.

Eventually they reached their first target, which they quietly surrounded and set fire to its thatched roofs. In a little more than an hour, they were on the way with forty-four captives, although one had to be shot to placate the others, usually the first one to rebel or the leader. Sixteen women, thirteen men and fourteen children and teenagers were shackled and led along the path to the next target.

Anthony was not pleased with his first raid, since the first raid usually brought about the largest catch. In subsequent raids, they would have fewer men to ambush the targets, since some would have to remain behind to guard those already captured.

To his pleasant surprise, the next raid was a little better than expected with fifty-four captured. Two slaves were shot due to their disruptive ways, as they marched them to the secluded area, they kept the others.

As they regrouped and made for their next raid, they came across a small cluster of houses, which they had no intention of raiding. The scouts had decided earlier on that it wasn't worth their trouble. For it to qualify as a target there should be a minimum of sixty people residing in the settlement, especially for a raiding party of their size, in order to be sure of at least twenty captives. In this particular settlement on the outskirts of a town, there were probably only twenty inhabitants. As they passed, they saw a tall slim figure outside a hut that stopped to look at the long file of people.

Tutu was sleeping in her mother's quarters, when she had an urge to urinate and went outside in front of the compound. If she had been sleeping in her uncle's quarters as instructed, she would have urinated at the back of the compound. Due to the fact that her parents' quarters were in the front of the compound, being the first to be built, she urinated in the front, near a passing path.

As she was returning to her sleeping mat, she heard clinking metal, shuffling feet and voices, which was quite unusual at the time of the day. Curious, she stopped to have a look at where the noise was coming from and saw some white men followed by some Africans. Oblivious to any danger, she squinted to see whether she could identify any one of them. The nearest person was less than fifteen feet away and was the one to react.

He went after her with lightening speed and she was slow to react. In her wildest dreams, she never thought of being kidnapped, having led a sheltered life. Moreover, it was a rare occurrence in her immediate neighborhood. The man caught and grabbed her with his powerful hands and she screamed at a very high pitch. Her scream, a loud shrill woke up her father and uncles, who rushed out with their cutlasses.

Because it was an unplanned attack, others were caught unawares as they found themselves under attack from cutlass wielding men. Reacting at the last minute, they shot down the advancing men and threw their torches onto the roofs as they hurriedly left.

Despite the commotion, the man carrying Tutu held onto her, as she screamed, scratched and kicked him, not dropping her once.

Anthony Smith was raving mad, when they got to a makeshift area, where they could rest the slaves and regroup, before moving on. "You must be out of your bloody, sodden mind. Who gave you permission to take the girl? For just one slave, you put the whole lot of us in danger, wasted ammunition and God knows what!" he ranted as he paced up and down. "Blinking Bastard!"

"I thought it would serve as a bonus, I intended no harm. Forgive me, I am sorry," pled Adam, a young impressionable fellow, who was one of the new members of the party. He had wanted to impress the boss, but it obviously backfired.

"That was too close to the main town and you plan your attack before you move, that's why we are better than the savages, you dumb imbecile!" Smith cursed as he looked around and saw Tutu, briefly assessing her; "You better make sure you fetch good money or I will make sure you breed a whole legion of slaves," he said, kicking a tree trunk angrily. "Damn! One frigging slave from one raid," he spat angrily and took a long swig from his bottle of rum. "Bloody idiot!"

After pacing for a couple of minutes, while everyone watched in silent trepidation, he stopped and spoke thoughtfully. "We've got to move on. That was too close to the town and we are not far away enough. They might send out a search party." He once again let loose a string of curses on Adam, "Just pray we get at least 50 more before dawn or I'll feed your balls to the dogs."

News of sporadic slave raids around the area reached them at the cult meeting, and Wura, feeling an uneasy premonition, asked to be excused. From half a mile away, seeing an orange glow on the horizon, she knew her worst fears had finally come true. She increased her pace as she got closer and broke into a frenzied run when she was about 300 meters from home and could clearly see the fire.

When she reached the compound, at first she saw her sisters-in-law wailing and shaking the dead bodies of their husbands. With a closer look, she sighted her husband bleeding profusely from chest and leg wounds being attended to by some women, including the second wife, who was wailing disconsolately. Kneeling beside her husband, she wiped his face as tears gently flowed down her cheeks.

"Wura, where have you been? The child snatchers have taken Tutu," Akin said weakly, coughing up blood as he did. Wura jumped to her feet in shock and let out a long anguished cry, before collapsing in despair.

"Aaaah! Tutu! No, they can't do this to me," she cried. She grabbed her weak husband and bombarded him with questions: "Who were they? Which way did they go? How?" she bawled at him.

"Oyinbo! The Oyinbos took her," Tutu's father, Akin, answered tearfully. Oyinbo is the Yoruba word for Caucasians but it literally means, "Peeled skin" because Europeans are sun burnt in the hot African sun.

"If he peeled his skin, did he peel his heart? For heaven

sake, my only daughter," Wura sobbed despairingly. "How long ago was this?"

"Not too long ago," answered the second wife on whose lap Akin's head rested.

"What direction did they go?" Wura asked, as she jumped to her feet, swiftly removing her head tie, which she tied around her waist truculently. Someone indicated the direction they saw the raiders flee.

"No, Wura! You can't go anywhere in this dark and they had sticks that spit fire!" Akin feebly objected as he once again coughed.

"We shall see!" She said as she picked up a cutlass and stormed off into the forest.

"Please, Wura! I have lost enough for one night," he cried as he coughed and collapsed. Wura didn't hear his plea or see him collapse as she headed into the forest with blind rage.

In her present mood, she would not hesitate to use the cutlass nor had any fear for her life. As she raged along the path, on two occasions, she met hunters that told her of some commotion further down the path, which was probably caused by the slave raiders.

Meanwhile, Anthony Smith had relocated his captives and was already carrying out his fourth raid three miles away. It was only after netting 28 more slaves that he was a bit relieved and placated over Adam's earlier folly. Once again, the party moved on to the next target, which before they executed, they secured the captured slaves at a predetermined spot just off the route.

It was nearly dawn before Wura caught up with the raiders. She was lucky to find them, because in the last couple of miles, she had met no one to give her directions and had nearly missed the clearing off the path. In fact, she had walked past the clearing, which was about 20 yards off the path, when she heard a gunshot followed by screams from its direction.

One of the guards shot one of the captives that refused to obey orders and was causing dissent. It was the women next to him, one of them his wife, that screamed, when his brain matter splattered on them.

Wura followed the direction from which she heard the screaming come, careful not to arouse attention. Due to the long walk and time taken to find them, she had considerably cooled down and was already losing hope of finding them, when she heard the gunshot.

Peeping from behind a tree, she was shocked by the number of captives and found it difficult to identify her daughter among them, but she eventually did. Thinking more focused, she counted the guards, who were twelve in number, all alert and walking around the captives in circles.

She had to think of a better way to free her daughter, with common sense now prevailing, she knew there was no way, she could use her cutlass against twelve men, even if they were unarmed. She realized that the only way to free Tutu was if they were sleeping or sufficiently distracted.

Being a member of a cult with supernatural powers, she was confident she could put them to sleep. Wura reached into her blouse and brought out a tiny gourd, which supposedly had magical powers and started incanting, "As the moon puts the sun to sleep and a rocking mother's breasts puts her baby to sleep.... I command you to sleep!"

As it appeared to be taking effect and four of the guards yawned and sat down to rest, some birds with high shrills alerted them. She tried once again, but with the birds fluttering their wings above them and continuing their high-pitched noise, the men rose again.

Wura sighed with frustration on realizing its futility. "Why are you working against me, you spirits of the realm? Please don't betray me," she whispered desolately as she looked up to the heavens.

A voice answered her. "She has to go. It's her destiny. Don't try to stop it or you will only stop your own life!"

Wura hissed disdainfully, "You are joking!" she said defiantly.

At that moment, she was startled by some noise coming

from behind, that of the returning raiding team. Hiding as well as possible, they filed past her, just a few yards away from where she crouched.

Anthony had another twenty-nine in his net and was feeling quite contented. He had done quite well for himself in one night as an independent raider, which was more than the average raider could do in one week. It normally took longer, sometimes it could take a couple of weeks or more for the slave traders to get their cargo and finalize agreements. This was the advantage that independent interlopers like himself had over the large state monopoly companies, who usually dealt with resident Europeans, mainly Portuguese.

Apart from the shorter time and greater efficiency of small independent slave traders, the large companies were usually cheated both by their own officials and their business associates, thus reducing the astronomical profit margin.

Therefore he was contented, when he shouted to the others, "Yeah, we shall move on and call it a day!" he said, beaming from ear to ear as he took a long swig from his bottle.

Relieved, the men ordered the sitting slaves to their feet, flogging the seemingly obstinate and slow. The captives weren't being difficult, but due to the chains and lack of movement, their legs had gone lame. With their chains rattling and many in serious pain, they were led towards the path by the guards and Anthony Smith. When Wura saw Tutu file past her in arm and leg chains tears flowed effusively down her cheeks.

Tutu was quiet and distant. She was still in a state of shock after seeing her father and uncles shot by her captors. Her mind was racked with self-blame and regret. "If only I had slept where I was supposed to, none of this would have happened," she thought. The thought of her mother grieving for both her and her father further depressed her.

The slaves were marched at a fast and excruciating pace, which caused them to bleed, due to the friction of the leg irons against their ankles. Occasionally, about every ninety minutes, they were allowed to rest for thirty minutes. Actually, the rest was not for their benefit, but for their captors', especially

Anthony Smith's. Two more captives had to be shot, when they refused to go on due to extreme pain, although their captors thought they were just being difficult.

It was just before dawn of the following day, nearly twenty-four hours afterwards, that they eventually arrived at the coast around Lagos, the slave port originally established by the Portuguese and named after a town in Portugal. The slaves were marched into a compound that served as a holding camp for slavers, and rented for a small price, before they loaded their cargo. In the compound, they were distributed into various huts, which had leg irons and cuffs secured to the walls and ground. Each hut was filled with twenty slaves.

By chance, Tutu was among the last twelve captives to be secured in a hut at the extreme end of the compound. A couple of sentries paraded the compound and there were two guards to each hut, although only one was assigned to Tutu's hut because it held fewer occupants.

After watching them from the top of a nearby tree for nearly two hours, Wura decided to make her move as the sun rose high in the sky. She could see that the guard placed in front of Tutu's cell as well as some of the parading sentries had dozed off from exhaustion or being drunk.

Her plan was to dash into the hut in which Tutu was locked and sprint away with her, thinking the only impediment was the bolt fastening the door from outside. The worst thing that could happen was to be caught by the lone guard, whom she believed she could take on with the cutlass, still in her possession.

She stealthily made her way to the hut, creeping low and dashing across the open space with the cutlass dangling by her side. On reaching the hut, she slowly pulled back the bolt, careful not to arouse the sleeping guard, she gently opened the door and closed it behind her.

Inside, she raised her hand to cover her nose as the noxious odors that filled the room hit and made her want to throw up, but she managed to hold it down. She was shocked to see the state of the room, which with no proper ventilation reeked of human excreta and misery. On the walls to which the irons were attached, there were also various bloodstains, both fresh and old.

Squinting due to the poor lighting, she saw her daughter, who was sleeping at the far end of the room. Crouching beside Tutu, she gently touched her forehead with the back of her hand. When she opened her eyes and saw her mother, Tutu was unsure of where she was, but soon recollected as she looked around her and felt the pain around her ankles.

"Mama!" She cried a bit too loud as she threw her arms round her mother.

"Shhh!" Her mother put a finger on her lips, glancing furtively at the door. Wura's confidence sank a bit lower on seeing the heavy leg irons, when she looked down from Tutu's face to her feet. This was an added obstacle, which she had not taken into consideration, when coming in to rescue her. "They are outside. Keep quiet!" She whispered nervously, "How do they remove these?" pointing to the leg irons.

"They put a smaller iron into it and turn," Tutu explained, pointing to the lock and looking to her mother, hopeful for a solution.

"Where is the small iron? Do you know?"

"They took it along with them," she said desolately as she realized that her mother's presence did not necessarily mean her freedom. "Ma, I am sorry, it's all my fault," she said with tears flowing down her cheeks. Wura patted her reassuringly, before moving closer to examine the lock, which she fiddled with desperately.

While trying everything possible, she mistakenly tugged on the chain of the man sleeping next to Tutu, which bit into the festering wounds on his ankles. The sleeping man let out a sharp cry, startling Wura into dropping her cutlass and causing a loud, chattering noise against the irons.

This woke the sleeping guard outside, who reluctantly decided to check what was going on. Wura heard him curse and spit as he dragged his feet sluggishly, with his gun and keys clinking loudly as he approached. Slowly opening the door, he looked inside to check the cause of the noise, but saw nothing out of order.

Wura had quickly lain down next to Tutu, putting her feet under one of the leg iron chains and pretended to be asleep. Being in the far end of the room, the sleepy guard did not notice the additional prisoner due to the poor lighting. Moreover, being sleepy and wanting to return to his slumber as soon as possible, once he saw that no one was protesting and nothing was out of order, he turned back and closed the door behind him. Neither did he notice that the door had been unbolted, which he bolted behind him.

After he left, Wura sat up and went back to the leg irons to try and figure out a way to spring Tutu loose. She soon realized it was impossible and the only way to loosen them was with the key that was with the guard.

"Did you see the small iron with the guard that just came in?"

"Yes! It was the little one beside the one that spits fire. The fire spitting iron that was used on Papa, Uncles Femi and Tunde!" she answered dispiritedly as she recollected the shooting of her family.

Wura remained silent for a few moments as she contemplated a way out of the desperate situation. Being no fool, she knew short of attacking the guard, there was no other way to spring her daughter free. She couldn't rely on her magical powers, which were being sabotaged by unknown sources. Neither could she attack him in the open without attracting the attention of the other guards. It seemed an impossible mission, yet she was not ready to give up on her daughter.

Like most mothers, she would rather die than have her daughter taken away as a delicacy, which was widely believed to be the reason for their capture. Otherwise, why would they need so many people, none of whom had ever returned, if not to eat them? Definitely, they were not being used as house servants, since no house could be that big. Even if they were house servants, one or two would have escaped, so they must all be dead, killed for food! That was her and many others' conclusion, not aware of plantation agriculture. Over my dead body would my daughter land on someone's table, she thought and even if she died, she expected Tutu to fight on.

"Tutu, I want you to take this," she removed two charm brass rings from her fingers and handed them over to Tutu, "and whatever happens always keep them on. Your wishes shall come through as long as you voice them to our ancestors or me, if it so happens I am dead. Unfortunately, today is not good, because someone or something is working against us, but whatever happens, I will be with you," she solemnly told her daughter, whose eyes continued to shed water as she spoke.

Wura was also brought close to tears looking at her tearful daughter, but she tried to put on a brave face. Nevertheless, a few tears were about to roll down her face, when she quickly embraced Tutu. Holding Tutu tight, with her chin on her shoulder, she bit her lower lip, not letting Tutu see or hear her cry. Wura held onto her daughter for a few moments, while she struggled to get hold of her emotions and wiped her face, before letting go of Tutu. Some other slaves had woken up and were staring at the heart breaking scene, which provoked tears from them as they also realized they were in the same situation.

Standing up with stoic determination, she instructed her daughter and those already awake to make some noise to attract the guard outside. She walked towards the door and hid behind it, then gave them a signal to start. About seven of them rattled their chains and shouted as planned.

The guard heard the noise, but initially decided to ignore it. He was enjoying his sleep, but could not continue sleeping with the noise and was eventually forced to check what was going on, much to his displeasure.

"Bloody frigging savages, can't a man just sleep in peace? Godforsaken bastards! You sodden animals behave, before you get shot!" He cursed angrily as he got to his feet to unbolt the door, which he flung open.

Standing in the doorway, he could not see the cause of the disturbance or anything wrong. They all kept still and quiet, pretending to be asleep. Furious, he thought they had just decided to disturb his sleep for the fun of it, which made him more irate.

"I am going to teach you animals not to play games with me," he said angrily as he stepped inside raising his whip, which apparently was his last act on earth.

Wura, standing behind the door behind him, swung the cutlass with all venom, precision and strength, cleanly taking his head off his neck. As he dropped to the ground, she hurriedly searched him for the key, which she could not identify until Tutu and the others pointed it out. The room was filled with excitement. They all clamored to be freed, but as expected Wura tried freeing her daughter first.

After fervently fumbling with the lock for a few moments, the leg irons came off. With Tutu free, Wura tried to free the man whose chains she had earlier tugged, which she got off more rapidly than Tutu's. The freed man subsequently set about freeing others, while Tutu and Wura made for the door.

Meanwhile across the court, the foreman was doing his rounds, when he noticed that the guard assigned to one of the huts was not in position. He decided to check what was going on, because sometimes the guards got carried away and raped some of the Africans. Most of them were sex starved due to the long periods away from home, considering the fact that European women were hard to find overseas.

He opened the door expecting to catch the guard with his pants down, but bumped into Wura and Tutu on their way out. Momentarily, he was shocked to find the guard's head down and his obvious assailants about to escape. Due to his shock, he was slow to react and not before a cutlass swung across his face, barely missing him. He fell backwards trying to avoid the cutlass and the women stepped over him and ran for freedom. The fallen foreman blew his whistle, raising an alarm as he tried getting to his feet, but realized rather too late that there were others.

The first freed man kicked him in the face sending him back down and stepped over him into freedom. The guard rolled onto his chest, drew his pistol, took an aim and shot the escaping man in the back. The others pounced on the guard's turned back, punching and kicking him to death.

6

Guards, who informed him of a visitor, a clergyman, insisting on seeing him immediately, disturbed Anthony Smith's deep slumber. After dishing out a long, scathing rebuke to the guards, he reluctantly agreed to see the visitor. He was quite groggy due to the walking, raiding and drinking of the past 48 hours, and staggered as he got out of bed.

In the sparsely furnished chamber that served as the living room, a tall, well-tanned man dressed in a cassock stood observing his surroundings. He was looking out into the forecourt when a door opened behind him and Smith came through it.

"What can I do for you, Reverend?" Smith asked grouchily on entering the living room, gesturing the clergyman to take a seat after exchanging handshakes. To clear his head, he resorted to his strong belief in the power of continuation and grabbed his half bottle of rum, from which he took a long swig, before fixing his gaze inquisitively on his guest.

"I am seeking passage to Jamaica and heard from the wharf that you might be leaving pretty soon," the clergyman said, returning Smith's quizzical look with his thick eyebrows.

For a moment, Smith had a blank look on his face, while trying to collect his thoughts as well as place the clergyman's accent and background. "Yes, that is true. We should be sailing tomorrow morning," Anthony Smith answered, pausing to take another swig. "Do you know where you are going in Jamaica? Have you ever been there?" His inquiring look returned as pulled his long nose over which he assessed the man, who appeared to have come from a good background, being well spoken and a clergyman, yet having some of the coarseness of a merchant about him.

"My family lives in the Westmoreland around the Abeokuta Waterworks area."

"That's where I am berthing!" Smith exclaimed in surprise, wiping off his grogginess. The returned state of alertness also turned on the business part of his brain. "Do you have money to pay me for the passage?" he asked in a guarded tone.

The clergyman was somewhat hesitant in replying, apparently unsettled by the sudden change to a business mode by his host.

"No! But I heard you do not have a pastor on board, which I think leaves much to be desired. God's presence is required in all endeavors, not to mention that the King requires it; otherwise the devil will use the idle minds of the crew to commit his evil desires. According to the book of Luke, chapter..." he stated eloquently, with his voice growing stronger with every word but was interrupted before he could complete his statement.

Smith was in absolutely no mood for a long sermon with his head pounding the way it was. He cut the priest short brusquely, "Yes, we lost our pastor to the fever. You know the dangers of this godforsaken land." He paused as he pondered on something else, slowly brushing through his redhead with his hands. "If I may ask, what were you doing before? I mean, how did you end up on this side of the world?" he asked keenly, but before the clergyman could answer a gunshot rang out and Smith sprang to his feet.

He ordered one of the guards to go and check out what was going on, while he went into the room to get his gun in case they were being attacked.

Wura swept the compound with her eyes as she stepped outside. Seeing no immediate danger, she ran towards the wall she came over, while Tutu turned the opposite direction toward the open space. "Tutu!" she called after her and in the confused frenzy, Tutu turned around to follow her mother.

Wura jumped at the wall without the slightest contemplation and in one move was on the top. Looking back, she saw her weakened daughter fall as she tried scaling the wall like she did. There was frustration added to the fear on Tutu's face as she contemplated the tall fence. As Tutu made another attempt with her sore legs and fell back again, a gunshot rang out, further compounding her fear and frustration.

With an extremely agitated expression on her face, Wura jumped back into the compound. "Come on baby, step on this and onto the wall", the desperate mother pled frantically as she put her hands together to hoist her over the wall. Tutu was petrified and froze as she saw guards pointing at them.

"Over there!" some guards shouted as they sighted them from the other end of the compound.

"Come on!" Wura shouted angrily at her dithering daughter. Startling awake, Tutu quickly stepped into her hands and Wura lifted her up, enabling her to hoist herself onto the wall. In one swift move, Wura joined her on the top of the wall as the guards ran towards them. She pushed Tutu as she contemplated the height, making her fall awkwardly to the other side.

Jumping off the wall, Wura pulled Tutu to her feet and they ran off as some of the guards were making it over the fence. While some guards chased them over the fence, several other guards went through the compound's main entrance to cut them ahead. Unknown to Wura, there was a small river that ran into the ocean three hundred yards away from the compound. Being a delta, it had quicksand on its banks and was unapproachable.

Tutu ran towards it as her mother followed closely behind, throwing darting looks at their pursuers. She was looking backwards, when she heard her daughter shout in disgust as she stepped into quicksand. Wura halted just before she stepped into it and hurriedly pulled Tutu out. As she did, the guards in pursuit steadily gained upon them.

The women turned away from the bank of the river and ran north along the bank. The guards seeing them head north, turned and cut their path. Also, the guards that had gone through the front entrance of the compound came running from the direction the women were running towards. With quicksand on one side and guards chasing them from both directions, the women were soon cornered.

The guards formed a semi circle and slowing closed in on the women. Wura, with a menacing expression and stance, waved her bloodied cutlass at the guards as she used her free hand to pull her daughter closer. Momentarily, there was a standoff as none of the guards dared move closer. Wura, occasionally jerked forward threateningly with the cutlass, making the men take a step backward whenever they came too close.

"Shoot her!" one of the guards suggested.

"No! Hold your fire, we will get them," one of the guards said confidently. Suddenly, two guards startled forward to attack. Wura faced up to them, making ferocious swings with her cutlass and cut one of them in the elbow. They both hurriedly retreated and Wura stood her ground as the face-off continued.

The guard that cautioned against using firearms dropped his rifle and ran to pick up a broken branch nearby. The guard next to him followed suit and broke off a branch. They both moved forward with their branches and approached mother and child very, very cautiously.

"Let's shoot the bloody bitches!" another guard insisted.

"We don't need guns, Ron. These are mere women," he answered, grinning confidently as he slowly approached Wura. Perhaps he would have not been that confident, if he knew these were not just 'mere' women.

In fact, soldiers who later had the misfortune of fighting women from the area called them the Amazons, "the amazing." The Amazons were fearsome women warriors on the West African coast, who would later face up to African and European armies alike. Although, unlike the Amazons that fought for king and country, Wura was fighting for everything worth fighting for and a lot more.

"Now!" the guard with the branch shouted and they swamped her, putting the branch in front to protect them and get the cutlass stuck.

Wura was quite agile and swung her cutlass deftly. Instead

of swinging at the branch and getting the cutlass stuck, she changed the direction of the cutlass the last second and buried it into the shoulder of the guard. The guard let out a scream as his arm was nearly completely severed.

Nevertheless, due to their numbers, she was unable to retract the cutlass before the others rushed her to the ground. Far from vanquished, Wura wrestled with the men in the mud. Tutu screamed as she fought off a couple of them that were not concentrating on her mother and tried to run away.

Wura grabbed hold of the closest guard's head as she wrestled in the mud and sunk her teeth into his ear. The man screamed as a chunk of his ear came off and gave her a punch in the face. Wura's head snapped back and she returned with a kick to the groin of another guard.

Tutu also kicked one of her attackers in the groin and made a run for it, but another guard leaped at her and brought her to the ground. Although, she tried fighting him off, two other guards soon overwhelmed her.

Meanwhile, Wura continued to fight her attackers ferociously. She had nearly clawed out the eyes of a guard, before the other guards jumped to his rescue. The guards subdued her, but only when they were able to cuff her. Breathing laboriously, they looked at her in amazement as they hoisted her onto her feet with handcuffs and a few broken bones.

By the time he loaded his gun and got outside, he saw some guards coming towards him with two African women that he assumed were his slaves. He turned back into the living room, where the clergyman still sat.

"Sir, there was an attempted escape and two guards and one slave are dead," one of the guards informed him as they came in. "We caught these women behind the compound, beside the river. The others were stopped from leaving." The gunshot and the sight of the fleeing women had alerted the guards, enabling them to stop the other slaves from leaving the hut.

"How could that have happened? You bloody idiots!"

Anthony Smith demanded indignantly, obviously prejudging his guards with irresponsibility.

"I don't know how this woman found her way into the compound, but she tried to free her daughter," pointing to Wura and Tutu respectively as he spoke, "I guess she must have followed us all the way here."

"That's strange, bring them closer," Smith ordered and they were roughly shoved forward by the guards. The mother and daughter dropped their mouths in stupefaction and looked at each other questioningly as Anthony Smith stood up and stepped closer. Behind him, he didn't see the clergyman slightly shake his head, wink and put a finger to his lips. Neither did any of the guards see the blond clergyman with piercing eyes strange actions and gestures.

On taking a closer look at Tutu, Smith frowned as he recognized her, "Where is Adam?" He demanded and looked around menacingly for him. Adam stepped out from behind some guards, trembling.

"Here, Sir!" his voice quavered in anticipation of the fury he had been expecting ever since he realized Tutu was the cause of the commotion.

Walking angrily up to Adam and shaking furiously as he spoke, "Isn't this the bloody bitch that you disrupted our planned raids for?" Smith bellowed into his face inches away.

"I think so, Sir!"

"What? You foolish bastard! You think so or it is so? If you afforded us the pleasure of your thinking, I wouldn't be standing here, having lost two guards and a slave!" Smith trembled with rage as he spoke. The more he thought about it, the more he lost his temper.

"Damnit!" he shouted after a brief silence as he threw and smashed his rum bottle against the wall near the clergyman, whom he noticed afterwards, was looking at him strangely. Pacing up and down for a few moments, he tried to control his anger, while everyone looked on in silence.

He sighed with frustration, took a deep breath and sat down before finally speaking with a greatly restrained voice: "Take them away and lock them in the gallows. I will deal with them after I finish my meeting." He waved them away in disgust.

The guards answered, "Yes, Sir!" in unison and in relief, and led the women away. No one noticed the faint smiles on the women's faces brought about by their renewed hope.

Once they left, Captain Smith turned back with a smile to the clergyman as if nothing had happened. "One can never find good help these days. That boy has cost me too much, too soon!" He said lightly and stretched to get his tobacco pouch on the floor, from which he lit a rolled one. He took a deep drag as if his life depended on it and for a moment, he was distant in his thoughts.

God! Barely having two hours of sleep and I have to go through all this rubbish, so much for this land, he concluded. With slaves being aided to escape from outside, the fever and the food, one is not truly safe until one leaves! He turned his attention back to the clergyman, "Reverend, you are welcome on board and I guess it is going to be rather sooner than later with all this nonsense going on," he coughed and spat some phlegm on the floor.

The gallows was a torture chamber for disobedient slaves or thieving guards and workmen. There were chains hanging from the roof used to suspend its unlucky occupants for flogging or simple torture. In addition, there were chains that were fixed into the wall and ground like in the slave holding huts as well as an assortment of whips and other torture instruments lying around.

Adam pushed Wura and Tutu into the room angrily, making Tutu trip and fall. He looked down at her with utmost contempt as she shrieked. She was the cause of his public humiliation and probably future disfavor and deserved no pity whatsoever, he contended.

The guards decided to tie their wrists, in order to suspend them in the air with the hook at the end of the ceiling chains placed on their wrists. Adam was irate because, in addition to his humiliation, one of the guards killed was a childhood friend from Liverpool.

The more he thought about it, the more livid he became. When Wura, who was in pain from a few broken bones, moaned the handcuffs were too tight as Adam put the first cuff on her right hand, that pushed him over the edge and he slapped her.

"Bitch!" he called her with all the hatred, he could muster. The slap was quite vicious and split her lower lip wide open, making blood drip profusely.

Wura, who had a slight cold, drew in a very deep breath and brought up a mouthful of phlegm, which she spat right into his face. This provoked a few chuckles from the three other guards that had followed him to secure the women.

The humiliation was too much for the adolescent guard. "You frigging bitch!" he shouted, giving her a backhand slap across the face, causing her to fall to the ground. Wiping the phlegm tainted with blood off his face. "You spit your venom at me, ugh? You know what, I will give you some of my venom, you stinking whore," he said hatefully as he bent down to where she was lying and ripped off her clothing.

"Hold her hands! Hold her down!" he ordered the other guards, who were somewhat confused and hesitant. "Come on! Hold her and stop looking like you are scared. I will show the black bitch whose got the venom around here. I've got to teach her who the boss is around here before she thinks she can come in here to kill our men and then heap scorn upon everything else," he grinned deviously as he removed his pants.

With Wura held down by two other guards as she struggled despite her injuries, Adam raped her in front of her daughter. Tutu cried and tried to wrestle free as her mother was sexually assaulted, but was held firmly down by another guard.

After Adam was finished and got up, he gestured to the other guard, Tim, "Come on! It's you turn. Have some of the African whore!" He told the other guards who were a bit reluctant to participate, although they overcame their inhibitions with little persuasion from him.

Adam walked across Wura and pinned her hands to the

floor with the help of one of the guards. Looking across the room to Tutu, he changed his mind and told the guard, Donald, "Go over to John and take that one. Let John hold her down, while you take her. I will try her myself later." The guard was undecided, but Adam urged him on, "Go on, I can handle this by myself." Turning to Tim, who was sluggishly pulling down his pants to rape Wura, he shouted impatiently, "Come on, Tim! We don't have the whole day!"

Adam took Wura's other hand, the cuffed one, which was left free by the other guard that was going for Tutu, and he pinned both hands to the floor slightly above her head. As the guard, Tim was erect and ready to enter Wura, she moved away, pushing her head closer to Adam. Adam, still naked from the waist down, struggled to keep the weakened and injured Wura down.

With her head pushing against his knees, Wura used all the strength she could muster to lift her head and upper back off the floor. Adam did not know what was happening and thought she was trying to get a view of who was about to rape her until he felt her teeth sink into his privates.

"Aaah! Aaah!" He screamed as Wura firmly sunk her teeth into his genitals. His whole semi erect penis and scrotum was in her mouth as he punched, kicked and even got on to his feet, but couldn't secure their release. Seriously in pain, he begged, cried and screamed, "Please!" but it was to no avail. Instead she sunk her teeth deeper and gritted them, making Adam stretch out his hands and clasping his head in the worst pain he had ever known.

The other guards were momentarily shocked. Initially, it was a funny sight to them, but when they saw blood dripping out of the corners of Wura's mouth, they realized the enormity of what was happening in their presence.

She didn't let go until his penis and scrotum were completely severed and he fell to the ground, writhing in pain and bleeding profusely. She spat his genitals at him and hatefully said, "Beesh," meaning bitch. Although she did not know the meaning, she guessed it was derogatory because he had used it against her repeatedly before raping her.

The guards recovering from their shocked inaction brought out their guns and opened fire. Just at that moment, Anthony Smith, the clergyman and a few others, who heard the screaming, rushed through the door.

"Hold it! Hold your fire! Halt!" he shouted, but it was too late for Wura, who had received multiple gunshots to the head and the chest.

As she slumped, Tutu free from the guard's grip ran to her mother's side, "Mama, Mama!" She tugged on her mother. "Please don't die! Please!" she sobbed as she examined Wura frantically. "Aaah! What have I done to deserve this? My mother! My father! Why God, Please!" She wept with profound sorrow.

Noticing Wura's hopelessly fatal condition, they moved on to Adam screaming in agony, leaving behind the priest, who was biting into his lower lip. Not able to control his emotions much longer, he moved on to join the others as they stared hopelessly at Adam in horror.

Wura opened her eyes and reached for her grieving daughter, "I will always be with you," she weakly said, coughing out blood as she took her last breath. Tutu was inconsolable, when Wura went limp in her arms.

With their backs to her, they barely took any notice of them as they stared at Adam still writhing in pain and bleeding profusely.

"Holy Shit! What happened here?" Smith asking no one in particular as he looked down at Adam, with his genitals close to his head.

"She attacked Adam and bit him in the groin, Sir!" Tim answered as he fastened his pants.

"How could she have done that with four of you around?" Anthony asked with a disbelieving look as he eyed him redressing. He looked around the room assessing the situation, unsure of what to make of it, especially with his unclear head.

"Somebody help this man before he dies!" Another of the guards urged them.

The reverend bent down and looked at the wound closer. "Jesus! How do you treat this kind of wound? I have never seen anything like this in my entire life," he said as he rose and moved away in an effort to stop from retching. He went over to Tutu, crouching next to her, he whispered, "It's alright. I will help you!" But she didn't respond.

"Please do something or shoot me," Adam cried and vomited due to the excruciating pain.

Anthony looked at him derisively, "I think that is the best thing. He won't want to live as a woman. Reverend, please bless him!" Smith slightly winced and turned around to look for the Reverend, who was beside Tutu. The clergyman came over and performed some Christian rites on Adam. When he finished, Anthony nodded to the guards giving them the go ahead. Anthony and the clergyman turned their backs and heard shots ring out moments later.

It was only afterwards that all attention turned on to Tutu and her dead mother. Sensing their eyes on her back, she looked up with deep hatred and bitterness and lurched at Anthony Smith. "*Pa mi*! Kill me! Kill me!" she shouted in Yoruba and English as she hit him. The guards threw her to the ground, drew their guns and were ready to grant her request. They looked at Smith to give the order.

"This damned piece of shit has been nothing, but bad luck since Adam took her. I have lost three guards and two slaves, all because of her." He turned his attention to the remaining three guards, "You have not told me what really happened."

"She attacked, Sir!" Tim insisted, but with his voice quavering and shifty eyes, he was unconvincing and Anthony let him know by shaking his head disdainfully.

"Don't give me that bullshit," pointing to Wura and looking at them accusingly. "You lot were fucking her, weren't you?" he barked at them, startling them.

They all looked to the ground to avoid direct eye contact, knowing the truth was out.

"That is what caused all this. That bastard was smitten by

her charms, once he set eyes on her," Smith said, pointing to Tutu on the floor accusingly.

"The nigger-loving bastard met his death in a nigger's cunt. May he rot in hell because he definitely isn't going to heaven," he snarled at them and punched a hanging chain dangling next to him in anger.

"What should we do with her?" Donald asked about the girl that he was restraining.

"Kill her! I have had enough of her rotten luck in a day," Smith ordered and headed for the door, while the guards raised and cocked their guns.

"Hold it! It is Sabbath day, let's not take life unnecessarily on the holy day," the pastor pled compassionately for Tutu's life.

Smith let out a small laugh as he turned around, "This is just a nigger's life, we are talking about here, Reverend! There isn't any soul lost here." He gave the clergyman a quizzical look. "Don't tell me you got a soft side for niggers. A nigger lover?"

Feeling everyone's gaze on him, he decided to change his approach. "God gave everything on this Earth for our wise disposal and I guess you don't want to go about wasting God's gifts. According to..."

"Rev, come..." Smith started, but was stopped by Parris' raised hand.

"Although, through no fault of yours, I believe you have had more than your own fair share of waste today and you should recoup a bit by selling her at the auction! It is my belief that, let no man put to waste anything, otherwise he shall gnash his teeth in need in the near future!" the clergyman counseled, although unsure of how he had fared, since it took a few moments before Smith answered.

Smith thought of the economic sense the clergyman made, even if he had little faith in the religious argument. He had lost too much and it wouldn't be a bad idea to recoup something, although he had a feeling there was something more to the reverend's argument. He felt he sensed a bit more than cold logic, like some emotion, there was some form of intensity, urgency, or was it desperation, in his voice.

Whatever it was, he wasn't going to bother himself, especially since it made economic sense, "Okay, the reverend wants her spared, but one more incident and I will serve her to the dogs!"

Smith looked down at her and the clergyman and shook his head as he continued for the door. "Clean up this mess and take her back to the others and make sure you keep your dicks in your pants," he ordered the guards before finally making an exit.

Reverend Samuel Parris sighed in relief when Anthony Smith left the room. He looked at Tutu on the floor and slowly shook his head with a mixture of guilt, disbelief and dismay. If only he had spoken when the guards brought them in earlier, he blamed himself.

His plan after seeing them unexpectedly was to find a way to free them, either through persuading Smith or helping them escape, but it was just too short a notice to devise an escape plan or persuade a total stranger, especially a mad one like Smith. The sooner he left this continent, the better, he thought and smirked as he remembered the veiled insult of being called a nigger lover.

He knew very well as an ex-slave trader that he was lucky to have been able to convince Smith against killing Tutu and that the insult was the price he had to pay for such a consideration. From his experience, slaves were spared for no cost, especially when causing the death of a European. The verbal attacks in the course of trying to do what was right, which gradually resulted in bodily attacks and finally termination, were the reason he was now seeking passage back to the West Indies.

Once a successful merchant on the "Triangular Route" of West Africa, the Americas and England, Samuel Parris had turned to Christianity and the clergy just a few years ago. At a young age, he had accumulated substantial wealth and set up sugar plantations in Barbados and Jamaica.

Due to falling output in Barbados exacerbated by the 1667 Bridgetown fire and hurricane, 1668 drought and 1669 floods, Parris and several thousand other planters moved to the newly acquired Jamaica in 1670. Thankfully, Parris found ample, fresh and fertile land in western Jamaica, where he set up another sugar plantation.

It was also in Westmoreland, Jamaica, he met and married Judith, the daughter of a successful plantation owner that gave birth to their daughter, Betty. Everything appeared to be going fine, when things suddenly soured and he had to leave everything behind to become a missionary.

After a long period of good fortune, he was struck with bouts of ill fate. Starting with the total collapse of his Barbados plantation he left in the hands of overseers and the loss of two consecutive cargoes, he was befallen by worse calamities.

The last and most serious struck his daughter. His six months old daughter fell to a strange disease in Jamaica, which grew worse by the day, with no cure in sight.

One morning in the summer of 1680 as Parris was sitting outside his compound in Jamaica, distraught and confused, a strange old black lady walked up to him and what she told him was to change his life significantly from thereon.

In the first instance, an old gray-haired black lady leaning on a cane was an anomaly in the land, where the average life expectancy of imported slaves was ten years. She had quietly walked up to him, as he bowed his head in thought and said, "Young man, I know your troubles and fears and was sent to tell you, there is a solution."

Startled out of his deep thoughts, he looked at the stranger scornfully, judging her to be one of the many fake psychics parading around the town. "Woman, I am in no mood for games!" he barked at her rudely.

"I do know that, Sir. The life of a beautiful baby girl is by no means a game, neither is the loss of two cargoes and fortune," she answered to a dumbstruck Parris, but before he could recompose himself, she continued.

"Some do evil and get away with it, while others don't.

Which is why we are told never to follow the multitude to do evil. Your trade does not go well with your spirit and I have been told that you need to make amends or you shall lose your whole family and fortune beginning with your baby daughter," she grimly warned a more perplexed Parris.

"So what amends are these? I will do anything to save my little girl," he said, knowing he could no longer endure the plague that had beset him.

"It is easy!" the old woman said, her smile revealing a near toothless mouth. "You have to give your life to God for the benefit of those whom you have deprived of so much." She slowly nodded her head affirmatively in response to Parris' confused, questioning look.

"What god? I am a Christian," he asked, fearing he was being asked to join one of the African sects practiced on the island. Considering his social status, especially his wife's family that would be difficult, although not impossible considering his desperation.

As if the lady could read his mind, she smiled and gently placed a hand on his shoulder. "Whatever you feel comfortable with young man. There is only one God, but thousands of languages and ways to speak to him."

She straightened up to leave, but Parris stopped her, offering to give her something in appreciation and dashed indoors. His intentions were not only to give her something, but also to call his wife for testimony.

To his dismay, when he returned barely a split second afterwards, she had disappeared. He ran to check the road, which was a long road with no turnings off for five hundred yards, but it was an exercise in futility.

It was the hardest decision, he had ever had to make, which was not made easier by his wife's unwavering objection. His wife having not witnessed the message and who was used to good fortune could not agree to her husband leaving a lucrative business for preaching. Neither did her family.

The following day, his daughter fell into a coma, thereby forcing his hand. He immediately went to the local church.

Although his initial plan was to join the local church and practice as a local pastor, the local minister told him there was no space for a new pastor. The local minister directed him to a visiting missionary from London, when he realized he was strangely persistent.

The visiting missionary, who also noticed his fervent scramble to join the ranks of clergymen, offered him what most people usually shunned—a mission in Africa. Apart from the fear of malaria, most clergymen preferred missions at home or the Americas, which had many social benefits as opposed to the relatively socially stigmatized African missions, which led most into eternal obscurity. Thinking of the old woman's forecast, Parris's raised no objections since it was the only opening.

He didn't need much further training since he had once attended Harvard University for religious training, but dropped out towards the end for more lucrative ventures. Nevertheless, he started a short induction at the local parish the following day.

From his first day of attendance, he noticed a marked improvement both in his daughter's health and some other problem areas, and despite his wife's continued objections, remained committed. Soon afterwards, he left for the West Coast of Africa.

His return to Africa in 1680 was a bit of a novelty, since he had never really stayed on land for more than a couple of days. Unlike some other daring merchants, he conducted most of his business from his ship or at best, on the shore, not worrying of the increased costs added by middlemen. He mostly bought slaves from other Europeans or their coastal operatives who many a times had slaves in hold, waiting for their European merchants.

He knew absolutely nothing of the hinterland or of its peoples. Like most slavers, he made sure he was emotionally distant from the products of his trade, in order to be able to make economic decisions free of unnecessary sentiments.

It was therefore to his surprise and profound regret to find socially advanced people, who were infinitely friendly and open in all their dealings. This openness and abundance of character, he realized was not due to their being primitive as believed by his contemporaries, but due to the abundance of nature, which had enabled them to develop an advanced society with minimal effort and disturbance.

Gradually, he fell in love with the land and its people; thus making him more committed to his mission. Contrary to his initial fears, it wasn't them that brought problems, but members of his old trade.

Before moving to Tutu's township, he was disrupted from two other towns due to slaving operations. After escaping from the mob in Tutu's township in 1686, he grew very intolerant and aggressive towards the slavers.

At his next mission, he actually gave chase to some slave raiders and relieved them of their kidnapped citizens. With acts like that, he soon became known and hated by many merchants, who after many unsuccessful tries on his life took the matter to his superiors in London.

Initially, London was supportive of him, although subtly telling him to keep his nose out of the slavers operations. Actually, they were surprised he had survived that long in a land, where most missions closed frequently to replenish their dead staff since the average life expectancy was less than a year.

Parris strongly believed them when he was told that the conversion of Africans to Christianity was of paramount importance, not only to the church, but also to the Crown. This belief strengthened his resolve against the slave raiders, whose relationship with him was deteriorating as fast as their tempo of raids in the area was increasing.

Unfortunately, the hands of those in London were eventually forced and they had to come down on him hard, instead of sitting on the fence. He was told in unequivocal terms to stop bothering the raiders as reported or face termination. Despite this, he didn't believe the church would support the raiders against him and believed the letter was to satisfy some people in London.

Therefore he continued his opposition to raids in his

area, but to his utmost surprise and dismay, he received a letter terminating his African mission and was ordered back to London. With much regret and pain, he packed to leave Africa and the people he had grown to love, although not heading for London as ordered.

Instead, he made arrangements to go back to his family in Jamaica, whom he had not seen for some time and fondly missed. It was this reason that brought him to Anthony Smith, one of the few slave merchants he hadn't met and fought. Although, it seemed to him their battle might be approaching.

7

E arly the following morning, Anthony Smith began making preparations to leave, ordering his crew to start loading his slaves and other cargo. Foodstuff and other provisions for the slaves were the first to be loaded, with the help of the slaves. Yams, beans, salted meat and loads of other food items were placed on the ship as Smith barked out orders to various members of his crew. The food and water provisions were very important for the survival of his cargo and, most importantly, his investment. No one was going to buy dead or extremely undernourished slaves.

The slaves were marched aboard and were seated on a lower deck, which was to be tightly packed with people, sitting in close rows and columns. Each person was to sit between the knees of the outstretched legs of the person behind him, and because of the overcrowding the men were loaded first. When the women, children and the sick were loaded and everyone was secured with chains that passed through their cuffs to the hull to prevent jumping overboard, they set sail.

As they set sail that evening, Anthony Smith and Reverend Parris stood on the top deck, looking thoughtfully at the fading port. On both men's minds as well as those underneath them was the thought of never seeing the land again, although with different feelings and for different reasons.

To Reverend Parris, it was a mixture of loss, bitterness and anxiety. He was to lose many good friends and freedom and was bitter towards the slave raiders, the church that betrayed him and the whole economic system. Lastly, he harbored anxiety on what the future held for him in the Americas.

To Smith, it was a mixture of joy, optimism and gratitude. He was overjoyed about being able to get much done in record time, optimistic as he calculated and made future business projections and lastly, grateful for leaving the White mans' grave alive.

Those below them felt anguish and fear.

Smith stretched out and yawned, "Not a bad start" he commented to the Reverend, who knew exactly how he felt. It was not a bad start considering that the cargo was eighty percent full and he was still to stop at the Gold Coast and if he wished the Ivory Coast, Pepper Coast and Grain Coast, then on to the West Indies, North America and finally England.

"Yes, not a bad start. Any partners?" The priest asked, although he was not really interested, he was trying to remain on good terms, knowing he wasn't much of a swimmer.

Smith shook his head. "No. I have passed that stage," he answered haughtily, "although I do have a partnership in a sugar plantation in Jamaica. Actually, I have been thinking, maybe that's where I saw your face, which looks rather familiar."

"Maybe," the priest answered reticently, suspecting it might be somewhere else, probably from the sketches circulated by some merchants to bring him into disrepute over his stance on raids in his area. He excused himself soon afterwards to retire to his quarters, although stopping briefly at the lower deck.

Parris saw Tutu looking haggard and desolate, her face was bruised and clothes were torn, her once beautifully weaved locks were now shabby and dirty. It hurt him seeing Tutu in the condition she was, but there was absolutely nothing he could do to help her. He moved on to his cabin heavy hearted and prayerful.

Anthony Smith stayed on the upper deck, watching the land move slowly as he mused over his business plans, especially being hours away from the Gold Coast. The business on the Gold coast always excited him, not only because of the relatively high cost and profit, but the sense of achievement he derived from it.

As a poor, young lad, he had always looked at the rich and

their gold and came to believe it was the most valuable item in the world. Having heard that gold came from somewhere in Africa, he had always dreamt of going to Africa to get gold and riches. Now, actually dealing in gold on the Gold Coast gave him a natural high.

Stifling a yawn, he stretched once again. That's strange, he wondered, I am a bit tired today and decided to have a quick nap. Usually the Gold Coast adrenaline kept him up thinking and absorbing the sights with occasional visits to check upon his crew at their various posts until they reached the Gold coast. On the way to his cabin, he contemplated various reasons, why he was so weak and tired and arrived at the conclusion that it was the long walk, Adam's folly and the slave girl.

The following day as they sailed close to the Gold Coast with dozens of flags of various ships and forts coming into view, the senior members of the crew stood on the top deck in a small group, wondering how to solve an abnormal problem.

Strangely, Smith had not been seen since he left the deck the previous day shortly after they set sail, and now they were about to berth at the Gold Coast over 24 hours afterwards. They were debating on whether or not to go and wake him up. They knew he had a bad temper and hated being disturbed when he was asleep, but they also knew how the gold trade excited him.

The problem was who was going to wake him up, and they kept passing the responsibility around since no one was willing to take the risk of being shot in the foot or continuously cursed and abused throughout the day. Eventually they decided to go in a group.

Anthony had been sleeping and when he was awoken, he was surprised he had slept for so long. As he tried to get up, he realized he was completely listless and was shivering. He touched his forehead instinctively and realized it was boiling.

"Oh God! I've got the frigging fever," he cried feebly, sinking back into the bed feeling really nauseous, weak and cold. Worse, he had a frightful sinking feeling.

The crew was lost for words on hearing it was the dreaded

fever that very few survived. They quietly retreated from the cabin, being unable to suggest anything to the sick man and a bit scared of catching it, since nobody really knew what brought it on.

For the next 24 hours, the ship sat still in the dock with no one debarking, because nobody could take on the responsibility of the gold trade. They could sail the ship without him, but the gold purchase was a different business. Neither could they continue sailing to the West Indies, as someone suggested, knowing Anthony Smith would go raving mad for missing the opportunity of gold trading. Therefore they sat down doing nothing on the ship or for the captain, apart from cooking and feeding themselves and the slaves.

The slaves, who had enjoyed a brief respite in their airing and sitting conditions while at sea, were now suffering due to the hot, humid and stagnant air, especially in their overcrowded deck. Once at sea where the possibility of escape was reduced, some women and children were let on the top deck for airing and exercise, leaving more room and air for those not allowed. Now, as they sat on the shore with no air coming into the cramped deck, which had headroom of only four feet, many were feeling sick or depressed. To make the dreary situation more bearable, the slaves began singing.

Eventually, Parris was able to convince the captain to order his crew to dock and get a cure on land. Smith was then aided on both sides onto land, where they managed to secure a bed for him in one of the numerous camps that littered the coast. Now a shadow of himself, he was growing weaker as the day progressed and unable to keep down any food.

Once they settled Smith in a bed, the priest and two senior members of the crew went in search of a cure for the fever. The fever was widely known on the coast by the mainly European traders, but no one knew a cure and after what seemed like eternity, they returned to a further weakened Smith. They tried to dilute the bad news to Smith, but Smith having seen so many die, gave up hope.

"Take me back to my ship, I would rather die on my ship

than on this godforsaken land," he said feebly but resolutely. "Moreover since I've got a week or so left, I will set my will straight." His wish was respected, and he was escorted back to the ship.

Walking the gangplank towards the ship, they heard the slave songs, which had changed in tempo. They were singing a very sonorous song, which was led by a sweet voice that the reverend recognized from the past—Tutu's voice. Her voice triggered off some memories of his stay in Ijebu, making his mind wander and his eyes nearly water, only to be brought back by Smith's talking.

"It always beats me how those Africans bring out such moving songs, despite one not being able to understand a word of it," Smith commented as they got on board. "I have to find someone to buy the slaves or exchange them for gold and have it sent to my wife."

They set him on his bed and were about to leave, "Wait! Reverend! Joe! I need you as witnesses to my will, while you write it down," he said weakly as he pointed to the third man, Ron. The three of them obliged him, as Ron picked up a quill and paper from the table, the others found a place to sit as they silently reflected their private thoughts on the situation.

The reverend was visibly disturbed by his thoughts as he weighed the pros and cons of some idea that had just struck him. Although he was not the only one with weighty thoughts as he was to discover after Ron fetched the writing materials.

"Those slaves!" Smith said ponderously after the long pensive silence, "Ever since Adam got that light skinned slave, I have got bad luck." The reverend that had been engrossed in his thoughts, startled as he caught the second part of the sentence.

Parris cleared his throat and visibly made an effort to fasten his resolve. "Speaking of which, I was thinking of bringing one of them in to diagnose the fever and suggest what to do," he said. He paused to see the reaction and was not surprised.

"Over my dead body would I let an African stand over me and tell me what to do," Smith objected in the loudest voice he had used all day. The overexertion made him retch in the bedside bucket and left him seriously drained. Parris noticed the lack of epithets or disgust on his face, despite his objections and suspected that with a little straight talking, the weakness in his body might influence his mind.

"Well, it's your choice whether you want to lie down and die in ignorance and arrogance," Parris said harshly, earning surprised looks from the other two men, but he was confident that Smith was too weak to burst out in anger. He continued less severely. "Or you let them treat you; remember this is their land, their sickness. I have been cured thrice by them and remain alive!" he stated as a matter of fact nonchalantly.

When he realized that there was no outright objection and Smith was contemplating it, he decided to force his hand. Standing up and straightening out his cassock, "one thing, I would not do is to bear witness to the will writing of someone about to commit suicide, please excuse me!" he said and walked towards the door.

Smith feeling very weak and helpless called out, "Alright! Alright, Reverend! Take one of the guards and have one of them brought here." He succumbed to the surprise of the others, who dropped their mouths. Smith was wise enough to know when he was beaten and did not want to die. As it was, he could feel life slowly drifting out of him and was desperate to stop it somehow.

The priest smiling as he left the cabin went towards where the slaves were being held. They were still singing when he reached them and ordered one of the guards to release Tutu. This had to be done by releasing the chain that bound her column from one side of the hull to the other.

Tutu walked up to him and looked fiercely into his face. Her countenance was one thing the priest had failed to put into consideration, while making his plan. He stepped back and was shocked by the hateful look on his once cheerful friend's face.

Ever since he saw Wura die, he felt strongly obligated to help and protect her, knowing he was her only hope. It dawned on him that he was the only person outside her family ever trusted by Wura to look after her.

He pulled her to a slightly secluded spot and looked into her eyes as he spoke softly, "I am sorry about what has happened to you. I hope you realize I have nothing to do with it and was just lucky to be there that morning, while looking for a ship home. This is one of the reasons I decided to pack it up and go home." He tried explaining to her, but there was no change in her countenance.

"Tutu, I am grateful for what you and your mother did for me and I want to help you too. It might not be as much as you need, but my best. First, I need your help to help you," he persisted.

"How can I help you?" she asked skeptically, although with less bitterness and anger. The reverend explained the problem to her and his plan.

"Let the mad dog die!" she said bitterly and angry that the priest could even suggest such a thing.

"No, Tutu! Listen, if he dies, you will be sold to another mad dog and I wouldn't be able to protect you, since I would also be looking for another ship to take me home. If you save him, I would work out a deal with him to make life easier for you. I don't think you can be freed here since it's too far away from home, and you would most likely be kidnapped again."

"Reverend, there is no easiness in the life of a slave and even if am freed, I have nowhere to go. My whole family has been killed! Thanks for the thought anyway," she said, devoid of any rancor or sarcasm. Parris empathized with her, shrugged and turned away to leave, when stopped by her hand.

"I will help. I don't know why, but I guess nothing should stop me from saving a life. Moreover, I think you are a good man and if it comes to the worst, I think I would prefer staying with you," she said smiling faintly at the reverend.

Parris was moved by the situation and momentarily tongue-tied. He silently led her towards the cabin and only stopped once they neared the entrance. "Don't act like you know me. It would only bring trouble to you," he advised her, not wanting to expose her to ridicule that was meant for him, which would come constantly unless he paid for her. Tutu was confused by the strange request, but nevertheless nodded in agreement.

He knocked on the door, although he did not wait for answer before stepping in with Tutu behind him. He paused at the doorstep to be sure all was right before stepping aside and letting Tutu step in.

"Oh, my God! Not her, reverend! Why did you bring her?" Smith whimpered and angrily turned away on the bed. The priest nudged her towards him as she stood looking around her surroundings, which were a world away different from theirs. She looked at Smith cautiously, before she approached his bedside, crouching beside it, she leaned forward to touch his forehead.

"Get her off me!" he muttered, but with no conviction or strength to do so himself.

"Ako Iba!" she said in Yoruba, meaning Strong Fever, thus confirming their diagnosis.

"Can you cure it?" Parris asked in Yoruba as Smith, who could pick out a few, words turned to look at them. She looked at him incredulously and rose to her feet.

"There is nothing that can't be cured. The question is does he want to be cured or is he man enough to be cured? There ain't any big women around to sit on him," she giggled, prompting the priest to smile at the veiled reference to him.

Smith was now lost in their discussion, "What does that mean, Priest? Can she do anything," he asked eagerly. The priest answered in affirmative, although not explaining her last statement. He requested permission to go on land with her, which was given, but on the condition that two guards be present.

"You can't be too careful with her, believe me! I have lost enough and I don't want you dead or her escaping." In order not to provoke unnecessary suspicions, the priest acquiesced.

Passing the busy port and forts, they walked towards the forest, which grew thicker as they moved away from the coast.

Parris and Tutu chatted along in Yoruba, much to the annoyance of the guards, who were excluded from their discussion and realized it had to do with more than merely searching for herbs.

After an eight-hour walk into the forest and a continuously fruitless search, the guards were about to call off the search and even Parris was getting skeptical, when Tutu exclaimed, "Igi Dogoyaro!" She led them to the tree she had sighted and reached for the guard's sword, which he refused to give up having seen what her mother had done with a cutlass.

"Hell No!" he strongly objected, but they all understood his fears and smiled. Tutu explained to him, they only needed the bark, which he tried to cut himself. Unfortunately, he couldn't get the bark off successfully and fumbled repeatedly, before Parris angrily snatched it from him and handed it to Tutu. Tutu deftly cut the bark off the tree, handed back the sword and made a cheeky gesture of feigning shooting with her fingers and mouth at the tree. The message was clearly, "All you know is shooting" and the guard glowered at her.

They didn't get back to the ship until well into the night, and Smith's condition had deteriorated further since they left him. Tutu immediately set out to work, demanding boiling hot water in a large container, which Parris ordered the crew to fetch. After everything was provided, she went about making the herbal concoction, which she washed, soaked and asked it to be left to simmer on mild fire, before being brought back.

Her giving instructions to the crew, indirectly or otherwise, did not go down well with them and soon malicious gossip and innuendoes were going around. To make it worse, the guards that escorted her into the forest, also contributed to the disparaging rumors.

It was rumored that the slave girl had bewitched the captain, and he was dying. Also, that he had handed over the running of the ship to the Priest, who was smitten by her evil charms. To make matters worse was the odor coming from the herbal concoction, which was repulsive to their unaccustomed European noses.

When the concoction was ready, it was brought to the captain's cabin. Parris woke him up, while Tutu stood at his bedside with a jug of the concoction. Several members of the crew hung around the door and outside to see what was going on.

As Smith sat up, he smelt and refused to drink the "evil-smelling, piss-looking magic potion." The priest gently persuaded him as the bystanders looked on. Smith was adamant that he wouldn't be drinking "that evil slave's piss" and was edged on by his crew.

Tutu saw the futility in trying to convince him and she spoke to Parris in Yoruba. "You have to force him, or he will die!" she admonished him gravely, but continued teasingly. "Only God knows where you spineless men come from." This earned her a feigned scornful look from Parris.

He thought back to how he felt the first time and knew he had to show tough love, but it would be difficult, especially with some sailors hanging around. They wouldn't understand just like he didn't initially, but had freely drunk it when he had other attacks after leaving Tutu's town. He thought of a way to get rid of the crew and ordered for more water from some, while sending the rest to his cabin to bring his bible.

With the crew out of his way, he quickly fastened the door with a bolt. He removed his cassock and sat up Smith, who was unsure of what was happening, but believed they couldn't physically force him against his wishes.

Of course, he found out that he was wrong and protested, "No! You can't do this to me, I am the captain!" He weakly struggled against Parris' strong embrace, "I will have your heads for this."

When Parris had him well pinned down, Tutu moved closer and grabbed his chin. Forcibly parting his lips, she poured the liquid through his clenched teeth. Not one to be easily dominated Smith spat out a mouthful at her, which she calmly wiped off her face. On her return to his bedside, she held his head back firmly and pressed so hard on his jaws, he opened his mouth wide open to stop further pain. He knew he had lost and co-operated, drinking the required amount, before being tucked into bed.

Smith's protests were heard by his crew outside his cabin, which promoted the loss of confidence in the ship's command. The following morning, his condition seemed to have worsened, and he was hardly able to answer his crew's questions.

He slept throughout the day and was only interrupted by Parris and Tutu, who gave him more of the concoction, which he readily accepted to avoid further humiliation from the hands of Tutu.

Later in the day, his crew started deserting the ship, but Parris, who didn't want to depress Smith, did not inform him. He reasoned it was more important to get him back on his feet, before bothering him with the ship's responsibilities.

The rumors increased in their intensity and absurdity, as they believed the slave girl was slowly killing their captain. This was an expected reaction since poisoning was the most feared slave weapon among slave merchants, especially in the Americas.

By the third day, chaos was reigning supreme on board since only Parris and Tutu were allowed to see the captain and by the evening, nearly seventy percent had deserted, leaving behind only his most loyal crew. Even then, the remaining crew did not stay to be subservient to Parris, but were planning a bloody revolt for the next day.

Fortunately, early in the morning of the next day, the fourth day, Smith rose from his sick bed feeling much better, but was extremely hungry. The hunger was a sign of his recuperation from malaria. As he made his way to the main deck, he noticed the absence of his crew and sounded a bell.

He was answered by only a few of his crew, who informed him the rest had deserted due to their belief that he was dying and had left the priest and the slave in charge. He was enraged and wanted to go ashore to look for them, but was stopped by Parris, who advised him to regain his strength, before embarking on any strenuous activity.

The priest explained that the next twenty-four hours were critical and he might relapse, if care was not taken. He was reassured by the remaining loyal seamen, who were pleased to see him recover, that they would retain control until he was fully fit to take over.

Reluctantly, Smith returned to his cabin, where he was spoon fed by Tutu with large portions of yam, beans and meat. Due to the depleted kitchen staff, Tutu was also called upon to help in cooking the food and serving the other slaves. Over the next 72 hours, Smith slowly regained his full strength and returned to his normal self.

He was overjoyed and grateful to be alive seven days after catching the fever, having lost all hope of ever beating it. He had only one person to thank, Reverend Parris, actually two he thought. Maybe the slave woman wasn't bad luck after all. He thanked Parris profusely and tried showing his utmost gratitude, before once again switching to top gear in his business pursuits.

He had a lot to accomplish, most importantly, to employ new crew and replace stolen equipment for the rest of the journey. He earnestly set out for business ashore, where some old members of his crew were shocked to see him alive after leaving him for dead. Despite being advised against it, he approached the captain of the ship, who he was told poached his crew and instruments.

"You have things that belong to me, which I don't think were rightly taken. I really don't care for the deserting rats, but I need my charts and instruments back," Smith gently told the captain, whom he found drinking among friends.

The Irish captain laughed in his face having heard the rumors. "My good friend, you don't need all those instruments when you have an African witch in control," he joked for friends, provoking laughter from them.

Embarrassed, Smith became very irate and very nearly shot him in the protracted argument that ensued, but in the end, left to hire a new crew at a higher cost. In order to cover the additional cost without digging into his reserves for the gold trade, he had to sell some slaves at a loss.

Smith was still irate, when he returned on board, pacing up and down the upper deck, while the new crew settled in and took over various duties. With the new crew in place, Tutu was taken back to the lower deck, where she resumed her place among the other slaves.

On seeing this, a disappointed Parris decided to broach the issue with the captain. When Parris approached him, he noticed Smith was in a foul mood and decided to find out the reason for his anger, before stating his own grievances.

"God is my witness. I will get everyone of those bastards, if it takes all my life. Nobody deserts and steals from my ship and then laughs in my face," Smith fumed. The priest, newly his confidante, tried to pacify him.

"You've got to keep a cool and collected head, plan and move on. Forgive whatever wrong anyone did to you as your life has been forgiven and handed back to you. You have it in your hands to profit more than you could have a few days ago," the priest paused, contemplating on whether to bring up what he had originally planned to tell him. "Which brings me to wonder about Tutu," he stared directly at him to see his reaction, but only saw confusion.

"What's Two Two, Father?" he asked genuinely puzzled.

"The name of the slave that saved your life. You never said anything about her and since the new deck hands have started, she has been returned to the hold as if nothing happened!" Parris raised his voice slightly in anger.

Anthony Smith sighed pensively. "Well, what am I supposed to do? You don't expect me to release her in the middle of nowhere, over 200 miles from her home," he said defensively, pausing as he looked at the priest and didn't like his expression.

"I am not a brute, Father, I have thought about it. She has lost her father and mother and even if she hadn't, there is no way she would make it across the Fon territory, Whydah and would most likely end upon another slave boat," Smith elucidated.

Whydah was the port of Fon territory, which was the small stretch of land of about 150 miles between Yorubaland and the Gold Coast. Its recently militarized inhabitants preyed on the heavily populated areas of their former overlords, the western Yorubas, whom they called the Eyo or Eso.

The Yorubas lost control of the area up to the Gold Coast, when the Muslim upheavals in the north and west drove the Akans southeastward around the same time Europeans from the sea landed on the coast. The Akans, previously involved in the depleted Northwest African Gold trade of Carthage, Morocco and Spain, effectively stopped the much larger Yoruba-Hausa Northeast Gold trade that fed the major world trade centers in the Middle East and the Mediterranean. Moreover, because they didn't have the population of the Yorubas that helped in effectively mining the gold, they resorted to slaves from Yorubaland sold by Europeans or from the Northern Muslims.

With the loss of the economic benefits of the Gold trade as well as the fishing trade, the small population of Fons, Ewes and some other distant Yoruba peoples on the western and southern fringes of the empires earned the coast its name—the Slave Coast—from the sheer volume of slaves sold. And they would definitely kidnap and sell Tutu on sight.

"So you would just pretend nothing happened. That's very convenient, isn't it?" Samuel Parris said with loads of sarcasm and scorn.

"Father, please get off my back. I will cut her a little slack, once we set sail and would get her a favorable buyer," Smith pled, hurt.

"Thanks for your generosity, my Lord," Parris bowed mockingly. "A little slack for just a little worthless life, you are most generous, your majesty!" He walked away angrily before the flustered Smith could regain his composure.

"She did what she had to do and don't forget I saved her life after all the losses she caused me," Smith shouted after the priest, who didn't bother answering as he walked away. Smith, realizing his folly, scratched his head in confusion; things were just happening too fast for his comprehension.

The priest shrugged in resignation, knowing he had tried his best and couldn't push too hard. He stopped at the lower deck and saw Tutu from afar; the sight of which made him wince. He noticed she had slumped back into the depression she was in before being released to take care of Smith.

Over the last couple of days, he noticed that her ebullient character, which he remembered from his days in Ijebu, occasionally resurfaced when she was around him. It greatly hurt him to see her in a trance-like depression seated among others in equal misery. He shook his head sadly and returned to his cabin.

The next day, Smith went ashore to conclude the final part of this business stop—gold. He went in search of a good price for gold, after which an exchange would be made, once he came back for the slaves or the agreed medium of exchange. The first part was quite a protracted affair lasting for four days. He went from camp to camp and fort looking for a favorable price, but was frustrated by the prevailing prices.

The exchange rate for slaves had dived further since his last visit, and it appeared the coast was flooded with slaves from the Benin civil war. Smith knew he would do much better if he took his slaves to the Americas, but due to the prestige he attached to the gold business, he ended up exchanging twenty-five slaves and some Pounds Sterling for gold.

In addition, he bought extra food due to the extra time spent ashore. Before leaving he had all the decks cleaned and made sure everything was in good order. Finally, he was ready to set sail, two weeks after they had berthed at the Gold Coast harbor, but not before he settled all accounts.

As the ship left the dock in the dark, he ordered it to stop about five hundred yards from shore and then let down a dinghy. With him were two of his most trusted men, who paddled the boat towards the dock, where the ship of the captain that insulted him still sat.

On reaching it, under the guise of darkness, he rigged the hull with limpets and quickly paddled back to his ship. Just as they reached their ship, they heard a series of explosions from the dock. Looking back, he smiled. "Let's see those bastards sail," he said with much satisfaction. There would be no casualties, but the ship would not be sailing anytime soon and perhaps never.

Getting on board, he went straight to the lower deck and ordered Tutu cut loose. When Tutu was brought out to him, he stood for a few awkward moments, not knowing what to say and just smiled. It was not easy for him, due to pride and the novelty of expressing gratitude to a slave.

Reverend Parris had seen Smith let down the dinghy and when he heard the explosions, he came to the conclusion that Smith had exacted his revenge. A few moments after he suspected he should be back on board, Parris went in search of him to rebuke him.

Parris found him on the lower deck standing in front of Tutu. Standing out of their view, he shook his head in sweet disbelief, not knowing what to make of the enigmatic captain, but it was no longer in him to rebuke him. He turned back to his cabin.

8

Although, they sailed along the West African coast like most ships heading toward the Americas, Anthony Smith instructed the crew to sail directly to Jamaica, with no more stops in Africa. The slaves were occasionally released for exercise on the deck and were encouraged to dance to enhance free blood flow to their cramped legs.

Following Smith's order, Tutu was free to move about at all times and was given the task of feeding and taking care of the other slaves. When she was not working, she was with the Reverend, of whom she once again grew fond and to whom she was eternally grateful. Tutu never allowed him to forget that it was his grace that allowed her to be able to move about and remain alive.

The priest completed the revival by once again teaching her to read and write English. To his surprise, she still retained most of what he had previously taught her and her remarkable intelligence to pick up new knowledge rapidly. She only had to be taught something once and she committed it to memory forever.

This new development did not go down well with the crew, most of whom were new and unaware of the incident that preceded their arrival. They found it strange and annoying that a slave was given such a free hand. Moreover, it was an affront to most of them that a slave was being taught to read and write, while they could neither read nor write.

Complaints soon reached the captain, who already knew, but had chosen to ignore them. When the complaints grew too loud, signifying widespread discontent among his crew, he decided to take it up with Parris.

"What are you trying to do, by teaching a slave to read?" Smith broached the subject one afternoon as they sat on the main deck. He didn't want to sound offensive but was beginning to believe that the priest was going too far with his sympathy for her. Knowing how Parris felt about her, he tried reasoning gently with him, "Do you want to cause revolts on the plantation?"

Parris, who had been expecting the topic to be brought up for some time, smiled as he took his time replying.

"I am not trying to do or cause anything, but I would not stop anyone eager to learn from learning. Remember it is my job to spread the good word to everyone who cares to listen," he answered pragmatically as the wind blew his cassock fiercely.

"If I remember well, the job is to spread the word to the crew, not the slaves. We are not Spanish," referring to the Spanish practice of converting and baptizing slaves, before they landed in the Americas. Observing the sudden tautness of the priest's face, he continued, "I don't really mind whom you decide to teach, but my main concern is that there have been many whisperings and complaints and I don't want another desertion or mutiny on my hands."

"None of those complaining wish to learn. It's hard enough to get them to recite the grace before eating!" Parris answered angrily, pausing to control his temper. "Don't worry. There isn't going to be another desertion unless you plan dying on us again," he said jokingly with loads of sarcasm. The salient point being well delivered and Smith could say nothing as he stared beyond Parris, fixing his gaze on something behind the priest.

"Good afternoon, masters!" Tutu sang sweetly as she walked past them, coming from behind the reverend and they answered. Tutu had undone her complex hairdo that had become haggard and plaited the locks into two long strands that reached the middle of her back, revealing her full facial beauty. She also managed to tack her torn blouse with loose threads from her wrapper.

Smith continued staring at her as she walked on. "Holy Cow!" he exclaimed as he looked at her from head to toe. "Damn, she has changed, she, err, err, looks different."

Parris slowly shook his head gravely. "She is more radiant and too beautiful for her own sake! I am scared to think of what trouble she is going to attract to herself." Once again Smith did not reply, but was staring and visibly trying to fix his gaze on something of interest.

"Is it my eyes or am I seeing smoke in the middle of the ocean?" he squinted as they both tried to make out what was rising above the horizon.

Smith excused himself and beckoned one of his seamen to bring his telescope. Looking into the telescope, he nodded, "Yes, there is surely smoke rising from Northwest North. Hey, set sail for it, but let's be cautious it's not a pirate trap. You never know with these waters."

Sailing closer, it became apparent that a ship was on fire, but strangely there was no one on its top deck calling for help. Actually there was no sign of life on it at all.

Smith cautiously maneuvered his ship to its side with all guns trained on it, in case there was a sudden attack from it. Moving closer, they saw a gory scene develop on the ship with bodies littering everywhere on the top deck.

"Holy Shit! It seems there was a pirate attack on it," someone observed with Smith nodding in agreement. "Let's board it and see, if there are any survivors that need help or anything worth our while," the seaman suggested.

"Yeah, but we better look around to make sure, whoever did it isn't hanging around," he cautioned and looked through his telescope 360 degrees, before giving the go ahead for an initial five-man investigative party. Ten seamen stood at alert with their guns trained on the ship to give the boarding party assistance, if required.

The boarding party was met with a more gruesome sight of dismembered body parts and blood. Ascertaining, there were no traps or pirates on the ship, they beckoned to the others to come over. Smith and the ten other seamen answered the call and crossed over onto the ship.

"Damn, look what I found," someone suddenly shouted,

startling the nervous men. They all went to where the man called out and saw that he had every reason to be flabbergasted.

"Who would rob a ship and leave these many slaves aboard?" queried one of the men in amazement.

"Pirates often prefer something light and valuable things than having to go through the trouble of taking slaves, especially Arab pirates. All they usually want are spices, gold or goods. They don't really bother with slaves," Smith, being the most experienced, explained to his men.

Truly, Arabs had an ample supply of slaves through their raiding of the northern grassland fringes of the forest kingdoms. However, they harassed European merchants off the coast of north West Africa, who had cut their supply of gold to their ancient Trans-Sahara route. Normally, they held the ship hostage until fines were paid. Although, it sometimes got out of control, especially when fierce, but unsuccessful resistance is put up, which appeared to be the case on this occasion.

"Search the ship for anything else, we will take the slaves," Smith ordered sternly, trying not to show his ecstasy over the find. The seaman searched the ship vigorously, but it appeared the raiders had conducted a thorough search. Moreover, the fire was spreading at a fast rate.

"Captain, see who we found in one of the officers' cabins. Do you think he would be of any good?" They dragged a huge African before him, who had sustained multiple sword wounds all over his body.

Smith examined him disdainfully, "Yeah, he is well built. He should go for a good price," he said as he continued assessing him. Then a thought crossed his mind, "but what was he doing there, while others were chained up," he puzzled.

"Well, he might be the slaves' foreman, like our priest's mistress on our ship," one of the seamen with a broken nose and sandy hair joked impishly, causing laughter among the others.

"Watch your mouth, before I have your tongue, you imbecile!" Smith snapped threateningly with a grim expression on his face, which made others stop in mid-laughter. "Now, take him along with the others and let's get the hell out of here, before it sinks under us."

Sometimes Smith found their antics amusing, but he never allowed them to get too lax in their words or actions, being a strong believer in discipline along the chain of command. Therefore, although he found the seaman's cheeky comments funny, the priest was high on the chain of command and he wouldn't be party to jokes at his expense from a junior officer.

He stepped aside as the men hurriedly led the slaves across into his ship, giving each one a cursory glance. After the last one left, he took the ships charts and ran off to his ship just as the fire totally engulfed the stricken ship.

Later, after they had continued their journey and everything had returned to normal, he went to observe the new slaves, who had been chained to the others. He met Reverend Parris on the deck, observing them from a distance.

"They are not mixing with each other. They are from another part of the Slave Coast. I guess they are Igbos from the Niger delta area, further east from where we set sail," the Reverend voiced his observations as Smith stopped next to him.

"I know some planters complain about Igbos' stubborn resistance and being prone to suicides. I don't give a damn. All I know is that the heavens are finally smiling down on me. I can't believe my luck," Smith replied, obviously in a better mood than he had been all month.

They stood in brief silence as they continued looking from a distance. "At least, even if they don't mix, it appears your friend, Tutu has found a new friend," Smith commented, referring to Tutu's nursing and doting over the injured slave found in an officer's cabin on the distressed ship.

Reverend Parris smiled smugly, "Maybe that's your source of luck. You went there to get her a friend and for your troubles were rewarded generously. I am happy for both of you."

"Rubbish!" Smith exclaimed and walked away, shaking his head in disbelief, but still smiling.

Tutu took care of the injured slave, towards whom she felt some empathy, as she examined and cleaned his numerous wounds. He was not chained with the others and was laid in the front.

To Tutu's surprise, he was a priest's slave and could also speak English, in which they conversed and learnt of each other's past. He told her he was an Igbo man, whose name was Emeka. The full name Chukwuemeka meant God's favor or gift.

He was reading the Bible with the minister in his cabin, when they were attacked by surprise. He had tried to protect the priest, but was overwhelmed and he was lucky to still be alive, while his mentor wasn't. The preacher was beheaded by those he called Moslems, but he had been spared his life, once he was overpowered and injured.

With a new friend, Tutu began to spend less time with the Priest, who constantly teased her over Emeka, referring to him as her husband. She learnt that in Emeka's village as in most Igboland, they put outsiders, especially coastal people from the south and east, in charge of their religious and judicial systems.

Over time Igbos abhorred and rejected monarchies, elaborate governments, their power trappings and abuse, for a system based solely on communal efforts contribution, coming together only for defense purposes. This system of sub-contracting government functions to outsiders, known as the Arochukwu Oracle, was to promote fairness, but it apparently went very wrong.

In his case, Emeka was wrongly accused of being evil and was forced to enter a cave on the outskirts of his town to address the gods to prove his innocence and probably beg for forgiveness. To his surprise, he was led out through another exit unknown to the villagers into the waiting hands of his slavers, who sold him on the coast to the priest.

"So no one knows of the back exit or slavers in your village. Wouldn't your family have wondered what happened to you?" Tutu asked bewildered, considering the large number of people that he told her had never returned from the cave.

He shrugged sadly, "They would believe I was guilty and the gods had taken my life."

Tutu told him of her own more dramatic story, to which his paled by comparison, especially with the killing of her parents. Being the first time she had recounted her story, she was overwhelmed by feelings she had kept bottled up. At a point, she burst into tears and wept her heart out. Emeka placated her gently, rubbing the back of her neck fondly to soothe her heartfelt pains.

She found it easier to open up to Emeka, who was her age mate and could relate more easily to her experiences, making her grow attached to him in their platonic relationship. Both of them being young, they had their occasional arguments, especially over facts of life, of which they neither had much experience.

It was the priest who adjudicated between them, although with time, he realized he was being asked increasingly tricky questions. Questions like why were they slaves when they were not prisoners of war, which was the accepted practice throughout Africa and most of the world. Or why were so many slaves needed?

As the new friendship between the young adults strengthened, the long-term friendship of Tutu and Parris was to be shaken to its foundations. On one occasion, Parris forgot his bible with her overnight and, by the following day, she and Emeka had read nearly the whole Book of Genesis. Normally, every preacher chooses the appropriate chapter for reading, and the church didn't encourage ordinary people to read and interpret the bible without guidance.

When she saw him the following morning, she handed the bible to a surprised Reverend Parris, who didn't even know it was missing and immediately bombarded him with questions. "Reverend, who is Noah? Is Noah, the father of the whole world?"

"I see you have being reading through the bible. You are

not supposed to read the Scriptures without the guidance of a priest!" Parris rebuked her in a stern tone.

Ignoring his scathing comments, she continued her line of questioning, "Tell me, now I am asking for your guidance. Is Noah the father of all people?"

"Yes," he snapped, but when he realized that she was unrelenting in her quest for knowledge, he added, "We are all descendants of Adam and Noah."

"Which of Noah's sons do black people come from?" she asked the priest, who suspected, but was not sure where the questions were leading.

"Ham!" he answered guardedly.

"So your God made black people slaves?" she more concluded than asked.

The Reverend caught unawares stuttered as he tried to give an appropriate answer, "No...errr. Yes, but that is in the Old Testament, Jesus came to give everyone salvation," he tried explaining Noah's story of Genesis chapter 9 verses 18-29 and Genesis chapter 10. This was in reference to the slavery curse placed on Ham, Canaan and their descendants and was often cited by slave traders and many others. The reply he gave Tutu was one he often gave since he became a clergyman against slavery.

She shook her head in disbelief, "So it was your God that told them to steal me and kill my father."

The priest knowing her well enough, knew there was no point trying to convince her otherwise, especially once she shook her head stubbornly as she was doing at present. Instead, he rebuked her and warned her never to take the bible away, "You will only end up more confused."

After Parris dismissed her, she returned to Emeka, who was taking longer than expected to heal. His wounds were infected, since they didn't know that the sword blades had been poisoned. It was only due to his strong constitution that he was still alive.

She told him about her discussion with the priest and how he reacted.

"I told you one has to be careful of these religions or you'll get sold down the river like I was," Emeka opined gravely, while Tutu remained silent. She had initially taken a different, more trusting stance, but with this discovery she was confused.

A week later, she gave in to her curiosity to once again read the holy book. Ever since her last experience, she was eager to read more and had started to believe the priest, who never let her into some secrets in the bible, had something sinister to hide. That could be the only explanation for his reaction, when he found out she had been reading the bible on her own.

Otherwise, if there were no secrets, why was she being kept from reading it freely, she asked herself over and over again, further fuelling her curiosity. Eventually, she stole the bible, one evening after studying with Parris.

This time the priest discovered the missing book before morning, since he had been expecting her to steal it. He prided himself on being able to read and predict her actions, having known her since she was just a child. He realized the folly of his reactions and guessed rightly that it would only fuel her curiosity.

Yet he knew he had to stop it because not only would it confuse her through misinterpretations, but also it was unheard of for a black slave to have a bible to herself, when the vast majority of the white populace did not have one.

It had only been interpreted into English less than a century ago and only clergymen and a privileged few owned one. Therefore he had to come down hard on her, unless it would provoke great resentment among the crew, if they found out.

Early the next morning, he went in search of her and found her, where she was about to begin her daily chores. She smiled knowingly as he approached her.

Disregarding her charming smile, "Tutu, where is the bible?" he demanded, "Didn't I tell you never to take it without my permission?" he tried feigning anger and disappointment. He grabbed her elbow to turn her round to face him, since she turned her back on him to continue what she was doing.

"Pharaoh, let my people go!" she said jokingly, because she could see through his mild attempt to discipline her. She was oblivious to the gravity of what she had done and saw no need to be serious.

Conscious of the stares of the nearby crew, he really became angry over the embarrassing scene. "Now stop being silly and give it to me, right now!" he said sternly startling her, but then again she believed he could not be that angry.

"Why are you angry, Father Parris? You are a person of God and shouldn't lose your temper easily", she continued playfully and even chuckled.

"Come on, young woman, give it back, before you...." Before he could complete his sentence she once again turned away, thus provoking him to yank her elbow a bit too roughly. Unfortunately her knuckle-kneed legs were awkwardly aligned and not firmly in position, making lose her balance and fall.

Tutu was shocked and hurt at what she believed was an overreaction, unbecoming of a friend, a priest and a gentleman. She got to her feet and stormed away angrily, leaving him standing awkwardly under the full gaze of the seamen, who wanted to see how it would all end.

Moments later, she returned with the book, which she thrust angrily at his chest as tears streamed down her face and she returned to her chores. The priest felt a bit guilty about overreacting, but knew he had to behave sternly to stop future embarrassment. Even if he wanted to, he knew he couldn't make amends in such an environment with so many onlookers. He knew they expected him to slap her or do something drastic for what they believed was disrespect, but he was too cultured for such a rash action.

Over the next couple of days, they avoided each other. Tutu was still hurt and disappointed, while he was annoyed over the ensuing embarrassment. It soon became widely reported throughout the ship that the priest and his mistress had a row, with so many distortions and exaggerations.

This was a development Smith did not appreciate and

he made his feelings known to the priest. "I heard you and the slave girl had a shouting match, leading to her hitting you, in the presence of the crew a few days ago," Smith stated gravely and held up a hand to stop the priest from answering and interrupting his planned speech. "It's got nothing to do with me, what happens between you two, but if disrespect is openly shown to seniors on the ship, it will be difficult to keep discipline on the ship."

Embarrassed by the captain's tone Parris said, "That was exactly what I was trying to do. I was...." he tried explaining, but was once again rudely cut off.

"Good gracious, if you call a shouting match with the lowest being on the ship an effort in disciplining, then I guess we are in trouble. No wonder you left the business for preaching," Smith said derisively, hurting the priest's feelings badly, thus making him blush and bow his head in dismay as Smith continued.

"Listen, I don't want to be brash," he said, noticing he had hurt the priest. "But I also want to avoid a situation whereby we have mutiny on our hands or my crew sleeping around with slaves and it appears that might happen, if we are not careful!" he admonished the priest.

The red-faced priest sighed as he finished. "I understand what you are saying and promise there would be no repeat occurrences," Parris assured him and left dejectedly for his cabin.

As if losing her close friend wasn't enough, Tutu found herself open to an avalanche of negative actions across the board and soon realized how vulnerable she was without the priest.

Many crewmembers were happy that the relationship between the Priest and Tutu had broken down, especially those who had sexual fantasies and those that simply despised her elevated position. Some junior members of the crew began scorning her in all ways and manners.

Ordinarily, being a beautiful woman she could not but attract unwanted advances on a ship full of sex-starved men in the middle of nowhere. To make matters worse, her blouse had become ragged due to the heavy toil exacted on it by her daily chores and she had to discard it. In its place she tied her head tie round her chest, leaving her midriff and shoulders open, which was more than enough to arouse sexual feelings among many of the seamen.

She constantly faced sexual innuendoes and harassment with her breast groped and her bottom pinched everywhere she went. It became increasingly difficult by the day to keep the sailors off her.

It all came to a hilt, one late evening when she went into the pantry to collect some items for use in the kitchen. It was part of her normal routine to move to and from the kitchen into the store several times a day and this was her final chore for the day. The pantry, whose only entrance was from the kitchen, was a small room with barrels and food containers stacked neatly, all the way up to its ceiling.

On this particular night, Tutu was in an introspective mood. She was finding it emotionally difficult to deal with the environment she had come to experience since falling out with her mentor.

Due to her mood, she took no particular notice of her immediate surroundings and people as she went about her chores. At least, not until she went into the store, the door slammed shut and she found herself staring at three lascivious sailors. These were three rugged looking new members of the crew she had recently begun to notice around due to their sexual advances.

Trying to keep her cool and remain her pleasant self, she greeted them, "Good evening!" With no intelligible reply forthcoming, they advanced towards her grinning lustfully. Seeing the looks on their faces, she asked nervously, "Do you want anything?"

"Yes, we want you, my love," one of them answered. His grin revealed a mouth with no front teeth due to the ravages of scurvy, a common ailment among seafarers.

"What do you want me for?" she queried, slowly stepping backwards apprehensively as they advanced.

"For your charms, the ones you used to give to the priest. If he doesn't want it, we do," answered another, while the other two murmured and nodded agreeably.

"We just want a little fun," added one of them, feigning sincerity and innocence.

"I don't understand. I got no charms or fun, please I just came for some sugar for the captain's food," she snapped, trying to bluff and turned to continue with her chore, but couldn't as they closed in on her.

"That's it! We also came for some sugar, honey! We might not be able to afford the captain's type of sugar, but I believe you could give us some of yours," the one with a broken nose and head full of sandy hair joked, provoking laughter from the others. Tutu could smell their repugnant alcohol laden breath as they neared her. With her back to the wall and nowhere to go, they gradually formed a semicircle around her. Left with no doubt of their sinister intentions, she visibly began to tremble.

"I've got no sugar!" she said with some desperation as sweat broke out on her forehead.

"Yes, you do! You are one heap of sweetness," the toothless one said and was backed with agreeing grunts from the other two.

"Don't be scared! We won't hurt you, unless you make us!" said the third one with freckles menacingly as he reached out to grab her.

She dodged his hand and backed herself further into the wall. "No! Please! Please!" she begged as she tried to avoid six hands groping hungrily at her. Inevitably, two sets of coarse hands grabbed hold of her and dragged her away from the wall towards them.

Tutu screamed at the top of her voice for help, but unfortunately no one could possibly hear her from the inner room—a consideration already taken by her attackers. Moreover, it was well after dinner and most people had retired to their cabins. She was only there to prepare the captain's regular nightcap.

The freckled sailor carried her off her feet towards the middle of the room as she screamed at the top of her voice, struggling and lashing out at them, although to no avail. If anything, it made them madder and more determined. "Oh! Bloody nigger bitch," the crooked nosed seaman shouted as he was hit in the eye. He grabbed hold of her head tie wrapped around her chest and viciously ripped it off.

"Look at those tits on the bitch!" exclaimed the toothless sailor as the freckled one laid her on the small floor space in the middle of the room. Tutu continued to resist and lash out at them until two of them were able to pin her hands down at the top of her head. Unable to move due to their stronghold, she became silent as she thought of what happened to her mother.

"That's good darling. Calm down and enjoy yourself." The toothless sailor said as he undressed to enter her.

Tutu with her eyes squeezed shut, quietly cried, "Yeye mi! Yeye mi"-another Yoruba word for my mother. The two men holding her hands on both sides sucked her exposed breasts, while the third now half naked and on his knees was grinning lustfully as he was about to enter her.

Suddenly, the ship was violently shaken as if hit by a great wave and about to capsize. This upset the barrels stacked on top of each other and made some fall off. One barrel full of oil came crashing down, hitting her attackers on their heads and knocking them unconscious, before rolling to the far end of the room.

Tutu, realizing what had happened, pushed off the men, who were momentarily knocked cold over her. She quickly got to her feet, grabbed her clothing, yanked the door open and fled.

With the inflow of fresh air, one of her assailants, the one with a broken nose regained his consciousness. He looked around, shocked and disoriented as he slowly rubbed the back of his head and saw Tutu running along the long kitchen. The freckled one also became conscious, and they both shook the third one awake.

"What happened?" he asked, startling awake. "Oh my head! My neck," he moaned as he regained his full senses. "What happened?" he inquired again.

"I don't know how she escaped. I think I remember us riding a wave," replied the toothless sailor, still massaging the back of his neck, "and something must have hit me." He struggled to rise to his feet, but since he was still dazed, he staggered a bit, before steadying himself.

"Damnit! She can't escape, let's go and get her!" he said as he got to his feet and headed for the exit, while exercising his taut neck muscles.

"How she did it, I don't know, but she is damn lucky. Let's go and get her. There is no one on the deck at this time!"

When Tutu ran out of the room, she initially headed for the priest's quarters, but on reaching his door, she changed her mind. Her pride and stubbornness prevented her from running to the priest for help.

"Not after him behaving badly towards me and refusing to apologize", she thought, "I might be a slave, but I've got some pride".

As she turned around and made her way to the top deck, she saw her three assailants pointing and running towards her. She once again broke into a run towards the main deck, but only to realize everywhere was deserted as she frantically looked around for help or refuge.

With none in sight and she couldn't run back to the priest, she ran haphazardly in circles trying to evade her pursuers, who were closing in on her, while she was trying to figure out what to do. If there were any chance of rescue, it would be with those who were still awake, playing cards and drinking somewhere below.

She realized that she had made a mistake by coming onto the top deck with one of the sailors standing guard at the only exit to the lower decks, while the other two chased her around the deck. She successfully evaded capture as they lunged at her every now and then, when they got close enough.

The freckled sailor with a stocky build cornered her, but she kneed him in the groin and escaped. The prolonged chase soon took its physical toll, and she became increasingly out of breath and tired, while the stronger, fitter men showed no signs of fatigue or relenting.

Eventually, out of breath, she was cornered under the main sail. Her face a mask of fear and determination as the men, laughing drunkenly, grabbed at her. Suddenly, she roared loudly with rage and lashed out ferociously, which gave her some space that she used to quickly climb the mast ropes. The sailor with no teeth, whose job was to maintain and repair the sails, climbed after her grinning as he thought of her folly.

When Tutu reached the top with nowhere to go, she started screaming and kicking at the sailor at her feet, who appeared to be enjoying the sick drama. All the screaming and kicking did not help as he grabbed hold of her leg and then her waist. Hanging on deftly with one hand, he tried wrenching her free from the mast.

Tutu realizing, she was fighting a losing battle against a much stronger man, who could expertly maintain his balance on the ropes, cried out in desperate agony, "Why? Why? Please!" The toothless sailor grinned and once again pulled her forcefully. This time, she lost her balance and grip and nearly fell free, but she held on desperately with one hand as her legs dangled freely. Looking into the cloudy skies, she screamed, "Mama! Mama! Yeye mi ooooh!"

Suddenly, the skies became alive with thunder and lightning, while the sea became rough and loud. A thunderbolt struck the toothless sailor, lifting him off the ropes and landed him on the sharp protruding end of a broken mast, which impaled his heart.

Those below were shocked by what they had just witnessed and began to back step away from the masts, with a mixture of fear and disbelief. Behind them, the chain of the anchor began to unwind fast, but the crooked nosed sailor, whose attention was fixed on the mast, did not notice it and stepped back onto it.

The rapidly unwinding chain wrapped around his left ankle, before he knew it. He lost his balance, and it dragged him away as he desperately struggled to free himself. Unable to free himself, as it dragged him to the side of the ship, he screamed out for help, but before his colleague could run to his aid, the chain dragged him overboard.

The last man, the one covered with freckles, on seeing what was unfolding before his eyes, was now devoid of disbelief and filled with fear. He turned around and ran for the exit leading to the lower decks, but never made it there.

Following a loud thunderclap, a thunderbolt struck a mast in the middle, breaking it with the sharp end falling through the air like a spear and impaling him to the deck. It went through his upper back and came out of his lower chest into the deck, killing and keeping him on his feet.

Tutu was no less surprised by what had transpired, but she managed a smug smile from the top of the mast and looked once again into the skies, this time with gratitude. She put her hands together with her fingers crossed and offered them to the heavens, a sign of thanks in the Yoruba culture.

After she came down from the mast, she noticed some blacks, who had remained unchained due to their ailments had come onto the deck, probably due to her screams. They looked at her in awe and parted as she walked up to exit leading to the lower deck. Without a word, she went to her sleeping space and lay down.

Tutu had hardly fallen asleep, when she dreamed of her mother sitting beside her sleeping area. "Mama?" she called out unsure, as it appeared so real.

"Yes, my daughter!" Wura answered, making Tutu draw in a sharp breath, "Have no fear! Shango, the god of thunder, Yemanja, the mother of the seas and all other gods are behind you. Nevertheless, you have difficult times ahead of you and need to remain strong, because you will encounter many more tribulations."

"You shall have war waged against you and will also rise and wage war against them, but you will not be alone. I will always be close to you. Lastly, I want you to know that although we, your parents might be gone, that reverend was sent to protect, nurture and lead you. Please put your stubbornness aside, apologize and listen to him!"

"Mama, I also have a new friend, Emeka, he is…" she said excitedly, but was interrupted.

"Yes, I know of him. He can't help you, and if he tries, he shall perish! Neither should you run away with him. Anyone that stands in the way of your destiny shall perish! Bye, my daughter and remember, all you need to do is wish and help will be there, bye"

"No, don't go!" Tutu cried, reaching out to hold and stop her from leaving, but was unable to do so. "Please Mama don't leave me. Please mama!" she bawled as the luminous figure faded slowly.

She jumped up from her sleeping position still trying to grab hold of her mother, when she realized she had been dreaming. It seemed so real, and she was more confounded when she noticed she had actually been crying in her sleep. Wiping off her tears, she went back to sleep.

The following morning, the seamen were shocked to find the two dead sailors on the upper deck and the third body, badly decomposed by salt water and bitten by fish, when they retracted the anchor. They immediately alerted their captain, but no one could explain what had happened.

Mesmerized, Smith ordered the bodies to be thrown into the sea and the masts to be repaired, while he conducted an investigation. Two sailors that were close to the deceased reluctantly told him there was a plot to rape Tutu the previous night, but they had backed out the last minute. They said the last they knew was when the three went to wait for Tutu in the pantry.

Smith remembered that he did not receive his nightcap the previous night and had made a mental note to reprimand Tutu that morning, but he was called to the upper deck before he could do so. He made a note to ask her what happened the previous night before everyone dispersed to carry out their duties.

Being a stubborn and proud person, Tutu found it difficult to go and apologize to the Reverend Parris, but she knew she had to do as directed by her mother. So she sought him out as soon as she was free and found him on the upper deck.

He was staring into the distance, engrossed in his thoughts, having just seen and blessed the three dead bodies before they were buried at sea.

"Father! Father!" she called him softly. When he did not respond, she tapped him on the shoulder, startling him out of his thoughts.

She dropped to her knees as done in the Yoruba custom, when apologizing to one's elders. "I am sorry, I was wrong, although you...anyway, I am sorry and ask for your forgiveness," suppressing an urge to apportion blame.

Parris was pleasantly surprised. "Good gracious, what happened, why the change of mind?" he asked, as he helped her to her feet and hugged her. He knew her to be stubborn and proud and never expected her to apologize. "What brought about a change of heart in my dear one?" he couldn't resist asking as he fondly looked at her.

As a matter of fact, he had been thinking over the last week and regretted his overreaction that led to the loss of his friend and was planning to call a truce later that day. Tutu was hesitant in replying to his question, not knowing how he would react. She didn't want to be laughed at, but being a spiritualist, she thought he should understand and decided to tell him.

"My mother told me to apologize," she blurted out shyly.

"Your mother? Your mother told you?" he asked, surprised with disbelief and might have laughed or cracked a joke, but he noticed she was uneasy and was nervously twisting her fingers together. It was a trait he associated with her, whenever she was embarrassed or nervous.

"Yes, she spoke to me in my dreams," she maintained, looking into his eyes for any trace of disbelief or ridicule.

Knowing this, Parris decided to play along and kept a serious expression on his face. "And what did she say about me?"

"That you are a good person sent to me. Would you still be my good friend?" she asked earnestly as she fondly touched him on his arm.

"That's nice of her to think of me as a good person. Yes, you will always be my close friend," putting an arm around her shoulders and pulling her closer affectionately, disregarding some surprised looks around. "Actually I think I owe you an apology for behaving rashly in public. I should have at least waited till we were alone."

Tutu smiled as she felt her pride restored and promised not to take the book again.

9

"We should be berthing tomorrow, Reverend," Smith informed the priest, as he looked pensively into the distance from the top deck.

"It's about time!" Parris replied curtly, staring inquisitively at Smith as he tried guessing why he had been summoned. Smith didn't appear to be someone that gave farewell speeches or entertained emotional goodbyes.

After a few reflective moments, "I have been thinking of what to do ever since our discussion after the fever and it has been difficult to decide what to do with Tutu, once we land. It seems I have been affected by your fondness for her and what she did for me. Contrary to what you think, I am not completely heartless." He paused to see whether the reverend appreciated his joke. He continued in his contemplative mood, "I promised to find her a good buyer, but that would be difficult and I simply don't have the time and patience, so I thought who is better than you."

"You are suggesting I should buy her off you?" the priest asked, barely concealing his surprise. "That would be nice, but the problem is I don't have the money to buy a slave at the moment."

Smith nodded slowly, indicating he had given it a thought as well. "If you are interested, you could take her for half the going price and pay me whenever you can."

On hearing the offer, Parris broke into a wide grin. "That sounds like a good offer to me," he enthused and accepted Smith's outstretched hand, which he shook warmly. He could hardly wait to break the news to Tutu, who had returned very much into his favor after their argument.

Parris had given some thought to her future and cringed at the thought of seeing her sold to the harsh regimes of the sugar plantations. She felt more like a niece to him. Now, at least he could protect her to some extent from the abuses and cruelties of the system.

When he told her, she was so overjoyed and relieved that she broke into tears. She had been apprehensive, like all other slaves, over her future as news of berthing reached her. Parris drew her nearer and fondly patted her on the back.

After leaving the priest, she ran to break the news to Emeka, who accepted it with mixed feelings. He was glad for her, but it heightened his fears over his own fate. "He is a good man, and you are lucky. I wish he could buy me, too."

"I don't think so because I think he said he doesn't have the money but would pay later. I hope we are in the same town and can continue seeing each other." Tutu expressed her sadness over parting with her friend, who had become like a brother to her.

The ship berthed at Jamaica's southwestern port of Savanna-La-Mar, Westmoreland in the early hours of July 7, 1688. Anthony Smith had slave-holding houses established in the Westmoreland area, especially in the Waterworks/Abeokuta area, where he had strong business partnerships with a few sugar planters.

He practically owned a sugar plantation in Abeokuta, through massive capital and labor investments in the once small and ailing sugar business of a relative, which had now grown into a successful medium-sized plantation. He left its management in the capable hands of the relative due to his other and more profitable businesses, although he still provided slaves and cash, when required.

He was able to derive massive profits from the Atlantic trade route due to the economies of scale and integration of all aspects of the route. For example, it was to one of these holding places with partners he directed his slaves once they disembarked.

The slaves were to be held in what was often referred to as the fattening house or factory, where according to its name, slaves were fed and treated 'well', before presenting them for sale at an auction. This was not the case for most traders and until recently for Smith, who sold their slaves at a slightly lower price from their ships due to the absence of fattening houses and most importantly, time and running expenses.

During their time in fattening houses, the slaves are gradually broken into light work, allowing the trader to closely identify the qualities of each slave that would be of advantage at the auction.

Smith advertised an auction for four weeks after his arrival as he grouped his slaves into categories of able men and women, children and the sick. One slave that was presently in the sick category to his dismay was Emeka, who if fully recuperated would go for top money despite being Igbo, due to his towering and well-built physique. Smith knew despite the Jamaican planters' aversion to Igbos, there were loads of Igbos on plantations across the island. Due to the slowness of his recuperation, Emeka was not sold at the auction and was transferred to Smith's partner's plantation, where he did light duties.

Shortly after the auction, Smith sailed to Boston, where his family was based and left dealing with Emeka until his return.

Reverend Parris and Tutu set out on horse to unite with his family, in a plantation not too faraway from Smith's plantation. He was totally unexpected when he arrived with a black slave and was to meet an unexpected and frightening scene at home.

On his arrival, he found his daughter on the sickbed, having fallen ill once again to another mysterious illness. She was very pallid and the disease had taken a high toll from her. Her mother, Judith, having tried all available remedies, was resigned to fate and was actually falling apart emotionally by the time her husband arrived.

Due to the problem encountered on arrival, Tutu was unceremoniously shown to the slave quarters, where she didn't see the reverend for some time. Initially, she was very lonely without either of her known, trusted friends, Emeka or the reverend.

Also, due to the family's preoccupation with their child's debilitating disease, no one instructed the foreman about her position or use in the slave quarters; therefore he put her to work on the plantation. As usual, she was started on light work but was soon upgraded to more exacting tasks.

On the plantation, Tutu met a number of Yorubas from her area and its surroundings as well as a number of Igbo and Akan (gold coast) peoples with whom she made friends. Tutu made friends across all ethnic groups, disregarding the normal pattern on the plantation and across the Caribbean islands of keeping friends and relationships within one's ethnic group.

One of the first slaves to approach Tutu and seek her friendship was Kojo. Kojo, a very dark, wiry Akan man with intense eyes, was quite popular among other slaves and was regarded as the rebel leader. Tutu's ebullient and compassionate nature as well as her sweet, powerful singing voice endeared her to many on the plantation, and she attached no special importance to the rebel leader's fondness for her.

Unknown to her, since nobody dared broach the subject with her, was that news of her spiritual powers had reached some slaves on the plantation through some gossips. The slaves, who had witnessed the attempted rape incident, had spread the news among other slaves and due to the nearness of the Smith plantation and fattening house, the news followed her almost immediately.

Regardless of her new friends and popularity, she missed the Reverend Parris and would have gone looking for him, if not informed of the policy of slaves not being allowed to go to the main house, unless invited. Meanwhile, Parris was being torn apart by the state of his daughter's health and had completely forgotten about Tutu.

By the third week, Tutu was upgraded to one of the most arduous tasks. This should have never been the case, but the foreman took a particular dislike to the newcomer, who came into their midst and immediately became royalty, whilst rejecting his sexual overtures.

Tutu, having spoken to others, knew the foreman was singling her out and her turning down of his sexual advances further compounded her problem. When she couldn't take it anymore, following an explosive confrontation with the foreman, she decided to break the rule and headed to the family house on Sunday, the one rest day given to slaves.

Parris was racked with guilt because he linked his return to his daughter's problems and thought it was a sign that he should never have left Africa, regardless of the problems he faced. Sitting on the porch that rainy afternoon, he brooded over a dream he had the previous day. Ever since his linking of his daughter's ailments to his arrival, he had taken to sitting on the porch, in the hope that the old lady would appear, but she was nowhere to be found.

The previous night, he had dreamt of the old lady for the first time. In the dream, she had turned up at his porch in similar circumstances and asked the reason for his unhappiness. "My daughter is very ill and close to death, and I have been looking out here to see whether you would turn up!" he answered.

The old woman burst into a long sarcastic laughter. "Silly man! What you are looking for in the horizon is right in your pockets. Son, don't look out here, but back there. It is someone who has not done his duty that looks to the horizon for help. You have fulfilled your duty and have nothing to worry about." On saying that she once again burst into laughter as she disappeared and he woke up. Over the course of the night, he had the dream thrice.

Now seated on the porch, he pondered over the dream and wondered if it had any significance and if so, what? He never really believed in the efficacy of dreams and was thinking of Tutu and her dream in which she said her mother spoke to her. He had just made another mental note to check on her well being, several of which he had made in the last month but failed to carry out, when a voice disturbed his thoughts.

"Good day, sir! Do you remember me?" Tutu said as she climbed onto the porch, startling him out of his thoughts.

"Good gracious! Tutu, oh! I am sorry for just dumping you back there. I have been facing serious problems since our arrival," he said apologetically.

"I was wondering what was going on with you, but was told I can't come here without an invitation. I risked being flogged by the foreman, who has been giving me hell," Tutu said, looking around furtively.

"You don't have to worry about that. I will take care of it!" he said reassuringly.

"You look sick. What's the problem with you?" she inquired compassionately as she moved closer and touched him.

"My daughter is dying!" he blurted out despairingly, holding his head in his hands.

"Your daughter you always spoke about?" she cried out in sympathy. "Can I see her?"

At that instance, he looked up at her with a puzzled expression as he thought of his dream. Ordinarily, he would have declined because of his wife, who might read something else into it, but he rose and told her to follow him. He led her to Betty's room upstairs, where she was lying on her bed. Thankfully, his wife was still sleeping in the adjacent room.

The eight-year-old girl, Betty, was sleeping on a small bed in the center of the room, which Tutu approached.

Looking down at her with heartfelt compassion. "She is very pretty!" she commented. Tutu bent down and touched her. "May the gods please come and save you! May Shango clear your way of all darkness and allow you to rise as he does for the morning sun. Osanyin, the great healer, heal this girl. Please answer me as you all promised!" she whispered quietly.

Looking up, she noticed Parris was looking at her strangely, but turned her attention back to the sleeping girl. He had not heard what she had said because she had spoken in a very low voice and the thunder that accompanied the rain as she spoke made her inaudible.

The door opened behind them as she stood in silence

looking at the girl. A medium built blond woman with a pronounced chin cleft, Mrs. Judith Parris walked in, but stopped in her tracks, shocked to find a black woman standing over her daughter. Because she was awakened by the loud thunderclaps, she was very irritable.

"What's going on here? Who the hell is she and what is she doing here?" she asked, not hiding her displeasure of finding an unknown slave in the privacy of her home.

"Tutu was one of my wards in Africa and she requested to see Betty, whom I had always spoken about," Parris answered as he gestured to Tutu to follow him outside, knowing his wife's foul mood was exacerbated by her girl's illness.

They didn't escape her wrath, "I didn't know you had the time and disposition to answer slaves' requests!" she hissed angrily, kicking the door shut after them.

When they reached the porch and out of Mrs. Parris's earshot, he told her to excuse his wife's harshness, which he attributed to the pressure of looking after their child. He promised to talk to the foreman about her mishandling and Tutu returned to the slave quarters.

Early the following morning, Betty was the one that woke her parents up, as she playfully ran into their room. Both senior Parrises were pleasantly surprised and overjoyed, although while Mrs. Parris was excited and talkative, the Rev. Parris was quiet and reflective.

Later in the day, he sent for the foreman and gave him a stern warning over ill treating Tutu and told him she was not to work on anything strenuous. His wife found her husband's orders and emotional outburst at the foreman rather odd and intriguing since she believed the foreman was only doing his job. Moreover, Parris had kept out of the running of the plantation until now.

When asked, Parris could not give a concrete explanation since it was awkward for a clergyman to give credence to spiritual powers outside the church. The silence made Mrs. Parris suspicious of the slave woman, who she suspected was more than an ordinary slave to her husband. Moreover, it was commonplace in the West Indies for men, both unmarried and married, to have sexual liaisons with their slaves.

The following day, Parris went over to the slave quarters to see Tutu. He informed her that his daughter was miraculously well and fit, while looking at her to see her reaction. Tutu smiled and thanked the gods, but did not claim any importance or role in her recuperation. Parris was unsure of what to make of it and did not offer any thanks, although he was grateful and vowed to improve her plight, if and when possible.

Once Tutu knew she had spiritual powers to heal from her experience with the Parrises' daughter, she set about putting it to good use among her immediate slave community. Most of the treatments administered were traditional Yoruba remedies, which she had learned from her mother's herbal practice. Luckily, she was able to find the ingredients in the tropical forest on the island. It was only rarely that she invoked her spiritual powers after everything else failed.

Soon her reputation spread across the whole area's slave community and people set out from faraway places to see her. In order not to attract unnecessary attention on the plantation, especially from Mrs. Parris, who had taken it upon herself to observe her, she met most of the outsiders at the African market after church on Sundays.

Most slaves on the island were given small patches of land on the outskirts of their respective plantations to plant their personal provisions, and they developed a market to exchange surpluses. The market was a feature in most towns that also served as a social gathering place. This point of social interaction for the slaves sometimes attracted up to 10,000 people and was where Tutu practiced her healing, which to many people's surprise, she did free of charge. Due to this, her followers dramatically increased, since they believed she was no quack out to swindle them.

Tutu's greatest followers came from the Akans, who had strong well-established religious sects and being close relations of the Yorubas and their traditions, she was easily understood and accepted. Therefore, due to her unpretentious nature, she made friends easily among them.

Although, one friend still very much close to her heart was Emeka. With Tutu's scaled down chores, she had more time on her hands than most slaves, which enabled her to visit Emeka on the nearby plantation.

Emeka, unlike Tutu, was not faring too well in his new home and was mostly in a depressed state of mind. The fact that there were many other Igbos in his midst did little or nothing to uplift his spirits since most of them also had the same or just slightly better dispositions.

The Igbo mentality was not much about being in a strange land or the hard work that accompanied it, but their pathological dislike of being subservient to anyone, even to another Igbo on their own land. This was an important factor that contributed to their unique political history and future.

It was only visits from Tutu that made him warm up and change him into a totally different person from that observed on the plantation. They resumed their friendship in earnest, with Emeka keen on taking the relationship to another level, but politely turned down. Tutu rejected his sexual advances by jokingly telling him that it was only for her husband to make babies, and unfortunately he was not nor going to be the lucky man. Tutu turned him down, not out of lack of feelings for him, but because she had her mother's warning at the back of her mind.

He was ultimately bound to lose his life if he became too involved with her. This was what she dreaded and determined to prevent out of her genuine feelings for him. Nevertheless, he continued subtle advances to court and marry her, despite her firm stance.

On one such visit about seven months after their arrival, Tutu arrived one early February evening to find him badly bruised due to a flogging he received the previous day. He had refused to carry out a task ordered by the foreman, who had run out of patience with the new slave's uncooperative disposition. The foreman reported this to his master, since he was unable to make corrections and enforce discipline by himself due to Emeka's size and strength, which he feared. The planter ordered six other men to carry and tie Emeka onto a tree, from which he was whipped and suspended for several hours.

On her arrival, Tutu was horrified to find him beaten, physically and spiritually. "What happened?" she cried as she tenderly cleaned the wounds. On quite a number of occasions, she had seen and treated similar wounds inflicted on slaves on her plantation. As a matter of fact, most of those she treated or prescribed herbs for in the Sunday market were those who had been inflicted with similar punishments by their masters.

"Massa flogged me! He said I was a no good slave," he answered weakly, although he was pleased to see his friend.

After cleaning the wounds in silence, she sat next to him, "Emeka, you must try to keep yourself out of trouble, otherwise these people will take your life," she cautioned him lightly.

"What is left of a man's life if his freedom and dignity are stripped from him? I would rather die than continue in this place," he said bitterly as he fidgeted on his bed, trying to find a suitable position where his wounds wouldn't rub against his coarse surroundings. This was not an easy task since his whole body was peeled by the cat-o'-nine-tails whip.

"So you want to die and leave me alone here?" Tutu said teasingly, as she tried to cheer him out of his gloom.

"No," he answered weakly, stretching out an arm with great discomfort to bring her closer, he continued with a lower, albeit pleading voice. "Tutu, let's run away into those hills. I promise I would be a good husband and take care of you as best I can. I am not a lazy man and would farm and work to make you and our family comfortable. Please, listen to me!"

Tutu pulled away from him abruptly, rose to her feet and walked to the far side of the room. With her back turned to him, slowly shaking her head, she bit into her lower lip as she tried to get hold of her emotions. She had heard of such ideas from other slaves, who spoke of escaped slaves further east, hiding and fighting from some hills, but she was lost and unsure of what to do.

"It is still not home and they would find and kill us," she expressed her fears. Moreover, she knew she stood to lose more, if recaptured. Among other things, she knew she would lose her privileged position with the reverend and was not entirely sure what would happen to Emeka after what her mother had told her about running away with him. Emeka persistently urged her to come with him until she left hours later and could only leave after promising to give it further consideration.

True to her words, she continuously pondered over the suggestion over the next several days. Even when she tried pushing it aside, conditions on her plantation were a frequent reminder.

On her plantation, she developed a close friendship with the Akan slave, Kojo, who slept next door. Much to her consternation, Kojo was to receive a similar punishment a few days later. When she went over to tend to him, she overheard identical plans from other slaves being discussed. Although she tried not to be a party to such discussions, Kojo pulled her into it.

"Mama Orisha," as she was fondly called by many, who took it for its literal meaning, Godmother, although it had another hidden meaning known only by a few.

"What can you do for us? What powers can you give us to fight against these wicked people or are you just going to be looking at us, while we suffer and you just treat the wounds? This can't continue!" Kojo beseeched, drawing consenting nods and attention to her. Caught unawares and with no ready reply, she shrugged.

Interpreting her shrug as a sign of indifference, another slave from Kongo commented, "Mama Orisha doesn't care or have the same problem as us. She has worked Juju on the master. Can't you see she is enjoying herself here," he said resentfully.

This greatly hurt Tutu's feelings, whose shrug was not of unconcern, but helplessness. Nevertheless, she responded gently, "No, my brother! Believe me, the chicken gets hot and sweaty, but its feathers hide its discomfort. I do care and although I may not bleed on the skin like you, my heart bleeds all the time seeing your suffering. It's just that I don't know what to do or how to go about it."

"We need advice of where to go, weapons to use, when to rise and a few other things!" stated another slave, Orji, of Igbo origins.

"I will ask the gods and let you know," she answered pensively, although she had no idea of how to go about the task, but with the prevailing mood, she knew she needed to say something. This gave her a respite as the other slaves continued discussing ways of bringing their plight to an end. Their discussions ranged from poisoning their masters to outright violent revolts and absconding into the hills.

Tutu's respite was brief as they constantly asked her whether there had been a response from the gods. She only managed to placate their growing discontent with reassurances that she was working on it.

Truly, she had called out to her mother and the gods, whenever she was alone, but with no response forthcoming.

By the end of the week, another incident occurred on the plantation, whereby severe punishments were meted out to three slaves. The three slaves had escaped the previous day but were recaptured in the hills. They were all suspended from pillories, where they were flogged, although one of them had an even more severe punishment meted out to him.

Orji, the Igbo slave, one of those that had accused Tutu of indifference, had his left foot amputated as it was his tenth failed escape in as many weeks. This was a punishment meted out to recalcitrant runaway slaves.

When Tutu went to administer treatment, he bluntly refused as he went ahead to heap scorn on her in the presence of others. "Leave me alone, Mama Orisha or whatever your name is. I don't need the help of any spiritualist, after all, they were the ones who got me here in the first place, and we can see the difference between us, even here. Just leave me alone, you evil, selfish people." Orji cursed her bitterly.

With his scathing remarks prompting derisory jeers and laughter among a few, Tutu stood rooted momentarily in front of him, not knowing how to reply to the slight or what to do. Tears welled up in her eyes, but she regained her composure and stormed off to her quarters, where she cried bitterly over her embarrassment and the state of her life. She cried all night until she fell asleep.

While she was asleep, her wishes were finally answered and she dreamt of her mother. Sitting beside her as she cried, her mother consoled her by gently rubbing her back as she spoke.

"My dear child, you can't take everything to heart. You have to be strong. I have heard your questions and know the problems, but the requests are difficult. There is no easy or immediate solution!" Wura told her frankly.

"But mother there should be a way out or to stop it!" she protested tearfully. "We can't just sit and do nothing."

"I understand how you feel, and I am not saying nothing should be done but just warning of the difficulties. This did not start on this small island nor will it stop here and even if you wage war here, help will come from distant lands to quell it. The war has to be fought elsewhere, although the roots could be planted here and other places."

"So how..." Tutu asked, but was stopped with her mother's raised hand.

"First, this is not your war. You are needed for more important battles. Secondly, it will take generations to finally win the war. Although, as I said, the roots could be planted now like the roots of the great Iroko tree planted many generations before it can give shade from the fiery sun. Now listen!" she said and Tutu sat up to be closer to her.

She spoke quietly, "You would direct them to a place in the hills, which should provide them sanctuary from the planters. Although they would be constantly harassed, they would prevail and be able to survive until everything is brought to an end. It would be no place or task for the meek and weak and they would need a strong leader."

"Me?" Tutu asked surprised.

"No! You are not to fight, but to plant the roots for the Iroko tree, which would later give shade from the scorching sun for later generations. You would not follow them, but move on to plant another tree elsewhere to give shade to others. Your friend, Kojo shall lead them, but you will take him to the land and show him. You should also advise him to choose Segun as his assistant, in order to be successful."

Segun was a vociferous Yoruba slave from the Egbado area, not far from Tutu's hometown. He was chosen because Yorubas were more numerous on the western side of the island and he was popular among them. He was more militant than the average Yoruba, who often resigned, but coped well with whatever their present predicament.

One could attribute this passive trait of the Yorubas to the underlying religious and cultural belief that everything was predestined and couldn't be change. Ori, meaning head, is the bearer of a person's destiny from heaven. This was the reason why most of the uprisings were orchestrated by Akans and Igbos, who shared nearly the same beliefs but less ardently.

"When are they to do this?" Tutu asked as she pondered over the scenario.

"I cannot say. Their hands will be forced when the time comes, but once again, you are not to follow. However, do not say this openly because they might lose confidence. Lastly, you should give them these armlets, which they must wear on their right arms and must always be removed before sex," Wura handed over a wrapped bundle. Tutu took the parcel from her mother, which she observed curiously, before she turned around to place it under her headrest. When she carefully tucked it under her bed, she turned back to her mother, but she had disappeared.

"Mother! Mother!" she shouted agitatedly as she looked around. Tutu startled awake to find out she had been dreaming. Depressed with a desolate look on her face, she remained sitting with her legs on her bed, placing her chin in her palm, as she thought of her dream.

After a few moments, her desolate expression turned into one of puzzlement as she remembered the parcel that was

handed to her. She excitedly lifted up her headrest and found
the parcel, which she then carefully unwrapped and examined
with great interest. She couldn't go back to sleep for a long time
as she thought of the ramifications of what she had just been
told and given.

She was unable to pass the message to Kojo until later in
the evening, since the slaves were worked from sunrise to sun
fall. Walking up to him in the circle of friends he sat among, she
requested to see him in private, but he insisted on receiving the
message there.

"Mama Orisha, say what you want to say. I am enjoying
myself as you can see. What is it? There are no secrets among
us men here," he told her brusquely. He was enjoying stories
during the remaining few hours, before they went to sleep in
preparation for another grueling day.

Moreover, Tutu was gradually falling out of favor among
many of the men, who believed she had no empathy for their
plight as voiced by Orji, the previous night. Therefore, Kojo
being the rebel leader, didn't want to be seen associating too
closely with her, which would be the case if he rose to follow her
into privacy as she requested.

Tutu understanding the politics, but not someone to be
outplayed. "Me? You aren't ready! You call yourself a man, Kojo?"
she scoffed, hissed and slowly clapped her hands derisively. "I
thought you said you needed help from the gods to guide you
in the fight for freedom, but it seems you aren't ready. You
are a waste of my time. You are nothing but a boy!" Tutu said
scornfully to his surprise and that of the other men, who had
never seen her as a saucy woman.

Although they were also pleasantly surprised by the
indication, that there might be a solution to their problems
as she had said. Before anyone could react, two women that
worked in the main house approached her.

"Tutu, we need your help, please!" one of them, Rebecca,
asked. Tutu looked at them questioningly, since she couldn't
really place them and had a policy of not treating strangers on

the plantation. One of them was pregnant and the other she couldn't place what was wrong with her since she had no visible wounds, but she guessed it was the most common ailment among her female patients—menstrual pains.

"Damn! Just as our Mama Orisha was coming alive to our problems after seven months of eating and drinking, the house niggers have to come and drag her away. God, please borrow me patience! Please!" one of the slaves looking to the heavens quipped, prompting laughter from the other men. The women being called house niggers enabled Tutu to identify them as household slaves from the main house.

"You girls ain't ready for me," she said waving the men aside disdainfully and turned to the women. "Maybe I should quickly try and deliver her baby. The gods might be merciful and give us a real man," she continued ridiculing them as she led the women to her nearby sleeping quarters.

This silenced the laughing men, who were sensitive to derogatory comments, especially from black women, due to the obvious Black male powerlessness in the society.

Tutu's pre-diagnosis turned out to be right. The pregnant one was having abnormal discharges for which Tutu gave some herbs and advice, while Rebecca was having abnormal and intense menstrual pains for which she also gave some other herbs. She was able to dispense of both of them quite quickly, and as they left, while she was tidying up, Kojo came indoors.

"Tutu, why did you insult me in public like that?" Kojo demanded angrily as he walked into the room.

"A person that buys a box of fancy shoes for his crippled mother receives a box of insults in return, not gratitude!" Tutu snapped angrily as she continued what she was doing. Finishing what she was doing, she rose to face him with an angry expression.

"You and the others choose to insult me over and over again. Thank god, my mouth was not taken away with everything else by the debt collector," she gesticulated passionately with her hands and head as she spoke.

"I am sorry, but everyone has been desperate and hoping you would do something. I am really sorry!"

"So, am I the one to blame for everyone's problem, uh?" Tutu raised an eyebrow, while placing a hand on her hip. "Open your eyes, I am in this with everyone else," she said with slightly less anger, which was actually feigned.

"Yes, we know you are in it with us, but for six years we had all prayed and hoped that you would arrive to help us. It is now over seven months..." Kojo couldn't finish his explanation.

"Olorun mi Ooooh!" she exclaimed, Oh My God in Yoruba with a mixture of surprise and fury and advanced menacingly towards him. "You have been praying that my family be killed and I sold into slavery?"

"No! No!" Kojo replied quickly, stepping back to avoid any attack. "The previous Mama Orisha had told us there would be some woman from the orishas to help us, who had real powers that would guide us out of here. She was an herbalist, but did not possess any spiritual power. We started calling her Mama Orisha since we needed one right away. She died the night before you arrived at a very old age in the next plantation. When you arrived the following day, we were shocked to see the resemblance and when we heard of what happened on the ship to those who wanted to rape you, we knew you were the real Mama Orisha."

The news made Tutu weak in her knees and she fumbled to find something to support herself. She rested on the edge of a nearby table, her face drawn and her eyes distant and watery. Her mind wandered from what he said to what her mother had said both during and after her physical life. Was it her missing grandmother? Could it be true? She wondered.

"What's the matter, Tutu? Are you okay?" Kojo asked with genuine concern as he observed her reaction, but could get no reply nor take any action.

After the long silence ended with a deep and heavy sigh; "I think she might be right. Now I see why you were angry. Who did she speak to and how many people know of this?"

"She spoke to me and told me to be prepared to lead our

people, when the time comes, but not before her replacement came! Not many people know of this, apart from those close to me and the trusted assistants."

"To begin with, your assistant from now on is to be Segun," she said authoritatively, which brought a baffled look to his face. She gestured towards the vacant space next to her, which he took. She continued, "I spoke to my mother...." but was interrupted.

"Your mother? I thought this was the works of the gods!" he said a bit disappointed.

"One's mother is one's god. Only she knows the route one followed from the gods to man and could be the best route back, especially if she is with them. Now, I was told to give you these instructions as well as these armlets," she explained and reached for the armlets, where she had hidden them under her spare clothes.

She told a dumbfounded Kojo all that she could remember from her dreams, which happened to be everything and more because as she spoke some other things she could not consciously remember, came out. When she finished, Kojo continued looking at her in awe until he recomposed himself and smothered her with kisses. Before he left, they agreed to go and check the mountains at daybreak. Being Sunday, a church and market day, their long absence due to the long distance would not be noticed.

Early the following morning before anyone woke up, Tutu and Kojo set out towards a northeastern direction that led them into the hills. Tutu followed her mother's descriptions, which weren't too difficult; they were to follow the rainbow in the sky to its source!

Although in the beginning, they reached impassable terrain and had to turn back on a few occasions. On a particular occasion, they were lost and were about to give up hope, when they noticed that a black bird that followed them all along was gesturing them towards a crevice. They had noticed the bird but had paid no attention to it and didn't think it was the same one. But when it kept landing on Tutu's shoulder and then flying towards the small opening, they realized it was a guide.

From thereon they made rapid progress towards their destination. Going at a fast pace, they finally reached their destination after midday. It was a plateau on a mountain with rugged edges, which was only barely penetrable unless guided as they were. The plateau was large enough to accommodate 20,000 people, and it appeared to be fertile enough to sustain them. They could hardly contain their excitement on what was to be the new home of the maroons — runaway slaves.

Eating the fruits and drinking from a spring, they darted around playfully, but due to their long return journey, they restrained their exuberance. They barely stayed for two hours during which Kojo made the necessary landmarks, before heading back to their plantation. Tutu was a bit subdued as she realized this might be her last time of seeing it. It was a return journey they both dreaded, not only due to distance but, having seen paradise, it was not easy going back to their hell.

10

Meanwhile, hell was being raised back on the plantation. The women, who came for treatment by Tutu the previous night, returned to the main house to tell Mrs. Parris what they had overhead while at the slave quarters. They told her that Tutu was the rumored leader, who had come from Africa to free her people.

Judith and other planters had heard such rumors before, but attached little importance to what they believed was fantasy. Although they feared if such beliefs were not curtailed, they could incite the already agitated slave populations. One of the agitators had already been identified in the person of Kojo.

Early the following morning, Judith sent for Tutu and Kojo before they were meant to head for church and the market, but to her surprise they were nowhere to be found. Judith Parris dressed up and went to her father's plantation, which shared a boundary with her plantation. Normally, she met her father at the church from where they left together for the Sunday family lunch either in his or her house. On reaching the opulent mansion, her surprised father took her into his study, where she told him her fears.

Judith and her father had already taken notice of Kojo and his activities and were only waiting for something concrete before coming down on him. It was only due to Kojo's shrewdness that he had been able to keep out of trouble, but this time as Judith and her father, Tim Lawrence discussed, it seemed they had him.

As for the female slave, Judith Parris had mentioned her once when she voiced her suspicions over the special treatment meted out to her by her husband. Her father disregarded it due to his own philandering with his black female slaves since his wife's death. How both slaves were linked he couldn't understand, but he had inkling from what he was being told by his daughter that something was brewing.

The daughter and father discussed the matter for a few hours, before the proud father accompanied her to church. Tim Lawrence was especially proud of his daughter, Judith, being the only one who had remained in Jamaica with him. Judith looked very much like him, especially with the blond hair and pronounced cleft on the oval face, although Tim was a much shorter man with an aura of aristocracy and pomposity.

His other children had moved to North America, which he resented due to its climate that mostly prevented sugar cultivation. Out of the other three children, only one, a male was in the plantation business, an Annapolis tobacco farmer and was believed to be less successful. His only other female child was in the north-eastern part and believed to be married to a merchant, while the last, a son, had disappeared for over ten years.

Therefore he had every reason to be proud of Judith who, despite being female, was the most successful and forged ahead where her brothers and husband had failed. Her husband always baffled him, once a good lad in his eyes, his son-in-law appeared to have lost his mind.

After church, they returned home and sent scouts to search the market to see whether Tutu and Kojo were there or not. As expected, the scouts returned to report of their absence at the marketplace. All day, Judith and Tim stayed together trying to fathom what the missing slaves were up to. They definitely hadn't run away, and it was absurd that they would just disappear, unless they were planning something.

Late in the evening, when the slaves started returning from the market, Judith and Tim both moved to a point, where they could see everyone returning. They made futile inquiries from a few of the trusted slaves, mostly mulattos and Creoles born on the island. This group of slaves believed they were superior to the new arrivals that they often labeled saltwater Negroes. Close to midnight, when it appeared all of the slaves had arrived, they decided to make a roll call to ensure the two slaves were the only ones missing.

While they were making the roll call, Tutu and Kojo arrived and stealthily joined the ranks of the other slaves. When the foreman finished calling the names, Tutu, oblivious of what had been happening all day on the plantation stepped forward.

"My name was not called," she stated to Mrs. Parris and her father's surprise. Kojo also, stepped forward to state the same and they were both ordered to follow the planters to the main house.

When the Lawrences reached the main house, they decided to sit on the porch to avoid disturbing Betty and her father sleeping upstairs.

"Where have you two been?" Judith Parris asked sternly as soon as they settled down.

"The market, Madam!" Kojo answered confidently, although he was having a queasy feeling being pulled up with Tutu.

"I am going to ask you for the last time, before I have the skin on your back peeled, where have you been?" Judith said slowly, but menacingly. Before Kojo could answer, she held up a hand, gesturing him to hold on, "Think well before you answer, because I searched the church and market for you two and you were nowhere to be found."

"Madam, honestly we were in the market, but there were..." Kojo was not allowed to finish his statement.

"Shut up! Bloody liar!" Judith shouted angrily and slapped him. Her father gestured to her to cool her temper and told the foreman to tie Kojo to a tree, meters away.

After he was suspended from the tree, "Now boy, where were you?" Judith asked, but no answer was forthcoming from Kojo. "John!" She gestured to the foreman to whip him. John obeyed and gave him two sets of twelve successive lashes of the whip made of animal skin and laced with nails. When it was obvious from Kojo's countenance that he would not confess, they turned their attention to Tutu.

Judith's father slowly walked a circle around Tutu as he puffed on a cigar. "So you are the leader from Africa, Tutu or whatever your name is?" he asked her in a condescending tone to match his disdainful look.

"Everyone is a leader in his own right until they are stolen away into slavery. As my elders say, a slave has a father, he is just far away," Tutu answered enchantingly, making father and daughter look at each other amusedly.

"She has some uppityness about her. Who taught her to speak so well? Is it Samuel?" the older planter inquired, which was answered with a nod from his daughter.

"So you have come to cause a slave revolt on my plantation?" Judith asked, but when no reply was forthcoming, she shouted. "Are you deaf? Where did you go today and what are your plans?"

"Madam, I went to the market and I don't know anything about what you are talking about. If anyone has said anything let them come out and say what I have done, otherwise please madam I am tired and want to sleep!" Tutu answered irritably to the wonderment of the planters.

Judith got up and gave her a vicious, back handed slap. "Because you are sleeping with my husband, does not mean we are equals that you can disrespect," she shouted at the fallen and crying Tutu.

"What have I done to deserve this? I am not sleeping with the reverend. I am not causing any trouble," she cried at the top of her voice as she lay on the ground.

"You are both leaving this plantation to separate plantations, you dirty bitch!" Judith Parris said as she kicked the crying woman, who once again screamed at the top of her voice. This woke up Rev. Parris as Tutu intended and brought him downstairs.

Walking on to the porch, he was surprised to find the small group, which included his wife and her father and most surprising, Tutu crying in the dirt. "What is going on here?" he asked lightly, trying to keep his surprise or concern out of his voice.

"This is plantation business and has nothing to do with you!" snapped his father-in-law, who despised him for leaving the plantation.

"Well, if you haven't been informed, that is my slave and she has nothing to do with your plantation," Reverend Parris answered with equal contempt and added, "nor with any plantation without my consent," when he noticed his wife was about to say something.

He had grown to dislike his father-in-law, whom he saw as domineering. Their relationship had changed considerably for the worse since he decided to leave the sugar cultivation business and Parris blamed him for the rift between him and his wife.

"It becomes plantation business when your harlot decides to lead a slave revolt, but you..." Judith Parris said acrimoniously.

"Harlot? Slave revolt?" Parris asked in surprise, looking from face to face and with no further explanation. "Can someone explain what is going on here?"

"Your slave here is said to be the messiah from Africa, who is supposed to lead the slaves out of bondage by revolt. I guess he over there is to carry out the plan!" his father-in-law explained.

"Nonsense! Where did you hear this from?" Parris asked, looking at their faces for answers, before looking at Tutu. "Tutu, what is this I am hearing?"

"Master, I don't know what they are talking about," she answered tearfully. Judith made a move to attack her, but her husband blocked her. "I went to church this morning and to the market, when I got back, we were told we went to plan trouble."

Samuel Parris sighed and turned to his wife, "Where did you hear about the alleged plot, because I have known her from a child and never known her to be a trouble maker."

"I guessed you wouldn't know her as a trouble maker. More of a bed maker, your lover!" Judith hissed.

"Is that why you are going through all this trouble? Because you think I am sleeping with her. Please don't be stupid!" Parris replied peevishly, "I am getting sick and tired of your childish..."

His father in-law interrupted to placate tempers, "This is not the place and time to straighten out family matters. Let's keep our heads and sight fixed on the problem. I guess if we called the eyewitnesses that overheard the plot, we would be able to move forward. Judith, please call the girls!"

Judith went indoors and on her way bumped into Parris intentionally and hissed as she slammed the door shut. Moments later, she returned with the two housemaids that came for treatment the previous night. Tutu's mouth dropped wide open, when she saw them and looked at them contemptuously. Tutu held a fixed gaze on her as her lips moved in a murmur.

Judith's father rose and walked towards the women. "Now, tell us what you heard when you went for herbs last night," he ordered them threatening, knowing that they might retract in the face of everyone due to shame and fear of reprisals.

Rebecca looked at Tutu and their eyes locked as Tutu murmured. As Rebecca made an attempt to talk, she grabbed her neck in pain and fell to her knees. She let out painful groans and her mouth foamed.

"What is all this playacting?" Judith's father asked in annoyance, while they all looked on at Rebecca, who soon collapsed. The other woman tried reviving her, by pulling her onto her lap and cleaning the foam that had come from her mouth.

"I am glad you can see that it is nothing more than playacting," Parris stood up and pointed to Tutu. "You go back to your quarters," he ordered Tutu, ignoring his wife who was about to protest. "If anyone has any concrete evidence wake me up, but until then no one should touch my slave. I cannot tell you what to do with your slaves." He made his way indoors but was stopped by his wife.

"Well, she better leave my plantation!"

"My plantation, which I turned over to you. She stays until

I find an alternative!" he said as he walked around her to go indoors.

"This is 1689, not 1681! And you didn't turn over anything to me, I saved it from ruins, when you lost your bloody mind!" Judith shouted belligerently, but she ran to hide behind her father, when she saw her husband turn around and head for her aggressively. Her father held out a hand gesturing for Parris to stop, and he did, only inches away breathing heavily, unsure of what to do.

"You see that? He wants to beat me up for his African lover!" Judith said from a safe distance. Reverend Parris shook his head in exasperation and turned around to go indoors.

Coming from behind her father after Reverend Parris slammed the door shut, "Father, you see what I have been saying. He has changed." she said and burst into tears.

Her father mollified her by gently rubbing her back. He spoke softly, "Look, I don't understand what is going on here. It's very late and I suggest that we all go and rest till tomorrow. I will take Kojo over to my place and assure you, I will break whatever is happening out of him. Keep a watchful eye on her since Samuel has decided he wants to be her Lord Protector."

"Okay father!" she made her way indoors, but stopped where the two women were. Rebecca was revived and they both looked down to the ground as Judith stopped and looked at them. "You two better find elsewhere to sleep tonight!" Judith said threateningly, before continuing indoors.

By the following evening, word had spread throughout various plantations that plans for a revolt were uncovered and the culprits were in custody. It was rumored that a lady messiah, who was unknown and Kojo, who was widely known were held in detention and may be killed. If the intentions of Judith and her father were to nick a revolt in the bud, it clearly backfired.

Many of the slaves, for the want of something to look for in the future in order to survive the grueling present, believed in the coming of a savior that would come to ameliorate their sufferings. For that savior to be linked with a figure like

Kojo, gave the story more credence, and made them more apprehensive. As often said, hope is a great force that could be directed both ways.

In this case, it made them frustrated, since their main hope was now in custody of their oppressor and was about to be put to death. In actual fact, it was a gross exaggeration, since Kojo was kept in solitary confinement pending Judith's father's decision. Tim had been busy all day and had actually forgotten about the whole issue. Tutu had returned to her room, which Judith Parris ordered locked to prevent any communication or further plans.

Shortly after the slaves returned from their daily work on the plantation, alarms of burning sugar cane fields were raised. One occurred on Emeka's plantation where the news had also reached, and raised tempers to a frenzy. The fire was put out before causing extensive damage.

On another plantation, they were not that lucky and the damage was nearly total. Although the fire was discovered early enough, there were a few scuffles between the foremen and some Igbo slaves, when the foreman tried to mobilize the slaves to put out the fire.

The planters hastily called a meeting to discuss the developing scenario, but believed it would soon blow over, especially when they were assured that the ringleaders were under lock and key. This turned out to be wrong, because the longer the slaves believed their ringleaders were detained, the more volatile the situation became.

The Parrises had serious quarrels amongst themselves. Rev. Parris demanded the release of Tutu from her house arrest. He claimed that the events over the last day showed she knew nothing and was incapable of inciting anyone. His wife remained resolute that Tutu was the cause of the trouble, and it had all been in their plans and would have been worse if she were free.

The third night brought about more fires and dissent and by the morning of the following day, hell was let loose. Judith's father, who became extremely angry when a fire was started on his plantation, inadvertently brought this about. Luckily, the fire was sighted and extinguished early enough to prevent any extensive damage, but he was enraged, especially when one of his loyal slaves told him it was done in support of Kojo.

Unfortunately, he made a fatal mistake by ordering the execution of Kojo at noon the following day, "to teach the bastards not to hold me to ransom." The news of the execution order spread like wildfire and was exaggerated to include the savior, Tutu.

In the morning, he ordered the foreman to bring Kojo from his confinement, while he had his breakfast. The foreman never made it back. As the watchful eyes of the slaves saw him take Kojo toward the main house, five of them attacked him with cutlasses and killed him.

With the success of the first open attack, many other slaves who were previously docile and unsure joined their ranks and followed the mob led by Kojo to the main house. By the time they arrived at the house, their numbers had swelled to twenty-five. The mob burst into the house to Judith's father's utter amazement.

"Good day, Mister Lawrence! It seems you are shocked to see us. Don't worry we are not here for the food but our freedom. Where is Tutu, our Mama Orisha?" Kojo said, smiling mockingly as he sat across from Tim, who was choking on his food.

"Where will you go? We are doing you a favor by keeping you all on this island. Otherwise you would waste away like your savage kindred back in Africa." He managed to keep a tough composure.

"For someone who I bet has never been to Africa, you seem to know a lot," Kojo retorted sarcastically, "but I guess there are no savages worse than you and your kind."

"Don't talk to me anyhow, boy!" Tim Lawrence admonished, brandishing his finger, which he retracted when he saw the look on Kojo's face. "You would never reach Africa anyway and as long as you are on this island, you will either starve to death or be recaptured when reinforcements arrive."

"I don't care if I starve to death. Lean freedom is better than fat slavery. Now where is she?" Kojo demanded impatiently.

"I don't know and as far as I care she could be dead!" the slaves dropped their mouths as he spoke of Tutu's death, unaware of the importance they attached to Tutu.

Kojo sighed and slowly rose from the table, turning to his followers. "Kill him and burn the place down," he ordered as he left the room, not looking back at Tim Lawrence, whose turn it was to drop his mouth.

Kojo had hardly stepped onto the porch, when he heard his scream. The slaves went on rampage and burnt the house down.

News of trouble on her father's plantation reached Judith Parris, even before his death. From her house she could see the rising smoke from the plantation fields, which had been set on fire by the other slaves that didn't go in to see Tim Lawrence. Sensing something was terribly wrong she called some trusted slaves to escort her there.

Meanwhile, it was not only she who knew of trouble in the next plantation, but also her slaves, who took it as a sign to let hell loose. Under the command of Segun, a Yoruba name meaning Victor, the slaves divided into two factions, one headed for the main house, the other to burn the plantation.

Segun and his small group of supporters met Judith Parris just as she stepped off her porch going to her father's plantation. A fight broke out between her handlers and the rioting slaves, but soon ended as her handlers ran off once their leader, John, was beheaded. They grabbed the screaming Judith and carried her to their slave quarters, where they released Tutu.

There was an argument on whether to kill her right away, but they tentatively agreed to keep her locked up in case they needed to use her for ransom. After locking Judith in the room, they decided to go on rampage and went back to the main house, but not before Tutu. While they were arguing and locking Judith up, Tutu used the opportunity to run to Reverend Parris in the main house.

Tutu told the reverend, who was hiding behind barricaded doors with his daughter, to leave immediately. She informed him that the house was about to be rampaged and burnt. "Your wife has been taken, but not yet killed. They are coming here for you. You have to leave immediately," she grimly told the father, whose daughter held onto him terrified.

"Please, you've got to help Judith. You can't let them kill her. Not for her sake, but Betty's," he pled.

"Save Betty first and I will see what can be done. I don't know anything about this revolt, but you have to leave fast."

"But where to?" he asked, looking exasperated. While they were discussing where he could seek refuge, noise of the approaching mob reached them and he hurriedly took one of the side exits to flee with his daughter. Although they were sighted and given chase, Tutu was able to considerably distract and delay most of them by coming out of the front door to make a speech.

"People, today you shall become free of fear and servitude. We shall chase them off the land, but first come inside and take what you wish," she addressed them in a fiery tone, which was greeted with roars of solidarity. They all rushed into the house, stripping it clean of it contents, before setting it on fire. This allowed the Reverend Parris to escape as he ran stealthily with his daughter toward Emeka's plantation.

Meanwhile, Anthony Smith had just returned from New England and England the previous day to find his whole investment on the island under threat of destruction. When the reverend arrived with his daughter, the slaves on Smith's plantation had just begun their own revolt.

They grabbed Smith's partner, who had come to the plantation to observe the damage done by the fire of the previous day. Although they killed the foreman immediately, they held the planter alive until they set fire on the plantation he had come to inspect before killing him. Then they headed towards the main house to pillage and destroy.

By the time they reached the main house, which unlike others was farther away from the plantation, Reverend Parris and some other planters that also sought refuge there had built up defenses with Anthony Smith.

Most of the planters sought refuge there because it was common knowledge that it held the largest ammunitions in the area, since Smith's dead partner also ran an arms shop. Hastily, they boarded the windows and loaded enough ammunition to keep the encroaching mob at bay, until hopefully reinforcements arrived. When the mob arrived, the planters fired at them from the house, killing a few, but not succeeding in driving them away.

Undeterred, the mob grew exponentially as mobs from various plantations joined them and were determined to fight their former masters to the bitter end, especially when they arrived to find a large carnage of fallen slaves.

Tutu arrived with Segun and slaves from the Parris' plantation to find the growing death count. She sought out Kojo, who had arrived shortly before her to take command of the rowdy mob of about a thousand into a well-organized siege.

"Kojo, why are you doing this? Why don't you leave them alone and lead the people to the mountains?" Tutu asked when she found him.

"They have to pay for the lives they have taken. Moreover, we need the arms in there to help us to protect ourselves in the mountains. Leave this to me, Mama!" Kojo replied peevishly as he issued orders.

Tutu shuddered as another slave was shot. "No Kojo. You have to stop this madness and leave," she urged him.

"They got to leave or starve to death inside there. We toiled on this land!" Kojo retorted strongly.

"This was not what was planned, but to save lives, I will go and persuade them to leave and accept your conditions."

"Don't interfere. Stand back..." Kojo replied, but could not finish his statement, because Tutu was not listening.

To his and others utter surprise and dismay, she broke the defense lines in a sprint, before he could stop her. They were dumbfounded as she raised and waved her hands to signify to the planters, she was coming over in peace. Despite her waving, a few shots barely missed her as she approached.

In the house one of the planters that did not know her continued shooting at her to stop her from approaching. "I bet it is a trick. The savages believe we are fools, sending a woman to do their job," he said aloud attracting Reverend Parris, who was guarding another angle.

"What? A woman?" He inquired as he left his post to see what the planter was talking about. Squinting through the hole since the sunrays were directly shining from that direction. "Oh my God! Hold your fire!" he ordered as the man fired again barely missing Tutu. "She is my slave. I say hold your goddamned fire!" he shouted angrily as the man fired once again.

"You don't believe she wants to remain loyal. They want our blood and their freedom!" the man scoffed at the distraught Reverend. Parris called the others and informed them he wanted her to come into the house.

"Of what use is it going to be?" one of them inquired.

"First and foremost, they have my wife and secondly, she might be useful in stopping this crazy situation," he explained to them, but they all shook their heads in disagreement, except Anthony Smith.

"We can't leave missus Parris in their hands and the slave woman could probably help securing her release and end this situation," Smith commented to Parris' relief.

"We don't need any help from any of those savages and I don't think they are offering any. I think she is coming to study what we have inside here. The governor should be sending us some reinforcements!" another of the planters strongly objected as Tutu knocked on the door.

"There is no saying when they would arrive and it might be too late for missus Parris. Moreover, if the soldiers arrive with her still in their procession, they could resort to anything. I believe there is no harm in listening to what Tutu has to offer," Smith argued.

Reluctantly, they agreed to allow Tutu to enter, by which time she was already turning around, accepting that it was a futile attempt. She was surprised when the door opened and the Reverend let her in. She gave Smith a slight curtsy as Parris led her to a corner of the room, while the others returned to their positions.

"What is happening, Tutu? Where is Judith? Is she still alive?" Parris blurted out anxiously.

"Yes, I think she is alive, but you have to stop this killing, otherwise there will be no one alive at the end of it!" Tutu told him with a sense of urgency and desperation.

"They started it. Tell them to go away and this would all end. They are the ones placing us under siege," he answered bitterly, wishing he were never around the fracas.

Tutu sighed, not knowing how to continue. "It is not that easy. They are holding you responsible for the dead and will only retreat if you agree to leave. In addition, they want all the guns and ammunition," she said.

"That's impossible. We can't leave all the weapons to them. Not that I care about anything here, but the others are going to want to stay to defend their property. There is no way I could possibly convince them otherwise. It would just..."

"What is going on outside there?" Smith interrupted the Reverend Parris, who explained Tutu's offer. "But there is no way they can get in here."

"Well, they will stay outside till you starve to death in here," Tutu startled him with the reality of the situation.

"I have had it with this sodden island and with everything destroyed, I would happily leave, but the others would object. Nevertheless, I would ask them." Smith returned to the other planters and Tutu could see from their long low murmurings, the plan did not go down well with them. After a while, Smith returned to Parris and Tutu, "They are not happy with the arrangement, but will go with it for Mrs. Parris's sake." Tutu returned to the slaves.

Kojo was not pleased with what he regarded as Tutu's reckless behavior and initially ignored her, when she returned.

"Kojo, you have got to listen to me or I will invoke the wrath of the gods on you, right now!" Tutu shouted at him in annoyance as she followed him around trying to get his attention. The threat stopped him in his tracks being a strong believer in the power of the gods and Tutu's ability.

"Okay, Mama Orisha. What is it that you want?" he asked in a resigned tone as he sat on a tree stump.

"I want you to stop this killing, right now! I am going to get Madam Parris, and they will leave taking nothing as you requested," she said, obviously angry with Kojo for his apparent disregard for her opinions.

"Well, if you say so!" he shrugged with a sly smile.

Tutu turned around and headed toward the plantation. As she passed the last flank she heard her name called, but did not stop to see who it was. Emeka, who had earlier seen her break the ranks and was eager to know what was happening, ran after her, despite her ignoring his calls. He demanded to know what was going on, when he caught up with her and she explained.

Not knowing what to advise, he decided to escort her to the plantation. When they got to the slave quarters, the slaves guarding Judith Parris initially refused to let their prisoner go, but after much persuasion and subtle threats, they eventually agreed.

Tutu and Emeka led Judith Parris, who was clearly distraught and scared, back to the Smiths' house. When they arrived, there was surprise on the faces of the slaves laying siege and some of them immediately took it up with Kojo angrily. He disassociated himself from the action, but before they could prevent the handing over, Tutu and Judith Parris had already passed the lines.

Their arrival was met with equal, if not greater surprise from the planters, who quickly opened the door before there was any change of mind.

Amid questions of how she managed to secure Judith Parris' release, which she chose not to answer, Tutu insisted, "the important thing is to continue with the plan and not waste lives. I will go back and talk to them and hope you will leave."

"It appears she has a knack for doing the impossible. No wonder they think she is a messiah. A real lifesaver, I can say!" Smith said in utter disbelief and turned to Tutu, "Yes, Tutu, tell to them to move back, and we will leave."

Tutu was once again let out, and she returned to the slaves.

By the time she got back, she found Kojo surrounded by complaining slaves. Squeezing through them, she managed to get through to Kojo, "Tell the men to move back and the masters will leave!"

"Sorry! The men have decided not to leave. They want their heads!" He smiled complacently, "Why should it be only us who have to die!"

"I don't care what the men want or not. You are their leader! Now move them to the mountains, or they will be the only ones to die and all of them!" Tutu shouted at the top of her voice, but Kojo ignored her. She continued pestering and cajoling him as she followed him around, but to no avail. She eventually accepted defeat and walked away into the fields desolately.

Indoors the desolation increased as time went by and there was no visible sign of a break in the siege.

"I knew that girl wasn't going to do anything. I should have shot that nigger ass off her," lamented the planter, who had initially shot at Tutu, when she was approaching.

"She set missus Parris free, she probably couldn't convince them to stop the siege," Smith cautioned them as they all derided Tutu.

"She is the leader. That's what I have being telling Samuel," Judith Parris said.

"That's unfair to someone who saved your life and if she were the leader, she would have been able to call the siege off," Reverend Parris pointed out to her.

The siege continued throughout the next day and was

beginning to be effective as the planters ran out of drinking water. They prayed for reinforcements from the Governor, which were taking longer than they had expected.

Unknown to them, the Governor had his hands full since revolts had also broken out in the central and northern parts of the island. Nevertheless, he sent out troops the day after he received the request, but they were not to reach the town for another three days. Meanwhile, the planters had to resort to unsanitary means to survive, while the slaves were living high on the hog with their food supplies.

The evening of the fourth day, government troops arrived at the Savanna-La-Mar port and news of their arrival reached the slaves, shortly before they entered the town. Despite this many of the slaves refused to leave, although Kojo was having doubts and wanted to pull back into the Mountains Forest.

The disarray and laxity of the past few days had weakened the discipline among them and his authority was called into question, when he told them to call off the siege and run into the forest. In frustration, he sought out Tutu, who had stayed away and in her room on the plantation.

"We have received news of troops marching from the port. I told those idiots to leave and follow me to the mountains, but they refused. I will be leaving soon. Are you coming along?" he asked Tutu, who was snubbing him.

"Now you want to leave after misleading the people into thinking they are untouchable. You have their blood on your hands, Kojo. You knew all this wasn't your own doing, but that of the gods. You wanted to be the boss and be popular among them, while disregarding instructions. You could go to hell and I am not coming. I would not leave the poor people, they might need me," she said and turned her back on him. Confused and hurt, Kojo remained rooted to the spot where he was standing in the doorway for some time, before shrugging and leaving.

When he returned to the siege, he once again made an appeal to the slaves to follow him, which only a few answered. He had barely moved a hundred meters from the siege, when gunfire erupted from the arriving force. With their little ammunition, the slaves held up some resistance, but it was no match to the well-armed government troops. Nevertheless, what the slaves lacked in ammunition and cover, they had double in courage and the battle continued for hours.

By midnight a hundred slaves and ten soldiers had been killed. Overnight, word passed around that Mama Orisha ordered them to make a break for the mountains in the morning, although some were reluctant. Around nine o'clock, 800 slaves fled into the mountains, while a 150 waited behind. The soldiers, who had planned a renewed attack in the morning, quickly captured those left behind.

The troops chased the escapees into the Mountain Forest, but soon retreated due to a sudden heavy thunderstorm. The thunderstorm turned the morning into night as the heavens roared and thunderbolts flew around. The soldiers had no choice, but to turn back for the fear of an ambush and postpone the search to another time, when the weather was better and they had more information about the terrain.

The planters, who were already gaunt, listless or frustrated, were overjoyed, when the troops secured their freedom. As the day went on, plans were made to return things to normal, but that was difficult since most of their livelihood had been destroyed. Most of them remained in Smith's house, since their properties had been razed.

The Parrises were in that category and were at loss at what to do. Tutu having been found away from the siege was not arrested by the troops and went to meet the Reverend, once order was restored. She was not well received by Judith Parris, who still believed she played a major role in the revolt.

Smith announced he was moving to Boston in the North American British colonies, since he was unable to run a plantation, even if he decided to rebuild and re-cultivate the plantation. Reverend Parris signified he would be leaving with him and needed little or no persuasion to convince his wife, because the loss of her father and all assets were enough to make her want to leave.

Not surprisingly, there was a disagreement over where they should go. Judith preferred to go to another Caribbean Island or Annapolis in North America to join her brother, who was also a plantation owner, while Samuel did not want to go to another sugar island or stay around any of her family ever again. He argued for Boston since they both had sisters around the area, but the Massachusetts coast did not appeal to Judith.

While some people like the Parrises and Smith were talking of leaving the island, some were talking of revenge and bringing those captured to justice. Tribunals were immediately set up to try the erring slaves, some of whom were switching sides and pointing fingers. Some of the fingers were pointed toward Emeka, who they claimed was one of the ringleaders. He was summarily tried, found guilty and sentenced to death by hanging.

The judgment was delivered the day, the Parrises and Smith planned to leave. On hearing the judgment, Tutu ran to meet Reverend Parris, who she found with Smith sitting outside the house discussing their travel plans. Judith Parris had spoken to Smith about going to Barbados to set up sugar plantations, and much to the Reverend Parris' chagrin it appeared Smith was very much interested.

Running up to them and out of breath. "Please master, they are going to kill Emeka. He is innocent. Don't let them kill him, please," Tutu begged as she breathed laboriously.

"How do you know he is innocent?" Parris inquired playfully.

The question initially baffled Tutu, and she had to think before answering, "He is innocent. He helped me in releasing your wife."

"That's no argument for innocence. He decided to help you, his girlfriend and couldn't care less what happened to anyone else," Smith countered.

"Yeah, but at least he helped save Madam Parris. Help me save him, too!" Tutu retorted insistently.

Smith let out a hearty laugh, "girl, that is good," he said and laughed once again.

When Parris couldn't say anything, he continued, "I guess that is reasonable, a lover for a lover. I like this girl!" he said as he continued his infectious laughter, which Parris caught.

"Since he is my slave and I am leaving, I would do you that last favor and ask for his deportation," Smith said after the laughter subsided.

Many of the slaves were to be sent to other islands, a policy prevalent in the West Indies, whereby those not found guilty of any serious role in a revolt were often deported. This is to prevent a situation where they tell war stories to the fresh slaves thereby causing a repeat occurrence.

True to his word, Smith went to the judge and pled with him to release Emeka into his custody and guaranteed his immediate removal from the territory, along with the other slaves scheduled for deportation.

Tutu was ecstatic when the Judge agreed to Smith's request. She ran to Emeka and embraced him as she shed tears in joy. Smith was also overjoyed, when he calculated how much they would be worth in North America or if he put them to use in Barbados.

Later that day, 16th April 1689, Emeka, Tutu, the Parris family and Smith as well as 52 deported slaves began boarding the ship to leave behind the ruins of western Jamaica.

In years to come, the area returned to sugar cultivation more than ever. Although Kojo and the others, known as the Maroons, became increasingly bothersome from the mountains as he raided the plantations, setting slaves free and stealing the planters' supplies. The Maroons continued from the mountains until they won independence generations later.

11

Shortly before Smith set sail from Savanna La Mar port for North America, news of the peaceful "Glorious Revolution" in Great Britain and its political effects in North America reached him. Several months earlier, the British Parliament had deposed King James the second, putting an end to the absolute power of the monarchy and crowning William the third instead.

When the news of the revolution reached Massachusetts, the people raised arms against Edmund Andros' regime, representatives of King James the second, who had deprived them of their autonomy and made them part of the large Dominion that extended to Pennsylvania. Led by a number of ministers, the people of Massachusetts waged war against Governor Andros.

Suddenly, Parris' realized that all his efforts to convince Smith against going to Barbados had been negated by the reports of anarchy in Boston. Having previously spoken at length with Judith Parris, who knew Barbados very well, Smith decided to sail to Barbados to check the possibility of setting up plantations there. This gave Judith immense satisfaction and hope, which her husband could do nothing about.

When they got to Barbados in May 1689 they stayed on Samuel Parris' former plantation, which was in a bad shape and on the verge of closing down. The partner he'd left in charge was making plans to move to North America like many other local planters. To ensure this, he had let the number of slaves dwindle without replacing them.

The slaves brought from Jamaica, the 52 deportees, were placed in a holding house and a few in the slave quarters, including Tutu and Emeka. They had little or nothing to do and Tutu merely cooked meals and did the occasional housekeeping. While Parris just sauntered around greeting old friends, Smith and Judith immediately set out to inquire about running a sugar plantation on the island.

To their dismay, everywhere they turned, they were met with gloom. They realized that the island was experiencing poor harvests due to the over-exploited soil. The huge ratio of slaves to white men also struck Smith as potentially dangerous having just survived a slave revolt. After about a month, Smith decided it might not be profitable or safe to set up anything on the island.

Moreover, news of normalcy returning to North America reached him. Therefore much to Parris' joy, Smith announced his intentions to leave for North America, despite Judith's insistence that they should try and make something out of the dire situation.

Smith, being a shrewd businessman devoid of unnecessary sentiments whenever he was making a business decision, insisted on leaving shortly. This was strongly supported by Parris, who informed his wife of his decision to leave with Betty if she insisted on staying. Left with no choice, she agreed to leave, but then again the question of where to go in America brought about another round of arguments.

This did not stop them from leaving with Smith, who decided to buy more slaves from the island that had become a major slave-trading center. Before leaving, he purchased 108 more slaves, bringing the total number to one hundred and sixty. In addition, he also bought large quantities of sugarcane and molasses, before heading for North America.

He planned selling the slaves in North America, but more important to him were the sugar products. Sugarcane was going at a high price and the by-product, sugar molasses was also in high demand up north in New England, where it was used to make rum for the slave trade.

Once aboard the ship, the slaves were kept in their normal hold and were given no slack for fear of a revolt due to their large numbers. Smith ordered Emeka and a few other deportees to be isolated and shackled round the clock, although the others were occasionally allowed on the top deck for exercise and fresh air.

Smith gave them less freedom than he normally would have. Due to the shortness of the journey, he could afford to keep them confined without suffering any loss or damage. Once they passed the Spanish colony of Cuba, he stayed near the North American landmass.

The rancorous and prolonged arguments continued between Reverend Parris and his wife over whether or not to go to Annapolis or Boston. Parris had a sister, Theresa, in the Boston area, but had not heard from her in over a decade, while Judith had a brother with a tobacco plantation in Annapolis. Eventually, Reverend Parris having no tangible argument for going to Boston or that he could put forward against going to Annapolis, agreed for the sake of peace. He could not come out and tell her that he did not wish to move into another situation, in which her family members would dictate what happened in his own household, so he reluctantly agreed with her plan.

Another argument, which Judith used to blackmail him into conceding was that it was bitterly cold up north and for the sake of their girl, who had lived in the tropics all her life, Annapolis would be more conducive to her health. It was also convenient, since Smith planned selling the slaves in Annapolis, which was a fast-growing town due to its tobacco plantations.

Judith was happy to once again get her way and couldn't wait to reunite with her brother there. Still being bitter and antagonistic towards Tutu, she had it in mind to avenge her father's death, which she blamed on her, once they landed in Annapolis.

Meanwhile, Tutu resumed the chores she had performed en route from Africa, taking care of food and welfare of the slaves as well as the senior officers. It depressed her that Emeka was kept in chains, but she knew she couldn't push her luck by asking for a more humane treatment from Smith after going out of his way to save his life.

Instead, she tried as much as possible to make him a bit more comfortable by serving him extra portions, and by keeping him company whenever she was not busy. She had more time to spend with him now than on the voyage from Africa, since she spent little or no time with the reverend. Reverend Parris was preoccupied with his daughter, and Judith Parris ensured that they had no private time to talk.

After weeks of sailing, Smith announced they would be berthing in Annapolis pretty soon to the relief of many on board.

In Annapolis, as Smith was announcing they would be berthing by the following morning, some activity not easily noticeable to a casual observer was heightening as the sun set. In one of the most palatial mansions in an area littered with rich tobacco plantation owners, people started arriving in two's and three's and were quietly ushered indoors.

The hostess, Angela Rogers, a petite thirty-seven year old brunette, was the wife of the largest tobacco grower in the area, who was currently in their other home in Philadelphia, Pennsylvania. All the visitors were women of equal or at least high standing in the society married to landowners and successful merchants.

Usually, whenever they came visiting in nice late summer evenings like this, it was for large society parties involving the entire attendant pomp and gaiety with horse-drawn chariots, evening gowns and beautifully decorated ballrooms.

Tonight is a different night, one with a sense of urgency and important issues at stake, a night for a selected few within the planter class. Angela Rogers personally ushered the eleven invitees into an inner room, having ordered all servants and slaves to their quarters. That is with the exception of her most trusted servant, whom she had monitoring the door. The servant was given a stern order that nobody, "absolutely nobody", was to

be allowed in or to disturb them while they were in the inner
room.

The inner room was a large well-decorated study with a long
mahogany table surrounded with twelve chairs. On the table sat
a fully lit candelabrum, whose flickering lights provided the only
source of illumination in the room. The atmosphere around the
table was tense and was clearly not a social occasion. The host
in her opening statement restated this.

"I called you here today as a matter of emergency. I might
have told some of you of an alien force that threatens to disrupt
our lives and prosperity, although we were not sure of its arrival
or the form it would take," Mrs. Rogers said and paused to drink
from her glass of water.

"What kind of threat is...?" asked one of the women, Pat
Lawrence, whose curiosity often got the better of her. She
was stopped from interrupting with a hand gesture from their
host.

"It is a spiritual threat from Africa that would cause a lot
of problems, if allowed to land on this coast. Luckily, we were
able to identify its movement toward our coast yesterday.
Otherwise it would have entered unnoticed and we would have
probably been too late. The vessel should be berthing within
the next twelve hours, which is the reason I called this meeting
so hastily," she paused to see, if she was being followed or for
any questions.

A woman at the other end of the table had one. "In what
form is the spirit embodied?"

"It is not certain whether it is male or female, but since we
were lucky to identify its presence on the ship, we have to sink
the ship and all its cargo. That is the reason why I summoned
everyone here tonight. We need the full strength of the coven
to command all the spirits and elements. So let's start. You all
know what to do." She said offering her hands to those seated
next to her. When a complete circle of linked hands was formed,
she started incantations in a low voice.

Most of the crew had retired, while those remaining were

exchanging stories or playing games as they drank hard liquor, when mayhem started suddenly. The captain, who was making his last rounds for the night, raised an alarm as he struggled to remain standing on the ship that was rocking violently from side to side. He was shocked since there were no warning signs of bad weather and the strong winds came out of nowhere.

The ferocity of the winds increased and the effect was pandemonium especially among the slaves, whose deck was soon flooded. Within two minutes, two sails were broken and badly damaged, prompting Smith to order the immediate lowering of the remaining sails. The storm was gigantic, making waves rise over 50 feet above the ship, resulting in the washing overboard of four sailors, who tried lowering the sails.

Standing beside Smith was Parris, who had rushed out of his cabin to see what was going on. "We must be in the eye of a hurricane," he said to Smith, who was busy issuing out orders to his crew.

"I don't know what the hell it is, but whatever it is, if it continues it might sink us or sweep us into one of those treacherous rocks that litter the coast!" he grimly answered, before turning his attention to one of his crew.

"Sir, the lower deck is filling up with water!" he reported to Smith.

"Free some of those slaves in the front," he ordered and turned to another of his men, "How far are we from the coast?" he asked, weighing his options as the wind continued unabatedly.

"From the way we are being blown around, we could be anywhere," the man answered. Smith ordered a couple of men to go down to block the leak, while he contemplated what to do, although he knew he was fast running out of time.

Moments later, one of the men returned to him. "Sir, at the rate we are leaking, if these winds don't stop, we will be fish food in no time," he told him ominously. Smith followed him to the bottom deck to check the damage and was shocked to see how extensive and threatening it was.

His immediate thoughts were whether he could manage to

save anything, but he knew it would be impossible to save his cargo, so they decided to get some materials to block the leaks. Beside him was Parris, who, being a former merchant, knew they were in grave danger. As they left the bottom deck, they bumped into Tutu.

"Sir, is there a problem?" she asked the men as they hurried along.

"Is there a problem?" Smith repeated sarcastically, "Reverend, did you hear that dumb question, if there ever was one?"

"Yes, the ship is sinking, the wind is taking us down!" Parris tried to explain as they walked on, but he saw none of the panicky reaction he expected. "We are about to die!" he snapped irritably, although she remained visibly unperturbed and continued smiling. Tutu turned back to the opposite direction towards the stairway that led to the upper decks.

"Where is she going?" one of the crew exclaimed.

"Wherever she wants to go," Smith snapped testily. "Now, let's get these leaks plugged, otherwise we will all be going down."

On her way to the main deck, Tutu met some slaves who were running down to the lower decks, because of the winds. Some slaves, without Smith's or the crews' consent or knowledge, had shifted to the upper deck after being set free due to the flooding on their deck. The wind blew a couple of them overboard, leading to their panicked exit back to the lower decks.

As Tutu approached the top of the stairs, she struggled to move forward as the wind blew against her. With great difficulty she managed to step on the top deck, as she slowly spoke, "the hands of evil shall not stop me as no hand can stop the wind, thou shall not stop my future as no one can stop the sun. Yemanja, the goddess of the sea, I call upon you since I am in your house. Shango, I also call on you to strike them down and all you gods, please don't turn your backs on me."

Tutu said her incantations as she moved towards the hull looking into the skies. Somehow, the wind no longer pushed against her, despite its continued ferocity. With her hands fully stretched out, "I, Tutuoba, silence you winds as a mother silences her crying baby!" she shouted.

At once, there was a thunderclap followed by sudden calmness throughout the horizon. She clasped her hands together and offered them to the skies. "Thank you," she said, smiling and turned to head for the lower decks.

Down in the bottom deck, the sailors were pleasantly surprised as the wind abated. Smith decided to go up to the main deck to assess the damage and the wind, if there was any. On his way up, he met Tutu, who was soaking wet, on the middle deck and shook his head, amused as he remembered her stupid question. He had passed her before it occurred to him that she was wet. He briefly wondered how she managed to have safely ascended to the main deck, but with more pressing problems at hand he discarded the thoughts.

In Annapolis, there were even more pressing problems at the Rogers house. Slaves and freemen alike could be seen rushing to put out a fire that had started in an inner room, but was fast spreading throughout the house.

A thunderbolt had struck the house, passing through the roof and striking the table into small splinters. It was counted as a miracle that no one was killed or seriously hurt, although they were all trembling. The women were relocated to another part of the house as the slaves struggled to quench the fire, which they eventually did.

After the fire was over, Mrs. Rogers returned to her guests. "I warned you, we are facing a powerful force and we are lucky to have survived. Anyway, I think they were blown off course and might not be berthing here anymore. We shall be on the lookout and I will let you know of anything that happens," she said, signifying the end of their meeting.

There was not much talk afterwards. This was not a good night and most of them were engrossed in their thoughts of how close they had come to death. It was not an experience that they would be forgetting anytime soon. Moreover, it was already past midnight, so they all left unnoticed as they came—in ones and twos, while Mrs. Rogers and her staff continued with the clean up.

The following morning, the crew made a full assessment of the previous night's damage. The situation was not good as they discovered that all the masts were damaged and there were several leaks in the hull.

"It is going to take a long while to repair this damage and that is if we even have enough spares in stock to repair it. Otherwise, we might need a tow, which I doubt would come out of the blue," Smith said. He shook his head ominously as he thought of the chances, which appeared to be slim.

"Where are we, is what I would like to know. The compass has been destroyed and without knowing where we are, we are doomed!" the navigator added to the sense of despair, which was prevalent among the sailors.

Unknown to them was that in the bottom deck, seawater had seeped into the pantry and destroyed most of their food. The cooks noticed it when they began their morning chores and sent Tutu to summon Smith. Seeing Tutu approach him, Smith remembered the previous night, "Here comes Tutu. I wonder what question she has for us this time around."

"I thought she would have gotten herself washed away after she tried to come up here in the middle of the storm," joked the seaman, who had questioned her direction the previous night.

"I think she did come. I saw her going down to the middle deck, when I came to check the sails after the storm died down," Smith answered as Tutu arrived beside them.

"Good Morning! Captain Smith the cooks want you," she said shyly, twisting her fingers nervously, having a feeling they were talking about her.

"What for, goddamnit? I have enough on my plate right now," Smith feigned more irritation than he actually felt.

"No Sir, there is going to be nothing on your plate. All the food has been spoiled by water, and he wants you to come and see it." Smith let out a string of curses, when he heard the latest in his pyramid of problems. He had no choice, but to go and assess the newly discovered leak and was followed by his men. As Parris was about to follow Tutu gently held onto him, although not without Smith noticing and shaking his head in mockery.

"Master, are we still in trouble, because I heard the cooks say we are going to die," she asked the impatient reverend, but with her charming smile he could not shun her.

"I guess things are not looking good. The ship is badly damaged, we are lost and upon everything, our food stocks are now destroyed. If we don't get a tow, we might die!" He explained and turned around to leave, but then a thought struck him and he turned back to her. "I heard you came out here into the storm last night. Why? That was very silly and dangerous," he gently reprimanded her.

She smiled coyly without saying a word, since she could not tell him her reason. He turned and left to join the men on the bottom deck, while she stayed behind. As soon as Parris was out of sight, she leaned against the hull's bulwark and whispered, "Please, help mother. Yemanja, we are in your house. Please help you gods!"

A few hours later, a ship was sighted by a member of the crew and was attracted by sending smoke signals. The ship was a Bostonian fishing vessel and the captain was an Irishman with a round figure and sandy hair.

"You are off the coast of New York," he informed them and could hardly believe their account of what happened, "Are you sure you were off the coast of the Chesapeake Bay, because I wonder what type of wind could have blown you so far off course." He was to be less skeptical, when he examined the damage to the ship, "Holy Mary! You are lucky to be alive," he exclaimed.

"Well, I would be grateful for any help that could be rendered," Smith said hopefully.

"Let's see what we can do, I would have offered to tow you, but I am going to Boston," the fisherman told him.

"Boston would be good! Actually Boston is my final destination. I was just stopping to sell my cargo in Annapolis. Prices are better in Annapolis, but Boston, it shall be," Captain Smith enthused.

"Let's make some repairs before we set out, so that we are not overburdened towing the ocean along with us," the fisherman advised.

They decided to plug the larger leaks and repair the main mast before embarking on their journey. This took several hours of hard work with all hands on deck. Eventually they set out and everyone was relieved and looked forward to berthing soon.

On the 25th of September 1689, the ship was towed into Boston Harbor to the delight of everyone on board, with the exception of Judith, who would have preferred Annapolis and the slaves, who were apprehensive about their fate in the new land.

A customs official came up toward the ship and met with Smith on the gangplank, shaking his hand warmly, Smith asked, "How are you O'Brien? Surprised to see us so soon? It is not out of choice. Anyway, how is the land treating you?"

"Fine! I cannot complain with good fellows like you treating me well. I am happy! The new king is happy! And I guess everyone should be happy! So what have you got for me? Remember you promised the last time to treat me better the next time you came this way!"

"Like I said this was not a planned voyage, but don't worry I will treat you accordingly," Smith said reassuringly as they spoke of the bribes that would enable him to pay less to the crown. The customs duties were usually exorbitant and most merchants connived with the officials to pay less through bribes.

"Let me hurry things up at that end and I will see you later," Smith excused himself and returned on board to supervise the unloading of the slaves. The customs officer remained at the end of the gangplank, positioning himself, so that he could see everything leaving the ship.

Soon the slaves began moving ashore, passing by him. Tutu was among the last of the slaves to come down the gangplank and as she passed him, he stopped her and gave her a discerning look from head to toe.

"Hmmm, a mulatto slave, I will be damned if I don't keep her for the king," he said, touching her gently on her midriff playfully.

"I am no mulatto and take your hands off me!" Tutu said as she cringed from his coarse hands.

"Holy Shit! She even speaks good English. I think I will keep this one for myself. My wife needs some help!" he grinned lustfully and grabbed her buttocks. Tutu slapped him angrily and he was about to return it, when he heard Smith.

"Keep it moving O'Brien, before I keep your head for myself," Smith shouted as the line came to a halt, extending back into the ship.

O'Brien startled and blushed at the threat. "That is no way to address an officer of the crown," he replied, trying to regain his composure as he swore under his breath.

"I will give you and the king what you deserve, now let the line move on. I need to catch up with some sleep," Smith answered brusquely. After the ship was completely unloaded, O'Brien calculated the duties and they haggled, before finally settling for an amount acceptable to both parties.

The slaves were led to a holding house behind Smith's mansion in Chelsea, where they were to be held until their sale. They were to be sold across New England through auctions and private deals over time. In the meantime, Smith ensured they were cleaned and rested.

The Parrises were welcomed to stay with him in Chelsea, which was on the northern outskirts of Boston, until such a time when they could get their own place. He had a big house, which at the moment was practically empty. This was all right with Reverend Parris, but his wife was not in the least happy having to stay anywhere, 500 hundred miles away from her intended destination. Especially, in a place with little or no large-scale farming, filled with merchants, small-time farmers and priests.

After much arguing, it was agreed between them, she could go to Annapolis by road, while Parris and his daughter stayed in Boston. Parris argued that Betty was travel weary and without a guaranteed comfortable abode in Annapolis, it would be better if Judith went alone to make arrangements, before they followed.

Knowing she could not get a better deal out of her husband, she left the day after their arrival. As soon as she did, Parris set out to look for a job as a minister, knowing it would be difficult for her to force a move down south, if he started working before her return.

12

Due to the absence of Anthony Smith's family, who were in London following the trouble in spring, Tutu and Emeka were in charge of the day-to-day running of the house. Tutu cooked for Betty Parris and the slaves, who were gradually sold off.

Most of the time, Tutu and Emeka were left to their own antics, since Reverend Parris was constantly on the road looking for a ministerial appointment and his sister, while Smith was always out on business or busy drinking with friends. They were alienated from the few remaining slaves, who regarded them as house Negroes, therefore not trustworthy. Neither was it easy to establish outside friends, since Tutu and Emeka rarely left the house for the fear of what might happen to them. Unlike in Jamaica, there were no universal black rest days or Sunday markets where all the slaves congregated.

The slave ratio was smaller around them, and they came to believe that they were treated as harshly, if not worse than in Jamaica. In Jamaica, many plantation owners were absent landlords and those around rarely had their family around. Therefore the black population was overwhelming, which was reassuring to them and other blacks. This was not the case here as they were to realize the day following their arrival, when they went to the local market and had an experience that instilled fear into their hearts.

Tutu had gone to Smith after finding out there was not enough food to cater for everyone and he took her, Emeka and two other slaves to the market. He told her to keep her eyes open, since he expected her to go to the market by herself or with other slaves to make purchases, when next anything was required.

On reaching Haymarket, they were astonished to see a large number of Europeans selling their wares. They, also witnessed the mistreatment of some slaves, some of whom were publicly whipped for offences they could not fathom. Observing her new surroundings studiously, she couldn't but wonder why they spat so much or smoked so much, nor why there were so many horses and carriages. It all seemed strange to her, having never seen a large European presence before.

At the end of the visit, she had so many questions, which she believed only her teacher, the reverend could possibly answer. Unfortunately, he was always so tired and irritable, when he came back at night that he didn't have time to answer her questions. This resulted in her keeping misconceptions, which led to unfounded fears, to herself.

Due to the isolated feeling and boredom, Tutu became depressed and at a stage, confided in Emeka that she was contemplating suicide, although he laughed it off, saying she was too strong a person to give up.

All through her life, she had been surrounded by lots of people and things to do, both in Africa and Jamaica, and she greatly missed the group feeling. Her inability to sing and socialize among people was killing her soul.

The only thing that was keeping her going was the presence of Emeka and her main fears centered around what she would do if her only companion, Emeka, was sold off to another person and she was left to herself in the new strange land. The mutual insecurity brought them closer.

Emeka intensified his sexual overtures and talk of escaping, which she began to give a serious thought, since it gave her the surety of never losing the only one she had at present. Emeka was confident of escaping and being able to cater for the wife and children he wanted so badly.

The thought increasingly appealed to her until another slave tried escaping and was caught in Lynn, a small town north of Boston and Chelsea near Salem. When he was returned, he was harshly dealt with to instill fear into others that might be contemplating such a venture.

It did have its desired effect. It put an end to any plans Tutu was contemplating, although Emeka still fancied their chances of success. While nothing concrete happened, the fear and loneliness of the new land deepened their friendship more than ever, as they found themselves alone in the big house with nothing to occupy them.

Luckily, a few weeks after his arrival, Parris located his long lost sister, Theresa, in the nearby town of Salem. His sister, Theresa, whom he hadn't seen for nearly two decades since his Harvard days, was now married to a wealthy merchant, who dealt in a variety of manufactured goods from England. While discussing what had been happening in each other lives since they last met, she realized he was currently looking for a ministerial job.

She was glad to inform him of an opening in the Salem parish, which she suggested he should apply for. Parris applied for the position, which was hotly contested with another candidate. In the end, he won the job with the help of his sister, but was offered a very small salary.

This, they explained, was due to what they regarded as his inadequate experience. They discounted his African experience, which they said was "not with real people." For some time, there was an impasse as they continued to haggle over his salary. Meanwhile, he continued looking for a better salary elsewhere.

Seeing his sister nearly every other day, Parris was soon to discover she had a brother-in-law who lived a few hundred yards away from Smith's house in Chelsea. On one of his visits to his sister, she requested him to help deliver a message to her in-laws, which he agreed to do.

Parris asked Tutu to follow him, because he wanted her to know the place, so she could take Betty there to play with her age mates. Betty was complaining of boredom and loneliness, and he wanted to relieve the monotony by finding her playmates.

Being a long time since they were alone together, Tutu was anxious to tell and ask him so many things she had wanted to for some time, which she wasted no time delving into.

As she spoke, gesticulating and laughing excitedly, she held on to his arm as they slowly walked down the street, oblivious to the stares they were attracting from passers-by. With the unseasonable, warm October weather, it was nearly like when they were in Africa and even Parris realized how much he missed Tutu's lively character.

It was supposedly a five-minute walk that took a blissful eternity, but it ended with a rude awakening, when Parris knocked on a house that looked very much like Smith's house. After four knocks, a middle-aged pale lady with a large bosom swung the door open and gaped at what was clearly a faux pas on her doorstep.

For a moment, she was shocked and looked at Tutu repugnantly, before asking for their business. Parris disengaged his elbow from Tutu's clutch and extended his hand as he introduced himself. It was only then the woman smiled, realizing who he was and invited him indoors.

"Welcome reverend. Theresa told me you would drop by today, which is why I have stayed home. Please sit down," she gestured to the chairs as she ushered them into a large living room. Parris, closely followed by Tutu, made his way to the chairs.

"Hey you! Go to the back and stay with your people. Tell Doris to come right away," she rudely ordered Tutu, whom she looked at despicably for having the temerity to try sitting on her chairs. "Is she your slave or...?" she asked, leaving the question open ended and insinuating, with the innuendo well understood by the priest as Tutu left with a scowl on her face.

"Yes, she is my slave. Although I have known her since she was a child, before she was taken as a slave and I took her off her owner, a friend. She is...," he explained uneasily as he tried to dispel the innuendo.

"I do not know how things are in Africa, but now you are in America; you can't be seen socializing freely in public with

Negroes and definitely not sitting together in a living room. You got to put them in their place," she cautioned him.

Doris, a thickset, middle-aged black woman entered, while she was speaking, but stood silently at the doorway waiting for instructions. When her madam noticed her, she paused and told the plump slave to serve the priest some drinks.

In the kitchen, Tutu found a teenaged girl bleeding and crying profusely. Studying the weeping girl from afar, Tutu noticed a side of her head was bruised and swollen as well as some other parts of her body. She felt awkward and didn't know what to say to console the distraught girl, with whom she empathized.

While contemplating how to approach and alleviate the girl's pain as she looked on pitifully, Doris came back and looked mockingly at the weeping girl. "You are still on this, girl! You better get over it and find something to do," she said disdainfully as she rinsed a cup and left through the door.

Doris returned moments later. "So who are you and where are you from?" she asked Tutu amiably although with a bit of arrogance as she wiped her hands on her blue apron, which was straining around her ample belly.

"I am Tutu and from up the road," Tutu answered curtly, with her eyes still set on the aggrieved girl. Tutu looked up and gestured by nudging her head inquiringly about the girl.

The woman scoffed, "Oh she? She got whipped for being uppity to madam. She is still young and has a lot to learn around here." At her age, Doris was used to the heavy hand of her mistress and saw nothing exceptionally heart rending about it.

"What type of name is Tutu?" Doris asked curiously, changing the subject.

"Yoruba!" Tutu answered brusquely. Tutu could not understand Doris' aloofness towards the girl and was beginning to dislike her, thinking she was a rather callous person. She decided to show some compassion and walked over to the girl. Crouching next to her, she put an arm around her in an effort to console her. This initially brought about a more emotive response from the girl, but she gradually mollified.

"Your master did not give you an English name?" asked Doris, a naturally ebullient and inquisitive person, who couldn't but continue talking and asking questions. Tutu ignored her and continued to placate the girl.

"What do you do in the church?" the woman wondered aloud. "It must be easy and for him to take you along visiting, he must really be a nice man." She continued talking unanswered as she went on to washing some cutlery. Lowering her voice to a whisper, "Or are you his mistress?" she asked with a mischievous grin and wink.

This caught Tutu's attention. "No, he is just a friend, a..." she said with some irritation. "Why is your madam so mean?"

"You are the one definitely having it easy. Going for a walk and visiting with the master," she shook her head in amazement. "Anyway, you are beautiful, so thank your stars!" She continued talking half to herself until interrupted by the madam, who came to inform Tutu the priest was ready to leave.

Later that evening, after Tutu and Emeka had finished their chores and were sitting under the moonlight, Tutu recounted what she had seen during her visit with the priest to his in-laws.

"I don't know why some of the women are so mean. I am just happy Madam Parris is not around, although I heard Madam Smith and the rest of the family would be back next week. I wonder, what she would be like," she voiced her anxiety. Remembering something, she excitedly tapped him on his shoulder, "Can you believe the old black woman there thought I was sleeping with the reverend, just like madam Parris?"

"I have heard that before and if I didn't know better, I might have believed it," Emeka said in a matter-of-fact fashion as he played around throwing stones into the distance. "I hope they are not right," he added teasingly, raising his eyebrows questioningly.

Tutu slightly stiffened on hearing the first part of his reply, but relaxed after he completed his statement. "Don't be stupid, you know you are my man!" she feigned indignation.

This made his stone throwing hand freeze, momentarily in mid-air. Emeka was surprised at the statement, because she had never formally agreed to have a relationship with him. To be sure he heard right, looking into her eyes, he dropped the stones and slowly moved closer to cuddle her, and she did not resist. For a brief moment, they stayed in an embrace and forgot all their problems as they dreamed of blissful coexistence.

Meanwhile, Judith Parris had reunited with her family in Annapolis as soon as she arrived by stagecoach from Boston. It was not difficult finding the Lawrences in Annapolis since they owned the second largest tobacco plantation in the area, second only to the Rogers. They were pleasantly surprised to see her, but were disheartened to hear the circumstances that led to her arrival.

Her brother, Frank, was willing to help her set up another farm, but there was the question of her husband. It was not commonplace for a woman to own and control a plantation and her brother thought it might be better, if her husband was around to manage it. She assured him the family would come down, once she could ensure their survival and prosperity.

As she spoke of her journey and how freak weather diverted the course of the ship, Judith caught the attraction of her sister-in-law, who later took her aside for more information.

"You said your ship was diverted by a storm off the Chesapeake Bay. On what day was this?" Pat Lawrence asked, while they were drinking tea on the porch the day after Judith's arrival. Her husband had gone to the plantation, leaving the two women to themselves. Judith answered without giving it any thought. "Did you have any Africans on board?" she asked and Judith told her they did.

The following day, Pat invited her sister in-law to a tea party at the Rogers residence, which Judith accepted.

On their arrival, a petite woman with short brunette hair called Angela Rogers welcomed them. She ushered them into a large, tastefully decorated living room, where there were three other women, whom she introduced.

After settling down and being served tea in some beautiful blue china, the women waited to converse until the serving slave left the room.

"Did you have a fire there or what happened?" Judith asked her host, when she saw the entrance to another room that showed signs of a fire.

"Yes, we had a thunder strike about three weeks ago?" Angela answered. After a pause, she continued, "I gathered your ship had some weather trouble at exactly the same time and was diverted to Boston."

Surprised that it was even mentioned, Judith nodded as she threw her sister-in-law a damning glance, castigating her for sharing the news too fast. "Yes, it was quite scary, when it started after midnight and continued for a long time, but thank God it stopped," she said and picked up her cup of tea from the polished coffee table.

"I was told you weren't coming from Africa, but from Jamaica due to a slave revolt. What caused the revolt?" Angela Rogers inquired amiably as she placed her short feet on a stool and relaxed into her seat. She tried not to appear too interested, but it was obvious, especially from the other women's disposition, that they were very much interested in gleaning information from Judith.

Judith took a deep breath before she launched into an issue that had given her sleepless nights ever since it had started.

"I was informed that a known troublemaker had joined forces with one slave that they believed was a kind of messiah. In order to cut any plan in the bud, my father and I had both of them locked up, but it seems that we acted too late and within a few days, Hell was let loose. My father was killed and our plantations were burnt. I was kidnapped, but was soon released," Judith recounted and towards the end had to wipe her eyes as she recollected the incidents.

"Who was this savior and what happened to her?" one of the women asked curiously, beating Angela to it.

"She is my husband's slave and nothing happened to her. She is still with him in Boston," she answered, prompting gasps around the coffee table.

"She is your husband's slave and is in Boston?" Angela asked, surprised and looked at the other women to see if they realized what the stranger was telling them.

"Yes, she is. Although the savior thing was all rubbish, I can tell you!"

Angela slowly shook her head as various thoughts raced through her mind. "I wouldn't be that confident, but anyway it is an interesting story," she told Judith. Angela and the other women, having confirmed their fears, changed the topic and shortly afterward everyone left for their homes.

The women planned to talk to her at later date, when all the members had discussed their plan of action, if any was to be taken. This was not to take place for a long while, because Judith fell seriously ill.

This was attributed, partly, to her changed environment and partly to the emotional strain, she had recently experienced. Although there were fears that it might be Tutu's spiritual handiwork, in an effort to get Judith permanently out of the way.

On November 3, 1689, Mrs. Helen Smith arrived with her three children and an equal number of slaves from England, where they had spent the last nine months. The woman of the house immediately stamped her authority over the house with her presence.

At five foot eleven inches and 190 pounds, she had an imposing presence that was augmented by her hazel eyes and long auburn hair. The children, especially the girls, Antonia and Helena, inherited their mother's looks, while the boy in the middle looked a bit more like their father with his redhead.

Anthony Smith took Emeka and some other slaves to welcome and help them from the port when they arrived, while Tutu was left at home to prepare for their arrival. For reasons unknown, Helen was in a foul mood, when she arrived home and immediately let it be known to Tutu, the first person she saw as she entered.

Ignoring Tutu's greeting. "Anthony, I see you found yourself an African mistress, while I was away," she said accusingly to her husband closely following her.

"Rubbish!" he answered peevishly, "she is not my slave, but she has being taking care of the house and cooking. You didn't expect me to do the housekeeping when you took everyone away with you, did you?"

"I hope she was only housekeeping, otherwise I would hang her with her bloody tits," she said threateningly. Anthony stopped for a moment and shot his wife a dirty look, before shaking his head remorsefully and walking away. She had been foul ever since she arrived and despite the fact that he had been looking forward to seeing his family, he was already getting tired of her constant cynicism.

She continued in the same vein, "Well, her help is no longer needed around here. Martha! Martha!" she called out loudly for her housekeeper and was told by a guard that she was outside. "She'd better get in here and start preparing supper."

"I think Tutu has already made some food, haven't you?" Smith asked Tutu, who stood silently, petrified over her future prospects with the lady of the house.

"Yes I did. I prepared some roast beef and potatoes, ma'am," she stuttered and scurried to show them the dinner that she had made in anticipation of their arrival.

Helena tasted the food and shook her head. "No, I will have Martha prepare us some food? Who taught her to cook, the ship stewards? The guards and other slaves could have that. Moreover, I don't want anyone to poison me and my children," she said stating her real fears, which were prevalent among the slave owners. She once again called out for Martha, who ran to her in the kitchen.

Slapping her on the back, "Do I have to remind you that it is time to prepare supper or don't you know what time it is?" she shouted at the 30 something year old black woman, who cowered beside a cabinet in anticipation of more beatings.

"Sorry, ma'am. I was told supper had been made and I was setting out the children's clothes," she quivered. Helena gave orders on what to make for dinner and left. Tutu sighed in relief as soon as she left the room.

Moving closer to Martha. "Hello, I am Tutuoba. Is your Madam always like that?" she asked, looking furtively at the door, in case she returned.

"Worse at times," Martha answered gravely, shaking her head ruefully, "You would know sooner than later." Martha, a light-skinned black woman, was normally reserved, but she found Tutu engaging and opened up to her quite quickly.

"How long have you been with her?" Tutu asked as she helped with the chores.

"I was born here. My mother tried running away with me, but she was caught and since she wouldn't give up, she was shot and died."

She told Tutu about her mother, Sally, who was impregnated by Helen's father and found herself subjected to increased mistreatment from the family, especially from the jealous wife and embittered children. She ran away to protect her newly born daughter from abuse, but it all ended sadly.

"So she is your..." Tutu couldn't bring herself to complete her question, but Martha nodded, knowing what she was about to say.

"I feel sorry for you and don't think I could stand it for all my life. I hope my master gets a job soon and we leave, although I feel sorry for my friend, Emeka," Tutu said thoughtfully, shaking her head.

"You mean that big man. He is your man?" Martha said with surprise and admiration. "You are lucky. If you don't move too far away, you could see him at the market or during holidays, like Thanksgiving and Christmas," Martha enthused.

Tutu did not know what Christmas was since plantation slaves were left out of the celebrations, but Martha explained it to her. "They are festivals that master and the family go out visiting. There are usually lots of eating and drinking, and it is a nice time, although it is cold."

The two women continued to talk and enjoyed each other's company while they worked. The pace of things around the house picked up over the next few days and Helen was always on their backs. Tutu could only pray that the reverend could get a job and get her out of Helen's way.

On Thanksgiving Day, they woke up earlier than usual to prepare food and do extra house cleaning. Luckily, the Northeast coast was enjoying an Indian summer and was much warmer than expected. Visitors started arriving early in the afternoon for the Thanksgiving dinner, which Tutu and Martha served.

As usual, when the Smiths were all together, they held an early lunch party before going into Boston to visit friends and family, leaving the slaves to enjoy themselves in what was considered their rest day; one of a few in the year.

Tutu and Emeka relaxed in each other's company, once the family set off for Boston. The Parrises had left the previous day to celebrate at Theresa's house in Salem.

"Ma'am Smith was nice to everyone for the first time since she arrived. She and Captain Smith even held hands when they were going out. You should have seen them. I wish I could have a family someday, when my husband and I could hold hands and be happy," she said dreamily.

"Well, we are together now and there is nothing stopping us from holding each other," he said softly, as he slipped a hand around her waist and pulled her closer.

"Yes, but I wish it could be forever with no master or madam, have children, my own house and just ride around in our carriage," she continued in her dreamy fashion as she playfully traced her finger along his bulging muscles.

"You don't have to bother about that. We don't have a carriage, but instead of a horse carrying you around, I would," and before she knew it, he lifted her effortlessly off her feet. "Where do you want to go, my ma'am?" he asked a giggling Tutu, who wrapped her arms around his neck affectionately. She pulled herself closer and gave him a kiss.

"Oh! Where did you learn that? You have been peeping at the master and mistress."

"Let's go to the water," Tutu suggested going to the Chelsea side of Boston Harbor. "Put me down. Let's go and see if any ships are coming today," which he obliged.

As they walked towards the shore, Tutu noticed that Emeka was trying to say something, but kept stopping.

"What is wrong or troubling you that you want to say?" she asked after it became apparent.

"You were talking of having your children and house and I was just wondering why not now and with me. Tutu...." He stopped and shook his head sadly.

"What? Say it!"

"I don't know what to say anymore than I love you and promise that nothing bad will happen to you and our children, if you follow me," Emeka stopped and held her shoulders firmly as he looked into her eyes. "Biko! Please! Jo!" begging her in Ibo, English and Yoruba as his eyes became misty.

Tutu remained speechless and buried her head into his chest. She gave it a thought and despite her mother's warning, she had decided it was with Emeka her heart lay.

"I would be your wife, but I am not sure how we could ever be free. I don't want our children to be slaves. You are the only one who I care about in the world and you know that," she said.

Emeka smiled and kissed her passionately, lifting her off the ground in an embrace. It was a dream come true after twenty months and he couldn't contain his joy.

Tutu, out of breath, pushed him away and straightened her dress. "Hold on! Do you want to start making the babies right here?" Tutu smacked him lightly in the stomach and ran away.

They playfully chased each other to the shore as they forgot all their worries. On reaching the deserted shore, Tutu fell to the ground as he grabbed her and they frolicked on the sandy beach. As one thing led to another in their dreamy world, they ended up making love in the beautiful sunset.

Afterwards they sat on the shore looking at the horizon in a silent embrace, thinking of freedom, prosperity, married life and their love.

"Let's go! We can leave before master arrives. By the..." Emeka broke the silence.

"No, not today. Tomorrow. I am too tired to be running in the forest today!" Tutu objected sharply, but softened when she saw disappointment on his face. "Don't worry. I am yours and so is the baby in me. We will always be together. Let's just relax and enjoy this town for the last night," she said, bringing a smile to his face.

After what seemed to be an eternity and in complete darkness, they rose and went back home. When they got back home, there wasn't a soul around.

Tutu was not ready to return to the dreary atmosphere of the house. "It is such a nice feeling, and I don't want it to end just yet. Let's take a walk to Main Street," she suggested, wishing to make most of their free time.

"I am tired. Let's just sit here," Emeka suggested otherwise.

"Come on! You know it's the last time we are going to see it," Tutu urged and pulled him to his feet from the porch step he was sitting. "Stop being lazy. You were all strength moments ago when you were making love to me. You have power to make babies, but you don't have any to take care of them, is that it?" she feigned anger.

Emeka sighed with mock exasperation and followed her. They strolled with their hands linked talking about their plans for the next day. When they arrived at the town center, they saw lots of people having a merry Thanksgiving.

The celebrations were prolonged and more public, due to the unseasonable weather. Many people were drinking in groups, while some were returning with their families from their celebrations.

After about ninety minutes of sauntering around, they decided to go back home as they got tired and bored. On their way home, as they turned off Main Street into a deserted side street, a group of drunken merrymakers also turned onto it, from the opposite direction.

Their noise filled the whole street as they walked towards Tutu and Emeka, who thought nothing of it. When they met halfway down the street, Tutu and Emeka gave them enough space for them to pass unhindered, but two of the drunks walked out of their way to block their path.

"Hey, honey! Hiyyaduhing love," they said boisterously in their drunken slurred speech. Yet, the lovers due to the festivities thought nothing of it and only split and walked around them, but one of them grabbed hold of Tutu as she tried walking around him on the other side.

"Honey, what are you gonna be giving me, so I can thank you or isn't that what Thanksgiving is about," the grabbing obnoxious drunk slurred, hardly keeping himself standing, while others who had moved closer were laughing and enjoying the spectacle. Tutu embarrassed by the awkward situation was lost for words, still smiling, she tried to wriggle herself free from the drunk's strong grip, but without any success.

"Please leave me alone, I am going home," she whimpered in frustration.

"Come on! Girl, be nice to us. I will pay, if you want!" As one of them groped her, another pulled on her clothing, inadvertently tearing it.

"Leave her alone!" Emeka shouted angrily and stepped towards them, but was blocked by one of them, who faced him antagonistically.

"And who the hell do you think you are, nigguh? Who do you think you are talking to?" asked one of them bellicosely. The man jabbing a finger at Emeka antagonistically continued, "if you say one more bloody word, just one more word and don't put your monkey tail between your legs and run back to the jungle, I will skin your hide right here!" he said, as he continued thrusting his finger into Emeka's face, which was a few inches higher up.

"Let me go. Stop! Stop!" Tutu shouted as she hit out at the groping hands and kicked another in the groin.

"You heard her. Leave her alone!" Emeka bellowed in a menacing voice over his antagonist. He was fast losing his temper seeing his woman, groped and crying in distress. He brushed aside the man in an effort to help Tutu out of the ugly situation.

"Don't you dare push me, nigger!" the guy threatened, but was ignored.

He angrily grabbed hold of Emeka's collar from the back, making him lose his balance and fall backwards. An enraged Emeka managed to keep standing and swung round with a heavy blow, which found a place on the man's temple. He followed it with an upper cut to his jaw in a split second, which snapped his neck and carried him off his feet. The drunk died before he reached the ground three feet away from where he was initially standing. On seeing this, three other men immediately attacked Emeka, who when vexed was fearless.

"No! No! Please Emeka! Don't fight," Tutu pleaded loudly, but the cat had already been let out of the bag as he took on the attackers. Tutu was alarmed, but things were happening too fast. Moreover, Shango, the god of justice couldn't be called since there was no injustice or any serious danger to her.

Emeka easily felled two of them, but not before the others who had continued walking, ran back to aid their friends. Out of the two he knocked down, one was seriously hurt, while the other had a few broken bones.

Within three minutes of the fight ensuing, a small crowd had milled around them, followed by the local constabulary and if not for the police, the mob was gearing to lynch him. The sheriff just managed to free him from the wrench of the mob, which brought about a lot of boos from the angry crowd. Tutu, now forgotten could do nothing, but follow the police and the crowd to the station.

When they reached the local constabulary, she requested to speak to him, but was refused and turned away. Distraught and confused, she went home to seek help. As she got home, she met Smith and the rest of the family, who were just arriving from their outing. Anthony Smith had had a bit too much to drink, although he noticed she had been crying and was still distraught.

"What's wrong with you, crying on such a nice day?" he slurred. Tutu recounted the events to him, but he was too drunk and was dozing off as she spoke.

Helen, who was more in control of her senses, was not impressed. "He attacked a White man? Then he deserves whatever comes to him," she said, uncaringly as she dragged Smith upstairs. "That's what happens when you give them too much freedom," she hissed.

The following morning, Smith, now sober, asked Tutu to recount the events of the previous night, which she tearfully did. "I made him go to the town center. It's all my fault!" she cried with self-blame.

"I am fed up with you two and being asked to bail out someone, whose good senses appear to have left him," he said vehemently, but Tutu beseeched him that it was her fault. Eventually, he agreed to go to the station to see what was being done.

She asked if she could follow him to the station, which he agreed to, but Helen refused her permission on the grounds that "there is too much cleaning to do today, maybe later or tomorrow." Not willing to countermand his wife, Smith promised to go in the course of his itinerary.

Later that evening, when Smith returned, he called Tutu, "I stopped at the precinct and saw the boy. All I can say is that he really got himself in trouble this time around. According to the police one person is dead, while two others are seriously injured."

"So what is going to happen to him?" she inquired eagerly.

"Well, that is up to the judges. I will try and see if I could get someone to defend him, but you don't kill a man and walk free here."

"They attacked him. They wanted to rape me and attacked

him," she protested loudly, which attracted Helen in the next room. Helen came and asked about the latest developments with regards to the jailed slave, which he told her.

"You might as well forget him and buy yourself another slave," she bluntly told him as she led him back to the living room, "You can't waste your time on these slaves."

Tutu looked at Helen with disgust for her callousness, a look that turned to one of hatred that neither of them saw since they both had their backs to her as they went to the living room.

The next day, Tutu woke up early to her chores and was given a helping hand by Martha, enabling her to finish in record time. To her utter dismay, when she went to announce she was leaving to see Emeka as planned, Helen gave her additional work, which she had no choice but to do.

At long last, she was free to go which she did as she half ran and half walked to the station. When she got to the police precinct, she walked to the desk constable.

"Good morning, sir," she greeted, for which she received a grunt and an inquiring look in return. "I am here to see Emeka," she continued nervously.

"Who?" he asked, with a mixture of irritation and indifference, as he slouched in his seat and picked on the food in front of him.

"Emeka, the black man who was in the fight," she answered expectantly.

"Oh, he was taken away by the people yesterday night," he said and sat upright to have a proper look at her, having heard that the man had killed the two men over a woman.

"Which people?" she asked with disbelief, "Please do you know where he was taken?"

"The park!" he barked. Seeing her puzzled expression, he said, "Make a left, when you step out of here and then your first right." He smirked and returned to his slouching position. Still perplexed but discouraged from asking further questions by the officer's indifferent attitude, she thanked him and left.

Walking briskly along the directions given to her, her heart pounded as she wondered what Emeka was doing in the park and who were the people said to have come for him. Why didn't he make contact with me, if he was free? She wondered. Turning around the last corner before the park, her eyes swept the small park, but she could not see anything.

When she got into the park, she gave it another sweeping look and saw what appeared to be a black hand from the other side of a tree, at the far end of the park. Slowly walking towards it, she turned around the trunk quietly, planning to surprise him.

Instead, she received the greatest surprise of her life.

13

Dangling from a low branch was Emeka, who had been beaten beyond recognition, before being hanged. His genitals had been cut and removed as a souvenir by one of his torturers, a common practice in lynching. Tutu let out a long scream and retched at the sight of Emeka.

Oblivious to the gruesome sight and smell, Tutu grabbed the bloody body. "Aaaah! Emeka," she bawled. "Who did this? Why? What have I ever done to deserve this? My father, my mother, now my husband." She dropped and rolled in the grass as she lamented in both Yoruba and English. She wept uncontrollably as she brought down and hugged the dead body of her lover.

Meanwhile, Smith, having gone into town earlier, had heard of the fate of his slave, which he took as lost property. Indeed, he had lost any hope of recovering him ever since he spoke to the police the previous day, although he never let on to Tutu.

He heard that one of those injured had died the previous evening, which provoked the locals into marching to the precinct and demanding instant justice. They demanded the release of the black man responsible into their hands. He was given up to them after little resistance by the police and was immediately jumped upon and lynched, Smith heard.

Smith pushed the news to the back of his mind until he got home much later in the evening and was told Tutu was missing. Helen believed she had eloped, but he thought otherwise. When he had first heard the news, he had wondered how Tutu would react; now he feared suicide. With the reverend and his daughter still in Salem, he decided to go and search for her and choose where Emeka was hanged as his first point of call.

Not knowing where Emeka was hanged, he had to go into town to inquire where and was directed to the park.

Turning into the pitch dark deserted lane that led into the park, Smith was contemplating on shelving the idea and returning home, when he heard some sobs and a voice, which he identified as Tutu's. He went to the area from which the sobs were emanating and found Tutu crying and talking to herself or the corpse lying on her lap.

Sitting under the tree with her back against its trunk and Emeka's head rested on her lap, the sobs racked through her body intermittently and he could see she was in a state of shock.

As hard-headed and cold-hearted as most people thought Smith was, he had a soft spot for Tutu ever since she saved him and her present mournful state greatly moved him. Especially knowing how she felt about Emeka.

Momentarily shocked, he initially stood transfixed to a spot and speechless as he bit his lower lip trying to get hold of his emotions. Once he did, he crouched beside her and placed a comforting hand on her shoulder without a spoken word. Acknowledging his hand by resting her head on it, she once again was racked by violent sobs, which in effect made Smith's eyes moisten once again.

When her crying subsided, he said softly, "Come, let's go!" lifting the dead man's head off her lap. With no response, he decided to be a bit firmer, "Come on, Tutu," he barked as he pulled her on to her legs.

"No, I want to die! Let me just die!" she cried as she slumped to the ground, but Smith was apt to support her dead weight, before it got to the grass. "Please let me just die, before I kill everyone who loves me."

"No, you know that is not true; you didn't kill anyone."

"I killed my family, my mother and now my husband," she

grieved, "please free me from this suffering and just shoot me." After slumping thrice within a few yards, Smith realized they were not making any headway and decided to carry her. Slinging her over his shoulder, he was able to walk faster towards home.

To Helen's surprise and disdain, he carried her indoors and laid her in the living room, instructing Martha to clean and feed her, while he went to clean the blood off himself.

Angry, Helen followed him. "Anthony, are you out of your bloody mind? What is happening between you and the slave girl?" she asked acrimoniously, but was ignored by her husband, who continued to clean himself. "Why don't you tell the truth and say you got yourself a nigger mistress like some of the sailors," she shouted as she stood next to him.

Still there was no reaction, apart from Smith's facial muscles that tightened in anger. "I am talking to you, bastard. Do not ignore me because of a stupid African whore!"

Flustered, but still biting his tongue, he looked for a towel, when he finished washing off the blood.

"Let me just tell you that bitch isn't sleeping in my living room," she said fiercely, wanting a reaction from him.

"She sleeps where I say!" he answered sternly through clenched teeth as he dropped the towel to leave the room.

Helen grabbed hold of his elbow, "No, she isn't! You godforsaken piece of shit, you...." She didn't complete the curses because Smith gave her a backhanded slap, which jolted her head backward and burst her lip.

He regretted his loss of control immediately. "I am sorry," he apologized, but she would not have it and stormed out angrily for the bedroom. Smith went back to the living room and gave instructions to Martha to take care of Tutu and not to leave her alone.

When he retired for the day to the bedroom, he was met with stony silence. "I am sorry, I lost my temper with you, but you pushed me. I am not sleeping with the girl, I just feel sorry for her because she has been through a lot of pain," he said remorsefully.

"Hmm!" Helen grunted cynically and said nothing more

as she turned her back on him. Due to Helen's philandering father's history with women slaves, she had grown up feeling all men had weaknesses for black women. She blamed her mother's early death on her father's philandering, which explained why she often treated women slaves with jealousy and cruelty.

"I am telling you the honest truth. I told you about the fever that would have killed me, if not for her help, that's why I am grateful and treat her differently," he tried explaining to his wife, who when he pulled her to face him, angrily smacked his hand.

"I knew it. That's why you started sleeping with her, to show your gratitude," she shouted accusingly as she sat up to face him. "I want her out of this house!"

"Helen don't you have a heart? She has lost a father, mother and now a lover or husband. That is why I feel sorry for her," he tried persuading her as he undressed.

"You talk as if she is your first slave. Don't they all lose their family? Why don't you think before you come out with stupid excuses? Upon all the insults, you slapped me for her, Anthony," she said tearfully as the thought of it came back.

Smith shook his head in exasperation. "Truly, they might all lose their families and whatever, but this is the first one, who although I made lose her family, did not let my family lose me! Helen, I was already dictating my will on my deathbed, for Christ's sake!" he said, raising his voice in frustration.

As an afterthought, he said, "I did not hit you because of her, but because you were swearing at me." They continued arguing until they fell asleep.

The next morning before Smith woke up, Helen was quick to put Tutu out of the living room, telling her to move back to her slave quarters. When Smith woke up and noticed what she had done, he let it go for the sake of peace. Moreover, he was running late for a meeting in Boston.

Martha tried her best to be supportive of her friend, Tutu, by telling her own painful experiences. She made sure Tutu sat with her through her chores, although she did so with a distant look on her face, occasionally bursting into tears. Martha also tried easing her pain with humorous tales and jokes, but Tutu's sense of loss and pain was too immense for her to appreciate any humor.

Meanwhile, Helen came around intermittently, looking at the grief-stricken Tutu with anger and spite normally reserved for one's husband's mistress, although Tutu was too engrossed in her sorrow to notice facial expressions and hissing.

The day dragged on slowly, but finally night fell and everyone retired to their rooms, with Martha and Tutu sleeping in the same room in the slave quarters. Martha, having worked all day was bone tired by the time they got to their quarters and fell asleep as soon as she entered the room. Tutu, on the other hand, lay awake looking into the ceiling, as she had done the previous night.

A few hours after they had lain down, Tutu rose and called Martha's name softly but Martha was fast asleep. Certain Martha was asleep, she got up from her bed and went to the corner of the room, where there was some junk and extracted a rope. Stepping gently in order not to alert her, Tutu opened the door and stepped outside carrying a small stool and the rope.

Looking around briefly, she sighted a tree, which she went to and tied the rope to a branch, while stepping on the stool. After she finished tying it, she put the loop around her neck and kicked the stool away. Instead of dangling and hanging, the branch broke and dropped her onto her feet. She tried it once more, but landed on her backside to her frustration.

Looking around once more, she chose the biggest tree in the compound that she knew would support her weight. The problem was that its branches were higher up. That notwithstanding, she decided to use it, and climbed it in order to secure the noose onto one of its branches.

From her deep slumber Martha startled awake and could nearly have sworn someone tapped her awake. Sitting up in the bed, she could not see the person, who had tapped her feet and after a while, realized she could not see Tutu in her bed.

As she wondered what had happened, she heard what sounded like the breaking of wood, followed by a thud as well as a muffled sound of pain. She thought Tutu probably had tripped over something on her way back from urinating. After waiting for a few seconds without Tutu coming back into the room, she decided to go and check on her.

As she stepped out of the room, she noticed the broken branches of the two trees in front of the room, which she ignored and called out Tutu's name. With no answer and still undecided on what to do, she heard the rustling of leaves from another tree at the far right end of the quarters. For some reason she could not explain, she decided to check out what was rustling the leaves.

Just as she turned the corner, she saw Tutu leaping off the biggest tree in the compound. "Nooo!" she screamed as she ran to hold up Tutu's legs, so that her body weight would not give the pressure required to strangle her. Martha continued screaming to raise alarm in the compound and woke slaves and master alike.

The slaves ran to her, while Smith brought his gun since he didn't know the nature of the emergency. When he got to the backyard, the slaves had just cut the rope and were bringing her down. Tutu looked dazed and defeated, as she lay helplessly on the grass with everyone looking down at her with different expressions. Smith shook his head in dismay as he remained momentarily speechless, but soon regained his composure and ordered them to carry her into his living room.

Helen met them as they were bringing her into the living room. "For God sake, what is wrong again?" she asked peevishly and when she was told Tutu had just attempted suicide. "All she wants is attention," she hissed dismissively.

"I can't believe you at times. It seems I married a different woman," Smith threw up his hands in confusion and shook his head in disgust. He turned to Martha, "Now, I want you to sleep here with her. Do you understand?" he said sternly.

"Master, I was sleeping in the same room when she sneaked out to be stupid," Martha protested against the accusing look

Smith gave her. Helen and the other slaves soon returned to their beds, leaving the three of them in the living room.

Smith sat next to Tutu. "Look! Don't be stupid, you have a lot to live for. Get hold of yourself," he said, trying to appeal to her but she was inconsolable. Smith decided it was only Parris who could shake her out of the fatalistic depression.

Early the following morning, because he had no idea of where the Parrises were spending their weeklong holiday in Salem, he sent a message through their in-laws living down the road. In the meantime, he restricted Tutu by placing a chain around her ankle and Martha constantly in her tow, even when she had to use the bathroom.

Later that evening, Reverend Parris returned with his daughter and his niece, Ann Putnam. He was shocked and very distraught, when Smith recounted the events of the past couple of days.

The messenger had not known the reason for the emergency and was just told to tell the reverend to return immediately.

Taking the chains off her, he led her into a room, where he decided to make a heartfelt plea to her.

"I know how you feel, you may not believe me, but I absolutely do," he said morosely.

"You do?" she asked skeptically in what remained of her voice, having cried to a point, where it was husky and barely audible.

"Yes, I do! Therefore, I will not sit down and talk rubbish about not killing yourself because I know that if I were in your shoes, I would be thinking and probably would have done the same thing a long time ago," Parris said, reaching out to touch her tenderly.

"But please, listen to me before you decide to do what you want. I promise I will not stop you," he said, as Tutu for the first time looked into his eyes, not sure what he was leading to, but could feel his genuine feelings.

"All I want to say is that I know there were a couple of

people, who loved you and who you loved very much in return, and unfortunately they are all dead, all with the exception of me. You know, before all this started, we were friends and it has been a friendship I greatly value. You have saved my life, and my wife's," he said, pausing to control his emotions, although a tear rolled down.

"Please, Tutu, I know it is hard, but at least let the last of your friends, myself, go before you decide to go. I don't know how I would continue if you go without me. You are my best friend, but if I don't count, then you can leave," he said and rose to leave, when Tutu reached out to grab his cassock.

"Reverend, please don't leave. You do count. I won't kill myself. I thought I had no one left, but I was wrong. I am sorry. I know you have been my friend, before I met Emeka or even thought of any man. It's just that I loved him, and we had just agreed to marry, when they killed him," she said desolately and broke into tears.

The reverend put an arm around her shoulder and tried consoling her, but her sorrow was beyond consolation and he let her cry her heart out. Afterwards, when the crying subsided, he pulled her to her feet and led her for a walk around the compound.

"So you two were going to get married? I always thought that would happen eventually. I wonder why it even took that long," he commented as they walked around the grounds, in order to keep her talking and thinking less of mourning.

"My mother warned me that if I let him come too close, he would be killed, so I refused when he asked in Jamaica. Ever since we reached here, due to my loneliness, I thought I could go ahead, but instead I killed the poor man," she said and once again became tearful.

After the crying subsided, Parris decided to change the topic to safer grounds, which he could control.

"I got the job in Salem, and we will be moving there after Christmas," he informed her.

His sister and her husband's family had been able to swing

some powerful political backing to his side and it was finally agreed that he should be the next minister of Salem, and he would be well paid. This had a divisive effect within the already politically beleaguered town, but nevertheless he won with a slight majority among the selectmen and other political and church officials.

"You would probably end up doing what I did for you — teaching little children. There is nothing like it. You make friends for life, and you never know what they might become in future. Although I don't seem to have done a good job with my wards." He said lightly as he tried to get her mind off her present sorrow.

"Stop it Reverend, you know you have done me a lot of good. You were the first to get me my freedom from my mother, and now you are the one helping me. I wish I could be like you to some child," she said.

This brought a smile to the pastor's face, who noticed she was already talking about making a difference in someone else's life, which he believed was a step away from her suicidal depression. They stayed outside until very late, when everyone had gone to sleep and before leaving her, he was sure there would be no more suicide attempts.

Nevertheless, Tutu was a shadow of her normal ebullient self as she often fell into depression, especially when she felt her loneliness and boredom. Parris ensured she did no chores, which was to Helen's deep consternation that couldn't understand why the men treated this slave so differently. When Parris noticed she was still very depressed, which he rightly identified as loneliness, he tried to spend more time with her. By the end of the week, he devised a plan to keep her busy, which was making her teach his daughter, Betty and her visiting cousin, Ann Putnam.

While Emeka was alive, although Tutu took good care of Betty, she rarely sat and played with her, despite Betty's cries for attention. Now with Emeka gone and no one except Martha, who was constantly overworked, the girls became her friends. They enjoyed her stories, especially the ones about Africa and she also taught them all that Reverend Parris had imparted to her.

They soon became an item as she taught and played games with them all day, everyday. They appeared to be having so much fun that the Smith children wanted to join them, but their mother would not have a slave girl teach and play with her children.

Helen resented the whole arrangement and made it known in clear terms, despite her husband's apparent disregard for her feelings over the matter. Parris, on the other hand, who could see a part of his wife in her, tried to allay her fears; otherwise she would have thrown Tutu out.

Regardless, things completely went out of hand on one particular occasion. It started when the Smith children disregarded their mother's restrictions and sneaked to meet the other children where Tutu taught them under the tree that she had made the final suicide attempt.

On her return from her outing, Helen sighted her children under the tree, where they had joined Tutu and the other children. Furious that her orders were flouted, she went to disperse the little group with a whip.

The children fled, when they saw their enraged mother coming, but that did not stop her from bringing the whip down on Tutu.

Initially Tutu backed away, but when chased around the compound, Tutu stood her ground and wrestled the whip away from her. While the two women wrestled for the whip, Helen not only lost the weapon but her balance.

With all the frustration coming to the surface, Tutu moved in to give Helen a taste of her own medicine. Tutu, with a foot over Helen effectively pinning her down, was about to bring the whip down on her, when her hand was held from behind. Parris, who had seen the whole incident unfold from his bedroom window and ran to stop it, held her hand.

"Let go, Tutu! Don't do what you will regret later," he implored the enraged woman, who looked at him, softened and let go of the cane. He then helped a baffled and scared Helen to her feet. She stormed off without saying a word.

Later that evening, Helen told her husband that Tutu had attacked her, but he didn't believe her and when pressed said, "if you push a dog to the wall, it would eventually turn back and bite you."

"Fine, I want her out of this house immediately, or I will shoot her on sight," she threatened, but Smith chose to ignore her.

It was Parris, who went to great lengths to pacify her and promised to get Tutu out of her way by the end of the month, by which time he expected to resume in Salem. In turn, he told Tutu to stay out of her way and not teach her children anymore.

"Master, I cannot chase away little children because their mother doesn't want them to learn from me. You did not, otherwise I would not be here with you today," she protested. The Reverend was initially dumbfounded by the reference to how they had established their relationship and stuttered, before regaining his composure.

"This is not the same situation and, for your own good, listen to my advice," he warned her unconvincingly and walked away shaking his head in frustration.

"Maybe we should pray for a little sickness," he heard her say as he was walking away.

The following morning, Helen came down with a serious flu, which made her bed-bound and unable to disturb anyone. The children were then able to join the other children without fear, although Helen occasionally saw them from her room window.

She accused Tutu of bewitching her, but no one took any notice of her grumbling, which they associated with her illness coupled with her pathological hatred for Tutu. Fortunately, for the children and Tutu, she did not recover until the day after the Parrises and Tutu left for Salem.

In Annapolis, by the time Judith recovered from her long illness in December, the women had decided it would be better to bring her into their camp to help fight the enemy. A few weeks after she had fully recuperated and was making plans to go up north to bring down her family, she was once again invited to the Rogers house.

"It may surprise you, if I tell you we were the cause of the wind that diverted your ship. Actually, we wanted to sink the ship due to the presence of that girl," Angela confessed to her.

Judith, surprised and confused, looked at her sister-in-law, Pat, who nodded in agreement. "How? Please, I don't understand."

"Well as they say behind every successful man is a woman, although not only successful men but communities. We come together to ensure the continued success of our families and communities by all means necessary, sometimes spiritually," Pat explained and stopped to look at Angela to continue.

"Although we have some outside psychics who help us, we learn and use everything to accomplish our aims. Some might call us witches, but we do no evil and work for the progress of all," Angela paused for the acknowledging nods and grunts to subside.

"A few months ago, we learnt that a strong spiritual force was on its way to wreck all that we have struggled to build. We put a watch out and luckily identified the spiritual presence on that ship, but since we could not say who embodied it precisely, we had to endeavor to stop it by all means. Unfortunately, we failed and were struck by thunder, which caused that fire," Angela told a shocked Judith.

"The force or girl is very powerful as you can see from what happened in Jamaica and the fire. Nevertheless, we need to destroy her, before she destroys us and we do need your help," Pat said.

"My help?" Judith asked in disbelief. "How?"

"We thought we were alright as long as she was not here, but our psychics saw otherwise. Unless destroyed, she will cause great upheavals across this land. Therefore, we need you to go along with your plan and bring her down here, where we can stop her."

"So please, whatever you do, ensure that you bring the family down and do not let her know you are onto her game; otherwise you and your family would be in great danger. Under no circumstances should she know any of this, which is why we are not making any spiritual incursions into her realm," Angela told Judith, who was finding it all strange but interesting.

"Can I join you? I also need powers to help me in my endeavors as well. Maybe if we had something like this in Jamaica, we could have stopped her beforehand."

The women surprised by the request, were momentarily dumbfounded, until Angela broke the awkward silence.

"We will look into that some other time, but I don't see any reason why you can't, once we overcome this threat. That is the first and most important thing we should concentrate on eliminating, otherwise we will have nothing left to build or protect," Angela said.

Shortly afterwards, the women set out for their different homes and destinations.

At home, Judith and Pat tried to convince Frank that it would be easier if a plantation were already in place before setting out to bring the family down. With a plantation, she thought, she might be able to convince her husband to come down, although she knew the control and running of the plantation would mainly be in her hands.

Choosing the appropriate land and making the necessary arrangements needed to set up a plantation took quite a while and Judith had to change her travel plans.

14

The Parrises and Tutu did not move into the refurbished Salem minister's residence until February 1690, because of a delay by the builders. The house was a two-storey building with four bedrooms on the top floor and a large living room, dining room and kitchen downstairs. At one side of the living room, closer to the entrance from the porch, there was a wooden staircase that led to the top floor. At the landing, there was a beautiful candelabrum that provided light for those going up or down the steps, at the top of which was the entrance to the first room that would become the girls' room.

At the back were the pantry and slave quarters for three, where Tutu was to reside by herself. Tutu was overjoyed when they finally left Helen Smith's house, and she looked forward to their new life in Salem. Moreover, upon their arrival, Parris' sister, Theresa, welcomed them and made Tutu feel at ease.

If Judith and Helen were Tutu's worst nightmare, Theresa came to be the complete opposite. Theresa warmly accepted Tutu once they moved to Salem, showing her around and always willing to help. This was partly due to Theresa realizing that Tutu was very much endeared to Parris, who had told her about everything that had transpired from Africa to the present. Apart from that, Theresa was a naturally fair and sweet person, who never said an angry word to her slaves.

In addition, her daughter, Ann had told her a lot about Tutu, of whom she was very much fond. Tutu was impressed to meet the first European woman she could call nice and friendly.

Theresa was never too distant from the newcomers whose house was nearby. The minister's house as expected was located next to the church in the growing town.

Salem was one of the fastest growing towns in North America being a seaport town that attracted many people from different lands. Its merchants traded in the West Indies, Africa and South-East Asia. It did not have any agricultural products of its own, but processed molasses from the Caribbean Islands.

Despite its growth and seemingly peaceful environment, it had a deep political rift that split the town into groups. The groups were aligned into two main camps—the Porter family and the Putnam family.

It was the Putnam family that supported Parris' appointment and the Parrises felt some antagonism from the Porters, once they arrived in Salem. This came, especially, from their defeated candidate, Michael Lewis, who became Parris' assistant.

One such antagonism surfaced when Reverend Parris decided to allow Tutu to teach the children in the church's Sunday school.

Although Michael Lewis never said anything to Parris, he went around telling people about the "new development" in the church, which was rather "asinine and objectionable." Many people raised strong objections over what they called "bringing a Negro to darken our children's perception."

To reach a compromise, Parris agreed to make an Irish woman, Sarah Good, the head of the Sunday school, while Tutu was her assistant. Notwithstanding, Lewis made it a point of duty to make things difficult for Tutu since he could not get to her master, Parris. Fortunately, she was able to ignore Michael Lewis' trouble-making intrusions most of the time, or she reported them to Parris, who was able to counter them.

She greatly enjoyed her role in the Sunday school, which gave her the opportunity to mix with a wide range of people. Once again, she was able to sing, which she taught the children. The school was a large one with churchgoers' children, up to the age of thirteen attending.

The colony of Massachusetts placed a high premium on education and enacted a compulsory education edict for all children. Therefore, apart from the education received during the week, parents sent their kids to the Sunday school. This also had the added advantage of allowing the parents to pay attention to their Sunday worship without disturbance from their children.

There were a number of other slaves who brought their owner's children to the school, where they were expected to stay and watch over them. Many brought their masters' babies and toddlers, who could not learn anything, but were part of a playgroup or nursery.

It was from these slaves that Tutu made new friends, with whom she often exchanged news and gossips, while their masters' children played with each other.

Apart from teaching and caring for some of the children, Tutu's chores included cleaning and preparing the church and its school before service or occasional meetings. Although it was heavy work, she was lucky to do it only once or twice a week and only did light housekeeping and cooking at home during the rest of the week. The arrangement greatly suited her and she was enjoying herself to the hilt, being able to push her horrific past to the back of her mind.

This blissful existence continued for a month after they arrived in Salem, but suddenly she withdrew and became moody. Parris soon noticed Tutu's depressed and sad countenance, which he initially regarded as only temporary in nature, but by the second week, he began to grow concerned.

On the first two occasions, Tutu claimed there was nothing bothering her, but knowing her well enough, he knew she was not being honest with him.

He noticed she could not look him in the eye when speaking and generally avoided him. Also, he noticed she was increasingly irritable with the children, who were also perplexed over her changed disposition, enough to ask him the reason behind her sudden change.

One Sunday after service, Parris decided to broach the subject again with her. "Tell me are you unhappy with anything here or what is wrong with you?" he urged her. Initially she remained adamant and said nothing was wrong, but with his persistence, she broke down in tears.

"I am carrying Emeka's baby!" she blurted out tearfully to the reverend's surprise.

She was able to push back all the painful memories, especially of Emeka, until she discovered she was pregnant a month after their arrival. When she realized she was nearly four months pregnant, all her painful memories came flooding back and she became very depressed. The most painful and prominent memory was the lynching of the father of her unborn baby.

To compound her desolation was the fact that she was scared to break the news to Parris. She was fully aware of the Puritan environment in which they existed, and the highly moralistic and intrusive values that prevailed in it. Parris being a custodian of those puritan values was not the best person to be approached by an unmarried mother, Tutu had thought.

Moreover, there was Michael Lewis, who, she believed, would surely make another campaign issue out of it. Keeping her secret to herself further depressed her as did the morning sickness that affected her physical and emotional well-being. Parris' initial silence that followed confirmed her fears of rejection by him on moral grounds and she quickly tried to explain herself.

"I did not plan it this way," she cried. "We had just planned to get married, when they killed him. Please don't be mad with me."

"Nonsense! Why did you not tell me all along? If anything, I am mad with you for not telling me you were pregnant. No one is going to judge you wrongly for carrying Emeka's child, at least not I, who clearly knows what happened. I am very disappointed that you have known for weeks and held back from me," he said gravely, showing his disappointment.

"I am sorry, I was just scared of what might happen."

Parris shook his head disapprovingly. "What is going to happen is no excuse for not telling the truth. Anyway, thank God it is all out and we can see to your proper treatment," Parris concluded to Tutu's relief. Although it all became too much for her, and she burst into tears.

Due to his lack of understanding of pregnancy and women's needs, he told his sister, Theresa, of the situation and she volunteered to help. Theresa came to talk and advise Tutu about how to take care of herself and the baby, having had the experience of three children herself.

"You have to stop worrying. Eat and rest to keep both of you healthy," Theresa advised and made sure she visited more regularly. Theresa instructed the girls to be more helpful in the running of the house, although Tutu wouldn't let them do much.

Over the next couple of days, she returned to her normal self and even began to find strength in the fact that Emeka was not completely dead, but was growing inside her. She objected to Parris' suggestion that she should reduce her workload in the church and Sunday school, which served as her social forum, where she met all her friends.

When Judith eventually arrived back in Boston just before the end of March 1690, she was informed that her family had moved to Salem, and she had to continue northward to reunite with them. Her arrival was quite a surprise, but a pleasant one only for her daughter. Parris had the intuition that his wife's return spelt trouble and the arguments that had been deferred were about to be reopened, a task he dreaded.

For Tutu, she knew the arrival of her madam would bring about changes that would be detrimental to her and was troubled by her arrival. To everyone's surprise, Judith was calm and pleasant in the first few days after her arrival, although Parris and Tutu were not fooled as they likened it to the calm before a storm. She was pleasant to Tutu and even asked about her well-being and her pregnancy.

After a week, she broached the subject of moving down south with her husband, who objected strenuously. She argued that he could always continue his preaching in Annapolis, and she needed him to support her on the plantation.

The income from the plantation would allow them to continue the standard of living that they were used to, but Parris claimed that the salary he was paid was more than enough to enable them live comfortably. A minister's salary in Massachusetts was quite high, and they were viewed as community leaders.

Gradually, the pleasantries were replaced with rancor, as husband and wife couldn't see eye to eye over the direction the family should take. They constantly argued late into the night and refused to speak to each other for days at a time.

As they both witnessed the return of the headstrong Judith, Parris and Tutu were surprised it did not extend to Tutu. Judith treated Tutu with some form of officious reverence, keeping her at arm's length most of the time. She refused to eat anything Tutu cooked, but did not say anything harsh to her.

The only other person to experience some antagonism from Judith was Theresa Putnam. Judith viewed her as an adversary, being the one who found her husband the job, who was capable of disrupting her plans. In addition, Judith was repulsed by the way she treated Tutu like a friend and family member. Although there was no open confrontation between the women, their relationship was frosty and they both avoided each other as much as possible.

After four weeks of no progress with moving the family, she decided to return to Annapolis, although she made it clear she was not giving up, but needed to take care of important business in Annapolis.

On her return to Annapolis, she informed the women of her problem, hoping they might be able to help.

"He seems to be fully entrenched in that stupid town and has started working as its minister. I am confused on what to do," she raised her concerns with the attentive women.

"Why is that? Is it the slave or are there some other problems you encountered?" Angela questioned with genuine concern.

"Yes! Although, his slave is still there with him, I avoided her as much as possible. She is pregnant for a slave I heard was hanged because of her. In addition, there is his sister, who he just reunited with, that has joined forces with them against me. You can't believe how I felt in my own house. I was like an uninvited stranger," Judith blurted out her frustrations to the visiting women, who came to her brother's house for tea.

"Pregnant?" Angela asked with some concern. "That is a problem! We can't allow her to bring that child into this land, for we do not know what the child might turn out to be," she said, prompting agreeing nods from the other women.

"So what do I do?" Judith asked the women in a helpless tone.

Following a brief thoughtful silence, Angela spoke. "I think you should hold on for some time, while we work out a better plan," she advised. "We can't work on her, but maybe we could use someone else indirectly. I would let you know how it goes."

In Salem, Tutu was at the center of the budding congregation, which provided her with a widening circle of friends. With Judith out of the way, everything was peaceful and amicable in Tutu's immediate surroundings, except for Lewis that took it upon himself to spread the news of the "unmarried mother." This near blissful existence continued until her sixth month of pregnancy.

Out of Tutu's increased circle of friends, she was closest to a particular black woman, who belonged to one of Salem's prominent families. The family had four children, ranging from ages four to eleven, while the slave woman, Carol, was eighteen years old.

Carol's main duty was to look after the four-year-old toddler during the service, although she frequently had to put the unruly older children in check. At home, Carol was experiencing gross mistreatment and abuse from her owners and found solace in Tutu, with whom she shared her horrid experiences.

Their friendship grew stronger over months as Tutu provided a shoulder for her to cry upon every Sunday, the only day she was "free" to talk to anyone. Although Tutu had the best in the slave world, she missed having an understanding person with whom she shared experiences. Moreover, Tutu was experiencing hormonal changes, which made her emotional many a times, despite Parris' efforts to make things easier for her.

Unfortunately, an incident occurred during the Sunday school session on 7th of May 1691, the fourth month of their friendship, which was to greatly affect them in different ways.

Two of the oldest children of the Andrews family started playing rough as usual, jumping from ledges, chairs and any high spots they could find. Carol, in between her talking with Tutu, tried to bring them under control, but to no avail since they had no regard for her. Unfortunately, just before the end of the day's service and school, they pushed their eight-year-old sister off a ledge, who landed on her head and fell unconscious.

While Carol panicked out of fear of what would happen when her owners arrived, Tutu remained calm and tried reviving the girl. She had just revived the girl, although still with a bleeding broken nose, when her mother walked in to collect them. Seeing her only daughter in the state she was, the mother panicked and rushed to her side as Tutu was cleaning her bleeding nose and forehead.

Panic-stricken, the woman turned to her boys, "what happened to your sister?" she demanded loudly. The guilt-ridden boys were too scared to tell the truth seeing their mother in the state she was, especially knowing her ferocious temper and quick hand.

After a second and increasingly agitated inquiry by their mother, the oldest boy decided to take the easiest way out. Knowing how their mother treated the slave, Carol, having whipped her just before coming to church, "Carol, beat her mother, because you beat her this morning," he stuttered. The mother looked at his younger brother briefly to confirm and he nodded in agreement to the lie. Before Carol could deny it, Beatrice Andrews pounced on her, raining her with vicious blows and kicks.

"No! No! Please, it wasn't me! Sorry," the poor Carol cried

as she tried unsuccessfully, to avoid the blows heading her way. Unfortunately, Beatrice caught her in a corner and she was unable to escape.

Surprised and at the same time disgusted, Tutu shouted, "Stop! Stop!!" at the attacking mother and rose from the side of the girl she was nursing to intervene. She tried to talk to the irate Mrs. Andrews, but with no success and had no choice, but to restrain her as Carol started to bleed from the nose and mouth. Tutu put her hands around Beatrice Andrews, pinning her arms to her side, but the big woman could not be easily pacified.

As Tutu tried to restrain her from hitting Carol and a struggle ensued between them, Mr. Andrews walked in. Gordon Andrews did not bother to ask what was going on for as far as he was concerned; a black slave was attacking his wife. He immediately jumped to what he thought was the rescue of his wife.

Throwing his six foot four inch, 250-pound frame into action, he yanked Tutu by her hair away from his wife and punched her right in the face. Tutu was stunned as she was jerked backwards and punched in the face. Followed with another blow to the head, she collapsed onto the floor.

Not satisfied, the couple turned their rage on her and continued to kick her in the head and stomach, until she lost consciousness. Luckily, Parris walked in soon afterwards and was shocked to find Tutu bleeding from her mouth and midsection. The Andrews were just about to leave.

"My God! What happened?" he exclaimed as he crouched beside Tutu.

"Your slave went wild and attacked my wife and I had to give her a good beating," Mr. Andrews answered, when he saw the other Sunday school pupils point to him.

"I find that hard to believe. She is not like that," Parris said expressing his doubts over the man's story as he lifted up Tutu, who was unconscious on the ground.

"Yes. She attacked me because I was disciplining my slave for beating and injuring my daughter. I know they were friends, but I didn't know she would have the effrontery to attack me,"

Mrs. Andrews said with an air of haughtiness as Parris carried Tutu away.

Tutu woke up six hours later to a swollen head, stiff neck, sore arms and most devastatingly, an empty womb. She lost the baby, having sustained numerous kicks in the stomach and hours of hemorrhaging from the womb.

To Parris' surprise, she never cried or showed any emotion in front of him, but he knew her heart was bleeding. He tried everything for her to show emotions, apart from her frigid expression, but he realized that something more than the baby had died inside her—her heart.

After the initial shock and confusion, when she discovered that she was pregnant, she had been overjoyed that something left of Emeka was growing inside her as well as having something, which belonged to her for the first time. She was hoping that the baby would come out looking like Emeka or one of her lost parents, the thought of which greatly excited her.

Now with the forced miscarriage, she felt empty and bitter with nothing to look forward to in her life, although to her surprise she remained cool and even aloof. She remained in bed for barely a week, despite Parris' objections, and resumed her duties. The priest suggested canceling the Sunday school, especially since the Irish woman, Sarah, had resigned following the attack, but Tutu insisted on continuing and assured him of her physical and emotional well-being.

Theresa came to talk to her and ensure that she was physically all right as her brother requested her to do. She was able to get through to Tutu and knew how she felt having suffered a few miscarriages herself and was crucial in making her feel at ease.

"I know you might believe everything and everyone is going against you, that we are all heartless people, but that is not the case. These are just a few mean-spirited people even we have been having problems with," she told Tutu, when she misconstrued her aloofness toward her.

The following Sunday, the Andrews did not bring their

children to the Sunday school, although they attended the adult service next door. Tutu missed Carol, although she mixed and joked with the other slaves that came with their masters' children. Everyone had heard of the incident and asked about her well-being, but she gave them more or less the same answers that she had given Parris.

Deep inside she was burning with rage and determination to exact revenge, but she knew she had to be careful. Due to the publicity the incident generated, she decided to let everything die down before she made her move. Notwithstanding, after service she tailed the Andrews home, always staying at a distance and out of sight. She saw they lived in a big mansion manned by a number of slaves, but never saw Carol. She decided she was going to exact her punishment slowly.

The following weeks as Carol and the Andrews children did not return to the Sunday school, Tutu established new relationships with other blacks. One of such friendships was with Jennifer, who was experiencing problems similar to that of Carol's.

About a fortnight after her violent miscarriage, a heavy May thunderstorm took place in Salem. The largest distillery in Massachusetts, belonging to the Andrews, was struck by a thunderbolt, and due to the presence of highly flammable materials it was completely razed.

When Parris raised it with Tutu, she smiled and said, "It is only the beginning of their suffering." Parris took it at face value and said nothing, believing she had every reason to be mad.

What he did not realize was she was not getting sad or mad anymore, but even and by all accounts, she believed, she was still far from getting even. In fact, he was even glad she voiced some emotions because he believed she was keeping everything bottled up. He really wished he could match-make her with someone, who might relieve all her stress.

Parris' wish seemed to be answered soon afterwards, but was met with resistance. Martin, a male slave of the Porters and new church member, became besotted with her.

One Sunday in July 1690, while Tutu was instructing one of the children, he came to sit next to her. He sat so close Tutu could feel the warmth of his slender body as he rubbed against her, despite her trying to move away. When it became obvious he was interested and wanted to say something, which reminded her of Emeka trying to express his feelings for her, she decided to bring it out in the open and put an end to any dreams.

"Martin, who is your wife?" she asked, catching him off guard and smiling at his discomposure.

"Uh...I do not have one. Why?" he stuttered as he tried to get himself out of the ambush, pinching his big wide African nose.

"That is strange! I was wondering who was loving a handsome man like you," she said, obviously patronizing him and enjoying herself.

Scratching his head out of habit, when confused, "I...I was thinking of err...girl, I love you, Tutu," he blurted out and felt relieved getting it off his chest.

"Hmm. How can you? You have only seen me twice before today," she asked seriously, but when she saw his expression, she could not stop herself from laughing.

"Yeah, that's true, but I have being looking for a woman like you all my life," he answered with all seriousness, but added, " and that is why I came to America," which provoked laughter from Tutu.

"Welcome! I advise you to keep looking," she snapped coldly to stop him from thinking his overtures were working, but when she saw him shudder and shrink, she decided not to be too mean.

"Listen, Martin, I think you are a nice man that deserves a good loving woman, but I can't love you. I can't love any black man anymore, otherwise I would bring him bad luck, harm and even death," Tutu said, and paused to let it sink in as she could see she had gained his utmost attention with the last statement.

"Everyone I have ever loved has been killed, and I can't do that to anyone anymore, if I really love him. That's why I advised you to keep looking or you would die," she told him calmly, but frankly.

"What if I say I don't mind dying for you," Martin retorted stubbornly, refusing to give up on his dream partner.

"Don't be stupid!" smiling, Tutu smacked him lightly on his thigh, before changing to a stern expression. "Listen, I appreciate how you feel, but it is not whether you are willing to die for me, it is whether I want another life to be lost on my account and the answer is no!" she said with a resounding finality.

She stood up and went to some other child across the room that needed attention. Although Martin said nothing further that day, the following week he continued and Tutu met all his overtures with at best, indifference and at worst, outright rudeness. Nonetheless, he continued his quest.

15

In Annapolis, Theresa tried to get the plantation up and running, but she met various obstacles being a woman. It increasingly became evident that without her husband around, she would not be able to make it a success of it. This greatly distressed her, as she didn't have a clue on how to get Parris to Annapolis. Her only hope was Angela Rogers' promise to find a way around it.

It took nearly a month before Angela Rogers and the other women got back to her with another plan on how to get Parris down to Salem and tackle Tutu. Knowing how most towns work in the Massachusetts colony, it was suggested by the women that Judith should go back to Salem and use local political connections to flush out Parris.

Toward the end of June the women met in Angela's house to discuss how to accomplish the mission.

"Well, she can talk to my brother in Salem and see if he could be of any help. I do know he wields a lot of influence in the town. Our family has been in Salem for fifty years and although I haven't been up there for sometime, I guess he should be able to help," Pat told the women as they discussed over tea.

Pat Lawrence was formerly Ms. Porter and grew up in Salem, before meeting Frank on a visit to Annapolis to see a friend. She and Frank developed a relationship and soon got married after they met.

"That would be the best thing to do," Angela admitted. "It is difficult to attack her from here, unless we have something personal of hers to work on, which is why it is better to get her down here."

"Isn't there anyone with spiritual powers up there that could help in attacking her?" Judith asked.

"Yes, there are a few women there, but they are not strong enough to take on this kind of challenge. They only formed a circle not too long ago and I would advise against it, although I informed a friend among them about Tutu's presence and cautioned them about going after her." Angela told her.

"Make sure you don't tell anybody to help you tackle her when you get back. It is dangerous. Don't even let her know you are aware of her powers, otherwise you would be putting yourself in grave danger", one of the women advised Judith sternly.

"You just have to work with my brother and others to get him out of Salem, unless you can get enough of her personal belongings for us to work with here in Annapolis", Pat told her sister-in-law.

Judith knew it would be difficult to lay her hands on Tutu's personal items, since she didn't have enough not to know some were missing. Therefore she was left with no other choice but to try the plan. She also decided to take along her niece, Abigail, so she could become acquainted with Betty.

It was hoped that once both girls became friends and Abigail was returning, it would also help to put additional pressure on Rev. Parris, when Betty decided she wanted to follow her cousin back to Annapolis due to her lack of playmates in Salem.

Immediately she returned to Salem in July, Judith set out to find Pat's brother, Mr. Porter, being her main hope of success. With hindsight, she realized the second part of her plan was weak, since Betty already had a close friendship with her paternal cousin, Ann Putnam.

To her pleasant surprise, it was not only easy finding the Porters, she found out they wielded immense political clout in Salem and only recently lost their grip on the town and church.

She found Porter to be quite friendly and willing to help her. Porter, a hefty middle-aged man with joined eyebrows and a cold stare of a merchant, was shocked and initially embarrassed to find out that the man he had fought against becoming Salem's minister was in fact an in-law.

"Your husband is in the wrong crowd. Those Putnam's are trash and we really fought against their candidate, not knowing that his wife was against his appointment," Porter told her as they spoke in his living room with his wife, Pamela.

"I guess you want to be near your family in Annapolis," Pamela commented. She was a tall, redhead, mother of three in her early thirties with an oval pretty face. Pamela was affable like her husband, but she sometimes came across as arrogant.

"Yes, but the point is if he was a merchant I won't have been against it, but we need the income from the plantation if he is to be a preacher. We have always had a plantation and when he decided he wanted to join the clergy, I took over the running of the plantation, which is what I am begging him to do now. He could preach in Annapolis, but he should give us a chance to make extra money. The work of which I don't mind doing".

Porter nodded in agreement as he thought of what he could do to help. "At present, there isn't much we can do, but we are working hard to secure back the control of the town hall and church. Once that happens, which I assure you would happen soon, we would be setting him on his way. So just wait around for a while and things will be all right", he assured Judith.

"You are going to have to stay around to take immediate advantage once that happens. Otherwise, he could easily find himself another job somewhere around", Pamela advised her.

"Well, it seems I have no choice but to wait. Things aren't working out in Annapolis with the plantation, so I just have to wait and hope things will turn out as you say", Judith said. She tried to cover her disappointment that nothing could be done immediately and hoped their assurances would not be in vain.

In the meantime, Judith and Pamela Porter took to each other and soon became close friends, although Judith told her nothing about witchcraft. She did not know how to broach the issue without exposing those in Annapolis.

At home, warning lights flashed, when Parris noticed that on the return of his wife, who did not bring up the relocation issue, she became an item with the Porters, his chief antagonists. He could not believe his misfortune when she informed him the Porter's were her brother's in-laws. Parris knew it was only a matter of time before they planned something against him. However, he was pleased that Pamela never came to their house.

If his wife's silence over their movement to Annapolis intrigued him, he found her continued attitude towards Tutu more baffling. It would appear to him she was scared of Tutu and treated her with some form of reverence he could not place. Still refusing to eat anything from her, she sent her on no errands and rarely spoke to her. He could not believe his eyes when they once bumped into each other, which was clearly Tutu's fault, but his wife was overly apologetic.

As months passed, Parris continued to be baffled by what brought about the change in his wife, who remained in Salem without mentioning anything about Annapolis or causing trouble for Tutu. Although it was a pleasant change, he felt uneasy about it, knowing his wife he believed she had an ace up her sleeve, especially with her unholy alliance with the Porters.

Tutu retained the distant cool aloofness she took on after discovering the loss of her unborn child. Although Parris noticed and continued to speak to her about easing out the pain, the change was not very noticeable to outsiders with whom she had increased dealings.

In November 1690, exactly a year after Emeka's death, Tutu took up her healing practice among black slaves and very few, mostly poor, whites. This did not bother Parris since he believed it was purely herbal medicine with no spiritual involvement.

At church, she continued her duties with no further incidents and actually ran the Sunday school mostly on her own. Her circle of friends continued to grow among the slaves, who often found her easy to bare their souls to over their sufferings in their new homes. In the absence of Carol, Jennifer remained her closest friend, probably due to the fact that she suffered the most horrible acts from her owners.

Martin, who despite the shabby treatment she continuously meted out to him to discourage his emotional and sexual overtures, was gradually winning her favor due to his persistence. He always tried to make her smile with his witty conversations and pleasant surprises, especially on New Year's Day and Easter 1691.

Nevertheless, she kept up, what was now clearly pretence, his mistreatment by shunning and embarrassing him. After nine months of his persistence, she knew deep down she was gradually becoming fond of him, his jokes and other mannerisms and was only pretending, which was getting harder for her to do.

One Sunday in May 1691, after service and school, Martin stayed behind to help her clean up after failing to attract her attention during school. Throughout the session, he had practically followed her around the class, but she was able to constantly avoid him or slip away.

Seeing him pick up trash after Sunday school, Tutu could not but comment. "Why are you so stubborn! Don't you have a better use of your life?" she asked as her frown melted into a smile.

"What is the meaning of life, if you can't love and live because of the fear of death. I have given up my body for the fear of death, should I also be forced to give up my heart, my love and my soul for the fear of death too?" he asked in such a melodramatic fashion that Tutu was moved.

"Stop! Please stop this, Martin," she clamored painfully and sighed before continuing, "I have already told you, I lost my husband and baby just over a year ago." Actually, it was a year to the day she lost her baby and it was making her somewhat emotional. The memory not only brought back the pain of the loss, but a yearning to fulfill her maternal instincts. There was a heavy silence between them for about five minutes, while he put the chairs together and she swept the floor.

"Martin, won't your master be looking for you?" she broke the silence with a measure of concern.

"I guess so. I'll find something to tell them," he said nonchalantly as he sulked.

"I don't want you to get into trouble over me, Martin. Please don't do this," she said in a worried tone.

"Okay, I will leave, if you give me a hug," he said, smiling and opening his arms wide. She hesitated, but knew there was no way out without hurting his feelings, which she did not want to do anymore. Therefore she walked into his open arms. As he kissed her on the lips to Tutu's surprise, Parris walked in and stopped in his tracks. Embarrassed, Martin released her from his hold and hurriedly left the room.

"I am sorry if I disturbed anything," Parris said, with a hint of sarcasm.

Tutu smiled as she noticed it. "No, you did not disturb anything. He was just saying goodbye," she answered.

"What a goodbye! With a goodbye like that, who would want to say hello?" he said as he sat on the table, while Tutu tried to look busy. "So, is that your new lover?"

With her back towards him, Tutu smiled, but turning towards him, she feigned sadness, "No! Nobody wants me."

"Come on! A beautiful young woman like you should have no problem attracting men in droves. Actually, I expect them to be pestering you every minute."

"Well, I was just joking," she smiled shyly. "Yeah, he has been pestering me every minute he sets his eyes on me, although I keep telling him I am not ready for any man." She confided in him.

"Why is that?" Parris asked curiously as he shifted on the table.

Tutu shrugged, unwilling to delve into her reasons, which she knew he would dismiss easily. "I just don't want any more of my people dying because of me."

"Come on, you've got to get over it and get on with your life. You are..." Parris feigned disappointment and irritation, but before he could continue, a church member came in asking for his help.

As weeks went by, Tutu and Martin became closer as he continued to pressure her, until she finally caved in to his demands. They began seeing each other outside church times and paid each other visits at home. Martin was a domestic slave and was usually able to squeeze in visits to Tutu, whenever he went on errands or to the market.

One day in December about seven months into what remained essentially a platonic relationship, Martin was sent on an errand and chose to stop over at Tutu's.

"Hey, what are you doing here at this time of the day?" Tutu asked, pleasantly surprised to see him. It was early evening, but due to the early winter that December, it was dark and cold, and the streets were empty.

"I have just escaped," he replied in a low guarded voice. "Are you coming with me, Princess?"

"What?" she exclaimed in surprise and was briefly at a loss for words. "I am not running anywhere with you unless you have a ship to take us back home," she said seriously.

"That's no problem. I can steal a ship," but he couldn't keep up the pretence and burst into laughter.

"You are crazy," she hissed, when she realized he was joking. "Anyway I knew you were joking," she said coyly. "So what are you doing here at this time?"

"I just miss you and told my ma'am I want to see you. If she wants she could hold my wages for the day," he said serious faced, provoking laughter from Tutu.

"You are a jester, ain't you? I guess that is why I like you," she said fondly as she placed a hand on his shoulder.

"No, I am not a jester. It's just that any time I see you, I feel so happy and try to make you happy as well," he said, as he pulled her closer to kiss her.

"Stop, you are going down that road again," she protested weakly and pulled away from him to his obvious dissatisfaction.

He followed her. "Tutu, if I can't go down the road of freedom, at least, I should be able to go down the road of love and joy and you, my Princess, are the vessel that carries me there," he said softly as their eyes locked.

Tutu was speechless as her head searched for words to discourage him, but her heart wouldn't let her do so.

"Tutu, I want you more than anything. I want you to be the mother of my children," Martin said, pulling her closer without any resistance and kissing her.

"Stop!" she said feebly, but did not push him away. "Please, don't let this happen."

Martin did not hear this and continued to kiss and caress her. He lifted her off her feet and carried her into her quarters, where they made love for the first time after his more than a year and a half pursuit. After making love fervently for a while, they both dozed off in each other's embrace.

They had been asleep for more than three hours when Tutu was awakened by the arrival of the Parrises from their family outing. Startling awake when she heard her name called by the Rev. Parris, she realized Martin was still there. He was deeply asleep and oblivious to the time and only woke up as she tried disentangling herself and her clothing from him.

"Sssh!" she put a finger on his lips as he spoke loudly from his disturbed slumber.

The Reverend called her once again and she had to shout her reply to prevent him from coming inside to check whether she was all right. "I am coming, sir. I am trying to get dressed," she answered as she frantically looked around, trying to find her clothing, since it was dark in the room. The heating fire that provided light in the room was burnt out.

Finally, she made her way out of the room, "I am sorry, Reverend. I had a headache and went to rest," she said apologetically as she fretted uneasily.

"Sorry for disturbing you. I am tired as well and just wanted to see whether there is anything to eat before I go to bed."

"I am sorry. I should have made you something. I just went

into the room to rest, before cooking and did not expect to fall asleep for so long."

"It's alright. Just make me something simple," he said and went indoors to the living room. Judith and the girls, having had something to eat during the outing, retired to their rooms upon arrival. Tutu went ahead and prepared a light meal as she thought of the trouble Martin was going to get into. After waiting on Parris to eat his meal, they both said their goodnights and he retired to his room, leaving Tutu to return to her room.

"God! I thought you were never going to come back" Martin said when she returned after her hour-long absence.

"It's very late, Martin. What are you going to tell your ma'am?" Tutu expressed her anxiety.

"I don't know, I will think about that when I get there tomorrow," he said nonchalantly as he pulled the covers over himself.

"Tomorrow?" Tutu repeated in surprise and shook her head slowly in dismay.

"There is no point going home now, everyone would be asleep by now. So let me enjoy myself with my darling. Come here, sweetheart," he said opening his arms. Tutu shook her head disapprovingly, but went into his hands and they cuddled and kissed, which once again led to their making love until they fell asleep.

In Tutu's sleep, her mother came in and sat on her bedside, tapping her awake.

"Mama, where have you been all these days? They killed my baby," she told her mother, who nodded knowingly.

"I have never left you, my child and have been seeing all that has been happening. The time is coming when you need to follow your destiny once again. Those that killed your baby are planning great wickedness and pretty soon you must face them and destroy them," her mother told her.

"How mother?" she asked with a confused expression on her face. "Who are these people and how do I know them?"

Her mother pointed to sleeping Martin, "When you go

to his house in a few days, you will encounter a meeting where they are making their plans to wage war on you and our people. Afterward, the gods will take control."

Wura tapped her shoulder to move closer. "It's often said, 'those who the gods want to destroy, they first make mad'. If you don't lose hope in the face of their madness, they will hand you the opportunity to destroy them!"

Tutu shrugged, not fully understanding what she was saying. She changed the topic to one that greatly excited her. "Mother, what do you think of Martin? I want to marry him. I love him!"

Her mother shook her head ominously; "You remember what I told you about the last one, Emeka, or what was his name? He died when he wanted to interfere in your destiny. I told you not to run away with him, but you ignored my advice. He is also the same, if he comes too close he will die like Emeka!"

This left Tutu distraught. "Why mama? Why can't I have someone to love like everybody else? Why do I have to suffer?" she lamented.

"We are all suffering, my child. We are all tied to our destiny. It's whatever our head choose before coming to Earth. You have to take whatever destiny serves you with your chin up. I have to leave, but before I do I want to warn you that two things can destroy one's destiny. They are alcohol and friends, be very careful of friends and do not drink the devil's water." As she finished, she rose and walked away, fading as she moved.

"Mama," Tutu tried to stop her from leaving, but she woke up with her hands outstretched and realized she had been dreaming. She lay back in her bed, but could not go back to sleep as she clearly recalled her conversation with her mother. Martin stirred in his sleep, making her look at him and shake her head sadly as she thought of what her mother had said about him.

Just before dawn, she woke him up and told him he had to leave before her boss woke up. Martin got up grumpily and made his way home. She decided that the next time she saw him, she was going to tell him to stop seeing her. I cannot let what happened to Emeka happen to him, she thought.

The following evening when she went to the market, her fears were confirmed when she met another slave, Michele, from the Porters' household. Tutu knew Michele through her bringing the Porter children to the Sunday school and although she was not as close to her as to Carol or Jennifer, she was still a friend.

Michele was a thickset, very dark woman in her mid-twenties who had an incredible sense of humor. She told Tutu she was brought over from Brazil after being kidnapped from Owu in Yorubaland. The Porters had renamed her from Ayobami to Michele. She and Martin were bought around the same time and since the Porters named their slaves down the alphabet, they both got names beginning with the letter 'M'.

"Ma'am flogged Marty this morning, and he is still hanging by his hands," Michele told her as they were buying potatoes. "Was he with you last night?"

Tutu slowly nodded. "Why is this always happening?" she asked no one in particular.

"I remember you warning him. I believe he will be all right. It's just that he will not be sleeping with you or any woman for a long, long while. Although you never know with that strong Igbo boy," she joked and laughed, but Tutu's mind was far away.

Martin had returned home the following morning to meet a fuming Pamela Porter. She had sent him on errands to the women, who were supposed to attend a meeting at her house. Because of him the meeting had to be cancelled and she was livid.

To make matters worse, he had no tangible excuse and refused to say where he was. She ordered him suspended from a tree and flogged with the cat o'nine tails until he passed out. He was left in the December cold to dry in his blood up until evening, just before Tutu met Michele who told her of his punishment.

Having heard too late in the day, Tutu was unable to go until the following morning. When she arrived, he was sleeping and woke up to slight pain, serious cold and flu. She consoled him for about 45 minutes before leaving, despite his reluctance to let her go, but she had lots of chores to do and could stay no longer. On her way out, Tutu, being quite distraught, did not pay attention to where she was going and bumped into Pamela Porter, who shouted angrily at her to watch where she was going.

After finishing her chores in the evening, she returned to check on Martin's progress, which although it wasn't drastic, he was definitely improving. The sores weren't too bad, but the cold persisted.

"Let us run away from these people! Let's leave," he whispered weakly but with conviction.

Wiping away tears of compassion for his plight, Tutu placed a hand on him. "No! I need to stay away from you, I told you this would only lead to trouble for you."

"Tutu, don't you love me enough to come with me?" he asked with great pain and emotion.

"Yes, I do, but it would not lead to anything, but trouble and even death for you."

"We can leave tonight, no one would know for sometime. She's having one of her stupid meetings, which is why she beat me like a rug," he said, ignoring her protests.

"No not tonight, I have things to do. Think over it for a couple of days, then we will see what happens," she lied. This was in order to give her breathing space, so she could plan how to disengage from their relationship. She kissed him goodbye, hoping it would be for the last time, although she realized how deeply she felt about him.

On her way out of the compound, she saw two women whom she recognized from the church go into the main house. Closely following their arrival were Mrs. Andrews and some other women, who looked around furtively as they went indoors. Tutu hid behind a tree and saw more women enter the house discreetly and wondered what was going on. She remembered Martin saying he was flogged, because of a stupid meeting as well as what her mother said in the dream.

Curious, she decided to find out what was going on, and why it required so much secrecy by the women. She sneaked to the side of the house stopping at windows to peep and listen for voices. When she came to what appeared from outside to be a well-lit room, she stopped to listen. From where she stood, she heard a voice and peeped through a crack in the curtains by standing on a boulder. In a room that seemed to be a dining room, she saw a number of women seated around a table.

"...With this our coast would no longer be called the barren coast. I gathered that the tobacco seed found from those Indians could provide us with three times as much yield than what is presently got in the South. Coupled with the cottonseed, we could expect an immense change in our fortunes. Although, until we are positioned to fully exploit the advantages, please keep this discovery absolutely secret," Tutu heard Pamela Porter counsel the other women.

"I guess we need to secure land and make arrangements for African slaves," commented a woman, whose voice Tutu could not recognize.

"We are going to need a whole lot of Africans, especially with the hard soil we have around here, but that should not be a problem," answered Pamela. "Should it?"

Mrs. Smith, the oldest and one of the richest out of the women, married to the largest gun and ammunition supplier smiled, as she spoke. "You know the arms for Africa or wherever is never a problem," she said confidently.

"Neither are the ships," quipped the wife of a major ship builder and fitter, Mrs. Campbell.

"It's really going to cost a lot!" cautioned Mrs. Morgan, an astute woman married to a family with large land holdings, although most were uncultivated.

Mrs. Hall, married to a big investment banker, assured them, "I guess financing wouldn't be a problem, according to Joseph." Her husband and his family brokered and financed deals for planters, shippers, distillers and most other big businesses.

"The rum and other liquor needed for the slave expeditions might initially be a problem due to the fire that razed the distillery, but thanks to the Halls, my husband is speedily rebuilding it and should start production in a few months." Tutu heard Mrs. Andrews tell them, and she smirked from where she was shivering and eavesdropping.

Pamela looked around the table. "Anything else?" she asked impatiently. When no one said anything else, she gestured to Mrs. O'Connor to talk.

"Yes, I heard from some sources that there is a powerful force in our midst here in Salem that is poised to cause great havoc among us. Although I was advised not to go after it, Pamela suggested we should search for the force and destroy it. Therefore it was agreed that we should consult the realm and see where it is harbored," said a voice that Tutu knew belonged to Mrs. O'Connor, Jennifer's owner.

"I heard about this earlier, but is it that important? I mean could anyone really come and destroy us?" Mrs. Simmons asked skeptically.

Mrs. O'Connor nodded assertively. "I heard the destruction might be devastating and to be forewarned is to be forearmed," Tutu heard Mrs. O' Connor say as she cautioned the women sternly. Inside, the other women nodded in agreement and joined hands to complete a full circle needed to start a séance.

"I call on the great spirits of...." As Tutu listened to Pamela recite an incantation, suddenly the heavens shook with thunder and lightening. One thunderbolt hit the window through which Tutu was eavesdropping and shattered it.

The shattered window left her wide open to the view of the women, and she momentarily stood rooted to the spot on which she was standing. Quickly recollecting her senses, she fled towards home, but not before a few of the women saw her.

"Who was that?" queried one of the three women that saw her before fleeing.

"I am not too sure, but I think I saw one of the slaves wearing that dress this morning coming from my slaves quarters," Pamela Porter answered pensively, clearly disturbed by the incident.

"What was she doing behind the window and what

happened with the thunder?" queried Beatrice Andrews, who never saw her.

"I don't know, but it is a good thing, the thunder exposed her, although she must have heard quite a lot," Mrs. Lake said reflectively.

"I wonder why a slave would want to eavesdrop on us? Maybe someone sent her to do their dirty job," commented another of the women, Mrs. Ramsay.

"We will never know until we find her and we must, otherwise our secrets will be out in the open. You know what that means," warned Mrs. O'Connor, the owner of the slave, Jennifer, who complained of maltreatment to Tutu.

"I think I know how to find her. Leave it to me," Pamela reassured them, before they all decided to disperse for another day. The consensus was that they should postpone the séance, in case there were others around eavesdropping. Moreover, a cold early December wind was coming through the broken window.

Immediately after the coven, despite it was past midnight, Pamela Porter summoned Martin. "Boy, who was that beautiful girl that came to see you this morning? The one with knocking knees," she asked him amiably.

"That is my wife!" Martin answered boastfully and noticed her sigh in relief.

"Where does she live? Whose slave is she?"

"Err...why?" he asked, surprised and suspicious of the line and manner of questioning. It occurred to him Tutu might be in trouble.

"Don't ask me questions, boy! I ask the questions around here," she said angrily. From her tone, Martin suspected Tutu was involved in some trouble; until he spoke to her, he knew he could not give any information about her.

"I do not know who you are talking about!" he denied stubbornly.

"What?" Pamela was astonished over his sudden denial. "Your wife! Did you not just say she was your wife?" she shouted petulantly.

"No, ma'am," he answered, looking at his feet with his hands folded behind him.

"Don't you dare, 'No Ma'am' me! Do you think I am deaf or stupid?" she yelled, jumped to her feet and came aggressively at him.

"Yes, ma'am," he said, with a smirk on his face which was wiped off with a smack from a now fully enraged Pamela. Martin looked down at her with all the hatred he had mustered over the last day and spat in her face.

Feeling the warm spittle hit her face, she lunged for his throat and rained kicks and curses on him. A kick to the groin made him drop to his knees, and she continued kicking and punching him.

"Bastard!" she kept on shouting as her alerted brother-in-laws came running to the scene. Her husband had gone on a business trip, leaving his brothers at home with his wife. They took Martin out and tied him to the same tree he'd been tied to before. He was left dangling from the tree in the bitterly cold weather, although he was not flogged.

Pamela and the other women were petrified over their unidentified eavesdropper, who now held information, which might lead to their disgrace and downfall. They all knew the laws in the Puritan colony regarding witchcraft, which was punishable by death. In addition was the question of their new discovery which, in the hands of the opposition, could mean great loss in their economic and political power.

These thoughts and their various repercussions kept Pamela awake throughout the night. She ordered Martin to be cut free at dawn when it became obvious he was not going to cooperate and she decided to use another approach, the soft approach. She had done it for fun in the past, now she intended to do it to save her life. Around noon, still lying motionless in bed, she sent for Martin.

"Yes, ma'am you sent for me," he said with a scowl as he entered the warm room, which was a world away in comfort from his own. A fire fiercely burning in one corner of the room provided the heat and only light.

"Yes I did. Martin, I think I owe you an apology over how I reacted," she said, sitting up in bed with the sheets held firmly to her chest. "I am sorry. Sit down," she gestured to the bedside space beside her.

Martin hesitated as he looked at her suspiciously at her unexpected change of heart. Moreover, it was not normal for a slave to be told to sit in the presence of his owner, especially not on their bed.

He shook his head adamantly. "Thank you ma'am," he said and remained standing.

"Martin, I say sit down," she said forcefully and he had no choice but to obey. He perched on the bedside like it was a bed of nails.

"Look, I am sorry. I have been edgy over the last few days. Alright?" she spoke softly and reached for him tenderly.

"Yes ma'am. Thank you, ma'am," he blurted out and hurriedly made for the door.

"Hold it! I haven't finished. Sit down," she shouted, stopping him in his tracks. Martin backtracked and sat on the edge of the bed. Pamela took a deep breath before continuing. "The day you slept out, you stayed with that girl, didn't you?" she asked coyly, but he just smiled and looked at the floor.

"Why don't you want to tell me?" she said softly. "She is a lucky girl to have a man like you. I have being admiring you myself," she said seductively to a stunned Martin, who dropped his mouth. There were rumors in the slave quarters that their madam had some toy boys among the slaves, but he had never believed them.

"Yeah, don't look so surprised," she said, as she swiftly got on to her knees on the bed, letting the sheets fall off to reveal her nakedness. She grabbed him by the shoulder and caressed his chest muscles down to the stomach ones, "Relax boy, ma'am likes you."

"No ma'am! Please! No ma'am," Martin said panicky as he tried moving away, but was held firmly by the naked woman.

"Don't be stupid! Is the girl better than I am?" she said with feigned indignation as she yanked his trousers open and felt him. "Come here, baby, and be good to ma'am," she urged him in a sultry voice.

With her hands in his trousers bringing him out, he lost resistance and although he kept repeating, "No ma'am," his voice lost its conviction. Eventually, he lost control and he had sex with her.

After sex, they both lay on their backs tired and in silence for a moment, before she turned onto her side to face him.

"Did you enjoy it?" she asked.

He answered with a nod.

"You see, I could treat you better than her. Moreover, I can make things easier and better for you around here. You can become a foreman or even not to do anything at all but to satisfy ma'am," she playfully traced a finger down his muscles as she spoke.

"Nice, ma'am. You are nice," he smiled as he fondled her breasts.

"It is up to you, if you want to be my lover. Anyway, I will see you tonight, if you think you want to be with me." Soon afterward, Martin left baffled but contented.

In the evening, he returned and they once again made love. After catching their breath, "I can see you are enjoying it more than err...?"

"Tutu's!" he completed the sentence without thought.

"And you don't need to go far for it? Where do you go?" she asked, a little too pointedly, which alerted Martin.

"Err.... I don't want to talk about her. You are the one on my mind."

"What do you mean you don't want to talk about her? I let you have me and treat you nice, and that is what I get in return?" she sat up angrily.

"I don't want anything to happen to her. I can't let you hurt her. I love her. I am sorry, ma'am," he blurted out with all sincerity.

Pamela, now very angry, said, "No, you are not sorry. I will make you very sorry, if you don't tell me where that dirty bitch is, two-two or whatever her name is." She stood up and picked up his clothes.

"What arrant rubbish! You don't want me to hurt her, but she is allowed to destroy me. Now for the last time, where does she live? You either say where she lives or you don't live anymore," she told him coldly, standing naked with his clothes in her hands.

"Please ma'am, Tutu is my wife, and I can't let anything happen to her. She has suffered enough," he pled.

"Now, I am going to count to three and that is it!" she threatened as she backed towards the door. After a pause following the count with Martin confused, but adamant, she started screaming at the top of her voice as soon as she wrapped a sheet around herself. The alarm brought people rushing to her aid, who were surprised to see her half-naked and even more surprised to see Martin completely naked.

"He raped me," she cried as they arrived. Her two brother-in-laws immediately pounced on Martin, who tried protesting his innocence, but to deaf ears.

"No, she asked me! No, please, I didn't rape her," he shouted as he was attacked. He was not given a chance to explain and was dragged outside.

A small crowd milled outside as he was beaten, some of who joined in, when they heard his offence. Eventually, he was lynched by the small mob. His genitals were removed before he was hanged, although he was already dead by then.

News of the alleged rape and lynching quickly spread through Salem and a church member, who came to visit the Parrises, was the one that told the reverend. Tutu was serving the visitor, when she overhead the conversation, and although she did not know Pamela's surname, she knew it was Martin.

Sick to her stomach, Tutu had to run outside to retch, where she cried for her dead lover. She had been expecting to see him turn up with his madam after the eavesdropping incident because she knew the madam saw her and probably identified her. After waiting all day, she knew he had not snitched on her, but at what price she did not know and was terrified for his safety.

Hearing the news, she now knew that he had paid with his life to protect her, another one dying to protect her. She did not cry for long and resolved to avenge the death of her loved ones, although she did not have a strong plan of how to get back at them. Her powers were limited to self-defense and unless provoked she could not really invoke them.

16

On hearing what happened to her friend, Judith made her way through the snow to the Porters' residence. She was happy to see Pamela was not too distressed, and they soon started discussing other things having not seen each other for a while. While they were talking, one of the workmen repairing the thunderstruck window came to ask for advice. Pamela rose and was followed by Judith to see what he was talking about.

"What happened there?" Judith voiced her curiosity as they returned to the living room.

"It was stuck by a thunderbolt a few days ago," Pamela answered.

"How come?" Judith asked, remembering the Annapolis story. "Or were you also chasing witches from the land?" she joked.

Pamela dropped her cup in shock and looked at Judith with surprise, "What are you talking about? Do you know? Who told you?"

"I was only joking, but it appears there is more to it than meets the eye. Is there anything you should be telling your friend that you are not?" she said lightly, and paused as she contemplated something. Continuing in a more serious and guarded tone, "Pamela, I have wanted to tell you something for sometime, but I have been holding back because I did not know how you might react."

"What is it? There is nothing you can't tell me, I am your

sister-in-law, remember? What have you heard about witches?" Pamela asked earnestly, sitting upright.

"When you told me about thunder striking your window, I remembered what I heard in Annapolis. My husband's slave is a witch and was responsible for the revolt that led to father's death. Pat, Frank's wife, and her friends told me that when we were coming to America they tried to sink the ship, because of the slave on board, but they were hit with thunderbolts, which is why I made that comment."

"This slave is still with you?" Pamela asked curiously.

"Yes, Tutu is still w...."

Pamela jumped up from where she sat across and held Judith's hand, "What did you call her, two-two?"

"Tutu, that is her name!" Judith answered, puzzled over Pamela's curious reaction.

"Yes, that is her, great!" she shouted happily, throwing her clenched fists into the air.

"My God! What do you know about her?" A bewildered Judith asked.

Taking a deep breath, Pamela launched into how she was having a meeting about a report of a powerful spirit in their midst, which they wanted to identify, when suddenly her window was thunderstruck revealing Tutu, who apparently was eavesdropping.

She told her everything, how she had tried getting the information out of her slave and how she had angrily had him hanged when he proved obstinate. Although she didn't tell Judith that, in desperation, she actually slept with him to win him over. Pamela told Judith the importance of getting to know who had sent the spy, although Judith allayed her fears that it had nothing to with the Putnams.

"I want to see her," Pamela concluded.

"I was told in Annapolis to be careful dealing with her, I do not think it is advisable," Judith cautioned her friend, who had already risen to her feet and was ready to go. Judith had abided by the advice ever since she had returned to Salem over a year ago.

"Don't worry, Judith. I can take care of myself. There is nothing an African slave can do to overpower me. Regardless of what they might have said in Annapolis, we are capable of dealing with her and I am one of the strongest around here. Trust me," Pamela said confidently, as she prepared to leave with Judith. Reluctantly, Judith rose with a queasy feeling to lead her sister-in-law toward her home.

When they arrived at the Parris residence, Reverend Parris had just left for the church next door, where he was to attend a meeting. Tutu was tidying the girls' room, when Pamela walked in and bolted the door behind her.

"Hello! Tutu, I believe we have met," Pamela said warmly, as she entered the large room littered with girls' dresses.

"No!" Tutu pretended she didn't know what she was there for and continued making the bed as her heart raced.

"You forgot eavesdropping on my meeting?" she asked pleasantly as if talking to a friend over the choice of her shoes.

"No ma'am. You know we Negroes all look alike," she said sarcastically.

"Cut the crap!" Pamela said, her voice hardening, "I know about you. You are the witch that wants to cause problems for everyone around here."

"I don't bother anyone. I don't go to other people's land to kill and steal their family. I am not a wicked witch!"

"Are you calling me a wicked witch?" Pamela moved closer to Tutu, where she continued making the bed, "We don't do evil. We work for the progress of everyone and harm no one."

"You do no evil, but you plan to go and destroy more of my people, because of your new plant and money. Sorry, I guess they are not people," Tutu sniggered and turned away.

"Don't you dare talk to me like that! We are doing you people a favor taking you out of that diseased land, where your souls would have been lost forever," Pamela said a bit flustered.

Tutu raised her eyebrows and shook her head pensively, "You are doing us a favor killing and enslaving us?" she grimaced, hissed and continued with her task.

Pamela remained silent. As she studied her, she realized Tutu was far more intelligent than any slave she had ever come across. "Tell me. What do you want?"

Tutu stopped what she was doing to look at Pamela, "What I want? It is for you to stop all this evil over money."

"Otherwise you would cause another revolt like the one that killed my in-law, Mr. Lawrence?" Pamela asked sarcastically.

"He was a stupid man that caused his own death, not me," Tutu answered with contempt.

"What? You stand in front of me and insult him?" Pamela moved closer aggressively.

"I have no respect for a murderers, like the one that killed my lover yesterday," Tutu answered, now standing and facing her.

Pamela raised a hand to slap her.

"Agbero!" Tutu sneered in Yoruba meaning 'halt'. "Amon!"

Pamela found her hand stuck in mid-air to her amazement and retracted her hand. Pamela, fixing a gaze on her, started reciting some charms quietly as both women locked gazes. Suddenly a trunk box was lifted from behind Tutu and went straight for Tutu's head, but dropped a few feet away her as she raised a hand and said, "stop."

Still with locked gazes, they slowly moved counter-clockwise as they recited incantations. Pieces of furniture began flying haphazardly around the room, but none hit either of them.

Tutu in the middle of her incantation stretched out her hands, as if drawing power from the skies, and slowly brought them down to her mouth. With the tips of her fingers touching her mouth, she opened her mouth and as if blowing a kiss, she started blowing from her mouth a small cyclone directed by her fingers.

The strong wind that came out of her mouth pushed Pamela off her balance and back towards the window. Pamela struggled vainly to maintain her balance, but it kept pushing her backwards.

About three feet away, the windows swung open and items

belonging to the girls, both heavy and light, were blown out of the window by the wind. Looking aghast at the window as she neared it, Pamela squeezed her eyes shut and her lips moved quickly as she said some charms in desperation. Suddenly the wind died down, and she stopped just at the edge of the windowsill.

Smiling, Pamela stepped away from the windowsill and toward Tutu before continuing to recite incantations. She flicked a finger and a big mirror came off the wall and headed in Tutu's direction. A yard before hitting her, Tutu clapped her hands and the mirror shattered into small pieces.

Before Tutu could continue with her incantation, three heavy pieces of furniture came toward her. She saw only two, which she commanded to fall with a hand gesture, but the last one hit her from behind and knocked her cold. She collapsed on the floor in a heap.

Cautiously, Pamela moved closer. "Do not fool with your superiors, African," she said triumphantly, placing her feet on Tutu's head and spitting on her as she looked down on Tutu contemptuously. Pamela looked around her, shaking her head in dismay as she assessed the damage they had caused in the room.

While looking around the room, she did not notice the unconscious girl turning green under her feet. Before she knew it, Tutu had turned into a large green python.

It was the cold, scaly feeling of the snake wrapping around her heels that startled her into realization. The python about 18 inches in diameter and 18 feet long, swiftly wrapped its tail around the bed and wrapped around her legs.

Shocked, Pamela frantically tried to free herself from the snake, but the snake was fast despite its size. She fell on the ground, still struggling to free herself as the snake began swallowing her. She tried to get a grip on the bed, when the snake swallowed her all the way up to her thighs.

Pamela was helpless, too flustered to invoke her powers and unable to stand her own, as the snake dragged her into its large mouth. Realizing she was coming to her end when the snake devoured her up to her chest, she screamed.

While Pamela had gone into the room, the Reverend Parris returned having forgotten something at home. Dashing to his room to get it, he heard noise of smashing things in the girls' room, but ignored it due to his haste.

On his way down, he heard a muffled scream. Unsure what it was, he decided to stop and see what was going on in the room, but it was locked. He started pounding on the door, but there was no reply. He was about to kick the door down when Tutu opened it. Smiling mischievously but clearly perturbed, she fled without a word, before Parris could compose himself.

"Hello, Reverend Parris!" greeted Pamela, who was quite flustered with her clothes torn and barely covering her. The little that remained of her clothing was stuck to her as if she had climbed out of a barrel of oil. Parris dropped his mouth on seeing Pamela emerge from the room. He was about to ask what was going on when a strong repulsive odor hit him, making him cover his mouth and nose. Pamela emanated the awful odor, which came from the snake.

"What the hell is going on here?" he asked through his covered mouth, but Pamela just smiled and walked past him. On her way, Pamela grabbed Judith, who was standing next to him and led her away. Parris, realizing he was keeping people waiting in the church, could not wait to find out what was happening and left perplexed.

After Parris left, Judith took her shaken friend, who had narrowly escaped death, into her room. She gave her a new dress to wear, and they both left in haste.

Tutu, watching from the side of the house, smiled as she saw them leave in a hurry. "I will get you," she said and turned around to go indoors.

The two women walked briskly in silence till they got to Pamela's house. On arrival, Pamela excused herself and immediately went to wash off the odor caused by the python.

After she finished, she joined Judith in the living room near the fire.

"Now, will you tell me what happened in that room?" Judith asked anxiously.

Pamela shook her head gravely as she thought about her close shave with death. "That girl is powerful. I nearly lost my life. She had already swallowed me up to my neck before releasing me, thanks to your husband," she admitted.

"How could she swallow you?" Judith asked with no small measure of incredulity.

"She turned into a giant snake. It was its insides that stank on me."

"Oh my God! I warned you not to go near her. Oh, what am I going to do? She is going to come after me. I am in trouble," Judith said, visibly agitated.

Pamela let out a deep sigh. "You are not the only one she is against; she confessed she is against us all. We need to seek help, before it is too late," she said.

"Where are we going to get help? Pat and the other women were trying to do something, but the plan was to bring her down with the rest of the family. They have being waiting for the past year to get their hands on her, but as you know I haven't been able to get Samuel out of Salem," Judith said, as she fretted in her seat.

As they spoke Mr. Porter arrived home. Greeting them, he excused himself to the bathroom.

Moments later, he rejoined the women in the living room. "Do I have good news for you? We've won control again; two members of the council have just crossed over to our side," he said ebulliently as he entered the living room. The women let out excited noises on hearing the news. Taking the seat between them, "Judith, I think we can finally do something about your husband."

"Sooner rather than later," Judith answered gravely, although trying to suppress her anxiety.

"He will soon be receiving a notice to leave. We can even make sure he does not wait till the order expires!" Porter said confidently as he rose. "I need a wash and a nap. I will see you ladies later." He excused himself and went upstairs.

"That is good news, at least," Pamela said after he left.

"Until we get rid of that girl, I won't be able to rest. I am not only scared for my sake, but for my daughter's and the other girl's. Until she dies or is locked up somewhere, nobody is safe," Judith said despondently.

Pamela held up a hand as an idea crossed her mind. "Thinking about it, we could just do that instead of trying to get her to Annapolis."

"Do what?" Judith inquired, raising her eyebrows.

Pamela smiled as she thought of her plan. "We could ensure she is arrested and maybe hanged for witchcraft."

"How do we do that? You cannot come out with your experience with her, although it would be a better alternative than having to wait for her to leave with Samuel. Knowing her powers, she could change the course of things and either he regains the job or gets another one around here."

Pamela nodded slowly as she acknowledged the issues raised by her friend. "Leave everything to me and we shall explore every avenue."

When Parris returned from his meeting, he immediately summoned Tutu. "What happened in Betty's room between you and Judith's sister-in-law, Pamela?" he asked as he walked toward the room.

"Sir, I don't know what was happening. You must ask the woman," Tutu answered innocently as she followed him. Parris flung the door open to find a neat room with no trace of the earlier pandemonium. He looked with bewilderment at Tutu and remained silent for a moment.

"I thought I saw you come out of the room." He looked puzzled at the ground, before walking towards the living room with Tutu following him at a distance.

"Yes sir, but you should ask the ma'am. I don't know anything," she insisted.

"I hope Judith did not bring her here to harass you," Parris commented thoughtfully as he observed Tutu, who was leaning against the wall and looking down as she played with her finger nervously. "Did she?" he asked, when she said nothing.

"I am alright, sir. I can take care of myself!" Tutu said defiantly, looking up and straight into his eyes.

Parris smiled and waved her away. He decided to speak to his wife and ask what Pamela was doing upstairs in Betty's room.

Judith returned late that night after bracing herself to face Tutu. Upon her arrival, Samuel Parris asked her what had occurred in Betty's room earlier in the day.

"I hope you did not bring your family members to harass Tutu. That would be totally unfair," Parris stated, before giving her a chance to answer or even sit down.

Perturbed, Judith looked around furtively, before denying. "I did nothing of the sort. I didn't even know they were in the same room. All Pamela told me was that she wanted to see how Betty's room was decorated, since she was decorating her daughter's room. Did Tutu complain of anything?" she asked innocuously.

"No, but that room when I saw it this afternoon did not look like a place someone would want to copy. It looked more like a hurricane had swept through it," Parris said cynically. "It surprises me that you never heard any of the noise coming out of the room. I do not know what is going on around here, but I hope you are not up to anything sinister," he voiced his suspicions.

Judith slowly shook her head in dismay and frustration, as she looked at her husband, who she believed was bewitched. Having thought of it all day, she believed she needed to make peace with Tutu, in order to be able to sleep peacefully.

"I know of nothing. Where is Tutu? Maybe I'll ask her myself."

"She probably is in her quarters, but I suggest you should just leave her alone in peace," he said, wanting to avoid any further harassment from Judith against her.

"I am not a warmonger, so I do not know what you mean

leaving her in peace," Judith said, as she rose and walked toward Tutu's quarters.

When she reached Tutu's door, she stopped and drew in a deep breath, trying to summon up courage before knocking on the door. Tutu swung the door open and was shocked to find her master's wife standing outside her room, for the first time ever.

"Yes ma'am? Is there something you want me to do for you, ma'am?" she asked politely with a faint smile across her face. Tutu had been thinking all day long how Judith would react when Pamela told her what had transpired in the room.

She knew they would not come out and accuse her of anything, since it would expose Pamela as well. Seeing Judith at her door, she decided to play innocent.

"Not really, I just came to have a word with you," Judith said in a slightly quivering voice. She was unsure of herself alone with Tutu, especially having heard of what she had done earlier in the day.

"Should I come to the living room?"

Judith wished she could say yes, but she did not want anything that happened earlier on, to be mentioned in the presence of her husband. "No, I will not take much of your time and could just discuss it with you here," Judith said, meaning at the doorstep, but Tutu turned around and walked back into the room.

With no choice, Judith had to follow her into the room, which she had never entered and felt like she was stepping into a lion's den.

The room dimly lit was shabbily decorated like most slave quarters she had ever entered, but in addition there were a few statues she had never seen. At the foot of one statue with a double-edged axe were various fruits, which Tutu used to appeal to Shango. Sweeping the room with her eyes, she had an eerie feeling and goose bumps appeared on her skin. Although the goose bumps were not only because of her fear, but the room was draughty and poorly heated in the cold winter.

"My husband just accused me of bringing my friend here to harass you, which is not the case, so I decided to talk to you to prevent any wrong ideas. I believe we have been getting on fine, and I would like it to remain so," she blurted out nervously. Pausing to see Tutu's reaction, which remained passive as she looked at her.

"I just wish to let you know, I did not bring Pamela here to quarrel with you nor do I know what happened between you two," Judith said amiably.

"Ma'am, I do not bother anyone and only wish no one bothers me. Thanks for coming down and I understand everything," Tutu answered, putting a sardonic stress on the last part of her sentence.

Judith made her way out of the room and was relieved she had at least made her peace. Nevertheless, she could hardly sleep that night and kept waking up in cold sweats after having nightmares.

On the morning of December 22nd, 1691, Judith was the first to wake up and go into the living room, filled with anxiety over how the day would unfold. She had being informed that some important meetings were to take place that morning and she could hardly wait to hear the decisions made.

Shortly before noon, there was a loud knock on the door, which she ran to open. It was Michael Lewis, who came with a letter informing Parris that his appointment as Salem's minister had been terminated earlier that morning in a meeting of selectmen of the town's council.

Parris was speechless, when he read the letter, not knowing what to do next. Initially, Parris chose to ignore his assistant's asinine comments and questions about when he planned moving out of the house, in order for him to move in his own family. When the questions became too patronizing and Parris could not stand the man any longer, he angrily walked him out.

Parris was still perplexed at the sudden termination of his appointment, trying to figure out what had happened, when another knock on the door startled him out of his deep thoughts. At the door was his chief supporter and brother-in-law, Mr. Putnam.

"From your face, I can see you've got the message," Putnam stated as he slumped into a chair next to Parris.

"What is happening?" Parris demanded sullenly.

Putnam shook his big head ominously. "Apparently some bastards were bribed and crossed over to the opposing camp recently. The Potters appeared to have used their first power of majority to get rid of you, but you don't worry."

"Don't worry?" Parris repeated in disbelief with a slightly strained voice, "I have lost a job and a roof over my family's head and all you say is 'don't worry'!"

"Yes, don't worry, because it is all stupid. The notice cannot be enforced until it runs out, which is after the next election. I believe we will win control back and have the decision overturned. That is why I said you should not worry, if you see what I mean," Putnam explained and lit a hand-rolled cigarette when he finished.

"Well, if you say it that way, I see what you mean. So my fate depends on the election," Parris concluded pensively.

Putnam smirked, "Not only your fate, but all of ours because if those bastards, the Porters, keep control, we are all in for a hard time! Believe me! We might as well follow you when you are leaving, even though my family and I have a lot at stake."

The Putnams and Porters had always had their differences. The two foremost families of Salem constantly vied for economic and political power and advantages over one another.

In recent times, the family competition had grown into an ugly feud with the winner taking all. Therefore not only the small Parris family would stand to lose with a Porter control, but the much larger Putnam family and their supporters.

Fully aware of the waiting game Parris and the Putnams would be playing, the Potters immediately tried to push out the weakest link in the Putnam network. A few days afterward, they ordered the immediate stoppage of the supply of firewood to the Reverend. This was easily achieved since his assistant Michael Lewis and selectmen from the Putnam camp were in charge of firewood and other small duties. It was also highly effective, being a few days to Christmas, with the bitterly cold December Northeastern winter.

When this happened, Parris was so mad he walked up to Porter in the street. "You are such a mean bastard. You stopped the firewood for your niece right in the middle of winter. Well, I hope you stock up the firewood and burn on it in Hell because you are evil Porter."

Porter, in the middle of his supporters, scoffed, "No, Parris. You are the one with no conscience keeping your family in such conditions against their will. Get the message you are not welcome in this town, never have been, never will be. Pack it up and forget about the loser you are following."

Parris shook his head in disdain. "You are the loser because you have lost the most important thing to a man, his soul. You wage war on children and men of God, there could be no hell fire hot enough to hold you, my friend," he said amid jeers from Porter's supporters, including Lewis, and angrily stormed off.

Taking advantage of the developments, Judith renewed pressure on her husband to relocate to Annapolis until he finally lost his temper.

"If this is what you and your friends hoped would happen, let me tell you right now, I am not leaving and, if I do, I am definitely not going to Annapolis. So you can scheme as much as you want. Although whatever you do trying to hurt me or for your selfish purposes, think of Betty. That is all I ask!" he shouted bitterly in frustration and left home to seek solace in the church. Tutu, having heard the developments and overheard her master and his wife argue, followed him to the church soon afterwards.

When she entered the church and found him praying, she waited till he finished. "Sir, I am sorry about what is happening, I know it's all because of me."

He looked up and was surprised to find her there. "No Tutu, it has nothing to do with you. The Putnam and Porter families have been quarrelling since long before we left Africa. Although, I believe my wife is instrumental in the sudden attack on me," he said. He went on to fully explain the politics that were at play in Salem.

After his explanation, Tutu rose to leave. "I will get enough firewood for us, if we have to move all the forests in Africa and would also find other ways I could help," she reassured him with her support. Parris could only smile and shake his head slowly in amazement and appreciation over her reassurances.

He was not to know the magnitude and sincerity of her reassurance until he woke up the following morning.

In the middle of the night, he had felt heat warming the house, although they had put out all fires before going to sleep to conserve the little firewood that remained. He had planned to go and cut some more firewood the following morning, but when he woke up in a warm house, he was surprised knowing what was left the previous night.

Immediately he got out of bed, he went down to check what was left and was going to rebuke whoever had burned the wood overnight. To his surprise, he found the largest stack of firewood, he had ever found in one place in the backyard.

Returning inside to the living room, he loudly asked Tutu in the kitchen, "Tutu, whose wood is that? What's going on around here?" While talking Judith walked down into the living room, without comment, she continued to the backyard and saw the huge pile. When she returned, she went to sit by her husband in silence as she looked in awe at Tutu, who was just coming into living room from the kitchen.

"It is ours, Sir. I had some friends help me," Tutu answered shyly.

"My goodness!" he exclaimed, "That is more firewood than I've ever seen. Thanks! Your friends must be very strong to cut all that wood."

Tutu smiled. "Yes, they are very strong!" she said looking at Judith, who avoided her eyes by quickly looking to the floor.

Not too long afterward, Judith left for the Porters house.

She met Pamela seeing off some guests and could hardly wait to tell her the new development. Once they returned indoors, Judith blurted out her story before she sat down.

"We have to do something about that girl, otherwise all your plans are going to fail. I was hoping that without the firewood, we would be forced to leave for Annapolis soon. Could you believe that overnight she got enough firewood to warm the whole of Massachusetts for a month."

Stupefied, Pamela let out a whistle. "She did? How did she?"

"She boasted in front of me to Samuel that she had very powerful friends. The way she said it and looked at me, made me realize the message was for me. She is really sure of herself and ready to take us on at anytime."

Pamela let out a small nervous chuckle. "Well, she could very well take us on, but let's see if she could take on the king's might and authority," Pamela said, pausing to sip what was left of the drink she was having with the guests. She waved her hand dismissively as she continued, "Don't bother yourself, Judith. Plans are under way to finally get rid of her and I assure you her powerful friends will not be able to help her."

Judith wished she could be as confident as Pamela, but guessed she was confident because she was not the one in the middle of everything. The whole thing was taking its toll on her, compounded by the nightmares and sleepless nights, which resulted in bags forming under her eyes and her being jittery.

She had thought it over and decided if she could get the plantation without a man, she would have taken her daughter and left Samuel Parris alone. She had returned to Annapolis a couple of times to see if there was a way to bring her plight to an end; unfortunately, she was forced to see everything through. At times like this, she really missed her late father, who was supportive.

Later that evening after Judith had left for home, Pamela held another meeting. The covens were becoming too frequent for comfort to many of them, who were particular about secrecy, but there was little they could do due to the nature of the problems faced. Luckily, Mr. Putnam was away again in Boston on business, otherwise the meeting would not have taken place in his residence.

The plans were gone over and refined, and it was decided that the plan would be put into motion the second Sunday of January 1692. Some opposed the use of the holy day to carry out such deeds, but in the absence of a better idea, they had no choice but to agree to the set date.

17

On the second Sunday of the year 1692, Tutu and Sarah Good organized the children into small groups and taught them as usual. Sarah, who had resigned following Mrs. Andrews' attack on Tutu, had returned. Being very poor with no other tangible income, Reverend Parris was able to convince her to return by promising her a weekly allowance. He had done this in order to give Tutu a helping hand and ward off criticisms based on the race of the teacher.

In between groups, Tutu spoke and joked with the slaves, who brought their wards. Everything went smoothly in spite of the harsh weather outside until shortly before the end of the session.

As Tutu sat and talked to one of the larger groups, that included Betty, Abigail and Ann, commotion ensued unexpectedly. Several girls in the group started convulsing, their limbs contorting in various directions and shouting in unknown languages.

Initially, she thought they were fooling around, but when they continued with some of them falling to the ground and foaming from their mouths, everyone panicked and raised an alarm. It was not long before the adults from the church ran to their aid, having just finished their Sunday worship, when they heard of the drama going on at the Sunday school.

"What happened?" inquired Reverend Parris, who was one of the first adults to arrive and allowed into the room.

"I do not know. We were reading, when they suddenly started. I have never seen this kind of illness before," Tutu answered, completely at a loss over what was happening.

Different remedies were suggested, but with no success. The girls continued convulsing and screaming in pain, making the adults send out of for a renowned physician, Dr. William Griggs, in Salem.

When Dr. Griggs arrived, he examined the girls, but after exhaustive examinations, the doctor could not diagnose what was wrong with them. This did not go down well with the priest and some of the girls' parents.

"It is sad that our doctor cannot tell us the illness that has beset our children. Maybe we should have you sent to Oxford for proper training," said one of the mothers cynically in frustration.

"Madam, if you would excuse me, this does not seem to be a natural sickness, if asked I would say it is caused by evil spirits," the doctor replied defensively to everyone's surprise. After contemplating what to do next amongst themselves, they decided to talk to a few of the girls, who appeared less distressed than others.

Parris sat his daughter up and asked, "Betty, what is wrong with you?" Betty could not answer as she continued to shake violently. Moving to another girl, he tried asking the same question, but was also met with the same response. Eventually, he was able to get a response from Abigail.

"They are sticking pins all over my body. Please tell them to stop," she said trembling as if seeing ghosts.

Confounded, Parris looked at the other parents, who stood over him and the girl. "Who are they? Who is hurting you?" They asked earnestly, but she said nothing. To be sure that the girl was not just hallucinating due to the effects of the illness, they went on to query the other girls. Those that could answer all said the same thing and more.

When one of the girls was asked who was responsible for her pain, she pointed toward Tutu. "She and the other woman are the ones using the demon to hurt me with pins. Mother, please tell them to stop!" the distraught girl cried. Immediately, the mother lunged at Tutu, but was restrained by the priest.

"I always knew that girl was no good. Let's lead her to the

stake or just stone her to death," Michael Lewis suggested
boisterously, to Parris and Tutu's disdain. Parris immediately
told Tutu and Sarah to leave for home, before the idea gained
support.

After they left, he discarded the girls' accusation as mere
hallucination, but as more and more girls pointed a finger at
Tutu, he found himself increasingly in a tight spot. He promised
to look into the accusations, hoping that by the following day
everything would have subsided and the true illness diagnosed.
This was not to be the case, because the symptoms persisted
and so did the girls' accusations.

At home, the three girls continued falling into fits
occasionally, at the end of which they always accused Tutu as
their tormentor.

"I don't know why you are surprised or don't want to
believe," Judith said when they were alone in their room. "The
signs were always clear to see."

"What are you talking about?" he asked irritably as he sat
pondering over the awkward developing scenario.

"The witch who killed my father and caused the revolt
that led us here," she came nearer and crouched beside him. In
a softer and appealing tone, she continued, "Samuel can't you
see the obvious? That girl is evil. She hates me and now wants to
kill my only daughter."

Parris shook his head violently, "That is absolutely untrue,"
he said and left the room.

Parris walked down to the living room and called Tutu.
"What is going on Tutu?" he demanded sternly when she came
into the living room.

Tutu, looking dejected, replied, "Sir, it is not true. I don't
know anything. They are just trying to get me in trouble." She
had been crying and was unsure about the turn of events.

"Why would all the girls try and put you into trouble? It's
absurd that seven girls would try and cause trouble for you for no
apparent reason," he reasoned as he looked at her quizzically.

"Sir, I don't know about the other girls, but do you think I would ever do anything to harm your daughter after all that you have done for me?" Tutu asked, as tears flowed down her cheeks.

Parris threw up his hands and sighed in exasperation, "I really don't know what is going on." This was a question he had asked himself over and over again, finding it difficult to believe Tutu could harm Betty after all that she had done.

"The evil witches are the ones behind all this, because they want to get rid of me."

Parris scoffed at her explanation. "Well they might be doing a good job, if this continues. I wonder why the witches would want to get rid of you?" He waved her away and thought about how he was going to resolve the issue.

Early the following morning, some senior church members, including Lewis, paid him a visit to discuss plans of bringing the scare under control, before it spread to other children.

"We cannot just sit around and do nothing while our children continue suffering!" An angry father objected, when the priest suggested adopting a wait and see approach. The others agreed with him and Parris found out that he had no choice but to do something fast. He knew they wanted him to hand over Tutu for lynching, but he could not agree.

After careful thought, he decided to play it safe. "Since they say it is done by evil spirits, I will call a meeting of ministers to verify the claims, and we will take it from there," he told them. Although they wanted immediate action against those accused, they decided to give his suggestion a chance.

Judith went over to Pamela, having not seen her since the whole thing started. "I know this is the plan you did not want to tell me about," she told Pamela, once they settled in the living room and were left alone by Pamela's husband. Judith was in higher spirits than she had been in a long while.

Pamela smiled knowingly, "I guess it is effective, and I promise you that we will soon be seeing her swinging from a tree."

"But what about the girls, aren't they suffering too much?"

Judith voiced the main concern that had been bothering her since the illness started. Seeing Betty scream in pain was a bit too much and she was hoping for a quick end to the whole affair. Although from what she had just heard from her husband's meeting with the church council, it appeared it would drag on for sometime. This was one of the reasons she quickly came to see Pamela.

"No, of course not. I wouldn't hurt my own nieces. It is all hallucinations, and they are not in any pain whatsoever," she assuaged Judith's fears as one of the slaves, Michele entered to serve Judith.

"The way they scream and writhe, it is hard to believe they are not feeling it," Judith voiced her doubts over Pamela's explanation. Pamela winked to Judith to let Michele leave the room, before continuing with the discussion.

Pamela smiled wryly, "You don't believe. Do you want me to try it on you to be sure? Come on Judith, the girls are perfectly all right!" She tried reassuring Judith, who shrugged helplessly. "Tell me, how is Tutu reacting?"

The question brought a wide smile to Judith's face as she thought of Tutu. "Very disturbed. You surely wiped the smile off that black face. She knows the people would lynch her, if given the chance." Judith went on to describe Tutu's every movement and action since the affair started.

Pamela had a hearty laugh over the description, "Although I am surprised that with all her powers, she has not been able to stop the children."

"I don't why. Maybe her powers are drained or she is waiting for something. One has to be careful," Judith said thoughtfully.

"There is nothing she is waiting for except for the tightening of the noose around her neck," Pamela said confidently, bringing both of them to uneasy laughter.

After the laughter subsided, they both turned serious once again and Judith told her of her husband's plan to bring ministers from other towns to decide what was going on.

Pamela shook her head slowly, "I don't know what is wrong with your stubborn husband. Anyway, he can only postpone her agony. No matter what happens, she is going to swing." The women went on to discuss a range of issues before Judith went home later that evening.

The ministers' meeting was called immediately, but couldn't convene till mid February, three weeks later, due to the various engagements of the busy ministers. While everyone waited for the meeting, Tutu could not leave home for fear of being attacked in the streets. The Sunday school was temporarily suspended, and she lived a dreary existence, crying most of the time.

Finding solace nowhere, she called to her mother and the gods, but there was no answer, which made her feel more deserted and desolate. To compound it, she noticed that Parris became increasingly distant by the day as he saw his daughter tormented and pointing to her as the tormentor.

Her friends from the Sunday school, especially Jennifer, paid her regular visits relieving the dreariness, whenever they came to see her. Jennifer was very supportive and Tutu realized she had a true friend in her. Her friends always endeavored to put a smile on her face, in appreciation of how she always tried to alleviate their pain. Nevertheless, most of the time she remained distraught and apprehensive about the church ministers meeting.

Eventually, the meeting date arrived and ministers from Andover, Boston, Plymouth, Portsmouth and many other towns all congregated in the Salem church to ascertain the cause of the girls' distress. The meeting was to be held in the meeting room that was used to conduct church and town meetings.

Chairs and tables for the ministers were arranged in an arc around a small table and chair, which was meant to seat those interviewed. There were only a few rows of seats behind the single table, so most of the spectators were standing. While they waited for the meeting to commence, the possessed girls and the accused women were held in separate rooms in the building.

Due to the ministers discussing both private and interchurch matters among themselves, the meeting did not begin until 90 minutes after the scheduled time. Most of the ministers were alumni of Harvard and hadn't seen each other for a long time.

When Parris finally ran out of patience, he called the meeting to order by raising his voice above the room's muffled chatting. "I called this meeting today to discuss and examine the strange occurrences being witnessed here in Salem." Pausing to let the noise die down further, he stared coldly at those still talking or not paying attention.

He continued, when the noise came down to a bearable level. "There have been allegations of witchcraft against certain members of our community, due to a strange illness that has afflicted several girls," he said.

After the opening statement and a brief outline of the planned proceedings, the interrogation started. The girls were first called in for examination and questioning, and the first to be called among them was Betty Parris. Due to his emotional attachment and for the sake of fairness, Reverend Parris decided to leave the questioning to the visiting ministers.

Betty was visibly nervous, when she came into the room with some twenty ministers staring directly at her and about double that number seated behind her. The minister of Boston asked her basic questions regarding her name and age, which she answered stuttering. Gradually the questions progressed to her present condition.

"So when you feel this pain, do you see those using pins on you?" the Boston minister asked benignly. The girl nodded, but was urged to say more with hand gestures by the smiling Boston minister.

"I..I was hurt with pins by Tutu and Miss Sarah. I begged them to stop, but they did not stop," Betty said tearfully.

"Are they doing it now or when last did they hurt you?" asked the Andover minister, whom Betty answered with a shake of her head. They excused her soon afterwards and called for the next girl—Abigail.

As soon as Abigail took the seat, before any questions

could be asked, she relapsed into the strange contortions and convulsions. Initially, everyone looked on in studious silence, but it appeared to be getting worse as she fell out of her chair.

The members of the public had to rush to her aid, when she fell off the chair onto the ground, writhing in pain. The amazed visiting ministers rose from their seats to more closely observe her as people milled around her.

"Could anything be done to stop it?" one of the ministers asked showing deep concern for the girl, but was told no by Parris. They ordered her to be taken to another room, where she could lie down more comfortably.

Another girl was called in for questioning. "Has Tutu ever performed any magic act while teaching you or have you ever heard her talk about witchcraft stories?"

The girl, Sheila Hanks nodded, "Yes. Tutu always tells us African stories, when we are in the Sunday school."

"What about doing any magic?" asked one of the ministers. She shook her head in reply. After a few more questions, they dispatched her and called for another girl.

Gradually, they worked through the girls, with another two falling into convulsions in their presence. After the last girl, the ministers told the members of public to excuse themselves, and they deliberated over what they had heard and seen.

"It all seems very absurd, and I have my doubts over whether it is witchcraft or simply an illness," the minister of Andover voiced the only doubts.

"From what I have seen and heard today, I have no doubt over the presence and working of evil spirits in those girls. The question is who is invoking evil spirits to disturb the girls," the Boston Minister said gravely. They agreed to let in the members of public and called in the accused women. Sarah Good was the first one interviewed.

As she entered, there was a muffled sound throughout the room as the members of public looked and spoke in whispers. Parris called everyone to order and the room resumed its serious atmosphere.

"Miss Good, you have been accused of sorcery and

witchcraft, do you have anything to say about this?" asked the Hanover minister.

"No! I know nothing about it," she said abruptly.

"Nothing at all?" inquired the Boston minister with some cynicism, and she shook her head in reply. The ministers looked at each other and since they were powerless to make her talk, they told her to leave.

Tutu was next to be summoned and was fetched by Lewis, who had ushered all the girls and Sarah to the meeting. Tutu was sitting in the room despondently, when the door swung open. She knew it was going to be her turn soon, once Sarah had been called.

"Step forward. A step towards the gallows," Michael Lewis sneered at her. "If given the chance, I would rather have you swing right away or stoned to death. What do you think?" he asked amiably like he was asking her what she wanted to eat.

"Whichever you prefer, Sir," Tutu said, smiling wryly.

"I like your spirit. It will be stoning!" He laughed as he led her into the corridor. Tutu was shocked to find the room crowded as she entered. Likewise the ministers were shocked to find that one of the accused was black. She walked to the chair as directed by Lewis, but remained standing until told to sit down by the Boston minister.

"Do you speak English?" the Bostonian asked, still reeling from the shock, although the first to regain his composure.

"Very well, Sir!" Tutu answered, looking at the Boston minister and others confidently.

"So you understand, when it is said that you are accused of witchcraft and responsible for the girls torment?" asked the Portsmouth minister.

Tutu took a deep breath, before answering. "That is not true. I have never hurt anyone in my life that did not deserve it. Some other people are the ones using the evil spirits and making it look like me."

"So you know there are evil spirits at work?" the Boston minister questioned her, mockingly.

Tutu nodded, but was prodded on to give a vocal answer,

"Yes, there are evil spirits, but are by Esu, who is tricking everyone into believing the wrong thing. The girls are being tricked into believing they are in pain and who is doing it to them."

Esu in Yoruba is the trickster god that causes unnecessary trouble and hallucinations in Yoruba mythology, although, frequently likened to the devil in western mythology and religion, Esu is not Satan.

The ministers were perplexed, both by her fluent, educated English and by her explanation, and could not say anything for a few seconds.

"You appear to know what is wrong here, but you claim it is not by you!" The Plymouth minister said quizzically and Tutu nodded. "So what and why can't you do anything about it since you know what is wrong?"

"No, I don't want to do anything. Esu has his ways, and I want those using him to see that it will come to no good," Tutu explained to an amazed audience and ministers.

"Do you know those who are responsible by any chance?" asked the Portsmouth minister sardonically.

"Yes, I do, but it is not for me to say. They would find out that Esu has no friend?" she answered. The ministers looked among each other and decided to dismiss her. They called for the third accused, but were told she was bed-ridden and would not be able to appear. Once again, they excused the members of public and started their final deliberations behind closed doors.

"I remain skeptical about the use of evil spirits. I believe either the girls are play-acting or there is a new form of illness. As of the women, the slave is an African. These are lesser creatures that are not in full control of themselves, not to talk of putting evil spirits to work," the Andover minister concluded.

The Plymouth minister shook his head in dismay. "I don't know where you have been or what you have been listening to. If it is the same as the rest of us, I think it is clear to all that there is the presence of evil spirits disturbing the girls!" he said peevishly.

The Boston minister nodded in agreement and raised his hand to talk. "Not only have we heard it from the girls. In addition, we heard the slave girl agree that it was the work of evil spirits."

"That I find interesting. She confessed to knowing the evil spirits responsible, although passed the blame onto some other people, who she refused to name" the Lynn minister contributed.

"I guess they work together!" the Boston minister commented.

"I would not come to the same conclusions knowing her," Reverend Parris cautioned. "Tutu believes there are some people out to get her and accuses them of causing this trouble to get rid of her." Arguments and counter arguments were put forward for nearly two hours as they tried to reach a conclusion.

Finally the Boston minister suggested, "The best thing to do is to ask the governor to appoint a judge to closely examine everything and pass judgment." Most of the priests agreed to his suggestion, except the Andover minister that admonished them for wasting further time. Parris had no choice, but to agree and would rather agree to a trial than having her pronounced guilty on the spot. Eventually, they agreed to pass it to the General Court judges to look into the matter.

Later that day, when Parris got home, he found Betty going through the convulsions once again. After trying to make her comfortable while the convulsions lasted, he went to Tutu's quarters. Knocking on the door, he entered to find Tutu sitting in front of a small statue and fruits.

"Tutu, what is going on? What were you saying or trying to say at the meeting this morning?" He questioned her, sitting down on the bedside.

"Master, I told the truth," Tutu answered as she put away what she was doing.

"Look, sit here," he patted the space beside him. "What do you know about this whole thing? How do you know it is by evil spirits?" Parris asked with a serious tone and expression.

"My mother and the gods told me before it happened that they would try to hurt me, but would only end up hurting themselves. The fly that wants to quench the candlelight will only end up quenching its own life," she spoke softly, but with emotion.

Parris sighed. He could never fully understand her Yoruba philosophy. "Who are these people causing these things to happen?"

"Master, I don't want to be in trouble. I would rather have them burn themselves up!" she said rising to her feet as if he had made an indecent proposal.

Parris shook his head in exasperation. "Listen! Tell me what you know. You know I will never leave you out to dry on your own."

Tutu, noticing the frustration and anger in his voice, walked to the door and yanked it open. Parris's mouth dropped, initially thinking she was throwing him out, but realized she was taking precautions against eavesdroppers. She came back to where he sat and moved closer to speak into his ears.

"Madam's friend, Pamela and her friends are responsible. Please don't tell ma'am, because she already knows and would go back and tell them. Although she is not one of them, her sister-in-law must have told her about it," she whispered.

"That is ridiculous. Judith won't do such thing to Betty," he objected distastefully.

Tutu laughed and shook her head in dismay over her boss' ignorance. "There is nothing wrong with the girls. It is just Esu, who is playing games and she knows that. That is why she is not that much bothered, if you've noticed. Compare her now to when Betty was sick in Jamaica," she said and moved away from him.

He reconsidered it and found the theory made sense. He left without saying another word and with a very troubled look on his face.

18

The details of the ministers' meeting, especially Tutu's statements as interpreted by the ministers, were soon spread throughout Salem and beyond. She remained indoors, but was visited by her friends from the church.

One pleasant surprise visit she received was from Carol, whom Tutu hadn't seen since she defended her and lost her baby. Carol explained that she had been placed under a strict regime and was unable to move around, as she would like to ever since the incident. Although, when she heard what Tutu was going through, she decided she had to find a way to see her.

Tutu brought her up on what had been happening since she last spoke to her. Carol was clearly distraught to hear Tutu had lost her baby trying to help her as well as the present trials. Before leaving, she promised to give any support Tutu might need.

Parris was confused, when he actually noticed his wife's lack of emotions over their daughter's state, but could not voice what Tutu had told him. He found himself believing Tutu's story more by the day and, when he told her to do something about it, Tutu seemed resigned to her fate.

Actually, to his surprise, she was the one pressing him to hurry up the whole process. This was already being done and the case had been passed to the General Court deputies, who had set a date for the end of February, a few weeks away.

When the February 29th court date finally arrived, the whole town congregated to watch the proceedings. Unlike in the ministers' meeting, all the girls were seated in the front row, although the women were brought in separately for preliminary questioning. As each woman was brought into the court, the girls lapsed into contortions with their arms, necks and backs turning haphazardly. Their mouths stopped, their throats choked and their limbs thrashed like never before. The deputies wasted no time passing the case on to the general court.

Once the deputies decided there were strong reasons for indictment, they arrested the charged women and took them to jail on suspicion of witchcraft. Tutu remained stoic amid jeers from the public, as she was cuffed and taken to jail. Parris watched from a distance with tears welling up in his eyes. When he realized he could not hold his emotions anymore, he walked away.

The trial date was not yet decided and until then, the women were to be kept in jail. Anyone who had ever been there would testify that the jail was hell on earth. In the front of the cells were iron bars that ran from one end to another. Inside each cell, the prisoners were shackled to a round pillar with a straw mat to sleep upon. There were ten pillars in each cell, five in a row and ten feet apart.

Tutu was shackled to the last pillar against the wall, which was good for its nearness to a high window that let in fresh air and reduced the stench. The bad thing was that it was colder around the area than anywhere else in the cell, especially in the middle of winter.

Normally two people were shackled to each pillar, but due to the smaller amount of women compared to men, Tutu had the pillar to herself like some others in her cell. The sanitary conditions were horrific since most people excreted where they were chained. This caused diseases to be rampant and easily contracted.

In addition, the food was pathetic and not fit for a dog to eat, but that is even if it is available. In the cold weather, things were simply deplorable for the inmates with no heating, inadequate clothing and food. Most survived on the charity of friends and families, if they were not too embarrassed to come and visit them.

Tutu was lucky to have her friends, especially Jennifer and Carol, bring her clothing, firewood and food every other day. To her surprise, Theresa Putnam came to see her one afternoon soon after she was jailed.

"I understand what is happening and believe in your innocence," Theresa told her. "Keep strong and you will come through."

Tutu was shocked by what she heard from the supposedly aggrieved mother, whose daughter, Ann was one of the afflicted girls. "You know? You believe?" Tutu stuttered, unable to get over her shock of how deep Theresa Putnam's friendship was.

"Yes! I know more than you would ever believe and I believe the truth will eventually prevail," Theresa said, nodding as she spoke softly and reassuringly. She promised to return, although she was secretly embarrassed over coming to the jail.

Likewise, her brother, Parris was one of the many who were too embarrassed to be seen in such environments, especially being a priest visiting an accused witch. Nevertheless, he came late one evening after a row with Judith.

Meanwhile, Judith was ecstatic having finally gotten rid of the girl she blamed for her present condition. This infuriated Parris, as it became obvious to him that it was a set up, although he decided not to talk about it. His boiling sense of injustice exploded, when Betty relapsed into the convulsions and contortions again. As he attended to her, Judith told him she was going to visit the Porters.

"Please tell them to stop harassing my little girl," he said acrimoniously, stopping Judith in her tracks.

Quickly regaining her composure, "What are you talking about?" she asked, nonchalantly as her voice went a bit off tone.

Parris rose and walked to her, pointing an accusing finger as he spoke, "Don't think I am a fool. I see you have no concern for Betty's condition and the reason is that you know that they are hallucinations. Hallucinations caused by your friends to get Tutu for whatever stupid reason."

"Rubbish! Who told you that kind of nonsense?"

Parris shook his head in dismay and walked back to the girl. "It is the truth and it is sad. That girl you are waging war on may have spiritual powers, but she is definitely not evil. There is not a single evil bone in her body, she cured Betty when she was really sick in Jamaica, but your bloody-mindedness wouldn't let you see that".

"All you want is your rotten plantation and to get that, you work with people to get me out of Salem, thinking Tutu might stand in the way. That is what all this is about! Money!" he ranted and gesticulated angrily, moving between his daughter and wife.

Judith was shocked by her husband's tirade. Although she knew he had been unhappy over Tutu's imprisonment, she never knew his feelings ran so deep. "Samuel, you are making a grave mistake supporting that girl and trying to find other scapegoats," she said sternly, leaving before he had a chance to reply.

In the evening, Parris went to see Tutu and was shocked to see the environment. He was relieved to see she was coping well, but seeing her in chains depressed him and he bribed the guard to release her chains, while he was with her.

Moving her to a side of the room, where there was no one to hear them, Tutu told him of Theresa's visit, which he brushed aside for more pressing issues.

"Tell me, do you have spiritual powers? I need to know," he asked in a serious tone as he locked eyes with her.

From his facial expression, Tutu knew he was genuinely concerned. She nodded. "Yes, I do. I found out after mother's death, but I have not and never will do evil with it," she said with all sincerity, which he found impossible to doubt.

"It was what you used to cure Betty, isn't it?" Parris asked. Locking eyes at a close distance, she slowly nodded as she bit on her lower lip and twisted her fingers. "So why don't you do something to get yourself out of this mess. You must have some proof about those involved or something!" he urged desperately.

Tutu slowly shook her head. "Let them burn themselves. I will be all right!" She said, managing a smile to ward off his pity.

Parris sighed over her stoicism. "Look, I don't know what is going on. Whether you want the government to help you commit suicide or you have a plan. It is difficult coming to this jail. Apart from the embarrassment, it hurts my heart seeing you like this. Therefore you might not see me that often. Nevertheless, thank you for all you have done!" Parris leaned forward and kissed her on the lips to her surprise. Before she could react, he was on his way out, struggling to keep his tears. Tutu sat staring blankly for a long while, after which tears slowly rolled down her cheeks.

When Carol came visiting soon afterwards, she found Tutu crying. "I never knew you could feel pain and cry," Carol joked as she sat down beside her.

Tutu smiled and wiped her tears. "It is not the wickedness of man that makes me cry in pain, but the goodness in man that makes me cry in joy," Tutu told her.

"Goodness? Where did you see that in this land? Weren't you the one who spoke of seeing wickedness in the land?" Carol asked light-heartedly.

"There is goodness everywhere, it is just that it keeps quiet for too long, while the wicked run amok," Tutu philosophized.

"And where did you find it?" Carol asked inquisitively.

Tutu smiled. "Don't worry!" she said, waving her hand dismissively and changed her countenance into a serious one. Speaking in a whisper, Tutu continued, "Carol, I need your help. Your ma'am is one of those causing these problems, and I need to find out all those with her, especially the ones she attends those meetings with." Tutu had previously told her of Mrs. Andrews' involvement in witchcraft, which Carol had said she already suspected due to some meetings held in their house.

"I will try, but you know that might be difficult," Carol said gravely as she thought of how she could do it, without necessarily putting herself in danger. Although she was ready to take any risks for her friend, she wanted to be sure it was worthwhile. "What are you going to do? You know people won't believe you, even if you tell them."

"Don't worry. You just do it and you will see what happens. Be careful and may the gods be with you," Tutu said softly. They talked about other things and Tutu opened the package brought for her. It contained enough food for the next day or more as well as some things to keep her warm. After an hour of talking, Carol left for home.

Not too long afterwards, Jennifer came visiting and Tutu told her the same thing. Another visitor Tutu appreciated was Michele, the Potters' slave she met in the market, who informed her of Martin's ordeal. She came to see her after overhearing Pamela speak with Judith about the incident and told Tutu about how she eavesdropped on the women's conversation.

Although, Michele didn't bring as many as provisions as Jennifer and Carol, she always brought a sense of humor that lifted Tutu's spirits.

"I heard you are on holiday. You know a slave in jail is one on holiday," she joked sitting next to Tutu.

"Why is that?" Tutu asked baffled, although she knew her to be a funny character.

"Because although you are still in chains, you are off work!" she answered. By the time she left, Tutu was in stitches with sweet tears rolling down her face. However, the after-effect was depression since her jokes reminded her of Martin, who always made her laugh when he was alive.

Tutu also sought Michele's help in her venture to know all those in Pamela Porter's witchcraft circle and she was willing to help.

While Parris went to see Tutu in the jailhouse, Judith went over to her in-laws house.

"Samuel was talking about the magic on the children today. I think Tutu has finally told him the whole truth."

Pamela shrugged indifferently. "What can he do? He already has enough trouble of his own," she said.

Judith sighed thoughtfully, "He might try to free her or get you in trouble. Moreover, I am not too confident with that girl still alive in there. I would have thought they would hang her immediately."

"In good time, they will hang her, don't bother yourself!" Pamela tried to allay her fears. "I will talk to the other women about what you told me and what could be done."

Around noon the following day, Michele came to visit Tutu. She brought no provisions this time around. "I can't stay long, if I don't want to be flogged. Ma'am sent me to her friends to tell them there is a meeting tonight, which I believe you wanted to know about."

Tutu was excited by the news, "I guessed they would want to meet tonight to discuss my case. Tell me the names," she requested and Michele obliged by telling her the eight names. "That is only eight, what about the rest?" Tutu asked, baffled.

"Those are the only ones I was told to call, maybe they will tell the other women that live near them," Michele suggested.

"Thanks, I hope we would get the rest of the names from the other girls. If you could help me find out, I would be grateful."

"So should I tell ma'am Porter you will be coming over? There are no more chairs, but I would get you a stool," Michele joked as she left.

"You can never be serious," Tutu shook her head slowly but with a faint smile on her face.

"If you don't think being a slave across the world is not serious enough, then you must be joking," Michele joked, finally getting a wider smile and chuckle from Tutu. She never failed to lift Tutu's spirits whenever she came, visiting. Close to midnight later that day, she returned with Carol and Jennifer, and they gave her the names of all those presently attending the meeting.

While some of their slaves assembled in Tutu's cell, twelve

women assembled in Pamela's dining room, undisturbed. Especially, with her husband in Boston, her in-laws out and the slaves retired to their quarters.

Candles lit on the candelabrum, placed on the center of the mahogany table, provided the only light in the room. Although since only a few of the candles were lit, the lighting provided was barely bright enough to see all the faces clearly.

"We have all heard that the girl has been put in jail until she goes to trial. When the trial date is I do not know, and I heard she told Reverend Parris about us. You know that might cause serious problems for us," Pamela told the women as they settled down to the meeting.

"That goes without saying. We heard her accuse us of trying to get rid of her, and for a moment, I thought she was going to mention our names. In fact my fear is what she can do spiritually, I believe she is still very dangerous. Forget about the Reverend, we can always handle whatever he comes up with, but the girl scares me," Beatrice Andrews admitted pensively.

Not until she saw Tutu at the minister's meeting did she link her to the girl, she and her husband had beaten up at the Sunday school. Having been told she worked with thunder, she instantly knew Tutu was responsible for the fire that razed her family's distillery and had a feeling that would not be the last, unless she was hanged.

She was terrified of the prospects of further revenge and to compound it, her husband was out of town on business and hadn't heard of the recent developments and the link between the fire and Tutu. Due to the fire, he had to process his liquor in a distillery in Connecticut and spent most of his time traveling between there and the reconstructed distillery.

"Tutu is far more clever than the average slave. Intelligent enough to know that no one would believe her, if she points fingers to us in this community, but with the Reverend I do not know what can happen," Pamela told them. "Initially she wouldn't even tell her master that she had a close relationship with, dating back to her childhood in Africa."

"So what do you think is going to happen?" Mrs. Simmons asked apprehensively.

Pamela sank into her chair as she thought about it again. "That I can't say for certain," she said blowing out wind in exasperation and shaking her head ominously.

"Does that mean we wait till she wages war against us?" asked Beatrice Andrews with deep concern.

"I think we should let sleeping dogs lie. We have other important business to deal with at the moment," Mrs. Campbell advised as she reached for something under her chair.

Mrs. Andrews moving closer to the table, "The point is we have already woken the sleeping mad dog and it is already chasing us," she objected strongly to Mrs. Campbell's passive suggestion.

"If we are going to do anything, we might have to work with Annapolis, who are stronger and washed her to our shores in the first place," Mrs. O'Connor suggested.

Mrs. Campbell finally extracted what she was looking for under her chair. "These are the seeds for the tobacco and cotton plant," she held out two small sacks, which diverted everyone's attention. "I believe it is time to start planting them and forget about this stupid girl."

Pamela frowned at the subtle criticism, "One does not disturb the other," she said crossly. "Arrangements are going on in full force."

Antonia Ramsay nodded in agreement. "My husband should be landing 400 slaves in the next few weeks as planned," she announced proudly. The Ramsays were the largest slave merchants in the land and were relied upon to supply the slaves required.

"That's sorted. I suppose the land to the west has been secured?" Mrs. Lake looked at Pamela inquiringly.

"Yeah, that is why my husband has been dashing to Boston every now and then. We need the governor's help to secure the land with soldiers against the Indians, and I can assure you that it is being taken care of," Pamela said with a bit of haughtiness.

"So back to this slave, what happens?" Beatrice Andrews

returned to the issue, being uneasy with having the matter swept aside, especially for her personal reasons.

Pamela raised her hands helplessly, "I don't know what to say unless you have any suggestions." Nobody suggested anything and they all looked at Beatrice Andrews for suggestions, since she raised it.

"I think it is a bad idea waiting for her to strike back, we might not have a chance to recover and we would find out that all these seeds and plans would come to no avail!" she admonished them before they all dispersed.

19

On the 29th of March 1692, exactly four weeks after Tutu was imprisoned, Ann Putnam went into convulsions and contortions to the surprise of her parents, who thought it was all over. After a few hours, it subsided to the relief of her parents, who were mystified.

"Is it that slave girl that is still bothering you?" her bewildered father asked concerned and she shook her head. "So who is it?"

"William's mother and Julian's mother," Ann Putnam answered feebly. When asked further, they realized that it was Mrs. Pamela Porter and Mrs. Andrews to their utmost surprise.

"I always knew and am not surprised," Theresa chuckled as she looked at her husband.

Mr. Putnam, disconcerted, shook his head in dismay. "The slave girl had always said she was not the real witch. Now we know who was behind it all along." He got up from the bedside and walked out of the house, very flustered.

Around the same time, Betty went into similar fits. When she was relieved, her mother in the presence of her father asked, "Are you better? That witch Tutu is still tormenting you. I wish that judge had ended it once and for all."

To Judith's utmost consternation, Betty shook her head, "No mother, it is not Tutu hurting me now. It is the wife of Mr. Lewis and Mary O'Connor's mother."

Parris let out a sardonic laugh, "Now the truth is surely

coming out!" He picked up his jacket and stormed out before Judith could say anything.

All around Salem, girls were falling into convulsions and mentioning different members of Pamela's circle. In most cases, their parents angrily stormed to the deputies to report the latest developments, although a few wanted to take the law into their hands. By noon, the Court was a rowdy arena with angry parents asking for instant justice.

Fortunately for them, the Governor was around to speak to Judge Sewall about other matters. When the news reached them in the judges' chambers, they both came down to address the angry parents.

Initially the Governor thought the recurring illnesses were caused by the three already accused women and told the Judge on their way down, he wanted a quick trial and the heads of the women. When they met the parents in the gallery of the courtroom, he realized he was mistaken, but not before he had committed himself publicly.

"I promise you that we will have them tried and hanged!" The governor shouted at the top of his voice as he tried to placate the small crowd.

Parris stepped forward. "Sir, you said 'tried'. These women have not been arrested at all. I guess they are the real witches."

The Governor was baffled and inquired more about their requests. "Who are these real witches that you talk about that have not been arrested? Have the girls mentioned new names?" There was a deafening chorus of "Yes" to his surprise and he asked for order, whereby each parent stepped forward and named two women each. A clerk scribbled down the names and at the end there were twelve names of prominent women in the society.

"This is very surprising, and I guess the only way we will get to the bottom of this is by setting up a commission of inquiry, which I will discuss with Judge Sewall," he promised the agitated parents.

"We hope it is going to be soon enough, and they are

punished to the full letter of the law. No partiality because of who they were," one of the parents voiced her doubts and was widely supported with grunts throughout the crowd.

The Governor nodded slowly. "I promise you it will be so," he assured them, before he and the judge excused themselves.

They went back to the judge's chamber, a large room filled with shelves of books and papers. Behind the judge's chair was a large window that overlooked the street below, and they could see people still talking in groups.

The Governor, an impressive white-haired middle-aged man, took the seat across the table from Judge Sewall and placed his foot on the second chair beside him. They each lit a cigarette in silence as they thought of what was confronting them. The bald, hawkish Judge Sewall offered him a cup of tea, but he declined, not fancying the new drink that had become a fad among the English gentlemen.

"We have got to handle this situation very carefully since it has the potential to bring disrepute to our institutions and its officers," the governor broke the contemplative silence. With his eyes on the list of accused, "If we don't prosecute properly, we will be accused of corruption and favoritism. Also, we can't disregard the fact that this list comprises of some of the most powerful people in this land, capable of bringing enormous pressure to bear on us," he voiced his observations.

Judge Sewall, holding his monocle, nodded in agreement. "I believe that we should prevent or disregard any pressure from the public and the accused and let justice take its course."

"I knew you would take that stance and I will give you all the backing you require. I shall be looking to appoint some other judges to support you since it is obvious you cannot handle all these cases on your own, but this might not be until after the election of the council," the governor said before leaving.

As soon as Judith could leave home, she made her way to her Pamela's house. This was not as soon as she had hoped because after Parris left, her niece, Abigail, fell into a fit similar to Betty's. When she was relieved, Judith asked her about her tormentors and she mentioned Pamela and Mrs. Morgan. Judith strongly rebuked her and told her never to repeat it to anyone. She told the girls to watch the house and she left.

When she got to Pamela, she found her normally ebullient and confident sister-in-law in a very distraught state, having heard of the latest developments. Some angry parents stoned her house in annoyance, and she was fearful for her life.

"What is going on? I thought you said you had stopped those hallucinations?" Judith asked Pamela, who had drawn the curtains and cowered indoors.

"Believe me, we stopped them immediately after the General Court deputies hearings," she answered in a shaky voice that was like nothing Judith had ever heard.

Judith raised an eyebrow as she looked at Pamela confused and waiting for more explanation, but when none was forthcoming, "So why are the girls mentioning your names?"

Pamela shook her head gravely, "That girl has turned it against us. That was the reason she never stopped it. She wanted it to go on, so when she turned it around against us, we would be in trouble."

"Do you think anything will come out of it? After all, they haven't done anything to her so far, so people like you have nothing to fear. Don't you think so?" Judith asked, although she knew the likely answer, she wanted to allay her distressed friend's fears.

"It was all a set up. Her performance with the deputies, which I don't know how she did it, has led to provoking the public into demanding for quick and stiff punishments for anyone else accused. Now, I heard a few minutes ago that they have forced the governor into agreeing to set up a commission of inquiry, which would give stiff punishments," Pamela moaned to her sister-in-law. Judith saw her reason for alarm and could not find anything to say to allay those fears.

"Can't you stop those convulsions or reverse them and let the girls mention her as their tormentor?" Judith asked, after a long period of silence during which she thought of every possibility.

Pamela shrugged. "I am not sure, but I have called a meeting for tonight. Although it is dangerous to meet under these circumstances since all eyes are on us. It is even dangerous to walk on the streets to go for a meeting, but we will try our best."

"You think people might attack you on the streets?"

"I told you they already stoned the house and shouted curses out there. It was Tom that went out to tell them that I was in Boston before they left. People, unlike in Tutu's case, are not only angry, but many are jealous of our success and would want to pull us down," Pamela lamented. Judith had no more suggestions or anything to say and they both kept quiet and deep in thought until she left.

Parris arrived home to meet the girls alone and asked whether either of them had fallen into the fits again. He was told that Abigail had fallen into a fit after he left by Betty.

When he asked Abigail who she saw tormenting her, she refused to tell him, but he eventually forced it out of her. He was mad that his wife had gone to the extent of coercing the girl not to tell anyone and waited for her return, despite having other plans.

As soon as Judith stepped through the door, he attacked her verbally. "I really do not know, whether I have a witch or a witch's servant under my roof. Why did you threaten Abigail about telling the truth?" he asked.

"I did nothing of the sort," she denied unconvincingly. Her voice quavered, and she was amazed and terrified by the intensity of her husband's emotions as he cornered her angrily.

Although Judith denied ever coercing the girl from saying anything, she did not escape his lambasting.

"We shall see how those spoilt friends of yours swing for their crimes, but swing they will, I assure you. And if you are not careful, you will be joining them," he said.

Parris was so flustered that he felt like slapping her, but

due to his profession and nature, he turned away to control his emotions.

"Pamela is innocent. It is that whore of yours that is making it look like them," Judith countered his verbal attack, when she suspected that the worst of his temper was over.

"Rubbish! They were the ones responsible from the beginning. It is just now the mask has fallen and their hallucinations don't work anymore that the girls can see their real tormentors," Parris insisted. The couple went at each other's throats for over an hour until Parris decided he had had enough and walked out.

Tutu received visits from her friends, who brought her news of the latest turn of events. To their amazement, she was not gleeful and took the news with no outward emotional display.

They all told her of their madams' panic, and how they were all hibernating and scared of venturing outdoors after being cursed and having things thrown at them. Doubts were raised on whether the meeting planned that night would take place.

"Let us see how they like the position they put me in," was the only sign of her vengefulness.

"How did you pull it off?" Michele asked curiously.

"I didn't, the gods did it," she answered smirking.

Michele hissed sarcastically. "Hmm? We must have given one of the gods the names then. Please can you make me disappear or white?" She said with feigned desperation as she grabbed Tutu's clothes in a groveling manner.

"The only thing I have left is a magic potion that would turn you into a dog. You want it?" Tutu played along, also feigning seriousness, while the others looked on amusedly.

Michele shook her head, "Even as a human being, I am being called a bitch. I wonder what they would call me when I become a real dog." They all laughed loudly as Parris turned up.

"It seems there is some celebration going on here," he said as he stopped in his tracks a few feet away from Tutu and her three friends. "Maybe I should come back later," he said, feeling a bit embarrassed being in such surroundings and turned around to leave.

"No, we were just leaving the boring girl. She's got no food or drinks to welcome us," Michele called out after him as they rose to their feet, still laughing. The women said their farewells and left him with Tutu.

"I hope I didn't scare away your visitors," he asked and rested his bulk on the nearby ledge. "I believe they must have told you about what is going on in town."

Tutu answered with a nod and said nothing.

"I am sorry I ever doubted your sincerity," he blurted out, feeling rather inept.

Tutu smiled. "You have never done anything wrong since the day I met you, so why are you apologizing?" she said softly and touched him fondly on his shoulder. "How is ma'am taking it?" she asked with genuine curiosity.

Parris raised his eyebrows scornfully. "I really don't know what's wrong with Judith," he admitted, throwing his hands up in defeat and dismay.

"She simply refuses to accept the fact that her friends are evil. She even tried to stop her niece from mentioning names of her real tormentors, but they are all going to swing. Governor Phips and Judge Sewall have promised to set up a commission and all because of her wanting to move to Annapolis for a plantation. Money, they say, is the root of all evil," Parris said philosophically as he confided in her.

"And ignorance, because they don't know what they are doing."

"That's true! Thanks for opening my eyes," Parris answered.

"Thanks to my teacher. You are too good a man," she said shyly and hugged him. The hug lingered for a moment too long and they only disengaged when the cell door was opened loudly by one of the guards, who brought in some visitors for another inmate. Parris said his good-bye hastily as soon as they disengaged.

While Parris was visiting Tutu, the various women in Pamela's circle were making their way stealthily to the meeting. One of the women, Paulette Lewis had a more difficult task than most. Living in the poorer and most distant section of the town without a horse, she had a long way to walk to the meeting.

Her husband, Michael Lewis was still struggling to climb the rungs of the society, which was being hindered by Parris, and they therefore could not afford a better and nearer accommodation until he became minister. As fate would have it, she had to walk past the houses of two of the agitated families accusing her of witchcraft against their daughters.

Paulette was definitely "the woman behind" the Lewis family, inspiring and nagging her husband to success. She was the one that introduced her husband to the Porter camp, where he got the chance to vie for the Salem minister's vacancy.

Paulette Lewis, an impressively built woman at over six feet, walked with a pronounced limp due to a horse accident. Despite covering her shocking red hair under a veil that also covered her face, she was easily recognizable with her enormous bulk and awkward gait. As she walked past one of the families' house covertly, she heard someone shout, "Isn't that the tall fat witch?"

She increased her pace hoping to escape before the person could draw attention to her, but she could not go fast enough. The man, obviously excited, shouted and gained the attention of everyone around. Within a few moments, a small crowd gathered and Paulette had to break into a run, but they gave chase, cursing and stoning her.

Being a tall woman with long legs in a run or die situation, she was able to gain distance on her pursuers, although some of their missiles caught up with her. After a few hundred yards that she had gained fifty yards or so, coming up to a corner, she was able to seek refuge in a nearby friend's house and lost her attackers.

After half an hour when she was sure of her safety, she continued her journey to Pamela's house. Although she was a bit roughened and disinterested, she thought it would be a better idea to continue to Pamela's and get a ride back home than walking past her antagonists again. When she arrived there, the other women were already seated and waiting for her.

"I was just chased by a small mob led by the Tompkins family. I narrowly escaped as I was chased and stoned," she said as she sank her bulk into a squeaky chair.

"It's a pity you have to come a long way. Stones were thrown at the house this afternoon and only stopped when someone went to tell them I was in Boston," Pamela told them. The mood in the room was quite somber, and there were mere grunts and sighs in reply to what she said.

Beatrice Andrews shook her head sadly. "I had some women spit at me. I wish we had done something before it got to this stage," she said ruefully.

Mrs. Hall, a petite blond lady married to an investment banker that brokered and financed business deals for the Porters and many big businesses, shook her head in dismay. "It is not what we should have done, but what are we going to do now," she said peevishly.

She had had a quarrel with her husband before leaving home over the scandal and was in no mood for recriminations. Her husband had blamed her for bringing the family name into disrepute due to her associations, but she pointed to him that it was those associations that helped him to where he was. Truly, her association with Pamela and the Porters had given him his first big deal that launched him into big business.

"Well, I think we should go into the realm and set those girls free or make them mention her, instead of us," Pamela suggested and was met with agreeing nods as she looked around the table for consent. Glad that there was no dispute, she quickly spread out her hands to be linked with those beside her to form a circle, before someone could raise a point of objection.

"We will be keeping our voices very low, since we can't be totally sure there are no eavesdroppers." One of the women near the window broke the circle and rose to check the window for any spy, but found none. Closing the window firmly, she rejoined the circle and Pamela started the séance.

Murmuring gently, she recited their incantations. As she continued, the candlelight began to flicker as if blown by some strong wind. Suddenly there was a loud thunderous clap and the window Mrs. Hart had just closed, burst open giving way to Tutu.

The luminous radiance of Tutu that appeared, smiled and brought her hand to her mouth from which she blew out a large swarm of bees. The bees attacked and stung the disconcerted women.

The coven was disrupted, and the panicked women tried to escape. The frenzied escape from the room led to the women falling over themselves and furniture. They shrieked and waved frantically to get the bees off themselves as they ran into the living room, while most continued for the front door and ran outside.

Some with horses jumped on their horses and fled, while those without transport took to their heels in the direction of their homes. Mrs. Lewis forgot about her return journey worries in the heat of the moment and fled towards home on foot, but luckily Mrs. Hart picked her up along the way with her carriage. At the end of it all, most were badly stung despite their quick exit.

The following day, when Judith went to visit, she became quite distraught when she found Pamela covered with sting sores. Her swollen black eyelids had closed one of her eyes completely.

"What happened to you?" she shouted aghast.

"Tutu set bees upon us," Pamela answered morosely.

"But I thought you said, you would not go after her without outside help," Judith criticized her sternly.

"We didn't! Honestly we didn't," she said tearfully.

Judith sighed, "This is going too far. I think we better go and speak to her before this gets out of hand. Come on!" she stood up, urging her sister-in-law to get on her feet.

"What for, Judith?" Pamela asked peevishly, "The girl wants

to destroy us and you want to go and talk? Are you crazy? Leave me alone!" she snapped sourly.

"Listen, he who fights and runs away, lives to fight another day. We have to make peace now, at least until we can find a sure way of winning!" Judith beseeched her angry friend. "Please, Pamela, let's do it before it is too late."

"I really don't know about this. I am not sure I want to speak to that evil bitch," Pamela said acrimoniously.

"Come on! Let's go and speak to that bitch or witch or whatever she is," she urged Pamela. At last, Pamela reluctantly followed her after much prodding and they rode in Pamela's carriage.

With their faces covered under veils, they entered the jail and were shown to Tutu's cell. Slouching, Tutu was daydreaming, when they entered the cell, but sat up as they approached her.

"Ah! See those who have come to visit me. Thanks!" she said sweetly, but laden with sarcasm. The women walked up to her frowning and obviously not appreciating her sarcasm, Judith was the first to talk.

"Please Tutu, what is it with you and my family? Why can't you leave us alone in peace?" Judith demanded earnestly, but softly. She was barely restraining herself from punching Tutu in the face.

"Me? I haven't troubled anyone, ma'am?" Tutu feigned hurt over being falsely accused.

Judith sighed and removed the veil covering Pamela's face, revealing her blistered badly stung face. "What do you call this? 'I haven't troubled anyone ma'am'," Judith mimicked her mockingly.

"That is not my fault. Those are bee stings," Tutu smirked. "She must have gone looking for honey where she was not supposed to. Did she go looking for my honey's?"

Moving aggressively towards Tutu as if she was going to smack her in the face. "You set the bees on us!" Pamela shouted accusingly, waking a prisoner sleeping at the next pillar, who let out a string of curses.

"No, she went to where she shouldn't have gone. It is none

of my fault!" Tutu protested strongly to Judith, but in a guarded voice because of her neighbor.

Judith asked pleadingly. "Why do you want to wage war on us? My father, now my sister-in-law. Why?" Judith demanded, close to tears as memories of Jamaica came flooding back.

"That is a lie! I have never set out to cause trouble for anyone. You are the ones making war. I am just trying to live. You are the ones who put me in jail after all," she retorted.

Pamela hissed loudly. "And you want to put us in jail or gallows, don't you? It would not work, I assure you," she said.

Tutu shrugged and did not answer.

Pamela shook her head disdainfully as she looked at her with hatred, "You came to this land to destroy what we have built for ourselves, but you will not succeed in God's name."

Tutu shook her head strongly in objection. "No, Ma'am. I was forced to come and I am trying to stay alive. You are the ones waging war on my people and me! And yet you are calling upon God's name. Genesis 9 and 10, ugh? You evil witches, planters and traders! You will all learn. Just hope it's not too late." Tutu put aside her inhibitions and feigned respectfulness and boldly faced up to them.

"We are just trying to stay alive, too. We didn't come to your house. Some of your people sold you lot. We are just working towards our prosperity and not going after you. We as traders, planters, bankers and mothers are only trying to live in prosperity," Pamela retorted insistently.

Tutu nodded sardonically. "Yes on our blood, ma'am." She paused and decided to continue. "I was taken by white men, but whether we were sold or stolen by our people or not, doesn't matter. It is not about the skin, but in the heart. They are evil people, and you are one of them. You are the ones enjoying the fruits of evil. Everything comes from that evil, which you live by and...." She decided against completing her sentence and just hissed and shook her head pitifully with a wry smile on her face.

Judith touched her gently on her shoulder, in a persuasive manner. "Please Tutu, you better stop this or we will all regret it.

There are others who will join the fight, and I don't think you could take on everyone."

"Next time, it would be total war," Pamela declared threateningly as she jabbed her finger at Tutu.

"If you say so, ma'am, but I would say I have never attacked anyone. Next time, I am attacked or disturbed it would not be bees that would be coming. That was just child's play protecting the girls!" Tutu answered her threat acrimoniously with hers.

"You must be really bold talking to us like this. Some uppityness! You think your little game could hurt us? You are making a mistake..." Pamela was saying, but was interrupted.

"Who is making a mistake?" Parris asked, startling them as he walked into their conversation. Pamela and Judith used their eyes to scornfully dress him down, hissed and walked out angrily without saying a further word. "Why do I always chase your visitors away?" he said jokingly, making Tutu laugh despite her anger.

Following her short laughter. "Who needs visitors like them?" she blurted out.

"It appears you were not enjoying their company," Parris continued humorously, but turned serious, when he saw Tutu's sour expression. "Did they come here to threaten you or something?" He inquired somberly as he looked into her eyes, trying to read her emotions.

"They can only threaten. They have done their worst. It can't get worse than this," she said bitterly, waving her hand around gesturing towards the squalid conditions, she was locked in.

Parris tried placating her, but couldn't find the right words to mollify her anger and pain. He stayed with her for a while until Jennifer and Carol arrived. When he left, Carol and Jennifer joked about their mistresses' new looks, which were the result of the bee attack. Tutu never told them she knew anything about the incident, despite their constant joking that she had stung them.

Despite Tutu's denial of spirituality, her friends believed without any doubt that she was spiritually active and strong.

Throughout the slave population, there were already whispers of a messiah-like leader currently in jail. The majority did not know her name or even if she was male or female and what they knew, they kept to themselves to prevent any trouble such knowledge could bring.

Even the few that had spoken to their masters about the Slave Queen were treated with disbelief and ridicule.

20

Michael Lewis was slowly making his way to the church grounds, enjoying the April spring weather that was breaking through, when a horse carriage pulled up beside him.

"Michael, how have you been?" bellowed a familiar voice warmly from the carriage. Michael was startled and initially could not recognize the voice or identify who was greeting him, because the person had a hat that covered his face. The person pushed the hat backward slowly with his finger to reveal his identity.

Pleasantly surprised to find out who it was, he replied beaming, "Oh! Mr. Andrews, fine. Thank you! Welcome back! How was your trip?" Lewis greeted his benefactor warmly.

"It was hectic, but profitable. Thank you! What has been happening in my absence? Are you going anywhere in a hurry?" Gordon Andrews inquired amiably.

"No," Lewis answered ponderously. "Not really. I was just going to the church to check on a few things. Anything, I can do for you?"

"Well, if you are in no hurry, we could have a few drinks, while I catch up on what has been going on around here," Mr. Andrews suggested and Lewis did not hesitate to accept the invitation. He jumped into the carriage and rode home with Mr. Andrews.

When they arrived at Gordon Andrews' house, Carol and two other slaves that met them outside took over the horses and carried in their master's luggage. Seeing him from their room, the Andrews children rushed to greet their returning father at the porch, while Lewis looked on cheerfully.

Carrying his youngest daughter, they followed the boys indoors as Mr. Andrews asked, "Where is your mother?"

Beatrice Andrews was sitting in a dark corner of the living room. "Welcome and how was your trip?" she asked flatly.

"What is wrong with you?" he asked, noticing his wife's demureness. He went towards her with his arms open, but halted as he noticed her blistered face. "What the hell happened to your face, Beatrice? What has been going on around here?" he asked with deep concern and pity.

Mrs. Andrews sighed deeply. "Settle down. We will talk later."

"I am sorry, Mrs. Andrews, I heard that the African witch gave you trouble at the Porters," Lewis greeted her. The women had agreed among themselves to tell all those that inquired that they were having tea in the Porters house, when Tutu attacked them with bees.

"Which slave witch is this? What kind of trouble?" he inquired seriously as he slowly let down his daughter, who immediately ran off to play with her siblings. "Would someone tell me what is going on?" He demanded as he sat beside her.

Mrs. Andrews sighed deeply again, letting the air out of her mouth. "The girl that attacked me in the Sunday school because of Carol is a witch. She is in jail now for tormenting some young girls with evil spirits and I found out that she was responsible for the distillery fire."

"What?" Gordon Andrews barked loudly, unable to contain his emotions as his face reddened.

His wife continued despite his interruption, "Anyway, we were at Pamela's place when she attacked us with bees." His wife moved her scarf backward to reveal the full extent of her injuries.

"My goodness?" Andrews whistled. "Where did you say she is?"

"She is presently in jail, sir. But it is obvious she is still dangerous and to make it worse, she is not being hanged," Lewis answered, before she could.

Andrews rose angrily to his feet. "Come on, Michael. Let's go see this slave that burnt my distillery and attacked my wife," he said. Not waiting for an answer, he headed for the door.

"Please take it easy, Gordon! Don't go to that dangerous animal," his wife cautioned him, but it was too late.

Lewis barely caught up with Gordon as he jumped on to his carriage and whipped the horses. Andrews rode in silence, like the enraged man he was, through town to the jail. When they arrived, he jumped down and ran towards the jail, but was stopped by one of the guards, who asked of his mission there.

Lewis was able to catch up and intervene at a point that Andrews was at a loss with the guard, not knowing the name of the prisoner and too angry to give a coherent response. Stating their business at the jail, Lewis was able to secure their entry into the jail and they were led to Tutu's cell.

Jennifer was with Tutu, when they arrived and they both had their backs to the door. The guard pointed the men towards where Tutu was shackled and on seeing the black hair from afar, Andrews broke into a run towards them. On reaching where they were seated, Andrews rained blows and kicks on whom he thought was Tutu, but unfortunately it was Jennifer. Tutu jumped up at him as their screams brought the guards running back. The guards tried to restrain Andrew with great difficulty, but eventually did.

"Next time you go near my family or property or anything happens to them, I will personally wring life out of your neck and not wait for the hangman," he shouted as he was restrained.

Tutu, crouching near her stunned friend, whose nose was bleeding, gave him a mean look. "You've really done it this time! You will regret it. Both of you!" she said coldly. "You want to squeeze life out of me like you did to my baby, ugh? We shall see who has life squeezed out of them!"

The guards dragged Andrews out of the cell as he shouted, "Ooh Yeah? I will kill you, if you mess with me. I promise..." He struggled to free himself from the powerful grip placed around his chest, but couldn't as the guards dragged him backwards and outside.

"Mister, you can't do this here!" one of the guards admonished him. He was let go once they were outside, and he and Lewis got into his carriage and rode away.

Inside, Tutu was checking and nursing Jennifer's wounds, "I am really sorry," showing deep concern and guilt.

"Don't worry. It is one of those things we all have to face," Jennifer smiled weakly at Tutu. "You know I am used to these beatings by now," she tried joking lightly, but Tutu only shook her head in dismay.

"It has to stop. It can't continue like this. That is what I was talking to you about, before the madman that killed my baby arrived. You have got to help me get all the other evil ones like your ma'am," Tutu told her imploringly.

Jennifer nodded, "But how do we do this?"

With a wry smile, Tutu placed a hand on her shoulder to draw her closer. "Talk to our people everywhere. I know a few in Boston. Just put the word out and give me the names of the rich and wicked ones that treat our people badly. I will take it from thereon," she said.

Jennifer nodded slowly, "I will do my best, but have you told the others? Michele and Carol?"

"Yes, they are working on it," Tutu assured her. She had spoken to the others of her plans to widen the witch-hunt to all over Massachusetts and they had already given her a few names.

The following Sunday at church a young girl walked up to Andrews and Lewis separately, and told them they were wanted in the freshly reopened Sunday school. They were surprised, because the girl did not tell them by whom, before she ran off. Nevertheless, they went to the school to see who had summoned them. Concerned parents that wanted their children to continue the Sunday school, due to no other alternatives, had appointed a new teacher.

The instant Andrews and Lewis stepped into the room, several girls fell into fits of contortions and convulsions and they quickly ran to their aid. While they tried to administer help to the girls, news of another round of fits among the girls spread to the church and concerned parents and members of the congregation ran to the school.

The fits were to continue unabated for 45 minutes, while the adults stood around in small groups complaining about the slowness of the governor in bringing the accused to court. They believed that it was the accused witches, who were still free that were continuing to bother the girls.

When the fits subsided the girls were asked who their tormentors were, and to the surprise of everyone around, they pointed to Mr. Lewis and Mr. Andrews.

"What? There must be a mistake here!" Lewis exclaimed in disbelief, but he could not exonerate himself.

Angry parents jumped at them and the two were only saved by the presence of local deputies in the vicinity. Although it was surprising that men were mentioned as the tormentors, it was easily believable since they were husbands of the women already accused and were present at the scene.

The news of the first male witches or wizards soon spread throughout the town as everyone wondered, what was really happening in their town.

The deputies took the two accused men to the court, where they were entered into their books and released pending trial. This was to increase public pressure on the governor and the general court to act swiftly over the witchcraft incidents that were afflicting their children.

Although on the other hand, due to the caliber of people arrested, there was also pressure on the governor, not to do anything and adopt a wait and see approach. Some of the people arrested had aided the colonial government in expelling the previous governor and winning a new charter for Massachusetts, which resulted in the appointment of this new governor.

The governor wanted his council, the upper ruling body, in place before he took any action. The governor's council was a body of wealthy landowners and respectable people at the pinnacle of the society, which was equivalent to the British

House of Lords, who the governor believed would be able to solve the problem.

Meanwhile, the number of black visitors to the jail was increasing by the day as Tutu's fame and network nearly grew to what it was like in Jamaica. Theresa and Parris were the only white visitors.

Most of the slaves followed Tutu's inner circle of friends to see her and talk about the problems they were having with their masters, while only a few came for healing. Tutu never promised anything, but just listened attentively to them. She then decided what she was going to do, if anything, and kept her decision to herself.

By the end of April, her second month in jail, more than 20 people had been accused of witchcraft pending trial. Out of the 20, she was directly responsible for 16 and realized that some other people were using the occasion to settle old scores by accusing their antagonists of witchcraft.

Tutu began to look beyond Salem and did not wish to have too many accused people from Salem, for the fear that it might backfire and the General court might not be able to handle it. Or, that the accused might sway the political machinery from prosecuting them due to their large numbers.

Her first alternative was nearby Andover, where her network had extended and names of wicked, prosperous masters had been handed to her. Some girls in the Andover church were afflicted with similar fits, but unlike those in Salem, they could not mention their tormentors. Due to this, the Salem girls were invited to identify those responsible, at the end of which 40 people were accused of witchcraft.

Her next destination was Boston, where she knew a few young girls, especially those of the Anthony Smith household and some mentioned to her by her network. Around the second week of May, she visited upon them the fits that were afflicting the Salem girls, but again like the Andover girls, they could not see or mention their tormentors. Therefore it was also suggested to bring in the Salem girls to help sniff out the evildoers.

Earlier in April, one Boston slave, Sharon brought by Michele had complained about how her ma'am flogged and ill-treated them. Although, Tutu was more interested in her description of how the household flooded with visitors.

She learnt one of the frequent visitors was Mr. Porter, who the slave followed to some parcels of land outside Boston with her owners. It was on the trip she met Michele, who was brought along by the Porters. The Porters and her owners made the trip to examine the land, which was to be used for plantations of tobacco and cotton.

"If you see the land, you wouldn't believe its extent. It took us over a day to go all over it. They plan to get it ready for the next planting season with new slaves," the slave told her.

This rang a bell in Tutu's head, and she linked it to the plans she'd overheard while eavesdropping on Pamela's meeting. Tutu thanked her and they left without any concrete plans, but a promise that the gods would look into the problem and soon shine their mercies on her.

When the Salem girls arrived in Boston, they were taken to the church, where most town meetings were held and told to fish out the evildoers. The girls broke into fits after which they mentioned the colony's first lady, Mrs. Phips, the wife of the governor. In addition, they mentioned Helen Smith and Mrs. Putnam, Parrises in-law that lived down the road from the Smiths. Tutu remembered how she had mistreated her young slave, when Parris took her to visit.

The witch hunting spread to Boston's aristocrats and caused great concern for the governor and other political heavyweights, whose wives were being accused of witchcraft as the specter continued. Like in Salem, many people also used the occasion to settle personal scores.

In Salem, Pamela and her friends were thankful that Mrs. Phips was dragged into the scene and saw the chances of their prosecution dwindle. They believed it would give more credence to their case that they were wrongly accused and knew the governor would never hang his own wife.

For the first time, they were able to sigh in relief and hold their covens, although they were still conscious of the envy and hatred from many people in the town. They also began a campaign to drag in others, especially from the opposition, namely the Putnams. They ensured Theresa Putnam as well as some of her sisters-in-laws and friends were also accused of witchcraft.

The accusations were soon to move to every corner of the Massachusetts colony, and it was increasingly difficult for the governor to continue deferring the setting up of a court, although the quantity and quality of those accused made a decisive move a political nightmare.

To appoint a special court, he would have to choose from his council, however most of its members' wives were being accused of witchcraft. This was a difficult situation for him, and the fact that his own wife now stood among the accused fuelled unsavory rumors that the Governor was tongue-tied because of his own personal involvement.

One evening when Michele and Carol met at Tutu's cell, Tutu realized she might have overdone her pursuit of the ruthless influential people.

"My ma'am seems to be happier than ever before," Michele commented during a conversation.

"So is mine. It appears they believe nothing is going to happen to them after all!" Carol said.

Tutu looked confused. "Why?" she asked.

"You remember Sharon that I brought to you a few weeks ago. Her ma'am is the Governor's wife, and she was accused of witchcraft. I heard my ma'am say that their case would never go to trial, since the Governor's wife is now one of them and the governor would never hang his wife," Michele explained to a sullen Tutu.

Carol nodded in agreement. "You can't expect the man to hang his wife. Instead, there will be no trial."

Tutu nodded and remained quiet for some time as she

realized she might have shot herself in the foot. After her ponderous silence, she arrived at a conclusion.

"Look we can't allow that to happen. I need you to get a gossip to Judge Sewall and probably the Governor that the Governor's wife was wrongly accused, and they should speak to the girls again," Tutu instructed them and they made plans on how to achieve their goals.

Word went through their network to Judge Sewall that some evildoers had tricked the girls into believing the first lady tormented them. The judge did not know the origin of the information, but nevertheless passed it to the governor, who recalled the girls to Boston.

When the girls arrived, they were taken through the same test, and the girls cleared the first lady. Some other women were accused of using the girls to get to the first lady. The girls claimed that they had been mistaken and were tricked into believing that she was the one responsible by other witches, who wanted to escape detection and prosecution. This initially raised doubts among some that believed the governor was merely trying to clear his wife, but was quelled by some of those that had witnessed the proceedings.

The governor was greatly infuriated that some evil people had dragged his name and that of his wife through the mud to escape punishment. This spurred the governor into action with a vengeance like never before. Moreover, the election of his council had just been concluded, and he was free to choose a special court from it.

The news of the enraged governor setting out to form a special court after the vindication of his wife caused great consternation for Pamela and her circle. A meeting was hastily arranged to discuss the latest development.

"That girl is playing games with everyone and we might be in grave danger," Pamela commented reflectively as they gathered around the table in her dining room.

Beatrice Andrews supported that view with her own, "I heard the governor is furious and vowed to punish all those accused of witchcraft for dragging his wife into the mess. We might be running out of time for something to do."

"There must be something we can do to stop her from causing us further trouble. I believe she got Mrs. Phips out of trouble when she realized the governor would not prosecute as long as his wife was accused," commented Mrs. Simmons, which brought about consenting murmurs around the table.

"I see what you are pointing out, which was why we decided to involve those close to her and the priest, but I am not sure what effect that would have," Mrs. Jones said.

"Let's wait and see what happens. I don't think she would let her master's sister hang," Pamela voiced her doubts hopefully.

Beatrice Andrews shook her head disagreeably. "I do not think it is wise to sit and do nothing, hoping she will do something to stop the hanging of the Putnams. This girl does not care about anyone and, if she does, she can always come up with something to let them off," she cautioned them.

"So what do you suggest?" asked Mrs. Lewis, but as usual there were no suggestions on how to tackle Tutu. The only other alternative was to fight spiritually, which all of them were scared to do from their experience with Tutu.

They put the issue aside and went on to the planned cultivation of tobacco and cotton throughout the Dominion of New England, hoping the witchcraft issue would sort itself out, when the time comes.

21

This turned out to be a false belief and sense of security when the governor announced in June, the formation of a special court to try all those accused of witchcraft. The number of those accused now stood at over 500 and was still growing, as others continued to use the occasion to settle old scores or remove their political and business competitors.

At the inauguration of the committee, the governor in his speech swore to leave no stone unturned and no sacred cows untouched.

"...the foundation of this colony, which was built in Christian traditions and brotherhood, has been shaken by evil people with their witchcraft and sorcery. These people have to be weeded out and punished severely, although, according to our Christian traditions, we are willing to forgive those who show penance and change their ways. Therefore, the judges are being instructed not only to adhere to the letter of the law, but also to that of the bible...." he told the crowd that came to witness the swearing-in of the commission of inquiry.

The court commenced sitting the following day and one instruction they were given, that was not mentioned in the speech, was the immediate arrest and detention of all those accused. The governor wanted to prevent the repeat of what happened to his wife, whereby he believed that some of the witches tried to frame her to distort the workings of the political and judicial systems.

The instruction was followed to the letter and over 500 people were immediately arrested when they appeared for the hearing, which they thought would be only to have their charges read.

Pamela and her friends were shocked to find themselves arrested, chained and led from the courtroom to the jail. They could not believe their treatment, both at the hands of the authorities and the general public, who booed and pelted them with the occasional tomato and egg on their way to the jailhouse.

The court ordered that all those previously in jail should be cramped into one part of the jail, in order to create space for the large number of the newly arrested. Therefore, Pamela and the other women were put in different cells from Tutu, which was a disappointment to them. They had hoped to strangle Tutu in her sleep, if given the slightest chance.

The instant they were jailed there was immense pressure from their families to secure their release through bail, but with no success since the court officials followed their orders. The governor purposely stayed out of reach to avoid being pressured to rescind his order.

When all their attempts for freedom were frustrated, some of them went to the extent of making representations to London, but those in London had their hands full at the moment. Moreover, the government in London, being grateful for the recent routing of opposition forces by the governor and the members of the Bostonian hierarchy, did not want to countermand any decisions made by its officials.

The mass arrests fuelled more accusations by the members of the public, who used the opportunity to get rid of those they didn't like or with whom they were competing. Within a fortnight, those arrested nearly doubled and Salem became a jittery town. Many people simply refused to venture outdoors for the fear of being labeled a witch and everybody wondered who was going to be the next to be arrested.

In the Parrises' home, there was increased friction between husband and wife as Judith's misery grew over her sister-in-law's plight.

"Your stupid girl is going to destroy everyone," Judith bitterly confronted him one day after returning from a visit to Pamela.

Parris angrily rose to the challenge. "No, it is you who always have to destroy everything for everyone. You started this, and you started the trouble in Jamaica. That girl, you are hounding is only reacting with a survival instinct," he bellowed as he wagged his finger angrily at her.

"Continue siding with the witch. We will see where it gets you or isn't your sister also in jail with them, waiting for the hangman?" Judith shouted, hissing and slamming the door as she left the room flustered.

Reverend Parris was very distraught over his sister's arrest and those of his in-laws. Now, he had more than one close person to visit behind the bars, making his visits there more frequent and stressful.

Later in the day, after visiting his sister, he stopped at Tutu's cell. Parris had to look around for a few moments, before he could sight Tutu and headed towards her. Due to the overflow from the other prison, they were no longer chained to a pillar, since there were now four people to a pillar, which was meant for only two.

"You don't have to carry the whole world on your shoulders," Tutu joked, when she saw his gloomy expression as he approached.

Parris shook his head. "This is becoming a nightmare. First, you now my sister, only God knows who's next," he said as they both leaned against free space on the wall.

"Don't worry, it will soon be over. There is nothing without an end," Tutu tried comforting him.

"Over with Theresa at the wrong end of a rope?" he scoffed and shifted uneasily at the thought of it.

"That won't happen! Believe me!" Tutu said confidently with a wry smile on her face.

"No! It would be a miracle if it does not happen from the things I have been hearing," Parris said, clearly distraught.

Tutu moved closer to him and placed a hand on his shoulder. "Listen, if you follow my advice, she will walk free," she whispered, looking at him expectantly for a reaction.

"Is this some of your mother's advice?" he said sarcastically, which annoyed Tutu and made her move away from him. She turned away from him and turned her concentration on a small wooden object she had in her hands. Noticing she was sulking, he blurted out his apology. "I am sorry. It is just that I don't see how it could be done. After all, you are still here."

"And alive! Have I ever told you something wrong?" she asked peevishly, hissed and turned away again.

Parris sighed heavily, "I said am sorry! Now what is it that you believe could keep them from the gallows?"

Tutu smirked and moved closer to him. "Promise, you won't tell anyone else and you have to make her promise as well that she won't tell anyone else, otherwise it will not work," she whispered into his ear, and he nodded in agreement. "No, I want you to promise," she insisted.

"I promise and cross my heart," Parris said, smiling over the awkwardness of the situation.

Tutu looked at him, unsure of his seriousness. She heaved a sigh, knowing she had to tell him nevertheless, since Theresa was a good friend to her. "She has to plead guilty," Tutu said.

"What?" Parris exclaimed loudly in consternation. "Absolutely no way!" He got to his feet as he strongly objected to the idea.

"It is the only way out, trust me," Tutu said softly and looked into his eyes for him to see her sincerity, but it was difficult for him to accept and he shook his head violently as the thought of it was repulsive. He sighed heavily and returned to his spot next to her.

"My sister is no witch, I have known her all my life and can vouch for her to the end of time," he tried explaining to her with a pained expression.

Tutu scoffed. "I know Theresa is no witch, but the judges don't know and everybody will be saying the same thing. If she pleads guilty and begs for forgiveness, she would be released and

have her life saved. Otherwise, she will swing like the others,"
she told him point blank.

Parris thought about it for some time and could see the logic,
but the stigma that she would carry all her life was unbearable.
"I see what you are saying and will talk to her about it, but it is a
bitter medicine to swallow," he admitted in resignation.

"Exactly! Just like the one you had to swallow in Africa that
saved your life," she said excitedly, bringing a smile to his face
with the analogy. "Just remember, no one else is to hear about
the plan," she cautioned him. He thoughtfully nodded his
agreement and left to talk to his sister.

When he told Mrs. Theresa Putnam, she felt slighted and
took it badly. Parris had to return subsequent days to try and
convince her with the idea. It was difficult to convince her
without telling her that it originated from Tutu, and giving
her the background knowledge, which he was not willing to
give. Eventually, she reasoned with him, but did not promise
anything.

22

The special court sessions were divided among various judges due to the size of the prosecutions. The first trial started with less fanfare than the deputies' pre-trial hearing due to Judge Sewall's stern approach. He kept the crowd to a minimum and in check. On the first day all the girls sat in the court, while the bailiffs were to bring in the accused women in turns.

The judge first questioned the girls and was told they still suffered from the evil spells cast on them. Then, their physician, Dr. William Griggs, was called to testify, which he did by restating his observations that what befell the girls was no natural disease known to man and could only be caused by demons.

The judge listened to various witnesses and experts who told the court that what was troubling the girls were demonic fits. After thoroughly questioning them, he told the bailiffs to bring the accused women into the court. The first to be brought in was Tutu, who also surprised the judge for not only being black but eloquent.

"How do you want to plea to the charges of witchcraft brought against you, guilty or not guilty?" The judge asked in his usual stern manner.

"I am not pleading!" Tutu's abrupt answer was followed by hushed sounds around the court, brought about by people catching their breath in amazement.

"You have to enter a plea. Do you talk to spirits or use them in any way or manner?"

"They can steal me away and stop me from talking to my

family, but they can't stop me from talking to the spirits of my ancestors and my creator."

"There are allegations that you are a witch, are you or not?" he raised an eyebrow as he rephrased the question with a hint of irritation.

"Sir, those that accuse me of being a witch don't even accept I am a human being like them. So how can they say I am a witch?" Tutu spoke, free of fear to an astonished judge.

The judge paused for a minute as he tried to figure out how to proceed. "I believe you are a human being like I am, so are you a witch?"

"Sir, anyone could be a witch, but there are evil witches and good ones. A witch is a messenger between the gods and man. He could be a priest or an evil one. I have done no one any evil!"

"So are you a witch?" he repeated slightly louder as he became impatient.

"Yes, I am a witch, only if a witch is someone who communicates with their creator and gods," Tutu said unabashedly, earning all sorts of comments from the gallery. Some shouted that she should be hanged, while some shouted she should be stoned. Samuel Sewall was not one to tolerate any form of laxity in his court and rapped his gavel.

"If I hear any more comments from you there, you will be the first leaving for the gallows," he threatened them angrily. It was rather very effective, as everyone kept silent. Then he turned his attention back to Tutu.

"So you plead guilty to being a witch?" The judge concluded, looking into her face inquiringly and she nodded in response. "Are you responsible for the girls' torment?"

Tutu took her time before answering, thinking of a right answer. "I did not do anything to the girls, but they are sick because of me. Some wicked witches made it look like I am the one who is doing it, so that you would kill me," she answered with all sincerity, which the judge noticed. Being an experienced judge, he could judge someone's character easily, but the girl in front of him baffled him.

"How could that happen? How could others torment the girls, yet they see and mention you as their tormentor?" he asked, throwing up his hand in confusion. Tutu explained the workings of a god, she identified as Esu and how he was the god of trickery and mischief. He was the one, she claimed, the wicked witches had employed to carry out their evil plan. "And who are these evil women, you mention?" he demanded.

"It is not for me to tell, but you shall surely meet them," she answered smiling.

"This is no laughing matter, woman! You better be serious and talk or you will soon be swinging," he scolded her sternly as he noticed her smiling and at ease.

"Sir, I am serious. I love those girls and would never do anything to hurt them. I teach and play with them, but the evil ones choose to strike them with tricks," she said solemnly.

Judge Samuel Sewall was out of his depth on what was being presented to him by Tutu. He was someone that always trusted his hunches and they were telling him that she was telling the truth. He excused her temporarily because he wanted to hear what the other women had to say.

The next to be called was Sarah Good. She came into the court looking very haggard and pallid because she had no one to visit and help her in the jail. Her face was covered with rashes, and she sneezed and coughed continuously. It was obvious she was diseased due to her incarceration.

"How do you plead to the charge of witchcraft, guilty or not guilty?" she was asked.

"My lord, I am innocent and don't know anything about witchcraft?" she answered morosely.

"Do you know what happened to the girls, when they suddenly fell ill in your presence?" and she answered with her head, she knew nothing. "Do you know whether any person you know is responsible?"

Sarah Good took her time as she thought of the question. "My Lord, I don't really know, but maybe Sarah Osborne. She is a bit weird," she told the court.

"What about Tutu, the black slave girl, who was with you?" Samuel Sewall asked curiously, expecting her to castigate Tutu.

Sarah Good slowly shook her head. "She loves the children, and I don't think she would do such a thing. She is a good person." The judge thought about what she said for a moment and when there were no further questions, he excused her.

Bailiffs carried in Sarah Osborne, the last of the accused persons for the day, because she was bedridden. They placed the aged woman down near the judge's bench and Sewall had to lean over his bench, in order to see her on the floor. He asked how she wanted to plea.

"Not guilty. If I knew about witchcraft, I would not be lying down here at your feet!" she answered grouchily.

The judge smiled for the first time since the proceedings started. "What do you know about the children and the strange illness that has befallen them?"

"Nothing! I was refused church membership 20 years ago and have never stepped in one ever since then. I have never seen any of the girls in my life," Sarah Osborne answered without any care or fear.

Judge Sewall called for a recess to deliberate over the strange hearings he had just sat through. He was faced with a dilemma over how to rule on the case. On one side were the prosecutors that were convinced beyond doubt, who the tormentors were and made a good case. On the other side were the accused women that raised significant doubts in his mind over their charges.

Tutu's eloquence and sincerity made a good impression on him and changed his impression of Africans forever, while it seemed unlikely that the bedridden Osborne woman could have the opportunity, either physically being crippled or socially being a non-church member. With doubts like these, it was difficult to convict, but the whole town was rooting for their conviction, placing him in a very difficult position.

The punishment of a guilty plea for witchcraft was imprisonment and the punishment of an innocent plea, when found guilty was death. Two of the women had pleaded innocent and he found it impossible to send them both to the gallows. Instead of passing judgment the same day, he adjourned the case until the next morning to give him time to sleep on it.

The following day, he called the accused women to the stand and asked whether they had anything to say before he passed his judgment. He told Tutu to step forward first and address the court.

"Sir, I do not have much to say except that it is strange that in a land where people like me are treated as mere savages, we could also be charged for being strong spirits. Ever since I was taken, I have been met with nothing but wickedness and now I am charged with wickedness," she said stoically and sat down amid hisses and curses.

The judge called the crowd to order and gave them a stern warning, which was usually effective for the whole day. He called on Sarah Good, but she declined the opportunity to address the court.

Sarah Osborne spoke from where she was lying. "How do you hang a crippled person is what I would love to know?" she asked in a nonchalant way that provoked laughter from both the judge and the crowd.

"Well, I have carefully examined and re-examined the merits of this case and have come to the conclusion that it leaves much to be desired in terms of solid evidence and counter evidence. While I sentence you Sarah Good to death by hanging, I withhold sentence on Tutu and Sarah Osborne for further deliberations," the Judge announced. He rose and left and did not bother to bring the court to order, suspecting that they would disregard him.

In the evening Parris went to visit Tutu at the jailhouse. "Congratulations!" he shouted from afar as he walked towards her with his arms open.

Tutu smiled shyly. "Am I going home?" she asked expectantly.

"Not just yet, but at least you won't be swinging," he said ebulliently as he found a ledge on which to rest his butt.

"I didn't do anything to swing in the first place, yet I have been kept here for months. It is just not fair!" Tutu vented her frustrations, which she rarely did in his presence.

Parris fumbled for something to say, "Well, neither did Sarah Good." When he noticed her sulking, he moved closer, "I would try and talk to the judge to speed up the deliberations, although I wouldn't want to annoy him into a bad decision," he spoke softly and brought a faint smile to her face.

"Leave him alone to the gods then," she said in a resigned tone.

"That reminds me. I was impressed by your performance in court today, and I guess the judge was impressed as well. It is the reason you are not on the way to Gallows Hill. You were quite impressive."

Tutu smiled shyly. "Thanks to my teacher!" she beamed and gave him a lingering hug.

Early evening the following day, Tutu's friends came visiting and they stayed with her for sometime joking and gossiping before they gradually left her. Michele was the only one left, when an unexpected visitor for Tutu turned up. They did not expect in their wildest dreams, who turned up and Michele scurried away.

Judge Sewall flanked by two guards moved towards her, once Michele left. He automatically put his hand over his nose as he was hit by the stench emanating from the cell, but soon got accustomed to it or decided to ignore it. Looking around he was shocked to see where he had sent many people.

Judge Sewall ordered the guards to leave him alone with her to give him privacy. Initially, they were hesitant because they feared for his safety, but could not disobey a direct order. The guards left to stand at the entrance, where they could see them, but not hear anything.

Tutu was shocked, but soon regained her composure. "Did

my master, the Reverend Parris ask you to come?" she asked, being unable to guess any other reason for his appearance.

Sewall slowly shook his head as he observed her with his keen judge eyes, "No, I came of my own will."

"Why would a powerful man like you want to visit someone like me?" she asked smiling and affable, showing no awe of the renowned judge.

Sewall smiled, "Maybe because powerful men do have their weaknesses. I have been thinking a lot about what you said in court and it has changed how I view a lot of things, particularly your people." The judge, being one of the fairest in the land, could not push out of his mind what he had heard in court from her.

Also, due to his sense of fairness and equality, the institution of slavery had always bothered him, but having no slaves of his own, he had never spoken or reasoned with any African. Like the majority of citizens, his impressions were derived from a few plantation owners and others that used them for economic reasons. Being an intelligent and independent minded person, he suspected they all painted the same picture due to the need to suppress the slaves and rid themselves of guilty consciences.

Tutu sighed in relief, "Maybe something good would come out of my problems, even if it is unfair."

He sat on a ledge nearby. "Tell me about where you come from? It seems I have a wrong idea of what Africa is, but seeing you so well spoken makes me realize you people might not be as primitive as I was led to believe. I am curious and want firsthand knowledge," he said candidly.

"Well, I speak like this because the reverend taught me in Africa how to speak English when I was young. I am Yoruba and we are not primitive. The town I come from is bigger than this town and Boston combined. God created us in the Ile-Ife meaning land of love," she spoke easily as if speaking to a friend or Reverend Parris. Telling him how Obatala and Oduduwa dried-up the swampy earth.

"The land of love does sound like the Garden of Eden, although I don't know what Eden means. You spoke of a religion that had the devil and other things. What do you worship?" He asked with keen interest showing on his face.

"God!" she laughed, but became serious, "The names are just different because of the language. For example, you have Mary or Mariam, whose son died for the people. We have Moremi whose son also died for our people. There are those that use the spirits and religion for evil or good in ours just like in your churches and cults. We are human like you!" She continued explaining the similar patterns of society and government, she had noticed for the next half-hour or more.

When she finished, Judge Sewall shook his head in disbelief and remained in thoughtful silence. "All I can say is that I have never met an African as intelligent as you, and I am delighted and grateful for the opportunity to be enlightened."

As he rose to leave, Tutu held onto him and said charmingly, "One thing we don't do is to imprison the innocent. You are a good man and you know I am innocent."

Sewall stopped and looked into her feigned innocent poor little girl face and smirked, "Like I said in court, I need to make more deliberations and investigations."

"You know I am not an evil witch and I believe when you see the real evil witches, you would not be letting them off lightly," she said, changing her expression into a sulking one.

Shrugging and raising his hands helplessly, "Well, it's not my fault that you didn't point them out. I am a judge, not a spiritualist and can only judge what is presented to me in court, which you failed to do!" he said in his normal court tone and walked away.

"You will be presented with them, but not by me!" she said aloud to his back and smiled in a knowing manner as she resumed her sitting position beside the last pillar.

"Maybe, but don't count on it!" he replied aloud, turning towards her, when he reached the door and guards. He felt invigorated having spoken to her, although he could not place a finger on why. Judge Sewall would in later years wage a war against slavery, first through high taxation and later by civil demonstrations, the first of their kind in Massachusetts that would eventually lead to greater things.

23

The next people to be arraigned before Judge Sewall, the following day, were Pamela Porter, Beatrice Andrews, Paulette Lewis and Angela O'Connor.

Unlike the previous day, all the accused were present in the court at the same time due to the judge's decision to try them in groups to save time. In his stern attitude, he once again warned both the accused and the public that he would not condone any improprieties within his courtroom.

"You will be asked how do you want to plead and you will step forward to answer, 'guilty' or 'not guilty'," he instructed them in an atmosphere thick with apprehension. Looking over his spectacles at the papers on his desk, "Mrs. Porter?" he read and looked up to see who would step forward.

"Not guilty," she answered boldly as she stepped forward and returned to the line. When all of them answered with not guilty pleas, the judge called for the afflicted girls to be brought into the court to start the proceedings against the accused. The serene court changed as soon as the girls were ushered in.

Immediately after the girls set eyes on the women, they broke into fits and contortions and fell to the ground. The members of the public forgot the earlier warning by the court and began surging forward to see the drama, making noisy comments.

"Order! Order! Silence!" Judge Sewall barked, but was mostly ignored. This infuriated the judge, who decided to make a scapegoat out of a few by ordering the arrest of one man and woman, who were to remain behind bars for two days.

"You are being held for contempt of court and are lucky to

be spend only two days in jail. The next will get two months!" This had a cooling effect on the crowd, and there were no further disturbances in Judge Sewall's court.

Thereafter, witnesses were called to testify for the girls, and the court heard how the girls were suddenly taken over by "demonic fits," which they blamed on the accused women.

Dr. Griggs was also called to the stand, and he testified that they suffered the same ailment. Like he did previously, he stated that there was no known illness like the one afflicting the girls and had to be satanic.

Another person, a clergyman, came to testify that the women were evil and probably had the sign of the devil on them. Two of them, Pamela and Mrs. Andrews were called to the stand and made to strip to the waist to check for the sign of the devil. The man pointed to blemishes on them as the sign of the devil, though unknown to him, the blemishes he pointed to around their necks were caused by the bee's attack sustained recently.

After the accusers finished presenting their case, the women were called to the stand to defend themselves. Pamela was the first one to take the stand.

"Sir, it greatly surprises and hurts me that after all I have done to help the prosperity of this town, I am being accused of being evil. I am not a witch and do not know any witches. This is all being caused by the black witch, who set out to get rid of all those that work for the prosperity of our town, land and people. I am not guilty," she said and looked beseechingly into the eyes of the judge.

"Is that all you have to say on behalf of yourself, Mrs. Porter?" the judge asked officiously, and Pamela answered with a nod.

The judge swiftly moved to the other women, who also claimed their innocence and blamed it all on a witch, who wanted to bring them down. After hearing all arguments, the judge adjourned the hearing till the following morning, when he would be giving judgment.

The following morning, the judge took his seat and

looked around his silent court. He managed a smile knowing his jailing of two people the previous day had stopped all the noisemakers. After asking whether the women had anything to say before pronouncing his sentence and they declined, he read his judgment.

"I have arrived at a conclusion, following careful deliberations over the arguments presented in this court before me, that the following accused women, Mrs. Andrews, Mrs. Porter, Mrs. O'Connor and Mrs. Lewis are guilty of witchcraft.

"It is a sad fact of life that those entrusted with much and supposed to embody all that is good in this land are the very ones that perpetrate evil in our midst. I hereby sentence you to death by hanging, may the Lord have mercy on your souls," this prompted an uproar in the court, while three of the women fainted on hearing the sentence. Among the crowd, more people collapsed including Judith Parris and Mr. Porter. The guards led Pamela Porter, the only one remaining standing, and carried the others out of the court.

While Pamela took her sentence stoically, her sister-in-law was an emotional wreck at home. She went home as soon as she was revived and retired to her room, where she wept all day and night. Parris felt sorry for her, but had no idea of how to console her. He was also scared of his sister's fate, which was yet to be decided.

The news spread throughout the town like wildfire and fear struck the hearts of many, who knew it could have been them. From that evening onward, Salem became a complete ghost town with no one on the streets, except for some slaves that had no fear of being accused and hanged.

The following week, more people were brought to court among them were Mr. Gordon Andrews, Mr. Michael Lewis, Mrs. Antonia Ramsay, the wife of the largest slave merchant in New England, and Mrs. Hall. This time they appeared before Judge Carl Thomas, who asked how they were pleading. The first three, Lewis, Ramsay and Hall, who came forward, plead not guilty without incidence, until it was Gordon Andrews' turn.

Looking pale and gaunt, Andrews stepped forward with a scowl. "Why are you wasting my time when you are going to hang me anyway, you stupid lot!" he spat, hissed and cursed as he returned to the others.

Having heard of his wife's sentence, he believed it was all a formality and even if not, he had no real wish to continue living without his wife. There was a hushed disbelief and shock throughout the court and everyone looked at the judge to see his reaction.

Judge Thomas was speechless momentarily, but regained his composure and readjusted his monocle. "Mr. Andrews, I will not tolerate insolence in my court. You might believe that you will be found guilty, which is presumptuous at this stage of the proceedings. Even then, hanging is only one of the options open to this court and I could make your death, if decided, more tolerable or otherwise," he sternly told Andrews, who displayed a defiant posture.

The proceedings continued with the girls brought into the court, after which they immediately fell into fits. The prosecuting side built up their case against the accused and then the accused were called upon to defend themselves. The first three pled their innocence as sincerely as they could and then the last, Mr. Andrews was called to plead his case, but once again shocked the court.

"I am no wizard. I have a successful distillery business and do not have time for that kind of rubbish. Having said that, I know you don't believe me so you can all go and sod yourselves. I won't stand here and grovel for my life, while you leave that damned witch, who is laughing over your stupidity," he told an astonished courtroom.

The judge asked for a recess after which he came back with the judgment. "I have heard the arguments and find all four of you guilty," he paused as Andrews laughed aloud.

"I told you!" Andrews repeated to his co-defendants.

The judge continued. "The first three, Lewis, Ramsay and

Hall are sentenced to death by hanging. In the case of Andrews, due to his utmost disrespect for the laws and institutions of this land, I sentence you to the most severe of deaths. I order you to be placed under weight of stones until it squeezes the evil life out of you."

There was an initial shocked silence throughout the court as everyone visualized the type of death that was being prescribed by the judge.

Andrews was also shocked. "No! You can't do that!" he shouted at the judge, who rose and left the court.

More cases were brought to court over the next few weeks, but not enough to free space in the jails, as people continued to be accused by their enemies. Therefore, it was agreed to hasten the whole process, including carrying out the execution orders.

On one bright summer morning in the third week of June 1692, the first four were led to "The Hill" where they were to be hanged. A large crowd of sympathizers and mere observers followed them.

Among them was Judith, who had been with Pamela, before she was taken by the guards to the hangman. They had shared a tearful final hour, before the guards arrived.

"I cannot believe that stupid judge could sentence good people to death, while he leaves that girl alive," Judith voiced her thoughts.

"She bewitched him. Didn't you hear he came to visit her?" Pamela asked.

Judith shook her head slowly. "That was her plan all along," Judith concurred.

"Don't let that girl get away with this, Judith!" Pamela kept telling her sister-in-law as she thought of her impending final journey.

"No, she will not step out of here alive. I am going to Annapolis immediately. It's war!" Judith assured her.

The guards finally arrived just before noon to lead the four women to Gallows Hill. Due to the announcement made beforehand of the execution, throngs of people followed the procession from the jailhouse to Gallows Hill. Partly due to the nice weather, there was a festive mood in the atmosphere as the crowd swelled as the possession approached "The Hill".

When they eventually arrived at Gallows Hill, the women were handed over to the hangman. The hangman, having set everything in place, led the women to their nooses, and asked if they had anything to say, before putting the noose over their heads. There was a brief cry of anguish as the women were hanged.

Tears trickled down Judith's face as she bit her lip, trying to control her emotions. Stern faced, she turned away and climbed into a carriage with one of the Porter slaves at its reins. Pamela had expressed as one of her last wishes to her husband to loan Judith their horse carriage. The horse-driven carriage immediately left for Annapolis with Judith as its only passenger.

24

Although Judith arrived in Annapolis exhausted, she immediately set out to business. Her brother was very distraught to hear about what happened to his in-laws and promised to give any assistance required, but his assistance was not what Judith came to Annapolis to seek. Pat told her not to disclose the type of help she needed to her brother.

A few hours after her arrival, the two women set out to see Angela Rogers, who was also aghast to hear what had transpired in Salem. She promised to speak to the other women, when she heard what Judith wanted and was to get back to them the following evening.

"I will see what can be done. Did you bring along what you promised the last time?" Angela asked, looking at them inquiringly. Judith nodded.

The last time Judith came down to Annapolis, the coven told her it would be easier to take on Tutu if they had something personal of hers to work upon. Therefore this time around, Judith made sure that she brought along some of Tutu's personal belongings, which she handed over to Angela before she left.

Angela did not to get back to them for another 72 hours, by which time Judith was already losing hope. When Angela turned up the third day, she looked exhausted and explained why she had taken so long to turn up as promised.

"I have been running up and down the whole place to organize how we could take on that girl. The other women were initially reluctant and not until a few hours ago could we finally agree to tackle her once and for all."

"I understand the reason for fear and caution. How did you eventually convince them?" Judith asked out of curiosity.

"Survival brings people together," Angela said smugly. "We were told by Mrs. Phillips, the psychic down the road from here, that we in Annapolis are her next target for destruction!"

Judith gasped, "I don't believe it? Who told you that?" Judith and Pat could not hide their awe and dropped their mouths.

"Mrs. Phillips, one of the best psychics around and, believe me, she has never been wrong. So Pat, we need to take the war to her, before she brings it to us. There is a coven tomorrow night at my place. Don't be late and be prepared. You could bring her along, but she won't be able to sit with us," Angela Rogers told Judith's sister in-law.

Disappointment showed on Judith's face because she had been promised a seat in the coven having joined them. Angela explained that the séance would be too dangerous for a beginner. She promised that Judith would be allowed to attend future meetings.

They discussed personal preparations to be made before the coven and listened to Judith's account of her troubles and that of Salem's for the second time.

Around nine the next evening, Judith and Pat set out for Angela Rogers' house. When they arrived there they met some of the women, sitting in the living room discussing their strategy, while they waited for the others to arrive. Gradually, the remaining women trickled in and finally the coven started in the dining room just before midnight.

On the table were some of Tutu's personal items and among other things included were her locks. To help them get into Tutu's spiritual realm, Mrs. Rogers and the other women had treated the items and hair. Some of the items were mixed with charms and a piece each was given to all the participants, to enable them to work on her individually, prior to their meeting that night.

"We all know what is to be done and I hope everyone is adequately prepared," Angela Rogers stated and paused to look around the table to see, if anyone had anything to say. When she realized there were no comments or anything to stop them from commencing, she continued.

"You all know this is not going to be easy, but if we stay steadfast, we will overcome her. Do not show any fear, and she will back down!" Angela said, sternly cautioning them. Having given out all the necessary instructions, she linked hands with the women and they commenced the séance.

Unlike before when only Angela Rogers recited the incantations, they all recited it together having been given adequate time to prepare beforehand. The atmosphere in the dimly lit room was intense, as the nervousness of the women was apparent.

In the Salem jail, Tutu was sleeping, when she began gasping for air. She threw her hands desperately in the air as if trying to get someone off her. She soon began to sweat profusely as she breathed laboriously. An old woman next to Tutu, woken up by her agitated movements, sat up and looked at her with puzzlement, not knowing what to do.

"...we call on you to help.." the women continued to recite their charms. Thunder and lighting roared outside them, the ferocity of which smashed the room's window open. Nevertheless, the women continued to recite their charms fervently and kept the circle intact. Suddenly a fireball exploded just above the table making two of the women shriek, but they continued only after a slight pause.

In Salem, the old woman noticed that Tutu's agitated movements were becoming weaker, although she was still struggling against an imaginary strangler. Gradually, her hands and body movements were reduced to mere spasms as she weakly coughed out some slime mixed with blood.

In Annapolis, the women smiled victoriously....

In Salem, on a closer look Tutu's cellmate noticed that Tutu was not breathing and her body appeared to be lifeless. She was just about to shake Tutu by the shoulder to find out if she was still alive, when there was a mighty thunder roar.

A thunderbolt burst through the nearby window and struck Tutu's lifeless body. The electrical force that passed through Tutu threw the old woman that had her hand on Tutu's shoulder to the other side of the cell, ten feet away. Tutu with blood dripping from her nose and the corners of her mouth sat up in a daze, staring straight ahead.

In Annapolis, the séance ended, mission accomplished and with the circle broken, the women relaxed and congratulated each other. As they congratulated each other, a vicious thunder roar was heard. Simultaneously, the window sprang open and Tutu, with blood running down her face, appeared. Looking around the table with rage and disgust, she moved forward.

"Form the circle! Form the circle!" Angela, stretching out her hands, shouted at the other women, who quickly linked hands with the exception of a younger woman, the closest to the window and Tutu. The woman, Kate had been searching for something in her bag, when the window flung open and Tutu appeared. Fumbling, she threw the bag down and tried to link hands with the others. Before she could do so, there was a loud hissing sound and Tutu transformed into a large black python right before their widened eyes.

"Come on, Kate!" the woman sitting next to the younger woman urged her to hold her outstretched hand. Unfortunately, Kate's eyes were fixed in awe on the transforming Tutu.

"Kate!!" about four women shouted, jolting her out of her stupefaction but before she could link hands, mayhem broke out.

The mighty black python disintegrated into over a dozen deadly Black Mambas, one of the most poisonous African snakes, which sprang at the women. The first to be attacked was Kate, the nearest to Tutu. One of the black Mambas leaped for her throat, where it buried its fangs. Struggling desperately,

Kate couldn't remove the Black Mamba and fell to the ground writhing and screaming.

The dozen or more other snakes went for the other women, some of who swiftly got to their feet and ran for the door. They were barely a foot away from the door and freedom, when bolts were seen and heard securing the door, both from outside and inside. The snakes leaped at the four dazed women at the door. The women screamed and banged frantically at the door as the snakes bit them from behind.

Outside Judith, having heard the commotion going on in the room, tried opening the door from outside, but with no success. With no help forthcoming, she looked around and sighted an axe, which she hurriedly picked up and used to smash the door and the bolts. After several ferocious swings, the door swung open.

In Salem, Tutu's cellmate thrown to the other side of the cell slowly got to her feet, brushed herself and cautiously walked towards Tutu. The look on her face was one of utmost awe as she approached Tutu, who was still sitting in a dazed state. Tutu suddenly jerked back to life, startling the shocked woman, who stumbled back in fear. Tutu looked around and resumed her sleeping position.

Judith managed to squeeze through the shattered door into the dining room, where many of the women were unconscious, while others groaned in pain and trepidation. Judith ran to her sister-in-law's aid, who was still alive, but in serious pain from the lethal snakebites. Beside her was Angela Rogers, also in a similar condition.

"It was a mistake...she came back..." Pat struggled with great pain to get the words out. As she was trying to make out what Pat was saying, Judith felt something tug at the seams of her dress and shrieked out of fear. Turning around, she realized it was Angela trying to get her attention.

"You have to...continue the fight...Ju..." Angela said in between coughs.

"Let me go and get help!" Judith said, looking around her frantically. Judith prepared to seek help outside.

"No! It's too late. You have to continue," Angela stopped her. "Here take my hand and the power will be with you," Angela stretched her hand. "Also, take the rings." Judith held her outstretched hand and immediately felt a shock, which passed through her body. She was stunned for a few moments and when she knew what was happening, Angela Rogers lay dead with her lifeless eyes staring into space.

"Take my hand too," Pat said weakly, startling Judith who was staring at the dead Angela Rogers. Judith turned back to Pat and only heard what she said after she repeated it.

"No, you can't all die and leave me alone with her," Judith said tearfully as she held Pat up by using a hand to support her at the back of the neck. "Please hold on, Pat."

"I will try," Pat coughed and paused a bit to stabilize her breathing, "but you have to take it and don't let it die with me." Judith looked confused for a minute and then decided to oblige the dying woman's wish. She grabbed hold of her hand and felt a shockwave go through her.

"Now you can carry me home!" Pat told her, smiling weakly, but contented. Judith, placing another hand beneath her thighs, carried the smaller woman with all her strength out of the room. With great difficulty and determination, she carried Pat into the carriage and jumped in the seat from which she rode furiously towards her brother's house.

As she pulled up outside the house, she shouted her brother's name and he came running to her aid.

"What happened?" he inquired, when he saw his wife barely unconscious.

"Just carry her inside. She was bitten by a snake!"

Although groggy and confused, he obeyed and carried his wife indoors, into the living room, where he laid her on some cushions. As he lay Pat down, she opened her eyes and smiled at him.

"What happened, darling?" he fretted around her, trying to make her comfortable.

Still faintly smiling, she touched him tenderly around the face. "I am sorry, Frank. Take care of the children," she said weakly as a round of bloody coughs racked her weak body.

"What happened? What is going on?" He looked agitatedly from his wife to his sister for an explanation.

"Judith will tell you everything. Please help her. I love you!" Pat answered, before slumping in his hands. For a brief moment, Frank was bewildered, blinking rapidly with his mouth open, but speechless, before it dawned on him, his wife was dead. On realizing, he burst into loud sobs as he shook Pat.

"No! No!" he bawled, holding her tight as if stopping life from flowing out of her.

After a few moments, Judith, who had been standing silently next to him, gently pulled him off her dead sister in-law. He turned around, still on his knees and wrapped his hands around his sister's legs, burying his head in her thighs. He wept disconsolately, while his aggrieved sister could only pat his head in an effort to placate him.

Judith looked down at her grief-stricken brother and his dead wife and shook her head sadly as tears streamed down her face.

In the evening, after her widowed brother had wept until he fell asleep and had finally awakened, they both sat on the front porch.

"So this girl is responsible for all this?" Frank asked his sister in disbelief as he drank from a big rum bottle and listened to her narration of all that had transpired since her husband turned clergyman.

Judith nodded pensively, "Yes, she is responsible for father's death, Pamela's and now Pat's."

Sighing heavily, Frank took another long swig from the bottle, the second bottle he had opened since he woke up.

"You have to be careful. I think you are drinking too much. Frank, you have to get hold of yourself. The family needs you strong!" Judith counseled her brother sternly.

"So you are going to take on that witch? How?" Ignoring her advice, he asked curiously as he took another swig.

"I really don't know. I was given some powers by Pat and Angela, but even if I had a clue as to how to use them, I still don't think they're enough," she answered as he took another swig. "That is enough!" she shouted at Frank. She snatched the bottle away from him and smashed it against the wall angrily, "This is going to weaken you. You need a strong mind to take care of everything, when I leave."

"Maybe you should give the witch some of that stuff to weaken her, if you believe that," Frank joked, obviously drunk.

"It does wea...." Judith was about to answer him angrily, when she stopped mid-sentence as an idea struck her. "Do you know any Mrs. Phillips?"

"Yes. She lives down the road. The psychic, isn't she?"

"I think so. I have never met her personally, but heard about her from Pat and Angela. I think I should go and see her before I leave," she rose and got further directions from him.

When she arrived at the described small building at the end of the road, which was dilapidated and showed signs of abject poverty, she knocked on its rickety unpainted door. After several loud knocks, an old bent lady yanked the door open.

"What?" she shouted rudely.

"I am Judith, Pat Lawrence's sister-in-law. I am..." she tried introducing herself, but the old woman turned around.

"I know who you are. Come in!" the old woman said distastefully as she walked slowly indoors. "I knew you would be coming and I was not going to open my door, but since you insisted on rapping on the door and nearly bringing the roof down on my head, I had to open it."

Judith was surprised, "You knew?"

"Yes!" Mrs. Phillips answered as she sat on a tattered chair that was the best in the living room, leaving Judith to choose from the remaining broken chairs.

"What is it you want? The other women are dead, aren't they?" the psychic asked once Judith sat down.

Judith nodded in reply as she took in her surroundings, which looked worse than slave quarters.

"I warned them about taking on that woman, but they were stubborn like you."

"I thought you told them to go ahead," Judith said with a puzzled look on her face, "that the girl was going to choose Annapolis as her next target. Or wasn't that what you told Angela?"

The psychic shook her head disagreeably, "No! What I told them was that the girl would destroy those in Annapolis, if things continued as they were. Those in Salem had picked on a much stronger entity, which led to their destruction and so have those in Annapolis."

"The girl declared war on us. That is why all this happened. Do you expect us to sit back and do nothing?" Judith protested.

"The girl would not have done anything unless pushed. The African has a good aura and would only attack when attacked. She is against evil; she is not evil!"

Judith raised her eyebrow contemptuously. "So are you saying we are evil?"

"No! It is a clash of good. She wants her people to be left alone and not in slavery and those here just want to survive here by all means. There are two sides to a coin!"

"You are on our side, aren't you?" Judith asked with a puzzled look on her face as she assessed the old woman.

"I am with nobody!" the old lady answered sternly. "I do not like the planters, who think they are next to God. Neither do I care about Africans. All I do is say what I see."

"I understand you, although without the planters, there would be no colony," Judith argued and walked over to her. Crouching next to the old woman, "Please, would you help me? Not for my sake, but the future generations, who would not exist if you don't. You can't just look on while the African kills our own people and takes over," Judith implored her, passionately.

"This is not about Africans and us," the old woman scoffed. "It is about money! Don't come here and try to say that it is us against them because it is not. It is about the rich and the poor. I can tell you that from experience, I am one of the losers of the war, the poor. You rich don't care about us unless you need us to support you to get more money from others."

"Please ma'am! I understand how you feel, but you've got to help. No matter the case, your future lies with us rather than with them," Judith implored her.

The old woman, setting her eyes in a fixed gaze across the room, sighed as she gave thought to Judith's plea. Still not looking at Judith directly, she asked, "What do you want me to do, young woman? This is a very strong force you are tackling and if you are not careful, you will soon be lying next to the other women."

"There must be something that can be done?" Judith insisted.

Mrs. Phillips shook her head thoughtfully, "there is no known force that could pick on her" she said and paused as she squeezed her forehead thoughtfully. "Unless a way is found to reduce her powers *before* she is attacked."

"How can we do that?"

"We?" raising her voice and eyebrows, the old woman moved away from her, looking at Judith as if she had an infectious disease. "Who talked about we? I am not going to be directly involved. I am no planter or merchant. After all you greedy lot take everything from us your people and then pour scorn on us. It is now that you try taking from elsewhere and face problems that you remember we are one people and beg for my support," the woman grumbled bitterly.

Judith gestured with her hands to the woman to forgive her mistake.

"You have to find a way. Probably when she is having her monthly period, pregnant, ill, drunk or whatever it is, that could disturb her contact with the gods she gets her power from," the psychic told her.

Judith nodded as she listened attentively to the old woman. After Mrs. Phillips finished, Judith told her about how two of the women passed their powers to her.

"I don't have a clue how to use them!" Judith told her helplessly.

"You don't have to worry about that. If it is real, they will show you how to use the power when the time comes. I think you will do well as long as you weaken her before attacking," the old woman advised, before getting to her feet signifying the end of the meeting. Judith still had a million and one questions to ask her, but the woman was not in a receptive mood.

"Please can I see you before I leave tomorrow? I still have a few questions to ask," Judith asked as she was being walked out of the hut.

"If I open the door," the woman answered dryly.

Judith went back to her brother, who was making burial arrangements for his wife, and told him what she had heard from the old woman.

"Mrs. Phillips? She is an eccentric and hates planters. She and her dead husband used to be planters, but lost out to some rich planter, who took over their land some years ago, while the creditors took everything else. Her husband couldn't take it and committed suicide. Although I heard she was a good psychic, what I can't fathom is why she's still so poor, if she has all those powers," Frank, who was more sober than before, told his sister.

"Some people just do it for other reasons, apart from money," Judith took a seat across from him. "What I can't fathom is what could weaken that bitch?"

"She told you the various ways possible. Chose one of them, although you have to be sure she has been weakened, otherwise I will have to come to Salem for your body," he said sardonically as he rose to his feet to leave.

Walking past her, he stopped and gently placed a hand

on her shoulder. "I really wish you didn't have to do this, but knowing the sister I've got, you would never back down...even if it is going to kill you. That is why you were father's favorite," he said amiably, although with a painful expression.

Judith believed he was leaving to avoid talk that would remind him of his wife and was being his usual self by pushing unsavory things out of his mind, instead of confronting and solving them.

25

Meanwhile, the trials continued in Salem, with more people sentenced to death by hanging, while new people were being accused and arrested. A couple fled as soon as they knew they were to be charged, while a heavily pregnant woman was allowed to go due to her condition.

Less than a week after the first hangings, Andrews was placed under an increasingly weighty pile of stones. After twelve hours, his screams could be heard a mile away as his executioners kept adding more boulders at intervals. Mr. Andrews was to endure the horrific torture for 43 hours before finally giving up life.

Judith arrived back in Salem in August, just over two weeks after she had left for Annapolis. After waiting for the burial, she immediately hopped into the carriage and headed for Salem with a vengeance.

On arrival, she hid her true feelings from everyone, including her husband and behaved amiably towards everyone. Parris asked about her journey to Annapolis, which he learned of afterward from a messenger she sent to him. He suspected there was something sinister behind her dashing to Annapolis and returning in strangely high spirits.

He tried to bring whatever it was to the surface by criticizing her harshly for leaving without personally informing him. He hoped she would react with anger and blurt out her intentions or whatever. Instead, she remained calm and even apologized, saying it was her brother, who sent her an urgent message. To his surprise, she went ahead to ask kindly about his sister's welfare and case as well as Tutu's.

He told her the judge was yet to decide on Tutu's charge, and his sister, Theresa was just about to attend the court for her charges.

"You don't appear to be too worried over your sister's impending day with the hangman," she observed.

"She won't hang," he answered assertively, but added with an afterthought, "I do pray, she won't?"

Judith, showing some puzzled amusement, continued. "Is there something you know that I don't because it appears everyone who sees the judge, sees the hangman," she said, adding curtly, "with the exception of Tutu!"

Parris wanted to lie, but couldn't be bothered to think of one. "Yes, there is something, we hope might work, although I can't talk about it."

"I guess it has to do with Tutu. That's why you ain't saying what it is!" Judith tried prying the information out of him teasingly.

"Why do you always have to link her to everything?" Parris asked, feigning irritation to stop the conversation, as he got out of bed and went to the living room.

This did not do anything to palliate Judith's curiosity and she made all types of designs to get the secret out of him. Parris knowing her fully well did not budge about the information, remembering that the last time she came back from Annapolis with an amorous attitude like this, she ended up putting into play events that led to his sacking and the present trials.

A few days later, Theresa and three others were brought to trial in front of Judge Sewall. Theresa Putnam, as advised, pled guilty of witchcraft, but insisted she had done no evil to anyone, in front of a shocked court that hadn't heard anyone plead guilty since Tutu.

When the judge returned judgment, he found the other three defendants, who had pled innocent, guilty and sentenced them to death by hanging. Theresa received a stern rebuke, a heavy fine and an order to seek help from the church but was released. She broke into sweet tears as she heard her sentence with disbelief that she would not be hanged.

Theresa Putnam was not the only one to be shocked in the court. Judith's mouth dropped, when she heard her sister-in-law's sentence. She looked beside her and saw her overjoyed husband run to the side of his sister to celebrate. Judith nodded meaningfully and left the court, leaving behind the joyous Parris clan as she thought about her lost friends and felt sick.

Later in the evening, Judith followed the family to the Putnams to celebrate, although she kept to herself throughout the small party. The hysteria that had taken over Salem limited the party to close friends and family.

Just before the end of the frolicking, Judith told Theresa that she needed to meet with her in private. A time and date was amicably fixed and Judith beseeched her not tell anyone, especially not her brother, of their conversation.

After his sister's release, the first of such releases, Parris started making moves to get Tutu released. After all, she pled guilty as well! Unfortunately, it was nearly impossible to see the judge, due to his hectic schedule and the barrier set around him to stop people from pressuring him into changing his judgments. Regardless, Parris kept on trying to get through with the hope that he would meet the judge one day soon.

For a few days after the attack during her sleep, Tutu was sullen and acted strangely to everyone. Although the inmates were also looking and treating her strangely after they were told everything by the old woman, who had seen her die, and resurrected by a lighting strike in her sleep. The woman had requested the guards move her to another part of the cell and would not even look Tutu in the eye.

Tutu knew she was attacked in her sleep and had nearly lost her life, but destroyed her attackers in the end. What she couldn't fathom was who they were, which greatly perturbed her, but after a few days she pushed it to the back of her mind. But, she had a nagging fear that those who came so close to killing her in her sleep could try again, if she didn't identify them.

When Parris came to visit her the following week, she asked about Judith and he told her she had just asked about her welfare. This puzzled her because she knew if there was anyone to instigate people against her, it would be Judith, and since she had destroyed all those Judith could instigate around, she would have had to travel. What Tutu failed to ask to solve the puzzle was whether Judith had traveled recently, but hearing she had just asked about her made Tutu believe that Judith had been in town all along.

Moreover, she had all her attention focused on being released and continued to harangue Parris every time he came to visit her. To further compound her anxiety was Sarah Osborne's death in her sleep, leaving her in the sole position of those, who had deferred judgments and had been kept waiting ever since. Parris kept allaying her fears and promised to do something urgently, but her distress increased considerably, when she heard of Theresa's release.

"Why was she released before me when I pled guilty too?" she grumbled, when he came to tell her the news the day after Theresa Putnam's release.

"Don't worry! Now that my sister has been released on those grounds, yours will soon be coming. I just need to remind the judge, who is probably too busy and has forgotten all about your case, but I believe that all will be sorted out as soon as I can get to him," he assured her, although feeling a tinge of guilt over what seemed apparently unfair to him.

As planned, Judith went to the Putnam's house for her meeting with Theresa. Theresa chose the day and venue, because she knew there would be no one around as requested by Judith. When Judith arrived at the large Putnam mansion, proudly sitting in well-trimmed gardens, a slave, the only one around opened the door and ushered her in. Theresa, who was waiting in her spacious finely ornamented living room, immediately dismissed the slave from the main house.

The women exchanged greetings, a bit stiffly, as they took opposite seats. They were both a bit uncomfortable this being only the third time Judith ever set foot in her in-laws house.

"You requested a meeting. What is it that you need to discuss with me?" Theresa asked abruptly after offering her guest a seat and a drink.

"I need..er..err..," Judith stuttered to a start, then stopped. She was too tense and did not have a clue on how to broach the issue. Clearing her throat, she made visible efforts to relax. "I am sorry, I need to ask a few questions, before I make a request," she said as she fretted under Theresa's cold gaze. Theresa lifted an eyebrow, gesturing her to fire on the questions.

"Please, Theresa, I would like to know who advised you to plead guilty?"

Theresa chuckled, when she heard the question. She was expecting something more absurd from her impression of Judith. "Well, I would say your husband," she answered as she got herself together and turned serious. "If I may ask, is it of any special importance?" Theresa added with curiosity.

"It is important, if you could see the whole picture as I do," Judith answered and paused to think before she continued. "Are you aware where that advice came from?"

"No!" Theresa answered impatiently and more curious. "I don't really think it was important, and I am a bit confused by these questions."

"Well, it is important and you would agree with me if you knew that the person responsible for your imprisonment in the first place was the one who set you free!" Judith blurted out.

"Samuel?" Theresa shook her head in disbelief, "I don't understand. I will appreciate it, if you can be clearer."

Judith sighed and paused thoughtfully before continuing, "I know you and I have been on opposite sides of the wall for some time, but circumstances have brought me to realize that you need to know what is going on, before it's too late."

Judith paused again to check Theresa's expression and when she realized it was genial, "Samuel's slave, Tutu, is the one that advised him how to get you released. She is the one who also started all this rubbish, and there is more to it."

"I have heard of this before, but I would not blame it on her, unless you know of other things of which I am not aware."

Judith smirked. "Unfortunately, I do, but please you must promise that whatever I tell you remains between us," Judith said in a pleading tone.

Theresa nodded, with her interest aroused she would promise anything to hear it all, "I promise!" she said with a wry smile.

"Well, Tutu has spiritual powers which she has used and will use in future to destroy us and all that we stand for. I know this sounds strange, but do you know why we left the West Indies for here?" she asked and Theresa shrugged. "Tutu was the one who caused the revolts that killed my father and destroyed many plantations."

"I heard something like that from Samuel, but not as you put it," Theresa countered her, for the sake of hearing it all.

"I guess you have, but believe me what I am telling you is the truth. Now, when we arrived here, I wanted to move to Annapolis, where we could set up a plantation, but Samuel would not oblige me. So I went to my family in Annapolis, and there I heard about Tutu and how they had prevented us from landing at the shores of Chesapeake Bay. From there, I learnt she was a powerful force sent to destroy us for the slavery and whatever they believe we have done to them."

"But that is not conclusive, coming from a jail after two months, I know one cannot believe all that one hears," Theresa countered.

"Yes, but they showed me what she did to them, when she attacked them. On my return to Salem, I met Pamela Porter, my brother's in-law, who had had a brush with Tutu and she said the same thing about her," before she could complete her explanation, she was interrupted.

"What happened to these people? What were they attacked with? The same fits?" Theresa bombarded her with questions.

Judith, smiling ruefully and readjusted her sitting position, before answering. "No, it wasn't with fits but thunder. She used thunder initially, before changing to more sinister ways."

"Well after everything failed to get her out or kill her, Pamela and some other women here in Salem tried implicating her with the girls' fits, which were mere hallucinations. I can tell you that the initial fits were caused to get Tutu," Judith paused to see her reaction, which remained passive.

"Yeah, go on!" Theresa said a bit impatiently due to her keen interest.

"Unfortunately, it backfired and Tutu turned it against them, which led to all these trials and hangings."

"I do not know what to say to that, and I still don't know why you are telling me all this?" Theresa gave her a quizzical look.

"It does not end there! When my sister-in-law, Pamela, and her friends tried to take the girls out of the fits, they were viciously attacked. Soon afterwards, they were jailed where they were to die. Having witnessed the various defeats suffered at her hands, I decided to go back to Annapolis to see if anything could be done to stop her. Unfortunately, when they tried she killed all of them, including Pat Lawrence, my brother's wife," she said. At this point, Judith was overwhelmed by her painful memories and burst into tears.

Theresa looked unperturbed from a distance and said nothing. When Judith pulled herself together, she continued. "I am sorry, but it is all too much for me to bear. Anyway, the point is this girl has to be stopped and she has already bewitched your brother. I need your help to tackle her," Judith said.

"I really don't see where I come into play with all this. As far as I am concerned Pamela Porter, who pulled me into all this rubbish has suffered and paid with her life, so it is all closed," Theresa pointed out calmly to her guest.

"No! You would be deceiving yourself if you think it is all over. She wants all of us to swing or our heads to roll. Look at what is happening in Salem, she killed a dozen women in Annapolis with snakes. What is next?" Judith demanded strongly, and Theresa threw up her hands indifferently. "Please, Theresa, believe me. You can find out yourself, but please do so quickly, before it is too late. I would not come here with a cock and bull story."

Theresa sighed ponderously. "The funny thing is that I do believe you and since you have let me into your secrets, I will let you into mine. Listen, I do know what happened with the girls because I do have powers of my own and when I checked out what was happening to my girl, I realized there was some trickery going on," she paused to smile, when she saw the astonished expression on Judith's face.

"Yes, I do have powers of my own!" Theresa restated before continuing. "I also heard of what happened in Annapolis because I had a friend among them, although I never linked it to Tutu, but I believe you. What I don't believe is that it has anything to do with me and even if it does, what can I do about it?"

Judith smiled in relief. "It does concern you because with the way she is going there would be no more plantation or prosperity after she finishes her plan. Secondly, when the women were dying, I was given some powers to continue the fight, which I might need your advice and help to use properly."

Theresa remained silent for a while as she thought of all that had been said. "It still looks like you are trying to avenge your relatives' deaths, which I find commendable, but can't find a good enough reason for me to join in. After all, these people or at least your in-law was against me ever since I met her and in the end, tried to make me swing."

"That is not the point here. Let's look at the bigger picture. Hundreds are to be hanged, dozens have been killed, all because of this slave girl. If your brother had not intervened, you would be among the dead. The nigress should not be allowed to destroy us all!" Judith passionately implored her.

Theresa shrugged, confused on what to do, "Okay, tell me what you want me to do. Remember I am not willing to die like your family chasing one black slave, but tell me what you want, and I will think about it and get back to you."

Judith stood up and walked to her, where she crouched at her feet and whispered in her ear. When she finished, Theresa shook her head disdainfully and said, "No way!" But when she looked into Judith's pleading eyes, she offered, "Listen, let me think about it. I will get back to you, but I am not promising anything," in order to get rid of Judith.

26

P arris continued to look for Judge Sewall and if his failure did anything, it was to increase his determination to get an audience with him. Eventually, his persistence paid off and he was able to see him one afternoon in the beginning of September 1692, as the judge was leaving after pronouncing another death sentence.

"Sir, I do gather from the way you sentence those accused, that you are using the Christian philosophy of forgiveness, only after repentance," Parris started amicably with the judge, who was in a hurry.

The judge thought about the statement carefully, before answering to avoid any entrapment by his seemingly cagey guest. "Yes, you may say so," he answered in a non-committal way as he looked at Parris curiously.

"Well, if so. Why haven't you seen it fit to release the first girl, who pled guilty in your court and sought repentance?"

"What girl are you speaking about?"

"My slave, Tutu, who appeared before you nearly three months ago. The Colored girl, if you remember, sir!" Parris tried to be as polite as possible, although he was irritated by the judge's attitude.

The judge squeezed his eyebrows as he tried to recollect what Parris was talking about. "Oh, my God! The brilliant African woman! Believe me, I could have sworn I had signed her release papers. They must be somewhere and I do apologize, I will give the order to have her released immediately," he promised apologetically.

That was how Tutu secured her freedom on September 5th 1692, after six months in jail. She was ecstatic, when she heard the news of her freedom that same evening. The release papers were being prepared, Parris told her, and she was to be released the following morning.

The next morning, everyone, including Judith and Tutu's black friends, came to meet her at the gates. They all hugged her joyfully and led her home. To Tutu's surprise, Judith showed some joy over her release, hugging her and saying good things to her. Tutu found her new freedom overwhelming and frequently became emotional.

When they arrived home, Parris proposed a toast and there was a mini-celebration among the family and her friends. Judith had prepared a small feast and drinks were served, although Tutu only drank sparingly, despite being prodded on by all to relax and enjoy the fruits of freedom.

The party continued well past midnight, since her friends were freer due to the hanging or imprisonment of their masters. Actually, most of them didn't have anything to do, since their households had been thrown into disarray following the witchcraft arrests and trials. Ultimately, they all left drunk, promising to see each other the following day.

Early the following day, Theresa came around to pick up the girls for a planned outing. Seeing Tutu, she greeted her warmly and hugged her.

"I do have a lot to thank you for and although I heard you had a celebration yesterday night, we would still have a special one for us, close family."

Tutu beamed shyly, unaccustomed to all the attention and good feelings she had been receiving since she was released barely twenty-four hours ago.

"We will have our own celebration later tonight, won't we?" Theresa asked pleasantly as she held Tutu's hand like a long lost and found friend. Truly she was one well-wisher that Tutu felt comfortable with, due to the past strong friendship.

"Yes, ma'am!" Tutu answered coyly in the presence of Parris and Judith, who were looking on fondly.

"It would be nice having a small family celebration," Parris commented.

"Yeah, although without the girls. We could surely do without them around," Theresa jokingly corrected him because they had made plans for Theresa to take the girls and her other children to Boston for the day. They would then return to her place, where they were supposed to spend a day or two. So only Theresa would be returning for the celebration. "I bet it will be fun," she enthused.

"I will make the best dish any one of you has ever tasted," Judith contributed to the cordial mood.

It was then agreed that they would have supper and drinks together, later in the day after everyone had concluded their day's business.

During the day, Tutu cleaned her quarters and slept since Judith gave her a week off to get her "health and strength back."

Judith mostly stayed in the kitchen preparing food and doing some chores, which she had been doing more often since Tutu was locked up and with the absence of the numerous house slaves that came with a plantation.

Meanwhile, Reverend Parris was out most of the day attending to various church matters, which he did not conclude till late afternoon.

Shortly after sunset, Theresa arrived in a cheerful disposition with three bottles of rum and strong wine each. Her brother opened the door and led her into the living room, while Judith was just finishing her cooking in the kitchen. Parris and Judith called out loudly to Tutu that Theresa was around.

"Good evening, ma'am!" Tutu slightly curtsied as she came into the living room.

Theresa rose to give her a hug, "It surely is going to be one," and she smiled and gestured to Tutu to take the seat next to hers. Tutu humbly obliged by sitting at the edge of the seat in a stiff position.

Moments afterwards, Judith informed them that the food was ready and she served everyone's portion separately from the kitchen. She called on Tutu to help her carry the servings to the table.

"That one there is for Samuel and that one is for Theresa," she pointed out the plates to Tutu, who carried them to the dining room. As Tutu turned around with the food, Judith reached into her scarf and brought out a small container. Hastily, with her eyes darting furtively between the door and the container, she opened it and emptied its contents into one of the remaining plates on the table and mixed it well into the food. Just as she closed the small container, Tutu walked back into the kitchen.

Startled, Judith scratched the back of her head. "Yeah, that is yours! I will bring mine along," she stammered nervously, although Tutu didn't notice her strange behavior and just picked up the plate pointed out to her and turned around, heading for the dining room.

As Tutu reached the dinner table, where Samuel and Theresa were waiting, there was a loud thunderclap that shook the house to its foundation. While everyone was startled, a brick fell from the ceiling and hit Tutu's plate out of her hand, making her shriek. Judith, who was close behind her, saw what happened and caught her breath sharply.

"Oh!" Tutu moaned as she looked at her food spilled all over the floor. She bent down to scoop it into the plate.

"Poor you!" Parris said with joking concern, "You can have some of mine."

"Don't worry. There should be some left in the pot, although I am not sure there are any lamb chops left," Judith said unhappily. Tutu cleaned up the mess and served herself a new portion, before rejoining them at the table. When she did, Parris said a short prayer and they dined.

Theresa poured the drinks, which were a bit too strong

for Tutu's taste. When she rose to get herself a drink, Theresa questioned her.

"Where are you going, my dear one?" she asked congenially.

"I need to get a drink."

"No! No!" Theresa shook her head firmly, but still with an amiable disposition. "The Parrises provide the food, the Putnams provide the drink. This is the best wine in the land befitting our celebration of victory, which you kindly helped to achieve. Therefore, drink and be happy, my girl." Theresa filled her cup, smiling and making faces at Tutu charmingly. Tutu could by no means refuse the hospitality being showered on her, especially from a friend like Theresa and with Parris nodding in agreement.

"You'd better enjoy it; it is not often that my lovely sister decides to be a loving person," Parris joked, earning him a contrived hurt look from Theresa.

Judith chuckled. "That's not nice," she also feigned dismay, but all three of them burst into laughter, which relaxed Tutu and made her join in the merriment.

Theresa told them funny stories about her time and experiences in jail, which cracked them all up, especially Tutu, who had experienced them as well. They laughed through their meal, which was cleared by Tutu and Judith after they finished. Tutu hoped to escape to her quarters after the food, but Theresa wouldn't allow her.

"Leave that alone for now!" Theresa ordered jovially, when she found Tutu washing plates in the kitchen after waiting for her in the living room. "This is our night. I don't care about tomorrow, but tonight we are all going to be merry," Theresa said as she pulled a giggling Tutu back to the living room.

They resumed the jokes as soon as Tutu was seated, and Judith poured her a drink. Judith made Tutu and Parris drink up fast, while Theresa kept them laughing.

Tutu was visibly enjoying herself and beginning to get tipsy by the third refill. When her fourth refill was given to her, she began seeing blurred visions, one of which was her mother's. As she was about to put the cup to her mouth, there was another loud thunderclap and in a jerk reaction, her cup flew out of her hand.

Judith, who had been looking at her and saw the action, had a puzzled expression followed by one of dismay on her face. She could have sworn, she saw something knock the cup out of Tutu's hand.

Nevertheless, she quickly gave her a refill as the jokes continued unabated. A few moments later, as Tutu once again tried to put the drink to her mouth, she saw her mother shake her head with dismay, and she moved the cup away from her mouth. She tried fixing her vision to make sure she was really seeing her mother or whether it was the drink playing games with her mind.

Unsure of what she was seeing and being prompted by Theresa to drink up, she once again put the cup to her mouth. Once again, there was a loud thunderclap that made her drop her cup again. Judith tried hard not to show her growing frustration and refilled the cup.

"From the day you brought her here, I always knew she would come to be something one day," Theresa talked on, disregarding the small scene created by the thunderclaps. "If she was white, I would have recommended her as a wife or mistress. I am lucky I was good to you, otherwise I would be swinging."

Theresa kept heaping praise on Tutu in between her jokes, making her feel at ease in their company. On some occasions, she put a hand around Tutu's shoulders like they were life long pals as she joked and frolicked with her guests.

Tutu became more and more disconcerted by the strange visions she was seeing of her obviously angry mother. She couldn't disengage herself from the merriment with Judith now sitting next to her on one side, while Theresa was on the other side and Parris directly across from them. With this sitting arrangement, Judith ensured that Tutu's drink did not spill again and was alert to shore her and her drink up, if need be.

In a flash, they finished two bottles of rum and went on to

strong wine. Parris began feeling drunk but continued drinking, while Tutu became drunk and was prodded to drink more. The women did not appear to be affected, although they appeared to drink as much as the other two.

Finally, Parris dozed off amid Theresa's jokes, while Tutu slumped in her chair. Judith got up from her chair and went upstairs to the girls' room. A few moments later, Theresa tapped Tutu on her knee and told her that Judith was calling her upstairs.

With her vision swimming, Tutu tried to concentrate and heard Judith calling her. She got up to answer but swayed and fell back into her chair giggling drunkenly, while Theresa looked on pitifully. Judith called once more and Tutu struggled to her feet, successfully keeping herself standing for a moment, before staggering toward the sound of Judith's voice.

Getting to the bottom of the staircase, Tutu stopped and took a deep breath as she contemplated the daunting task of climbing the stairs in her state. She steadied herself, before climbing slowly, but Judith's persistent calls made her quicken her pace.

Meanwhile, Parris was snoring in his chair where he had fallen asleep.

When Tutu got to the top of the stairs, she made a serious effort to steady herself once again, which was not an easy task. Hearing Judith call her again, she staggered towards the girls' room, where she heard her calling. As she walked into the room, she saw Judith standing and saying something she could not hear.

"Sorry, ma'am! What did you say?" she asked as she swayed. Judith did not answer, because she was not directly speaking to her but reciting some charms.

In Tutu's swimming vision, she saw four boxes flying toward her and she tried dodging two of them. Unfortunately, she chose to duck the wrong ones and was hit smack in the head by the two boxes, which sent her off balance onto the floor.

On the floor, she saw two Judith's circling her and reciting incantations. Wiping her face with her bare hand to steady her vision, Tutu tried reciting charms to countermand Judith's, but she was too drunk. Most of the things she was sending Judith's way were totally off mark because her focus was swimming and duplicated. To her credit, she was able to stop some of the things flying at her, although a few hit their target. Actually, the missed targets also had to do with Judith's novelty as much as anything else.

Unable to fight back effectively nor even stand properly on her feet, Tutu backed away slowly on her ass as things kept flying at her. Now and then, when her vision stabilized, she was able to send things flying directly at Judith. This frustrated Judith, who increased the intensity of her charms and things flying, which pushed Tutu back into the corridor leading to the staircase.

Following her, Judith made a mistake of standing in the doorway, making it easier for Tutu to target, since the missiles could barely pass through the doorway without hitting her. Tutu sent stools and other furniture from the room to hit Judith, which found their target and stunned her momentarily, especially since they hit her from the back unexpectedly.

When Tutu realized Judith was stunned, she quickly tried to escape by heading for the stairs to Parris, but Judith was not going to let that happen. In her rage, with blood dripping from her nose and temples, she forgot all about the charms and dived at Tutu.

"I am going to kill you bitch! My father, my family.... Die!" Judith said hatefully. Pinning Tutu to the floor, she wrapped her hands firmly around her neck and squeezed in an effort to strangle her to death.

To Judith's surprise, she found that Tutu was changing and before she knew it she was squeezing a huge snake that slipped out of her hands. The snake recoiled and poised to strike her. Judith backed into the wall in terror, but the snake struck her several times, before retreating and sliding away.

A few inches away from the staircase, it changed back to a swaying Tutu, who could hardly keep her balance. Tutu looked at her antagonist fiercely, for a moment as she decided whether to continue to attack, but due to her swimming vision hesitated a bit. At that moment of hesitation, she heard a movement behind her, coming from the other end of the corridor that led to the other rooms.

Turning back swiftly, she saw Theresa and smiled at her, believing she was no threat. Still swaying badly, she turned her attention back to Judith, who was backed into the wall, writhing in pain as she held on to her snakebites.

Being a few inches from the stairwell, Theresa gave Tutu a sudden push backward. Tutu tried to stop falling backwards and for a brief moment, she balanced on the edge with a look of utter surprise at Theresa, whose face seemed to be changing to Pamela's and Pat's.

"I am sorry!" Theresa said with a pained expression, seeing the look of surprise and disappointment on Tutu's face. Then, it changed to Pamela's laughing face. Tutu blinked, unsure of what she was seeing. Eventually, Tutu lost her fight against gravity and was sent flying downstairs screaming. She landed with a sickening thud as she crashed into the candelabrum that pierced through her lower neck and collarbone.

The noise woke Parris, who ran over to where it came from. Seeing Tutu in the twisted way she landed and the blood, he instantly burst into loud cries of desperation, despair and grief.

It was obvious from the way Tutu landed she was dead!

27

JULY 7, 2010: BOSTON, MA.

That was what happened to you the first time. You have to watch out, if you defile your mind with substances, God can't work in it to help you," the old woman told Tutu as she lay on the bed.

"Very interesting! She looked and thought exactly like me. What happened to the others?" Tutu Oba asked curiously.

"The trials were stopped soon afterwards, but not before nineteen had been hanged. The Rev. Parris was sent packing and moved to Braintree, but came back less than two years later, although not as a minister. Judith died a few minutes afterward from snake poison. Anyway, I have to go and you have a lot to do!" The old woman stood up from the bedside and walked away.

"Wait one more thing! What am I to do?" Tutu shouted after her and was about to get up to stop her, when she opened her eyes to find herself in strange surroundings. She realized she had been dreaming all along, but could not fathom where she was. Her body felt stiff and numb and she had some bandages around her neck.

Suddenly the door swung open and Professor Parris walked in. "Here you are, our sleeping beauty! I was beginning to think you weren't coming around anymore," he said pleasantly as he walked to her bedside.

"Where am I? What happened?" she asked weakly.

"You are in Boston General Hospital and have been in a coma for sixteen days after falling down the stairs in a drunken state after your first night out in America," Professor Parris said mockingly.

"You are Reverend Parris," but she corrected herself as she put her hand to her throbbing temple, "No, Professor Parris."

Parris, in a blue blazer and red tie over a blue striped shirt, smiled. "That's right, I'm the Professor, not the fumbling Pastor!" he joked.

"The pastor was a good man, a really good man!" Tutu said pensively.

"It appears you are definitely going to survive," Parris stated, ignoring her remarks. "Let's hope you are out of here soon. I just dropped by to see if you were all right. I'm going to a meeting in the Cambridge area," he rose from her bedside and walked towards the door.

"Do you have a wife, Professor?" Tutu asked as he leaned forward to pull the door open.

He was surprised over the line of questioning, which he thought of as flirtatious. Smiling, he turned around to face her. "No, we divorced and she moved 3,000 miles away!"

"Thank God!" she exclaimed. Not meaning to say it aloud, she covered her mouth with her hands in embarrassment. Parris shook his head in mock dismay and opened the door to leave.

Shortly after Parris left, a team of doctors came to examine her once the nurses told them she was fully conscious. The team, comprised of a consultant and two resident doctors, started examining her and asking questions.

"It appears from your x-rays that you had a previous injury around the same area. When did this occur?" asked the consultant as he peeled the bandages from around her neck.

"No!" Tutu answered with a curious look, and then continued, "That is from my previous life." The doctors laughed, thinking she was joking, but she kept a stern face.

"You are from Africa?" he asked and Tutu answered with a nod. "Have you ever been treated for any diseases?" the doctor inquired as he continued to examine her.

"No?" Tutu answered abruptly.

"No smallpox, chickenpox, Ebola, AIDS or anything of that sort?"

Tutu's expression changed into one of disdain and irritation on hearing the question. "No!" she answered firmly.

The doctor moved down her body, pressing and feeling for broken bones or anything abnormal. "Any foot ulcers or infections?" he asked as he felt her soles, "Surprising, your soles are quite smooth and soft...."

"For an African?" Tutu interrupted and angrily pulled her feet from his hands, "You think I am a deer-riding, spear-throwing, tiger-chasing, bare-footed primitive person!" Tutu raised her voice and struggled to sit up.

The consultant took a step backwards in shock from the angry barrage. "I was only trying to find out your medical history," he stuttered.

"Yeah right! Like you ask every woman that comes in here why their feet are smooth and whether they have foot sores? I don't know what foot sores have to do with falling down the stairs."

"I just wanted...," but he was unable to complete his sentence as Tutu continued, obviously irate.

"You just wanted to do what, ugh? You are the one going to get foot sores! Bloody idiot," she hissed and turned the other way. The doctors, not knowing how to deal with the situation, filed out in silence.

The following morning, Professor Parris came visiting, bringing along a bouquet of flowers. He apologized for not returning the previous day, which was due to his busy schedule he did not conclude till late in the night.

"I heard on the way up here, you had some trouble with Professor Raja yesterday. What happened?"

Tutu scoffed, still a bit irritated over the matter. "He came in here and started patronizing me. Asking me why my feet were smooth, whether I had AIDS, Ebola and all that rubbish?"

Parris shrugged, "But isn't that all part of a medical examination that is given to everyone?"

"No! That is racist and ignorant. I can bet my life that he doesn't ask everyone if they have feet sores, AIDS or Ebola. He is just ignorant thinking all Africans walk barefooted and have AIDS. I grew up in a city larger than Boston or any other one here, apart from New York."

Parris, noticing she was getting agitated, raised his hands in surrender and gestured to her to cool down. "Take it easy! You can't blame anyone for the media stereotypes, even many black people around here have that impression."

Tutu shook her head in disagreement. "He is a doctor and well educated; he should be more informed," she said. Parris changed the topic on to safer grounds since it was obviously annoying her. He stayed for an hour and a half before leaving.

As soon as he left, Tutu did what she had been hoping to do since she arrived. She picked up the phone beside her bed and dialed. "Yes, please I want to find out if you have a listing for Emeka Obi in New York."

An hour after Parris left, a nurse came to take her for X-rays ordered by her newly appointed doctor. Placing her in a wheelchair, the nurse pushed her out of the room towards the radiography department. They were coming out of an elevator, when they ran into Dr. Raja, although Tutu did not take any notice or recognized him till he spoke.

"Please madam!" he shouted from the wheelchair in which he was being pushed. "Forgive me! Take the curse away from me. I am very sorry," he groveled.

"What?" Tutu was taken by surprise and only recognized him from his Asian accent. "What are you talking about?"

"Oh God, please!" he bawled. "Look at my feet, you did it. I know these things I am Asian. I know!"

Tutu, her nurse, a man on a gurney and his nurse all leaned forward to see what he was talking about. His feet were hugely swollen and wrapped in soggy bandages that were soiled with a yellowish substance.

Arriving at home the previous evening after work, he had first felt tickling sensations in his soles, but thought nothing of it. To his deep consternation, he was woken by pain from the two-hour nap he always took before attending his private practice in Brookline. On getting up, he realized he couldn't walk with his swollen feet, which were giving him excruciating pain. He tried several remedies at home but with no relief and had to call an ambulance, which brought him to the hospital just after midnight. Various tests were carried out, but nothing concrete could be diagnosed, except that his feet were producing enormous amount of pus.

His feet, which were rather dainty for a man, had swollen to seven times their normal size. He was told that, if it continued at the present rate, they might have no choice but to amputate his feet before the infection spread to his whole body.

Tutu was embarrassed and confused as she glanced at his bandages and his face. She couldn't believe she was responsible. "Please, I don't understand what you are talking about."

"Don't do this to me! You are the one that cursed me yesterday that I would have foot sores. You know you did it! Please just forgive me and tell the foot sores to heal," he pled tearfully.

Tutu sighed and smiled. "Okay, I forgive you. May your feet be free of any curse and sores," she turned to her nurse. "Please can we go?" The nurse perplexed over what was occurring was jolted out of her stupor and pushed Tutu away.

The Professor on the other hand was pushed on to the elevator, where another patient was waiting.

"So she did that to you?" the patient asked curiously.

"Yes. She is from Nigeria and fell down the stairs and broke her collarbone the day she arrived," the professor told the three other people in the elevator.

"What is her name?" the patient asked keenly.

"I think it is Tutu Oba," he squeezed his eyebrows as he tried to recollect, "Yes, it is Tutu. Her professor is my friend!"

"Goddamnit! It is her, I thought I recognized her from somewhere," the patient said aloud to himself. "She is studying law or a lawyer or something?"

The professor nodded, "I should think so because Professor Parris is a law professor."

"Shit! They let her in," he turned to his nurse. "Please can you take me to the nearest telephone?"

"When we finish with your tests, Mr. O'Brien!" the nurse said curtly, fed up with the constant demands of the immigration officer. O'Brien had been revived from his coma, a couple of days after he had been initially taken for dead. He was recuperating and was being taken for tests to decide whether he was well enough to be discharged.

In the luxurious Scandinavian style office of the chairman of Empire Bank, Bill Jones studied the photographs of George Forrest taken with various heads of state that adorned the walls, as he waited for his boss to continue their discussion. It was a large enough office, with immense character and style, to keep him busy, while George Forrest was on the phone following the umpteenth interruption to their meeting. After many years, Jones was accustomed to the long wait he had to endure, whenever he came to see Forrest.

Forrest dropped the phone and sighed, it was not easy being the head of the largest bank in the world. Clearing his throat, he said, "I was telling you before I was interrupted that the witch girl has been located in Boston General hospital. These are the details." He pushed a paper across the table, which Bill picked up and gave a cursory glance.

"I want her placed under surveillance, although absolutely no contact should be made. We do not want to alert her. My wife has strongly advised against confronting her and I insist absolute nothing should be done to provoke her," he stressed with his finger as he spoke. "Otherwise, we might inadvertently be courting trouble, you understand?" Forrest said sternly.

Bill Jones smiled nervously as he nodded in reply, "Yes, Sir!" He paused, before asking obsequiously, "And how is Mrs. Forrest?"

Forrest visibly relaxed as he grinned widely over the mention of his wife. "Fine, Thank you! She should be discharged by the end of the week." Just as his expression softened quickly, so did it harden as he turned his attention to some papers on his desk, signifying the end of the meeting without a further word.

"I thought I should let you know. The boss just informed me that the Nigerian girl has been located," Bill Jones relaxed into his recliner as he spoke on the speakerphone. The large oblong office, tastefully furnished in brown oriental fittings, had a scenic view of the New York Bay, befitting of the director of security for the large conglomerate.

"So what is going to happen?" the voice asked with anticipation over the speakerphone.

Jones swiveled on his chair slightly as he played with a pen in his hands. "Nothing! I have been told," he smirked.

"Nothing?" the voice belonging to Anthony Pierce boomed in anguish over the phone. "I can't believe we are going to fold our hands and do nothing."

"That is what the boss ordered. He said categorically that he did not want to disturb the waters and that she should only be placed under surveillance. Which was the reason I heard about it in the first instance."

There was a short silence on the line, while Jones tapped his pen nervously against his thumb. He knew he shouldn't be revealing the information to Anthony Pierce, but being the closest to him by age in the top hierarchy, they often exchanged favors.

"We have to do something. We can't let the girl move first. Forrest is growing too old and senile and we have to provide the muscle needed," Anthony Pierce insisted.

"What do you suggest?" Jones asked with a wry smile, knowing what was coming before he asked the question.

"I think we should move to nip any threat in the bud. Have your boys neutralize the threat immediately," he answered with a touch of ruthlessness and finality.

"Done!"

"You have been moved to another room since you are

no longer in a critical condition," the orderly informed Tutu in the elevator, as she pushed her back from the radiography department. They had been to various departments for tests over the last three hours and were just returning to the private ward where she had stayed since she was admitted.

"But I need to get my things," Tutu insisted strongly. She was feeling stronger with the bandages removed leaving only a small scar.

"You need not to worry about that. Everything would have been moved to your new room," the orderly smiled reassuringly as she pushed the wheelchair out of the elevator.

Tutu shook her head stubbornly. "Please I would like to check myself. There are some things I hid in the bathroom," Tutu remaining adamant, implored her. "Please!"

"I don't know about this because I was told someone else was to be moved into the room this morning," the orderly answered, stopping hesitantly in front of the elevator. Looking down at Tutu, who was putting on a sad, innocent face, she had no choice, but to turn around. "We will check only if there is no one there already."

When they arrived at the door, they found it was slightly opened and the nurse pushed the door open with the chair. The door swung open to reveal two men firing their guns, with silencers attached, at a fire victim whose head and face were covered in bandages. The sight of the men and the muffled shots made both women wince and draw sharp breaths.

The gunmen were surprised to be caught in the act, but quickly recovered and turned their guns toward the women. The orderly squeezed her eyes shut in fear, while Tutu fixed a gaze upon them. Without a word said, they pressed on their triggers to waste the unexpected eyewitnesses, but all that happened was a click in the guns.

Realizing their guns had jammed they looked at each other and appeared to nod toward the women. The gunmen walked aggressively toward where the women remained transfixed at the door. The orderly winced as they approached, expecting to be hit or dragged, but the two men barged through them, sending Tutu sprawling on the floor as they escaped from the area.

When the orderly realized they left without harming her, she tried to get Tutu and the chair upright, but realized she was not conscious. She immediately raised the alarm, screaming and pressing a panic button, but the men had already left the area.

"That was close!" the shorter of the two men said, as the door to the elevator closed.

The stocky one just shook his head in exasperation, "Imagine the bloody guns jamming at the same time!"

"You should have seen the face on that nurse," the shorter one said jokingly.

"Yeah!" his partner agreed, but had an afterthought and he raised his eyebrows, "the patient was a tough one though!"

Suddenly the elevator came to an abrupt stop on the second floor and the lights blinked.

"What's going on? They couldn't have got to us so quick, could they?"

"That is what you thought!" Tutu's voice sounded in the elevator.

"Did you hear that? What's going on?" the shorter man asked, looking around searchingly to see where the voice was coming from.

"Why? Why did you come to kill?" the voice asked.

The men looked at each other in amazement as they tried to figure out what was happening. "Let us out. I want a lawyer. We haven't done anything," the taller one said nervously but defiantly.

"I am a lawyer! Now do you want to answer or do I have to get it out of you by force?" the voice said sternly.

"I am not talking! I take the fifth!" the shorter one said stubbornly toward the ceiling, where the voice was coming from.

"Okay the fifth!" Suddenly the elevator started moving and raced upwards at a neck-breaking pace. The neon light showing the floors in the elevator was changing fast and was barely keeping up with the movement. The elevator came to an abrupt stop on the fifteenth floor.

"Oh! Sorry the fifth, not the fifteenth," the voice said, when the elevator stopped for a moment. The men were sweating and very distressed. Before they could say anything, the elevator went on a free fall, making the shorter man fall to his knees and grab hold of his head. The taller one held tightly to a bar in the elevator, closing his eyes in fear, expecting to be smashed into the ground at any moment. This did not happen as the elevator came to a jolting stop at the second floor, throwing both men off balance. Their guns dropped and slid to the other side of the elevator, but they made no effort to retrieve them as they held on for dear life.

"Damn! This thing doesn't work well. This is the second, I suggest we go back and start again." The men raised their hands to protest, but the elevator once again headed up at high speed. Stopping at twenty-five for a moment, it made another free fall to the third floor. By the time it stopped, both men were retching.

"When you are ready to talk, let me know. I hope it is before we reach the floor you wanted. What was it again, the fifth or fifteenth?" Before either of them could say anything, the elevator began another fast ascent. By the time the elevator returned to the lower floors both men were lying on the floor.

"Please don't kill us. Enough! I am ready to talk!" the shorter one said weakly as he tried to wipe the vomit off himself.

"Don't say anything!" the taller one admonished him severely.

"Listen here, I don't know about you, but I don't want to be splashed in an elevator like a tomato on the sidewalk. Prison isn't that bad. I don't want to die. I got a family, and Bill isn't worth dying for!"

"Don't!" the taller one insisted.

"Please, I am ready to talk!"

"I am listening!" the voice said firmly.

"What do you want to know?" he asked, while he tried to

pull his shirt over the wet patch in front of his trousers, having let go on himself.

"You are not yet serious. I told you I want to hear you talk!" she hissed and the elevator once again started a quick climb.

"Please! I will talk! Please!" the man screamed as the elevator raced upward. It raced all the way up before dropping once again. When it came to a rest at the second floor, the short man blurted out, "We were sent to kill the girl from Nigeria. We are from New York! Please don't kill us." The man wept as he looked around for an answer from his tormentor, which was delayed.

"Who sent you and why?"

"Our boss in Empire Bank, Bill Jones. He is the head of security at the head office in downtown New York, but I don't know why. Please don't kill us!" the man groveled.

"You don't want me to kill you, but you wanted to kill me, ugh?" the voice demanded fiercely. The men looked at each other in surprise.

"Kill you? But....," the short man stuttered. "How come you are doing this, if we shot you? Oh my god! It's a ghost. A ghost is haunting us! We are going to die." He whimpered in panic.

"Yes, you are going to die! Bye." The elevator sped up as they both screamed along the way. Suddenly the elevator stopped, and the door opened at the floor where they had committed murder. Looking up, they saw security officers standing in the corridor. Their screams attracted the cops, who were slow to identify them, not believing that they would turn up at the crime scene so soon. The tall one tried to reach for his gun across the elevator but was too dazed.

One of the officers saw their guns and sprang alert, drawing his gun as he bellowed, "Freeze! Don't you dare move boy!" With his gun drawn and covered by others, he approached them carefully. Both men were cuffed, brought to their feet and led out of the elevator.

Tutu suddenly regained consciousness to the surprise of the nurse and doctor attending to her. Ignoring protests from them to remain seated, Tutu got on to her feet and walked towards the security officers and the arrested men. The arrested men were just being led away, when she walked up to them.

With nobody noticing, she bent down and picked up a small wallet that dropped from one of the arrested men. Pocketing it, she returned to the doctor, requested her clothes and to be discharged immediately. The doctor discouraged her, but she was adamant and they had no choice but to let her discharge herself.

"I don't know why you discharged yourself. You have not fully recovered and I think it is ill-advised, regardless of what happened in the hospital. This is America and shootings happen all the time," Professor Parris admonished when he picked her up. She did not tell anyone what she heard in the elevator and was already thinking far ahead and not listening to the professor.

Moments after he finished his rebuke without Tutu saying anything, she cleared her throat. "I am going to New York for a couple of days. Please, can you drop me at the airport?" she asked.

"New York?" he asked in surprise. "Why the sudden rush to New York, and who do you know in New York?"

"I am sorry Professor, but I can't fully explain my actions at present," Tutu said softly as she gently placed a hand on his shoulder. " I need to sort things out in New York before I can settle down to my studies. I will be staying with an old friend for a few days."

The professor looked at her quizzically, but did not say anything as he drove her home to pick up her luggage and then to Logan Airport, where she boarded a plane to La Guardia Airport in Queens, New York.

28

Coming out of the Delta Shuttle terminal at La Guardia Airport, Tutu looked around for the friend she had called from Logan Airport. Not seeing anybody she recognized, she dropped her luggage in exasperation.

"Hello, Princess!" she heard somebody say from behind her as she felt a gentle touch on her shoulder, startling her.

"Oh! Emeka! I was just wondering whether you were going to turn up or not," Tutu said smiling, evidently relieved to see him.

Emeka, her ex-boyfriend was a six-foot four-inch, well-built handsome man in his late twenties. "Why would I do that to my baby?" he opened his arms to hug her, "You look stunning as ever!"

"Hmm!" Tutu murmured sarcastically, "I am not your baby! A baby you have forgotten for all the beautiful New York girls. Anyway, how are you?"

"Fine thanks! It is not as easy as you put it, but I do agree I have lots of explanations to make. Let's start by getting out of here," he said as he picked up her luggage and led her to his convertible BMW, which was parked a few yards away.

"I don't know your living arrangements, so I wouldn't mind being taken to the nearest hotel," Tutu said as she followed him and added, "I don't want to be shot by some jealous wifey."

Emeka shook his head in dismay as she giggled behind him. "You are staying with me. All the mamas are going to disappear when the real queen appears."

"Flattery will get you nowhere with me. You know I know you well enough not to fall for your sweet tongue. You leave me broken-hearted and think you can just turn up and flatter me back into your arms," Tutu said lightly as she entered the car.

Starting the car, they turned onto the Grand Central Parkway and drove to Farmers Boulevard in Queens, where he lived.

In a well-decorated living room with black leather furniture and African figurines adorning the wall and cabinets, Tutu sat across from Emeka after refreshing herself.

"I still think it is bad that you couldn't write or phone all these days," Tutu paused to sip from her cup of orange juice. "Anyway, let's forget about that for the time being. I need to go to Empire Bank's headquarters downtown. Do you know anything about them?"

Emeka shrugged as he leaned forward to switch channels on his large screen television. "Not that much, apart from being the biggest bank in the world. I know a girl who works for them though. What do you need to know or do?"

"I need to get in there," she said. "You know I don't like lying, and I can't tell you everything at this moment."

Emeka furrowed his bushy eyebrows as he looked at her quizzically, shrugging indifferently, he answered. "A girl I know, Tameka, works there. We used to do things together some time ago. She might be of help."

"That's nice! Can you ask her about the recruitment agency that the bank uses to employ temporary staff," she paused as an idea crossed her mind. "What is her name and where does she work? Maybe she could make herself useful, apart from taking my man."

"She is not my bitch!"

"Bitch? Emeka, when did you start calling women bitches? You've really become American!" Tutu exclaimed. 'Where you at?' Nigger! " Tutu mimicking him.

This prompted laughter from Emeka, who shook his head as he looked at her fondly. "There is nothing strange about 'where you at'. That's a direct translation of Yoruba's 'where are you'-'ebo lo wa'. It's Yoruba English called Ebonics here".

"Yeah, but what about the swearing?"

"Nigger is not really swearing. You are from Nigeria, ain't you? Nigeria means nigger area, like India being Hindi's area, Algeria, Algiers area and Liberia, liberated slaves area. Nigeria is the largest black area in the world, so it's called Nigger area," Emeka argued.

"Point taken. But if you ever call me a bitch, I will definitely be calling you an ambulance, Nigger!" she said, and they both burst into laughter.

"No, I meant she wasn't my woman", he said, when the laughter subsided. "She should be at the comedy club, Manhattan Proper, around the corner. We will see her later, and you can ask her whatever you want to."

The Manhattan Proper, a small comedy club at the corner of Linden Boulevard and 219th Street in Queens was swarming with people by the time they arrived around ten o'clock. The club had different programs for different days of the week, although the most popular was its comedy club on Tuesdays. When they arrived, there were more people hanging and frolicking outside the premises than there were inside. This was a common occurrence in the summer, when many Queens' natives use it as a hangout and meeting spot.

Tutu and Emeka slowly made their way into the club as he greeted various people, whom he obviously knew from the area, along the way. They found a seat near the stage where the few remaining seats were. Most people shied away from sitting close to the stage due to the fear of being picked on by the comics.

Just before the program started, Emeka sighted who he was looking for and beckoned to her to come across. The tall, dark-skinned woman in the company of two other women waved from afar and made their way to a table next to them. While her friends sat at the table, she came over to Emeka's table.

"What's up, nigga? Where've you been? I just got your message on my pager," Tameka nodded a greeting to Tutu, whom she quickly appraised and realized she was a new face. "What's up? You got some business for me? I need some money, yo!"

"Meet my friend, Tutu, from Africa," Emeka gestured

toward Tutu. "Tutu, this is Tameka. She is not as mad as she seems, so don't be scared to ask her whatever you want." As he spoke, the first stand-up comic came onto the stage.

"Don't tell me, she's in the same game. It seems all you Africans are some dodgy mufuckas," she said jokingly, but when she noticed Tutu wince. "It's all good, I'll take care of all my African brethren as long as I get paid."

Emeka laughed heartily, "No, she is not interested in that...."

"Look at this player right here. He got one fine sister sitting next to him and another standing over him, while the brother over there has only got Palm-ela and her five sisters," they heard the comic joke. The comic came close to them, "My brother, what do you do and where are you from?"

Emeka was a bit embarrassed over the attention that was now focused on his table and especially over him, "I am a businessman and from Nigeria!"

"Oh! Oh! An African brother! Business? I think we all know the business our African brothers do around here. Now we have African brothers living the thug life, they have chased all the American brothers off the street corners," he said, prompting laughter from the audience. Switching to a mocking African accent, he said, "Me, I don't need gun; am a bloody murder-fucka; just one touch of this Juju and you disappear." Amid laughter from the audience, they agreed to meet after the show.

The program ended around midnight, and people slowly filed out to join those who never came in and were hanging out around the area. Outside in the parking lot, across the road and the side roads, cars were parked with music booming out of them as everyone was enjoying the warm weather. Also, present were members of the police force and sheriff departments, trying to clear the roads of cars parked haphazardly, as well as to seize cars that had outstanding fines.

Tutu and Emeka waited in front of the Chinese restaurant next door, while Tameka tried to free herself from friends and admirers along the way toward them.

"Yes! Sorry for the delay. Niggas keep bugging me. This place is more packed than normal," Tameka said as she joined them, and they walked toward the parked car.

"Yeah, she wants to talk to you about Empire. I think you two can get along with it, while I get something from the shop," Emeka said, leaving them to discuss.

"So what's up, cousin?" Tameka asked warmly.

"I am alright, Sis! I need to know a bit about your bank. Where do you work there? How do you get to work there and you know..." Tutu said.

"What? And you say it isn't fraud. Are you a terrorist or something?"

Tutu laughed. "No, Sis! Terrorized! The Muslims have been terrorizing us for centuries and still do. Their Christian brothers came and left them there. So I know all about the wild sons of Abraham, Ibrahim in Arabic, and am trying to fight them."

"Well, I work in the computing department, but I am on leave and not returning till next week. What do you want to know exactly?" Tameka asked curiously.

Tutu took in a deep breath before answering, trying to explain her interest without giving anything away. They talked for about fifteen minutes before Emeka returned.

"I hope you two got along while I was away?" he asked as he entered the car.

"No doubt! Like we sisters always do when you brothers aren't around," Tameka answered as she and Tutu giggled.

Opening the door, "Well, I got to go. Niggas are going to the Q club and I got to bounce. I will see you guys around." They said their goodbyes, and Emeka zoomed off.

Stopping at the traffic lights at Linden and Springfield Ave, Tutu noticed the large police presence outside the gas station across from the McDonald's restaurant.

"You always see them, wherever you see niggas partying. They are like vultures waiting to pick on some dead meat. You remember how vultures used to swarm around and sit on the walls back home, whenever there was a large party going on, waiting for the cow remnants" he asked, making Tutu laugh.

"You mean any nigga caught is dead meat?" she asked and Emeka nodded.

Slowly driving on Springfield Avenue, when he got to a traffic light, he stopped and indicated he was turning left onto Hollis Avenue to take him back home to 109th Avenue and Farmers Boulevard. As he turned a car followed him, which he took no notice of, as he and Tutu spoke of old times. About three blocks from the turn into 109th Avenue, in front of a grocery shop, the car overtook them and blocked their path. Emeka had to slam on his brakes to avoid colliding with the white car.

Three white men jumped out of the car with their guns drawn and shouted at them to get out. Emeka being a New Yorker knew what was going on and quickly came out of the car, but Tutu was perplexed and remained seated. One of them yanked her door open and dragged her out.

"Get on to the floor!" he barked. Tutu angrily jerked her elbow from him and refused to obey. "Get on the ground!" one of them shouted. "Or can't you understand fucking English?"

Emeka was already lying on the wet road with his hands behind his back, while he was frisked.

"Why? What do you want? Who are you?" Tutu demanded stubbornly.

"New York Police, if you don't know! Now get on the motherfucking ground!"

"Yeah, so what if you are police. What have we done? You don't have the right to harass us. We were just coming from a night out."

The tallest of the officers walked right up close to her and held her firmly by the chin. "Look, don't make things difficult for yourself, girl. You are coming from a night out, eh? Well let me tell you, we own the night. Now, do as you were told," he said menacingly, after which he released his grip on her jaw.

As he let go of her jaw, Tutu spat right into his face. "Bastard," she cursed him. "I am a lawyer and you don't have any right to abuse us like this."

"Tutu, don't! Obey them, please!" Emeka called out from where he was lying.

"Fucking Bitch!" the officer shouted and walked back to their car to get something to wipe the slime off his face. Returning soon afterward, "I am placing you under arrest for assaulting an officer. Your stupid ass is going to jail!"

"I promise you, you will regret this, if you live long enough."

"Threatening a police officer. A lawyer? When I finish with your ass, you won't be practicing any more. Actually, you'll be needing a public defender." He brought out a pair of handcuffs, cuffed and led her toward the car, while the others searched the car for drugs or weapons.

Moments later, a marked police car arrived to carry Tutu to the station. Emeka was left to go since their search brought up nothing, but he insisted on knowing where Tutu was being taken and drove after them.

Tutu was taken to the Jamaica Avenue Precinct, where she was booked and detained. Meanwhile, Emeka was phoning frantically to his friends for help, both those in the legal profession and otherwise. Unfortunately, he could not secure her bail till early the following morning.

When Tutu stepped out of the precinct about eight o'clock, she had a defiant expression as she hugged Emeka.

"Welcome to America!" he said.

"I can't believe I just spent seven hours in jail for doing nothing."

"You assaulted an officer, they say. You should have obeyed. It would have saved you all the hassle. They would have conducted their search and found nothing and let us go!" Emeka put an arm around her shoulders and led her toward the car.

"I can't believe what I am hearing from your mouth. You don't think it is a gross abuse of my rights as a human being to be yanked from a car and made to lie in a puddle without any justifiable cause. I am sorry, I can't take such indignity, and I am disappointed you do without a fight. I don't care how many times they lock me up," Tutu said with apparent dismay.

"You might lose your license to practice if convicted of

assaulting an officer, and if you continue like this, I don't know what might happen. The same police unit shot a young man outside his home 41 times with nothing coming out of it, and the guy did not do as much as you did to provoke them," he told her as he turned off Jamaica Avenue onto 188th Street, which became Farmers Boulevard.

"So why is that? Why hasn't someone stood up to do something about it?"

"Listen, it is not only in New York, it is all over, all the way to England. It stems from the new thinking that is being pushed by your friends at Empire Bank. They have a conservative think tank, the Empire Institute, which pushes the policies starting with the war on drugs and now quality of life crimes. They call it zero tolerance policing and anything goes," he explained as he parked outside his house.

"What do you mean push? Aren't they a private company? How come they are making laws?"

Opening his front door, he smiled. "Well, they sponsor politicians, who sympathize with their views and have gradually taken over governments, both at local and federal levels across the western world." He continued to explain the political climate and how ultra and pseudo-conservative views were leading it.

"Well, they might be getting away with you lot, but I won't be standing for rubbish," Tutu said, dropping into a seat exasperatedly, "Emeka, I need an I.D to go there. I can't use my name."

"A fake I.D?" Emeka asked in disbelief, "God! I don't know what you are up to, but please be careful. I can do an I.D for you here at home, but please don't bring them to me, if you get arrested."

Tutu smiled, placing a hand on his shoulders fondly. "Don't worry, nothing is going to happen. I can take care of myself and won't do anything stupid. Please can you do it for me now?"

"Now? Ain't you going to sleep before you set out?" he asked, raising his eyebrows, and Tutu shook her head to reply she wasn't.

The reception on the ground floor of the Empire Bank's headquarters was bustling with people, both customers and members of the staff, when Tutu arrived. Passing the reception, she headed for the elevators as if she was a member of staff. Some other people, who were returning to their workstations or coming for business, joined her in the elevator.

When the elevator reached the seventh floor, she alighted and walked along the corridor. The door leading to the office was locked and a 'Staff Only' sign was placed on the door. Opening her wallet, she brought out the plastic card she had taken from her attackers back in Boston and slid it in the groove on the door.

The door sprung open and she walked into an open plan office, which held about 50 workers, who were busy typing away at their terminals. She swept the office with her eyes and located the supervisor, who was in the only closed office at the end of the room.

"I was sent by the agency for a temporary placement, I have just been to the security department and they gave me this," showing the entry card. Tameka had told her the security department vetted all new employees before they were allowed into the computing center.

"They already sent us a replacement for Tameka, I wonder why you were sent. Did the security department phone them?" the middle-aged bespectacled woman asked and Tutu nodded in reply. "We asked for only one replacement," she angrily reached for a phone, but paused as Tutu raised her hand and spoke.

"Please ma'am, I need the money. My man has disappeared and I have to feed my daughters. Please I will be grateful if you can help me, even if it is just for a day. I won't disappoint you," Tutu implored her in her most persuasive voice, making her drop the phone back on its cradle.

"Okay, sit at that terminal and I will see what you can do. You are lucky, we are a bit short staffed," she said as she answered a ringing phone from the array of phones.

Tutu left the room to sit at the terminal she was assigned. A few minutes later, the woman came with a thick pile of printouts, which she instructed Tutu to check against entries on-line for errors. She explained to Tutu what was required and how to go about it, before leaving her on her own.

Initially Tutu was scared that someone or something might turn up and give her away but gradually, she gained confidence and settled down. She took her time going through the printouts without talking to the other women around.

Eventually closing time arrived, and the office gradually emptied as Tutu continued to work at her terminal. At about 7:30pm, the supervisor came to her terminal carrying her handbag, obviously ready to leave for the day.

"You don't need to finish that today. You could leave, if you want and continue tomorrow," she said, leaning against Tutu's monitor.

"Thanks ma'am," Tutu looking up with a charming smile. "I will leave as soon as I finish this page. I see you are leaving, goodnight." The supervisor returned the greeting and left.

Soon after she left, Tutu moved to another terminal, which was a direct terminal. She switched on the terminal and started going through the database. Going through the menu, she came across "Empire Institute" and tried to gain access into the file, but was denied as the screen flashed "incorrect password." Squeezing her eyes shut, she slowly moved her lips and began to type. The flashing stopped and another sign appeared telling her she had gained access into the top security file.

The file revealed payments to various politicians, most of whom she had never heard of before. Quickly skimming through the file, she came across various payments and policy statements. After going through the file, she tried to get the names of the directors and members of the institute, but came across another security restriction, which she by-passed once again.

Knowing she had nearly achieved what she planned for the day, she made a quick call to Emeka to come and pick her up.

On the twentieth floor, Bill Jones was about to leave for

the day, when he decided to check the computer and security systems as he usually did before going home. Going through the system, he realized that someone was accessing a top security file. This alerted him, knowing that there were only three people in the bank allowed access.

The file had nothing to do with the day-to-day operations of the bank and unauthorized entry could warrant immediate firing. He traced the violator to the seventh floor and tried to shut the person out of the file but couldn't and decided to catch the person in the act.

Why would someone be accessing the file in the computer department? He thought as he entered the elevator.

Tutu was scribbling down the names of the members of Empire Institute, when she heard a noise, which she identified as the closing of the elevator door. She continued to hurriedly scribble down what she was reading on the screen. She had just finished writing the names, when the door burst open.

"Hey you!" a short man in a gray suit shouted as he came through the door, "Who are you?"

Tutu was initially taken aback and could not answer as the man approached her, but quickly hid the paper in her bra. "I am Angela White. I am a temporary staff."

"And what are you doing in files that you have no business with?" he asked in a stern tone, standing over her threateningly. "How did you get into that file?" he demanded, staring into her eyes coldly, having caught a thief in the act.

"What file, sir?" Tutu tried to bluff her way out by putting up an innocent front.

"May I see your I.D and security pass?" he stretched his hand as he appraised her. Tutu went into her wallet and brought out her fake I.D and security pass taken from the man in Boston. Bill rudely snatched it from her and examined it, "This is not the security card we give to temporary staff. Please can you tell me where you got it?" He held on to the I.D and security card as he continued to look at her searchingly.

"From the security department, sir," Tutu's voice quivered a bit as she answered, unable to look at the man directly.

"I am Bill Jones, the head of the security department, and I am nearly 100% sure that we didn't issue this card to a temporary staff. Please follow me," he ordered her.

He was not totally sure that his staff did not give her the card since they often made mistakes and disregarded procedure, but whether or not they issued it, was not the point. She had entered a file that she had no authority to enter, which was tantamount to hacking in his view and was a sackable offence, if not prosecutable.

"Where to, Sir? I was just about to leave to pick up my son at the day-care center," Tutu said. She picked up her handbag and rose to follow him, trying to quickly figure out how she was going to get out of the situation. Bill Jones contemplated calling the police, but it was late and he wanted to go home soon as planned.

"I will walk you out of the building, although don't think you are going to get off free," he said as he opened the door and gestured to her to walk out into the corridor.

He called for the elevator, which wasted no time in arriving and they both entered. "You could go to jail for this, you know. That is a criminal act you have committed, and I still don't know how you came across this security pass or the passwords. I am letting you go home now, but if it turns out tomorrow there is anything sinister about any of this, you could expect the cops."

When the elevator pulled to a stop on the ground floor. "On your way, girl, and pray that the police don't come knocking on your door," he said despicably.

Tutu stepped out of the elevator slowly and pressed the topmost floor button. Stopping and turning to him. "Before you call the police, I advise you to think of what you would tell them about the men you sent to kill me in Boston, Mr. Jones," she said.

Bill Jones' mouth dropped in shock, and he stepped back in trepidation into the elevator, away from her. "No, I didn't.

Please don't hurt me," he stuttered as he thought of all he had heard about her powers.

"That wasn't very nice, was it? Anyway, you can experience what they did and more," she said with a wry smile at the scared man, whose mind was racing over many possibilities, but before he could bring himself to answer, the elevator door closed. Tutu ran out of the building, where she met an already waiting Emeka.

Emeka and Tutu decided to spend the night at home, catching up on old times and because it was agreed Tutu needed rest, having spent the previous night in a cell. After a romantic dinner, they drank Bailey's Irish Cream and talked.

"I am really not sure that I should give you another chance, but I will try," Tutu said, as they cuddled in front of the television.

The 10 o'clock news was just starting, when he rose to his feet and offered her a hand, "Let's go to bed. It has been a long day."

She took his hand, and he helped her to her feet, but as they were about to leave, Emeka stopped to listen to what was being said on the T.V.

."...there are reports just coming in of a freak accident at the headquarters of Empire Bank in downtown Manhattan, where an elevator went through the roof killing its sole occupant. There will be more on that story as we go on," they heard the newscaster report on the television.

"That's where you are just coming from, Tutu," Emeka shouted in surprise, "Damn! You're very lucky. You could have been in it!" Tutu did not answer, but had a smirk on her face.

."...Also, another freak accident happened in Queens, this time on the road. Three NYPD officers died in a crash this evening, when their vehicle lost control and flew from Jamaica Boulevard onto the Cross Island Parkway rush hour traffic. They were hit by a fast moving vehicle and died on the spot. Preliminary reports say that the pedals to their car jammed, while approaching the flyover..." the newscaster reported and photographs of the dead officers were shown on screen.

"Hey! Those are the cops that you had beef with yesterday!" Emeka exclaimed once again.

"Come on! They tested the best and were put to rest," she said coyly, switching off the television and pulling him toward the stairs. "Let me test you."

THE END

The epic non-fiction book highlighting the Black Race...
THE BLACKWORLD: EVOLUTION TO REVO-
LUTION by Prince Justice

THE BLACKWORLD: EVOLUTION TO REVOLU-
TION starts with solid proof that the true Garden of Eden/
Evolution site was between the West African Negro Delta and
the Land of Love—the Slave Coast where most Africans in the
Americas came from!

THE BLACKWORLD then goes on to breaking down the
past, present and future of Black America from the Chicago's
Millionaires row to Californian Death rows; the East, West,
Gulf and Slave Coasts; the all-Good, the Bad and the damn
Ugly of Nigeria, Jamaica, Sudan, Trinidad, Haiti, Ghana, South
Africa...the real deal, no B.S. or Bamboozles of mainstream
media, academia...

THE BLACKWORLD: EVOLUTION TO REVOLU-
TION offers a fresh empowering perspective to help us achieve
our full potential moneywise on Black or Wall Streets (econom-
ically) and with our relationships (culturally) on all levels—personally, locally and globally. It empowers us with loads of useful
easy-to-understand information to free us from cultural and
economic restrictions, as it analyzes every major Black community in the world—from their inception to present-day.

Check it out...if knowledge is power, then this book will
make you a fully kitted one-man army to deal with your money,
honeys, phoneys and attorneys...

http://www.amazon.com/gp/product/1419629115/002-
6048855-5900803
http://www.ebookmall.com/ebooks-authors/prince-
justice-ebooks.htm